All That is Solid Melts into Air

DARRAGH McKEON

PENGUIN BOOKS

PENGUIN BOOKS

UK | USA | Canada | Ireland | Australia
India | New Zealand | South Africa

Penguin Books is part of the Penguin Random House group of companies
whose addresses can be found at global.penguinrandomhouse.com.

Penguin
Random House
UK

First published by Viking 2014
Published in Penguin Books 2015
001

Copyright © Darragh McKeon, 2014

The moral right of the author has been asserted

Set in Garamond MT by Palimpsest Book Production Limited,
Falkirk, Stirlingshire
Printed in Great Britain by Clays Ltd, St Ives plc

A CIP catalogue record for this book is available from the British Library

ISBN: 978–0–241–96467–5

MIX
Paper from
responsible sources
FSC
www.fsc.org   FSC® C018179

sustainable future for our business, our readers
and our planet. This book is made from Forest
Stewardship Council® certified paper.

PENGUIN BOOKS

All That is Solid Melts into Air

'An outstanding debut novel . . . portraying inconceivable horrors and acts of incredible beauty in luminously understated prose. McKeon makes us care . . . skilfully drawing us into their worlds before and after the explosion. Devastating' *Metro*

'A heartbreaking love story . . . Very accomplished and moving' *New Books*

'An accomplished debut that provides a snapshot of the Soviet Union during the Chernobyl disaster. A powerful story of interwoven lives through a momentous episode, McKeon is an exciting voice' *Bookseller*

'A book to be devoured, tragic and funny and sad and beautiful and sensual and shocking and, ultimately, utterly transcendent . . . Crackles with the whip-smart propulsion of a thriller, while immersing its reader in the rich inner turmoils of its characters' *Image*

'An extraordinary story of truth and tragedy during the Chernobyl disaster' *Stylist*

'Fascinating, beautifully written . . . [a] flawless pearl' *Irish Independent*

ABOUT THE AUTHOR

Darragh McKeon was born in 1979 and grew up in the midlands of Ireland. He has worked as a theatre director, and lives in New York. This is his first novel.

For Flora

In memory of my mother

All that is solid melts into air, all that is holy is profaned, and man is at last compelled to face with sober senses, his real conditions of life, and his relations with his kind.

Karl Marx, *The Communist Manifesto*

To my mind radioactivity is a real disease of matter. Moreover it is a contagious disease. It spreads. You bring those debased and crumbling atoms near others and those too presently catch the trick of swinging themselves out of coherent existence. It is in matter exactly what the decay of our old culture is in society, a loss of traditions and distinctions and assured reactions.

H. G. Wells, *Tono-Bungay*

He comes to her daily, slipping into her mind between breaths. She draws him in as she draws in air, pedalling along the Quai de Valmy, as she draws in her new surroundings: the glow of a Paris summer, the jigsaw of shadows thrown across her forearms when she sweeps beneath a canopy of poplars.

She can never say what it is that triggers a recollection, they come into being in such stealthy ways. Perhaps there was something of Grigory in the man with the cigarette at the lock just passed, a familiarity in the way this stranger brought a flaring match to his face. But then the breadth of their marriage contains a corresponding moment for any of the thousands of minute actions that surround her.

His image is lost to her now, belonging solely to the photographs he inhabits. She can no longer see him in resemblance, but only in the motions of others, so that when she chains her bicycle to the railings by the canal and steps towards the café terrace, he is echoed in the man who looks towards her: not through the dark Gallic features, but in the nod of the head, the opening of the long, deft fingers, the downturn of the eyes.

These are the small consolations that death offers. Her husband still turning the key to an undiscovered chamber of her heart.

April 1986

When Yevgeni closes his eyes, the world comes in.

The world rattling and banging, whispers and footfalls, the hiss of trains, the bleep and slide of doors, announcements on the tannoy cracked and frail and distant, people saying 'Excuse me,' or, less polite, 'Out of my way,' 'Move in.' Sound in tides. The train comes, the crowd boards, the train goes, nearer silence now, new people striding down the platform, the train arriving again. Escalators relentlessly creaking, jumping in pitch, constant in rhythm.

A clasp unhooks on a bag, resonating timidly.

He can make out all the individual noises, this is the easy part, a recognition game. But Yevgeni can also block out all associations, can bathe only in pure sound, the patterns it weaves down here. This is the child's special gift, although he doesn't know it yet – how can he, nine years old.

Yevgeni's head is tilted back, he's standing ramrod straight, arms by his side, an unlikely statue in the centre of the concourse.

He opens his eyes to see a parachute jumper shooting towards him face first, his chute rippling behind him, caught in the last few seconds before the cloth would unfurl hard and taut and the man would be yanked by his shoulders right way up and float silently in the clouds, abandoned to the whims of the wind. Yevgeni can hear this too, block out all the noise around him and listen to the bulging drone of the passing plane, to the darting air currents, the sound of the man's fall, sound stretched in time and air and speed.

He is in Mayakovskaya station, gazing at the oval mosaics overhead, each one forming a part of the overarching theme: 'A Day of the Soviet Sky'. Yevgeni doesn't know the scenes have a title and it doesn't matter. He can just stand and look and let imagination fill in the rest. Down here there is no music, only noise, pure sound, the passing plane has no orchestral sweep, the man has no sonata accompanying him to his destiny. Down here Yevgeni is free to put together melodies from all that surrounds him, the tumbling effluvia of daily life. There are no crotchets and quavers down here. There are no staff lines and indicators of tone: forte, pianissimo. There is just sound, in the fullness of its natural expression.

Smack.

A raw stinging in his ear. A shrill industrial note, the same one the TV makes when programming is finished for the evening.

Yevgeni knows what to expect before he even looks.

Two kids from school, a couple of years older than him. Ivan Egorov and his friend Aleksandr. Everyone calls him Lazy Alek, he has a lazy eye. There are a thousand jokes about Alek. *Why was Alek late for school? His eye wouldn't get out of bed.* Alek gets this all the time, but not when Ivan is around. Nobody messes with Ivan.

Alek speaks to Ivan. 'My mother says why can't you be like that other boy, play an instrument, like that Tchaikovsky boy. That's what she calls him, "the Tchaikovsky boy".'

'Tchaikovsky. I know that name. Tell me again how I know that name.'

'The ballet. *Swan Lake.*'

6

'That's right, *Swan Lake*. There's another one, though, what's the other one?'

They're having the conversation for him but not to him, like Yevgeni just happened to sidle along as they were talking. Yevgeni thinks about running, it might be the best way out. But he isn't afraid to fight. These kids could kick the hell out of him, no question, but he'll stand and fight. He just wishes they'd get on with it. People wandering by, no idea of Yevgeni's situation. No way he can ask for help, that would mean an extended beating; other kids would hear about it and join the fun. Not here, but later. Nothing is more certain.

'What other one?'

'The other one.'

'I can't remember.'

'Hey, Tchaikovsky, what's the other one you're famous for?'

A sigh. Here we go.

'*The Nutcracker.*'

Ivan fakes a punch to the groin and Yevgeni flinches. Basic mistake.

'I hear you have two mothers. You need a lot of looking after or what? You get a scrape, one blows, one kisses, this is what I hear.'

'One blows? I hear they both blow.'

Alek always has his head tilted to the side, compensating for the eye. It makes him look like a chicken. Flipping his head one side to the other. Yevgeni wants to slap it back to straight.

'Show us your hands, maestro.' Ivan says this. Ivan once beat a boy four classes ahead of them, no small fry either, a full fight, caught him hard on the windpipe, even the teachers watched it.

Yevgeni clasps his hands against his back and Alek slinks behind, digs into Yevgeni's wrist separating the hands, displaying one of them to Ivan. They have to be careful how they handle this: maximum pain, minimum attention.

Ivan grabs the smallest finger of the right hand, cranking it slowly back towards the elbow.

'I hear he wears a bow tie. You hear this?'

'I hear this.'

He moves left, steps tight to one of the arches, using Yevgeni's body to shield the action. Yevgeni is forced to perform an incremental twist, elbow following shoulder – an agonized version of the twirl he sees his mother do when she dances, the few times he's seen her dance – until he rounds to face Ivan.

The older boy changes his grip, considers the punishment. Breakage is not out of the question. Yevgeni knows this, Ivan knows this. Testing the flexibility of the joint. Testing the will of Yevgeni.

'So where's your papa when your two mamas are home?'

'He died in Afghanistan.'

A pause. Ivan looks at him, sees him for the first time.

'My father went to Afghanistan.'

A stabbing note of woe in Ivan's voice. A glance towards somewhere distant.

Yevgeni may be OK.

It's just the two of them now. Their joined experience, a father in a war zone, separating them from everything else. Ivan holds the younger kid's pinky. Holding it in his fist. An odd point of contact, he realizes, looking at it, holding the finger in a baby's grasp.

The Tchaikovsky kid is staring at him, really looking now, like he's trying to discover something. Like he wants Ivan to repeat what he said. Ivan can feel the tension releasing in the kid's hand. There is the possibility of letting him go. There is definitely that possibility. But Alek's here. And word would spread.

He takes in the kid, measuring everything. Fucking pathetic really: sprawly limbs; a body that looks like it was made from spare parts; angled joints; everything at a slant. Ivan's father taught him to stand square, be grounded. Another lesson to be thankful for. When his father speaks, Ivan listens. A man who went to war.

'There's a difference, though, between our fathers. Know what it is?'

Calmness glazing Ivan's eyes. Yevgeni can see his own reflection in them, the vague shape of his hair. The moment turns, irrevocably. He takes a breath, a fleeting image of his tears stored in a small, dark reservoir near his brain. His words create a surface ripple as he speaks.

'No. What?'

Ivan grasps Yevgeni's wrist with his other hand. A fist around his pinky, another around his wrist.

'Mine came back.'

Silence. Stillness. A jerk from Ivan, his lower lip clamped between his teeth.

The sound of a branch snapping.

Yevgeni doesn't cry out and he manages to be proud of this – in the middle of the pain – to let out a sound means they'll see him again, maybe next week. These are the rules.

A station guard walks up, asks their names. Yevgeni is bent over, hand folded into his stomach, cheeks puffed. The guard repeats his question and they answer him. 'Pavel.' 'Yuri.' They know better than to give their real names. They look at him blankly: 'So what, no problems.' Alek scuffs a shoe on the floor, tugs at his crotch through his pocket. Yevgeni raises the good arm to the man. 'I'm fine,' the gesture says.

'He's got some cramp. We're just waiting on him.' Ivan

9

says this. Alek hangs back in these situations. This is why Ivan is Ivan and Alek is Alek.

The man walks off. Alek gives Yevgeni a final ear flick, a little bonus pain, and they make for the platform as the train pulls in.

Lazy-eye fucker.

Yevgeni's tears come as they saunter away, overflowing the lip of the reservoir.

He stumbles forward, away from the arch, breath leaking from him, saliva bubbling down his chin. He wants to go somewhere dark to hide, maybe to sleep, but there's no place to be alone in this city. Even if he went home and locked himself in the bathroom, there'd be a fist banging on the door. He might get five minutes of peace. Definitely no more than ten. People living in each other's lives. In his life. Sharing his bath, his toilet. His mother tells him he's lucky to have his own bed. She says this to him and he doesn't know what to reply. Maybe his bed will be the next thing. Maybe he'll have to curl up beside a stranger someday soon. He never knows when the rules will change again.

Yevgeni tucks the wounded hand under his jacket. The pain has its own heartbeat. He cradles it inside his jacket like it's not a part of him, it's something else, a wounded bird, an abandoned kitten. He feels an urge to let out a whimper, to give voice to the stricken hand, but what if his test isn't over yet? There's always someone who might hear.

Mr Leibniz, his teacher, will be waiting. Yevgeni can see the old man sitting on the piano stool, looking out into the yard, checking his watch.

Maybe he should still go there. Mr Leibniz would certainly be annoyed, but surely when he sees the finger he'd understand the pain involved, do something about it.

He needs to go somewhere. He knows this. Stand around

here much longer and the station guard will come back. Never attract attention. The great rule of this city. Blend in. Walk in a group. Speak quietly. Keep your good fortune to yourself. Queue patiently. These are things that no one has ever said to him, at least not directly. Yevgeni picked them up from simply being here, alive to the quick of his skin.

The city reveals itself to him all the time, slinging its patterns across the most innocuous things. On sunny days, when shadows sit sharp and defined along the ground, he sees people following lines of shade, scuttling along near walls, slinking away from the glare of the light. Or waiting at traffic lights, everyone hunched together, inhabiting a small rectangle of sun-starved concrete. The things he knows, he knows from being alone amongst others. Walking, listening, watching. Last summer he sat on a step and looked at a queue that stretched out in front of a fishmonger's, everyone sweating and gossiping. And when it was too hot to talk, they stood in silence, breathing. Taking air in and pushing it out together, like they were all part of the same thing, some long, straggled creature. Sometimes he thinks that people stand in line just to be part of a line. To become part of the shapes that are created to fit them.

His mother spends her day working in a laundry and then comes home and washes and irons the neighbours' clothes. People call round at all hours with baskets of dirty garments. His mother didn't choose this. He knows she hates it. But someone has to do laundry, to keep clothes clean, keep them free from creases. Why not his mother? Everyone adapting to need.

And still they all want him to play Mozart and Schubert and he can't help asking himself: *Where's the need in that?* But he's too young to ask questions. This is what he's always told. So he asks them to himself and doesn't look for an answer. There are questions that float down to him from the mosaics. He has so many questions. He used to write them down but his mother found the sheets in his scrapbook and burned them. She said he had other things to concentrate on. She may as well have kicked him in the stomach. Still the questions keep bubbling in his brain. He straightens and asks himself: *Why did anyone feel the need to put a mosaic of a parachute jumper on the ceiling of a Metro station?* But it somehow feels more fascinating down here. The rush of clouds and sky has an intensity to it, in a place without fresh air, a chandeliered tunnel.

Mr Leibniz would have plenty of questions. He'd treat Yevgeni like a broken artifact, a precious heirloom that had fallen off the mantelpiece. He wouldn't be concerned about the pain, at least not at first. He'd think of the weeks of rehearsals that would be missed, the competition schedule that would have to be rearranged. He'd place a hand on his forehead and bring his fingers together by running them across his tufted eyebrows. And then he'd look at Yevgeni with disappointment.

Yevgeni hates that look.

People cascade down the escalators again, pour on to the platforms. Someone jostles his hand and Yevgeni lets out a stunted moan and then allows the surge to sweep him up, before finally coming to a stop at the platform's edge. He stands there and leans gently towards the track to catch a look at the incoming train as it rounds the curve, headlights bulldozing through the darkness.

He'll go to his aunt Maria. He's not sure at what point he made this decision, but he's standing here now and this is what he'll do.

Around him, people are tweaking their nostrils, chewing their nails, tugging at their earlobes. All of them looking into nothing.

The train pulls in and as it stops the woman beside him bares her teeth to the steel panels of the doorframe. She's checking for lipstick marks. Yevgeni knows this because his mother does the same thing fifteen times a day, even if she's at home for the evening, even if she isn't wearing lipstick. She looks and asks him to check for stains and then unconsciously runs her tongue over the front row, because just in case. The doors open and the crowd surges and squeezes. Yevgeni hunches over, protecting his finger with his elbows and shoulders. He stands, waiting for the shunt when the train moves forward. He can't use his free hand to grasp one of the hanging straps, it would leave him too exposed, so he spreads his legs wide, lets them soak up the movement of the carriage.

He may be nine years old, but he's ridden the Metro on his own countless times. It's been at least a year since he convinced his mother to allow him to travel alone. He goes to Mr Leibniz's four times a week and waiting for his aunt or his mother to pick him up and bring him there was cutting into his rehearsal time. Yevgeni knew that if he could relate his argument to music, he was on strong ground. He got Mr Leibniz to agree with this, in front of his mother, which took some doing, because Mr Leibniz didn't like agreeing with him on anything. He didn't want Yevgeni getting ahead of himself.

So, his mother bought him a map and gave him a little perfume bottle that he was to spray into the eyes of anyone who came near. Of course he threw it away as soon as he could. Bringing a perfume bottle to school was just inviting pain.

The things he's seen since, especially on Tuesdays and Fridays, when he comes home late. He's seen men with matted hair stretched out over a row of seats. He's seen couples bundled together under blankets that reflect the light with their dirty sheen. There are people who have loud conversations with God and people with no teeth, their faces sucked into the hollow of their mouths.

A man took out his penis once. In the end carriage this was. Took out his penis and pissed against the driver's door. A weighty slub of flesh. Yevgeni kept looking at it, then looking away and then looking back. He couldn't help it, such a secretive thing, out there in the air, in the light, alive. Steam coming off the stream of his raw piss. The liquid flowing down the train, fanning out into skinny tributaries. Yevgeni didn't want to pull his legs up, didn't want to draw the man's attention, so he let the piss lap against his shoes, flicker over his toes. Nobody raising an objection in the carriage, everyone else wrapped up under blankets, closed off from sensation.

He changes trains at Okhotny Ryad, his steps reverberating into the broken bone. By the time he gets on the red line aches are flaring up in other places. His shoulders and ribs are held by a numbness, as if he had unhinged them and left them in ice for a few hours. They too are turning in on themselves, preventing the vibrations from the tracks reaching the spongy insides of the bone. The screeching metal claws at his ears, pitched to the same intensity as his pain. All of this going on inside him, inside this train, as it bullets along, deep under the Moscow streets.

They reach the Universitet stop and he slumps on to the platform, makes his way to the escalator. He pauses before it, secretly afraid of escalators, afraid he might fall down backways if he doesn't place his feet fully on the step. Once through the gates, he walks up a flight of wet steps, into the air. Rain is coming down in blustering sheets, thrashing on to the tarmac of Prospekt Vernadskogo.

14

Water sweeps across the roofs of passing streetcars. It's evening, which he hadn't expected. Time has slinked along and now Yevgeni begins to worry that he might be too late, perhaps his aunt has finished with her class, maybe he'll have to go home after all, face the full force of his mother's questioning.

Through the trees of the campus, he can see the central tower of the Lomonosov, but it's further away than he expected, a ten-minute walk. The rain keeps building momentum and as he reaches the campus gate, he decides instead to dash for shelter on the opposite side of the road, underneath the concrete canopy of the State Circus.

Thick streams of water fall from the rounded folds of its roof, mooring the building. Sodden ticket-holders bustle into the glass auditorium, shedding their coats as soon as they're inside. In front of the steps below him, a man walks past pushing a bike with one wheel, half carrying, half coaxing it along, drops clinging to the strands of his thick beard. Yevgeni thinks at first that the man might be one of the performers, but then takes in his state of dishevelment and decides he can't be. Besides, what kind of tricks can you do with a clapped-out road bike?

He tucks his damaged hand under his armpit. He wants to be at home, sitting beside the radiator, warming his hands with sweet tea. A wave of nausea rushes over him and Yevgeni realizes he hasn't eaten since breakfast. His hand is consuming all his concentration and strength. It's the only thing that matters right now. Café tables and chairs are abandoned all around him. With the sleeve of his free arm, Yevgeni wipes the rain off a nearby chair and plants himself on the metal seat. Even though he knows his location, he feels lost, he's not where he needs to be and can't think of how he'll get himself to his aunt Maria's classroom, or back home. And he can't go to the hospital on his own; there would be three hundred questions. They might even start questioning his mother, which she could definitely do without.

He doesn't know where his aunt's classroom is or even which building it's in. What was he thinking, coming here? He shouldn't even have been standing on the concourse, doing nothing, shouldn't have put himself in a situation where someone could harm his fingers. His rehearsal schedule will be thrown off and then what's to become of them? Will his mother have to do laundry for ever? She works so hard. He's the man of the house. What kind of man is he who comes to a place looking for his aunt and doesn't even know where to start and ends up in a wet chair watching the rain?

In the apartment blocks across the road women are whipping clothes off washing lines strung over balconies. They pluck pegs off their lines, holding them in their teeth, then turning to call indoors for help, identical bursts of movement that happen on different levels of the building, independent of each other. Across the city, his mother is probably doing the same.

Below them, at ground level, a woman walks past, sheltering under a navy-blue umbrella. Yevgeni's eye is drawn downwards from the intermittent chaos that unfolds above her. She wears a grey coat and black shoes. Yevgeni recognizes the swivel of the body, the pace of her stride. It has to be her. Finally some luck. He stands up and shouts over to her, 'Auntie!' She doesn't hear and keeps moving. He shouts again, 'Auntie Maria!' Still nothing. Yevgeni doesn't think he has the strength to run after her. He needs rescuing from his little island of gloom. He waves his good hand in the air with broad strokes. Still nothing. She's moving past now, the moment quickly becoming lost.

The pavement becomes washed in a yellow glaze. Carnival music blares from the overhead speakers.

Yevgeni, momentarily disorientated, looks up to see the perimeter of the concrete canopy lit up with hundreds of individual bulbs. The steel tables around him glisten, stagnant puddles turn into blobs of molten gold. Across the street, his aunt Maria stops and looks over at the circus building, charmed by the electric surge that radiates out into the damp evening air, and pays particular attention to a sodden boy sweeping an arm above his head, as though waving out to sea.

Grigory Ivanovich Brovkin stands at the edge of the cold pool in the Tulskaya baths, gazing at the flat sheen of the undisturbed water. The slap of flesh surrounds him: feet sticking to the wet marble floors, the large hands of the old masseurs pounding and kneading thick wads of skin in the adjoining treatment rooms. All men, mostly older than him, walking with a certain gait, paunches swaying, shoulders bent back, chests out, bodies freed from restrictions, uniform white bath towels cosseting their waists, corners flipping around their knees from their languorous stroll. To his left, two men play chess, partially obscured in the steam, half the pieces ivory white, the same colour as their skin. The pieces gathering condensation, looking as though they too were sweating out their impurities.

The pool water inert and translucent, so clear he can see the tiled bottom, six feet below, so solid-looking that the idea of it opening itself to him, parting to his weight, seems absurd.

The day has been a long one and it's not finished yet. He climbed out of bed at 5.25. He stood at the window in the cobalt light and watched as the day unfurled, the morning growing paler, routine activities billowing out, bakers checking on bread rising dutifully in ovens, janitors pulling on their overalls, mechanics in depots tinkering with delivery trucks, testing the engines patiently until they greet the day with spluttered complaints.

He leaned his forearms against the glass and watched as a

pigeon lifted above some beech trees, its outstretched wings gathering invisible currents, carrying a heart disproportionate to its body size. Such contradictions that nature can hold in its effortless order.

He has always appreciated order. It was this aspect of his nature that probably, on reflection, drew him to surgery. In the operating theatre, he takes great comfort in the physical rituals. The tools being handed to him in a specific way, held at a particular height. Placed into his hand with just the same amount of force. Everything scrubbed and disinfected. Everything shining clean. A room that is beyond, if not error, then carelessness, everything in it the result of careful deliberation.

He showered and ate a breakfast of black bread and two boiled eggs and drank some tea. He put on his suit and tied his tie, ran a comb through his gradually receding hairline; the years moving ominously forward.

His thoughts had a bitter taint to them this morning because it's his birthday today, he's thirty-six years old. Skilled. Respected. Alone. A chief of surgery with a failed marriage behind him.

He chose a set of cufflinks from the drawer of the bedside locker and stared at the empty bed, the discarded blankets funnelled along one side, as though there were a body underneath them, as though she were still there, that they had emerged from the raging arguments, their love made stronger through the heat of their marriage; refined into something purer, more enduring. But the shape in the bed was merely a reminder of her absence, one which he feels most acutely in the mornings; from when he wakes in the same position as he did in the years she was there – cradling nothing now – to when he turns the key in his door, facing the day without Maria's tender words of encouragement.

He walked to the hospital. Forty minutes from his apartment. He likes to take in some air, even though his path is mostly along the third ring road, with traffic spitting out its fumes. Snarling. Even at such an early hour. He stopped in the centre of an overpass and looked down on the motorway, holding on to the metal rail. A lorry bellowed as it passed underneath him and he felt the urge to spit on it, a habit from childhood which he thought had been extinguished, but it turns out it was lying dormant all the time, only to rise up in him now, on the first day of his thirty-seventh year.

A man stood at the far end of the overpass taking photographs of a gravelled section that overlooked some scrubland beyond the boundary wall. He'd never seen anyone in this spot before, as it has no practical use, an unnecessary extension alongside the stairway that drops to the footpath. Grigory walked towards him. He was curious to see what the man was photographing, but there was also the fact that the stroll provided a slight aberration from his usual routine, an acknowledgement of this particular day.

Before Grigory reached him, the man with the camera turned and nodded in greeting and descended the stairs. Grigory continued to the boundary wall, and leaned on it. The sky had almost fully lightened, the sun cresting the horizon. Grigory knew he was running later than usual. He liked to get a couple of hours of office work done before the committee meetings and the rounds and the demands for his signature and the funding applications and the consultations and the operating theatres. All of it racing along. His days streaming by. He crossed his fingers and thumbs to form a rectangular frame, a viewfinder, something he hadn't done in years, but the idea of someone taking a camera to such an indistinct place intrigued him.

A nothing place of scorched grass. A pylon planted in its centre. A crumbled wall.

Then Grigory looked down, almost directly underneath, and dropped his hands from his face to take in the whole sight, trying to see it in its entirety, framed by the field, the perimeter walls beyond which traffic streamed along, oblivious to the image.

A grid of shoes, a whole cityscape of shoes it seemed, was decked out before him, evoking a sensation that he couldn't quite articulate. How many shoes were here? Perhaps a thousand? All neatly lined and spaced.

He was no longer in a hurry. These shoes were placed there, carefully, to be looked at. And so he looked at them. The leather stitching or plastic moulding, the laces and flaps and the contours of the openings, the finely curved lines. There were slippers and ballet shoes, work boots with exposed steel toecaps, children's sandals. The shoes not filling the landscape but emphasizing absence, such personal items, as if a whole battalion of people had been ghosted away. There was, he was sure, a rational explanation for such a sight. Maybe it was a memorial of sorts, or perhaps the work of some radical artist. He was sure he'd hear about it at some point. But for now he could stand and marvel at what you could stumble across, just off an anonymous motorway, on a routine morning. Aware all the while that he himself formed part of the scene, a forlorn figure in a worn suit, staring at this wonderful absurdity.

He rarely thought of how he looked to others. It was a side effect of having the responsibility of delivering grave news. Walking into a room to meet fraught parents, or a wife who hasn't slept for a week, required only an outward gaze. You lose all authority, all assurance, if you worry about how you'll be perceived. He thought how the life that had silently formed around him seemed such a solid thing now, how rarely he ever brushed against the element of surprise any more.

Down, to the right, almost outside his range of vision, his attention was drawn to the sheen of a pair of glossy black stilettos. A regular staple of her wardrobe. The sight of it transported him to the night at the river. The night of their first real encounter. Grigory's younger self, hunched alone on the frozen surface, only a paraffin lamp for guidance. A small wicker stool, the same one on which he sat many years later in the eye of their unhappiness. A rod. A hole in the ice.

The place is Kursk. The river named after the city. He's a junior registrar in the hospital and a new arrival. He comes to the river to rid his brain of Latin terms, of the smell of the wards, antiseptic still clinging to his skin. Nothing to concentrate on other than the dark circle before him, half a metre in diameter, his line plunged into the ambiguous depths. He holds the rod loosely in his hand, engrossed in his waiting. A glass bottle rests between his thighs and he puts it to his lips but receives nothing, his supply exhausted. He shakes his head in annoyance and places it under the stool, resuming his position.

A cry from the bank. 'Hey!'

He turns to see buildings foregrounded against the streaked indigo sky, passing cars sweeping their halogen light over the streets. The cry again, coming from a walkway along the bank. A figure emerges from the darting shadows, shrouded by trees, a woman with long, dark hair, moonlight skimming over it, woven into the night.

He reels up the line and balances the rod on the stool and

approaches her. As he nears he can hear a flurry of giggles as her hand rotates a small rectangular object. Closer now, he sees it to be a silver hipflask. The light separates her face into planes, each angle revealing its own beauty.

'Dr Brovkin, you looked lonely and thirsty,' she says. 'I thought I could help.'

She says this with a slight lilt in her voice, a subtle challenge. She's wondering if he'll recognize her, which he does. She's a cleaner in the hospital, they've made eye contact in the lobby, excused themselves as they manoeuvred past each other in the canteen, both carrying laden trays. Of course he knows who she is. He imparts warm familiarity with his eyes, looking straight at her.

'With which part?' he asks, and she pauses, not understanding. 'Are you offering to help with the loneliness or the thirst?'

'Oh,' she laughs, a flush to her cheeks, a softness around the eyes, 'maybe both.'

She wears a thick shawl over a long, grey dress, cut to her figure. She is returning from a party, which has left her not drained nor drunk but effervescent, radiating life and curiosity.

He takes a mouthful from the hipflask and feels a hot flash spread through his chest. His head judders with surprise.

'Whiskey? I was expecting vodka.'

'Well, it's good to be surprised. Has it warmed your insides?'

'Yes. Yes it has.'

'So it has done its job.'

He nods, looks at her again.

'I have never fished,' she says. 'It looks peaceful.'

He raises his palm gently to his waist, cupped, as if he is offering something. 'Show me your shoes.'

Warily, she lays her foot into his hand and he cradles it for a moment, running his flattened fingers along the curve of her instep, then over the long stiletto heel and lingering on her ankle, gripping it as though in greeting before replacing it gently on the ground, a blacksmith's motion. He looks into her lean face, so twitchingly alive, a thoroughbred, and shakes his head with disappointment.

'Your heels are too sharp. How can you wear these shoes in weather like this?' he says.

'Women are well-balanced creatures. Didn't you know this?'

She stands on one leg, then the other, and removes them, hanging them on her fingers. He laughs. A light chuckle, boyish, which surprises both of them.

'You can't come out, you'll freeze with no shoes.'

'I'll be fine, there's a doctor present.'

She stands expectantly. And so he scoops an arm underneath her legs and carries her on to the ice. He takes wide steps, bending his knees, keeping a stable base underneath them. If they fall in, there is no one around to help.

When they reach the stool she half kneels on it, tucking her legs beneath her. She places the shoes on the ice and then unfurls her shawl. For an instant it hangs horizontally in the air, swelling in the middle, just as when the nurses change beds in the wards, a suspended sheet gathering together everything in proximity.

She twirls the shawl as it descends and its thickness falls across her entire body, no part of her distinguishable beneath shoulder level. When she is wrapped and seated, he stands behind her and places the rod in her hands, then unclasps the spinner and they listen to the mechanism rotate until he thinks the depth is adequate, then flips over the metal spur, causing the line to brake, and he encourages her to loosen her grip on the handle by gently pinching her fingers.

'Now what do we do?' she asks.

'Now we wait,' he says, and she feels his breath streaming over her neck and he sees the black stilettos lying askew on the white ice, giving off an air of bewilderment.

The memory carried Grigory all the way into the hospital lobby. He glanced at the clock above the reception desk. There was work to be done and he was late. It was almost 9 a.m., a full hour and a half past the time he usually arrived. The place was already moving in the ways it always did. People were sitting, clutching their numbered tickets, waiting to be registered. The administrators were walking behind the counter pressing bundles of paper to their chests. Somewhere in the room a radio broadcast a combination of static and muffled conversation. He brushed through the double swing doors of the ward corridors and passed rooms with nurses handing out medication and saw patients sitting up expectantly, their arms linked to intravenous drips beside their beds. Usually he would turn into one of the wards and have a word with a few of them, a reminder that the surgical staff didn't just see them as skin and bone. He'd ask where they were from, read their medical charts and reassure them, tell them they'd be out of here before the weather changed or the hospital food became too much for them.

People looked up as he passed but he avoided all eye contact. He caught himself mid-pause gazing blankly at an empty wheelchair, still carrying this morning's vision, the very unlikeliness of it turning inside him. He'd have to shake himself out of it.

An attendant crossed in front of him pushing an empty gurney. It shimmered noiselessly across the lime-green linoleum, a twig drifting on a river.

The smell. The place always had the same smell. It usually hit him as soon as he walked through the doors. Disinfectant and boiled vegetables. Earthy and sickly clean. He couldn't smell it without thinking of his aunt, his father's eldest sister. Walking into her house as a child. The stink of her old, unbathed body covered over with the perfumed powder she put on her face.

Family in everything. History bundled into the basic materials of who we are. His was a job where he could trace the origins of things. He often stood and looked at X-rays and saw lesions in a patient's lung, opaque spots dotted around the chest, as if someone had spilled water on to the film. Or coronary arteries that had been whited out, the clotting looking like unthreatening, blank space. He saw the origins of illness. And in many cases he saw family here too, the hereditary nature of these conditions bearing a whisper of those that had gone before. History and family carrying on into the present, into the future, and he never failed to be fascinated, to reflect that our upbringing is apparent not just in our manners or mannerisms or our speech, it is there too on a cellular level, proving its presence on an acetate sheet, laid against a lightbox, fifty years after our birth.

Raisa, his secretary, heard the cartoon squeak of his approach and was already standing by her desk holding a bunch of notecards as he rounded the corner. He nodded his greeting and walked into his office, leaving open the door for her as she trailed him. She began reciting the messages as he took off his jacket and settled himself at his desk.

Some referrals. Replies to referrals. A message from the editor of the state medical journal. Requests for responses to new initiatives from the hospital management committee. Invitations for lecture slots.

He stopped listening after the first few.

He made some calls, dictated two or three of the most pressing letters and then left for the theatre.

His first task was an endoscopy on a young woman. She had come in the previous afternoon, certain that a chicken bone had lodged itself in her neck. Nothing had shown up on the X-ray but it was possible that a bone fragment had lodged itself in her trachea, obscuring itself from view. He had spoken to her the evening before. A young woman full of certainty. A trainee dentist. Sharp-featured. Thin. Her bones discernible under her skin, her clavicles running a straight line under her shoulders, so distinct that when he had spoken to her he couldn't help picturing an artist's sketch of her body, the construction lines as prominent as those of her features.

She was adamant about the pain and would gag involuntarily every now and again, sometimes in mid-sentence. When this happened, though, it barely interrupted her speech. She was unshocked at the reactions of her body, adapting to them.

It was her first stay in a hospital, but there was no sign of nerves. She had a faith in professional procedure, she clearly understood the precautions they would take, trusted in the skill of the surgical staff. Usually he would leave this type of job for one of the registrars, but he had volunteered to do it himself. After speaking with her, a part of him wanted to repay her faith in them. She expected them to be expert and so he would match that, bringing his personal talent and experience to bear. And, besides, he welcomed the easing in. Doing something routine would be a way of warming himself up for the larger tasks of his day.

On the operating table Maya Petrovna Maximova lay on her side, anaesthetized, her lips fitted around a mouthpiece

27

with a hole in the centre, ready to take in the tube of the endoscope. Patients always looked so different in their vulnerable state; the personality she had shown the night before was all but erased.

The viewing screen was placed just above her head, to her right. Stanislav Nicolaevych, his new junior surgeon, stood beside him. Not that there was any need for his presence here, he too could practically do the procedure in his sleep, but it was his way of marking his territory, reminding Grigory that he was more than capable of it.

The tube was handed to him and Grigory began to feed it through the plastic hole in the patient's mouthpiece. He pushed it forward slowly and steadily, careful to maintain a slight momentum but cautious also not to puncture any tissue. The insides of her mouth filled the screen and the short journey began, past the flap of the epiglottis at the back of the mouth as he gently forced it downwards. Maya, although unconscious, gagged, her muscles doing their job. Past the opening of the larynx and the two protrusions of the vocal cords, like small internal fangs, and into the oesophagus. He slowed here, searching for a foreign body. And finally he could see it, a tiny piece of grey gristle that had embedded itself into the wall. Using the pincers attached underneath the camera he plucked it out, drawing a pinprick of blood. He pulled the tube back out, released the fragment into a steel dish and entered once more, checking to see if there were any ancillary pieces, but he found nothing.

Job done, he handed the tube back to the attending nurse and took his leave, moving on to another patient in the adjoining theatre.

He liked the quick satisfaction that came from routine procedures. No thinking to do and minimal risks involved.

The patient would be freed from all discomfort. In a couple of days, she will have forgotten all about that area of her throat, forgotten about him, free to go about her normal days. Nothing in this job was mundane. And it never bored him. Every tiny element had a purpose.

The next hour was taken up with placing a catheter in a man in his mid-forties with subclavian-vein thrombosis. He let Stanislav close this one up to show him that taking on the endoscopy wasn't a judgement on his competency.

Finally, before lunch there was a stent insertion. Usually he played music at this time, but he wasn't in the mood today. The change in routine had an effect on his junior surgeons and nurses though. They were left to guess why there was silence.

He ate a large lunch in the canteen with his old friend Vasily Simenov, an endocrinologist. Grigory rarely ate much but indulged himself because of the day that it was. He and Vasily had served in the military together. Ran and cleaned their guns and ran and stripped them down and put them back together and ran some more. They forged their friendship by holding each other up as they scaled the snowy climbs of the Urals, half their bodyweight strapped to their backs.

When a position had become vacant in his unit Grigory had seen to it that Vasily was transferred in. It was one of the few times he had used his influence to sway things. He needed someone in the hospital who he could be himself with, who knew him before he was who he was. Of course there were mumblings from the rest of the staff, but they quietened over the passing months as Vasily proved his expertise.

After lunch there was a triple bypass that took almost four hours, which he struggled through, feeling bloated after his meal and sweating through the later stages of the operation, the nurse constantly swabbing his brow and offering up the drinking straw attached to his bottle of tepid water.

Until finally he left the hospital and made his way to the baths.

So Grigory needs this swim even more than usual. From the middle of the afternoon he has looked forward to this immersion in the chilled water. And now that he's standing on the edge of the pool, he savours the moment, drawing it out.

He'll swim and then go back for some night reading. It's his favourite part of the day, his mind cleared of practicalities, his body placated by exercise.

The curve of his spine is pulled sideways with idiopathic scoliosis, a condition he's had since childhood. It acts as a personal weather system, dictating his mood and tone with its fluctuating activities, and this is another reason for the routine. He thinks of it as a peace offering, a plea for respite, a secret pact with his troublesome vertebrae. Raising his arms above his head, he traces a wide circumference through the air. He relishes this moment, the moment before entering into a new state, from air to water. Fine blond hairs riffle along his limbs. He dips his back into a concave curve and lowers his head into his shoulders, bending his thick legs as he does so. Grigory cuts through the air until he feels the wholeness of the water sluicing around him. A body of water. He's always liked this phrase; on the news, when snowmelts flood the regions; or in geography exams, when he was asked to compare the size of lakes and seas and channels. We inhabit bodies of water – he thinks when he hears the term – with all our fluids and juices. We have an aquatic mass of our own: tides, maelstroms, undercurrents.

Once submerged, he takes aggressive strokes, lengthening

his arms to their limit, stretching his fingers, tearing through the undulating surface, wanting to temper the water or for it to temper him.

He reaches the far wall and tumbles in expert fashion, flipping his heels over his head, his legs shooting him through the pool, torso corkscrewing to right himself, bulleting underneath the surface.

In the first years of his career, when Grigory was gaining experience as a physician, the pool was a great source of inspiration for him. Often, if a patient had remained undiagnosed for more than three days, he would dive in and wait for the water and motion to provide an answer, which, invariably, it did.

And he's an exceptional swimmer, a fact that has spread among his acquaintances. A story surfaced in the hospital recently about his time in the military, when he and his comrades showed up to a grand party in a dacha somewhere near Zavidovo. Grigory got so drunk that he couldn't stand upright, so his comrades threw him into the swimming pool for safety and Grigory floated there, unaided, for the rest of the night. He couldn't remember the party, a fact which, considering the circumstances, didn't make the story any less true.

Of course it made good gossip in the hospital. He knows it hasn't come from Vasily. They never talk about their military life to anyone else – it's a point of honour between them – so Grigory has no idea how it emerged. But he doesn't care. Maybe it's good for them to see him in a different light, to see him as something other than their responsible superior. It would remind them that he's a man going about his duty, just as they are.

He has never heard the story told inside the hospital walls. He hasn't caught a snatched conversation in a nurses' station, or two orderlies whispering by the coffee machine. But he knows it's there, in the ether, the same way he knows when one of the registrars sneaks in late to rounds or when a junior surgeon is unsure of the exact location of the intercostal nodes.

The rush of silence as, eyes closed, he listens to channels of water passing his ears.

Grigory understands the power of the unspoken. To progress is to become fluent in the language. His rise in stature increased its pace when Grigory noticed that people in positions of power could hold almost an entire conversation with only a few simple words. He gained influence by understanding what his older, more junior, colleagues did not: that power lurks in silences, in whispered conversations in the corner of a room, in contained gestures: a dip of the head; a pat of the forearm. It has often struck him that the most powerful men he has met also have the greatest range of physical articulations, a vital ability in a sphere where a misinterpreted comment can end even the most celebrated of careers.

He cranes his arms over his head and plunges them under the surface, limbs travelling from water to air to water, bubbles leaking from his nose. After a few lengths the actions become automatic and his encounter this morning re-emerges. He sees the shoes again, ghosts standing in formation.

He couldn't begin to guess – and would never want to – how many of his patients have had their lives cut short. And although it was never something he had fully articulated, even to himself, it was no coincidence that he had chosen a job that valued human life in a state that had always disregarded it so readily.

Simple physical actions. Arms and legs. Head and torso. No thought required, just motion in water. He places his arms by his sides, paddles gently with his feet and opens his eyes to the space that envelops him, lined in white ceramic.

The old silences are echoing. In the past year there has been a steady stream of young men coming through the doors with knife wounds. The emergency rooms now have to deal with drug overdoses. Sometimes, on weekends, there are full fistfights in the reception area. Secret bars are popping up in abandoned factories or unused rail depots. Anger is beginning to seep out. People aren't so careful with what they say any more. Grigory sees traffic lights burst apart by rocks, road signs that have been scrawled over. Public property used to be an almost sacred thing, collective property. No one touched it before. That too has changed.

He doesn't feel any revulsion towards the present or nostalgia for tradition; anger is a presence to be welcomed. Everyone, including himself, has spent too long denying the accumulation of commonplace evidence. Injustices have mounted up on everybody's doorstep.

He pulls himself out of the pool, water funnelling down.

In the steam room sits Zhykhov, chief of administration at the hospital, talking to an acquaintance. Grigory knows the man's not a friend because Zhykhov's laughing that laugh of his, barking it out, obviously trying to ingratiate himself.

The acquaintance is smoking a wilting cigar. The smoke drifts up and mingles with the steam, the two substances circling each other in a formal dance. His lank hair droops over his forehead. Grigory finds something quite familiar about the man, something that engages him, the way he looks to the ceiling when he speaks, the rhythm of his smoking. Something.

Zhykhov raises a hand and beckons him over. Grigory is a good twenty years younger than him and Zhykhov wants to be cast in the light of youthful vigour.

'Our head of surgery, Dr Grigory Ivanovich Brovkin.

Look at him. A brilliant career ahead of him. Everything he could wish for at his fingertips.'

Grigory laughs dutifully.

'Perhaps the brilliance is all behind me.'

Zhykhov raises a thumb to his companion and waggles his hand.

'Don't worry, Vladimir, he's rarely this modest. This man, such ambition I have never seen. A python, this man. He squeezes every breath of rationality out of you. Arguing with him is a full gloves-off affair. This man is a fucking word-smith.'

The acquaintance looks bemused. 'I like my surgeons to be good with their hands, I'm not looking for someone who can dominate a debating chamber.'

Grigory remembers.

'You like a surgeon who can remove an inflamed appendix.'

The man lowers his cigar and stares at Grigory. Unconsciously he runs the tips of his fingers along the neat scar to the right of his stomach. He's trying to figure out if Grigory has mentioned this because he noticed the mark. But the way he said it implies a familiarity.

'Have you been to Kursk?' he asks tentatively. Grigory can tell that the man is rarely unbalanced like this. He's a man who knows things about other people. He's not used to them having some insight into his life.

'Yes. I operated on you.'

'I don't remember you. But then I hardly knew where I was at the time.'

He offers his hand and Grigory shakes it.

'I owe you some thanks, Dr Brovkin.'

Zhykhov cuts in. 'Vladimir Andreiovich Vygovskiy has recently been appointed the chief advisor to the Ministry of Fuel and Energy.'

'Then we've both come a long way from Kursk.'

Vygovskiy takes a long pull from his cigar, holding the smoke, which gives him a moment to consider his answer.

'Yes and no, comrade. There I was in charge of a nuclear-power plant. I had real things to look after: equipment, operational procedures. I had a building to run. That time, when I was sick, my wife was getting calls every hour, asking advice, wondering when I'd be returning. Now, I think I could go missing for months without anyone really noticing. The department would just carry on without me. Someone else would be happy to offer the advice I give. I'm sure, comrade Brovkin, you've never experienced such feelings. Every day you have people's lives in your hands. You've never come home in the evening wondering, *What's the point?*'

'We all do what we can do, comrade. It's good to meet you again in full health. I don't remember the circumstances of your case, but it can be an awkward procedure. I'm pleased to know you are well.'

Grigory wants to move on to a spot of his own, to close his eyes, let the steam filter in, but he can see Vygovskiy is interested, lining up another question. It would be disadvantageous to provoke Zhykhov's displeasure, so he stays.

'You feel a sense of ownership to your cases?'

'I feel a responsibility. If an operation goes wrong, who else is there to blame?'

'Many people blame fate.'

'Yes, they do.'

A pause. Vygovskiy is a man who knows how to read a pause.

'But you're not many people.'

Vygovskiy turns to his associate.

'You have an excellent surgeon here. My wife had nothing but praise for him, even though he was about twelve at the

35

time. And my wife is not an easy woman to please. Apparently he talked everything through with her so calmly. I remember when I was back home in bed, she said a tornado could have blown through the building and the young surgeon wouldn't have flinched, he'd still have sat there, answering her questions.'

Zhykhov laughs, slapping Grigory on the shoulders, his prize pig.

'I choose well, Vladimir. I keep telling you we have the best medical staff in the city. Imagine what results we could achieve if we had some proper funding.'

Grigory remembers the man's wife. There was a thing she did with her mouth, a certain turned-up disdain that showed on her lips and, even if this were not the case, people could tell by the quality of her clothes that she was married to someone with influence.

He had lied about not remembering the circumstances. It was a crucial moment in his career. He could recall it all in great detail.

By the time Vygovskiy checked into the hospital, his appendix had swollen up like a balloon. No one would take on the procedure. The man was a high-ranking member of the regional section of the Party. It was well known that he had connections to the highest levels in Moscow. Any mistakes could have serious consequences for the surgeon or his family. Even the administrative staff were reluctant to handle his records. Everyone knew that perforation of the organ was very likely, and that peritonitis, which was often fatal, could set in. So the responsibility was passed down the line, surgeon to surgeon, until the file landed in Grigory's hands.

A few hours later, Maria approached him outside the break room, placed her mop against the wall and walked out through a delivery door. He knew her signals well enough by now to understand he should follow, even though he had a patient waiting, even though he'd get a dressing-down from one of his superiors for being late. They sat in the car park, behind a beige Moskvich with a drooping headlight. She wore a padded overcoat with her thick plastic apron showing through underneath, her hair in a net, some loose strands clinging to her face. She smelled strongly of bleach.

'I'm hearing things,' she said.

'About me?'

'Of course.'

'What things?'

'Don't ask me "What things?", you know what things.'

'So then. You want to talk about it.'

'Yes. I want to talk about it.'

'I can't discuss it. I have to respect the patient's privacy.'

'Don't. I'm not just some stranger. I'm thinking about your safety. Don't. They say he's powerful. They say his wife is feeling guilty that it took them so long to get help, she wants to blame someone.'

'They say a lot.'

'Yes, they do. I hear things and I've been here long enough to tell the difference between gossip and something real. When people talk about you now they shake their heads. They're pitying you. They think you're being offered up as a sacrifice.'

Grigory doesn't say anything. They sit in silence for a few moments.

'Are you?'

'Yes. Probably. In their eyes at least.'

And they were quiet again.

When they fought she hunched in on herself, took time to choose her words, to calm her temper. It was something he

37

admired at the beginning, that ability to be both articulate and angry at the same time. Later he came to hate it. She always had an answer, even when she was wrong; even at the end, when her actions were unforgivable.

'Why you? Why should you take this on and not someone else?'

'Why not me? If we delay it much longer the man might die. Someone needs to make a decision.'

'There are others with more skill.'

'I don't believe that.'

She looked at him, laughed at his arrogance.

'There are people more experienced than me, yes, but not more skilled.'

'You haven't even finished your training.' She said this in exasperation, breath filling her voice.

'It's a routine operation, I've observed it dozens of times.'

'Oh. Well, if you've *observed* it. Well, in that case, you're the perfect surgeon for the job. "I've *observed it*," he says.'

He put a hand on her arm.

'Do you trust me?'

'Yes. But I don't want you to take this risk. I don't want to imagine what might happen.'

'I'm a doctor. I can't walk away from this because I'm afraid. I'm a surgeon and he needs surgery and no one else will do it.'

'It doesn't have to be you.'

'It doesn't have to be, but it is. Do you trust me?'

'Yes.'

'So . . .'

He clapped his hands against his thighs. There was no more to be said. He didn't want to rationalize it, to turn a medical decision into something that should be weighed against political risk.

'When will it happen?'

'In the morning.'

'You'll find me afterwards.'

'Yes. Of course.'

'You'll be careful.'

'Yes.'

He kissed her, a consoling kiss, a faint taste of chemicals on her lips, and then walked back to the building alone. More scared than he'd ever been.

Sweat runs down Grigory's eyes and he wipes it away and sees the steam room has filled. Two men sit across from him exchanging stories. One is mapping out the terrain of their conversation by tracing his finger through the air.

He hears Zhykhov's exaggerated laugh again and turns and watches Vygovskiy. After the operation, responsibility was thrust his way. He was allowed to scrub in on the most difficult cases. His learning accelerated and promotion came quickly. How easily, he thinks, our lives hinge on single incidents. Grigory stands and offers his hand.

'Good to meet you again. This time in better circumstances.'

Vygovskiy stands to shake it.

'I had hoped you'd stay. I'm interested to hear about you.'

'Unfortunately, comrade, I can't this evening. I really must get back to the hospital.'

Grigory nods his goodbye to Zhykhov and leaves.

In his office Grigory can't concentrate. He realizes that a full hour has passed, staring at the same page, the words divorced from him, seeming to float above his consciousness. Studying has been a part of his routine for so long that he can pore over dense texts for hours without losing momentum. Usually he opens a page, scans it for the relevant facts, a sentence buried in a dense paragraph, makes some brief notes and moves on.

Not tonight, though.

He raises his head and considers the room.

He takes pleasure in his office, especially at this time of day, when it's cocooned in the soft amber light of his reading lamp, text books and journals arranged chronologically on dark wooden shelves that take up an entire wall, the most recent publications nearest his chair, so he can check a case study without standing. A couch and coffee table in the corner, which he never uses. His certificates framed and evenly spaced on the opposing wall, standing proudly over three well-ordered filing cabinets. Beside the door, across from his desk, are the only personal items in the room: three photographs of beech trees, the same image taken at different points of the year, their colours in stark contrast. Photographs he had taken as a teenager, when photography was an obsession for him. A passion he keeps promising himself that he'll return to someday, if he ever finds the time.

Grigory swivels round in his chair and looks out of the window. It's not yet fully dark and he walks over to take in the view, placing a hand on the thick blue curtains. The window overlooks a park. On the grass below two lovers roll over each other. Not a sexual tryst, rather a childlike tumble, their laughter carrying upwards.

The night after the operation he and Maria experienced a similar joy, an unburdening taking place through each other's touch. He had found her that morning and delivered the good news, how it had been a success, the man would recover, but they were in public, the conversation taking place near the nurses' station in the orthopaedic wards. He could only relay a short message, their eyes speaking for each of them, relief expanding their pupils. When his long shift finished he met her in a railed garden near her apartment. She waited for him on a bench. No other life nearby. He stood and looked, an outsider to the scene, an onlooker, drinking in the sight of her, as she stamped her feet on the ground in cold and anticipation. When he approached he took her hands and tipped backwards into the snow, his momentum lifting her from the bench, pulling her on top of him. His hands propping up her shoulders, her chest, feeling the volume, the density of her. Her breath streaming into his collar, radiating down into his chest, regions of their clothes being peeled away. All of it slow and deliberate. Blending their skin. Both of them reaching for the place of most heat, her fluid running like warm oil, gathering in the cleft of his hand. Until finally she enveloped him, condensation hovering over them. And they collapsed into each other, a dark form on a pristine canvas, pulsing together, their individual elements becoming erased.

And afterwards he wrapped his fingers around the parts of her within his reach and named the bones that formed her. Manubrium. Ulna. Radius. Scapula. And she listened to the inflections of his voice, felt the vibrations of his words in her ear. Their breathing slowing, calming.

A siren wails in the distance. Grigory watches the lovers stand and leave, brushing grass off each other's backs, still laughing. He opens the window and puts his head outside, the evening air refreshing him. He shouldn't still be here. He knows he won't get any more work done this evening. An impulse comes over him to go and see a play at the Kirov, but it's too late now.

41

He wants some company. He could call on Vasily, have a drink at his kitchen table, but the man has a family, there'd be kids to be bathed. Besides, Vasily's wife would probably remember it was Grigory's birthday. How pathetic he would look, calling round because he had nowhere else to spend the evening.

No. He'll go home, go to bed early, something he hasn't done in an age.

In the corridor visitors are leaving the wards, coats slung over their arms. They have concerned conversations: couples, siblings, parents. Telling each other their impressions of how their loved one is progressing, saying all the things they can't say in front of the sick. We put on our most positive front in the face of weakness. He sees this continually. Around each corner people are leaning their backs to the wall, crying silently, a hand to their faces, their companions standing beside them, a reassuring touch on their shoulder or arm. Inside the wards the patients are silent. In time they'll pick up a conversation again, introduce their visitors in retrospect, summarizing them in brief biographies: their son's career; the intolerant men their daughter always chooses; the older brother who still treats them as though they were a teenager; the grandchildren they're still waiting on. He passes through Intensive Care, stopping at the nurses' station to inquire about the progress of his patients for the day, something he does every evening. All are stable and have reacted well, so far, to surgery. He decides to round off his day by checking in on this morning's endoscopy, making his way to the ENT ward. The nurse reminds him of the patient's name, Maya Petrovna, and points him towards her bed.

She's sitting up, knitting, her needles clicking time.

'A scarf?' he asks.

'It was supposed to be a sweater. But they all end up as scarves eventually.'

'You're not following a pattern?'

'I'm just following the needles.'

'How are you feeling?'

'Relieved.'

She stops her knitting and leans over conspiratorially.

'I had a thought, before the anaesthetic. I knew it was a routine procedure but I began to fear the worst.'

'Don't worry, you're not the first.'

'No, that's not it. I wasn't worried about it all ending. I was worried about the funeral. I couldn't bear the conversations. "Death by Chicken Bone" – what a fate. Everyone doing their best not to laugh. I thought, if I have to die early, I want it to be from a condition with a complicated name.'

Grigory smiles.

'I'm not sure you get to choose.'

He puts a hand on her shoulder.

'Good night. I'm glad to see everything's OK.'

'Thank you, doctor. It's good to be back to normal.'

'Good luck with the scarf.'

'You should wish the scarf luck instead, it has no idea what's ahead of it.'

Grigory passes through the lobby, filled with people waiting to be admitted. Those without chairs sit against the walls, framing the perimeter of the room. There's a chorus of coughing. A pool of tea lies in the middle of the aisle. He walks past it, it's not his responsibility and, besides, he's finished for the day. Three steps more and then he stops. He can't bring himself to ignore it and walks back to the admission desk, asking the receptionist to get some attendants to clean it up. When he sees her making the call he turns to go.

And she's sitting there, in the front row.

Talking to a kid with floppy blond hair.

Pushing it away from his forehead.

Her hair is short, sharply cut; it still has its dark lustre, with the odd rogue strand of grey. Her face is slightly more defined, sinews in her neck beginning to show. She's talking to the boy and he realizes it's Zhenya, her nephew, his nephew still, technically, an older version of the child he knew, beginning to take on the heft of a teenage boy, broader shoulders, a thicker face, and he can hear the inflections in her voice as she talks to the child and they reach him in waves, warm, subdued, utterly her.

Maria.

He says her name.

She turns and looks at him, and he realizes what an advantage it was to have noticed her first. She can't control her reaction. The flicker of naked shock across her face, which softens into pleasure, familiarity.

'Grigory.'

He takes a step towards her.

'What are you doing here?'

She gestures to Yevgeni to hold up his hand, which he does, the fifth digit red and swollen, possibly fractured.

'He's telling me he caught it in a door. Which is code, of course, meaning some kids attacked him.'

'You should have called me.'

'I didn't want to bother you. We can wait.'

'Come through.'

'We can wait. We'll be called soon.'

'Come on through. Please.' Grigory turns to Yevgeni. 'Let's get you looked after. I bet it hurts.'

'It's not too bad,' Yevgeni says, attempting bravery.

'Do you know who this is, Zhenya? It's Grigory. Do you remember him?'

Yevgeni looks at the doctor. He remembers the man

44

carrying a present into their apartment. A large, wrapped box. But he doesn't remember when this was or what was in it.

Grigory picks up an admissions form, indicates to the receptionist that he'll take this case and leads them through the doors.

They walk in silence to Radiography. It feels too casual for them to speak while moving. And the boy is there – they need to get reacquainted on their own before they can talk in front of others.

Grigory steps aside for a short conversation with a radiographer then returns and speaks gently to Yevgeni.

'You're going to get an X-ray of your hand. Do you know what that is?'

'Yes. It's a photograph of my bones.'

'That's right. Sergei here will look after you. It'll only take a few minutes. When he's finished, he'll bring you back to us. Is that all right?'

Yevgeni nods. 'Yes.'

'Come on then,' says Sergei. 'Let's get you fixed up.'

Sergei offers his hand to Yevgeni, but he doesn't accept it, so instead Sergei begins to walk and Yevgeni follows.

Grigory hands Maria the admissions form to fill out and they both sit and she starts writing.

'He's grown up. He's not a child any more. I barely recognized him.'

She takes a minute to reply, checking she's filled in the form correctly, then places it on the small table beside her. She turns and looks at him, settling into the chair.

'Yes. He'll be a teenager any day now. Mood swings and masturbation are imminent.'

Grigory laughs.

A pause.

'I knew I might run into you,' she says.

'Did you look forward to it?'

'No. Maybe. I don't know.'

Another pause.

'Yes. I wanted to see you. If I'm being honest.'

'I'm glad you came. You look well.'

'Thank you. I feel bad for keeping you working though, your days are long enough.'

'I'm sitting here, talking with you. This isn't work.'

'Well, thank you anyway.'

Another pause.

'I thought about you on my way here this morning.'

'Really? Why?'

'I saw a pair of high-heeled shoes. The same as those black ones you used to wear all the time.'

He thinks about describing the sight to her, but stops himself. It would be too complicated to explain.

'Just one of those reminders that come from nowhere.'

Maria would like to ask if there were others, ask how often he thinks of her.

'Happy birthday,' she says instead, softly.

'Thanks.'

'No parties?'

'What do you think?'

'It's possible. Maybe there have been changes I don't know about.'

'No. No changes. And you?'

She leans back and rubs her neck, something she does when a conversation ventures into uncomfortable ground. They know all each other's signals.

'Yes. There are changes.'

'A new apartment? A new job?'

'I'm doing some teaching now, a couple of days a week at

the Lomonosov. I'm still living with Alina. That's not what I meant, though.'

'I know.'

The texture of her skin. He can bring forth the sensation of touching it just by looking at her, it feels as if he were keeping perfect time to a long-forgotten dance.

The ceiling is made up of square foam tiles, one or two dislodged, revealing the darkness of the roof space above.

'I bought an allotment. I've been growing potatoes.'

'Good,' she smiles. 'I'm glad. Where is it?'

'Out in Levshano. I go there on weekends and turn the soil and practise for when I'm deaf and half senile.'

She laughs her laugh.

'He's become quite the talent.'

'Who?'

She nods in the direction of the radiography room.

'His piano playing. He's now a fully blown prodigy. There's talk of a scholarship to the Conservatory.'

'Really?'

He looks to see if she's joking; he can't hear it in her voice.

'Really.' -

'It happens that quickly? I remember he used to plonk away with gusto on my old upright, like any other kid in front of a keyboard. Three years and he's a potential genius?'

'I know. It makes me wonder what the hell I've been doing with my time.'

'He looks so uncoordinated.'

'Well, they never look like athletes, do they, all that time spent tinkling away. He's kind of a marvel, though. Alina's got him a teacher in the Tverskoy. An old Jew. Tough as a boot. I've seen him at lessons. The teacher plays something, then Zhenya sits down and plays it back. Straight away. Without hesitating. No notation either.'

'Just like that? From nowhere?'

'From nowhere. I'm constantly having to fight away my jealousy. We're saving to buy him a piano.'

'You're saying the boy doesn't even have a piano?'

'No. Nothing. When I said "prodigy", I wasn't exaggerating.'

Grigory flattens his hair with his hand. She can tell he's irritated.

'Why didn't you ask for mine?'

'I couldn't.'

'If he needs it. You know I can hardly play – it's just gathering dust. You're too afraid to pick up the phone?'

'Not afraid. Of course not. But maybe you'd moved on. Maybe there's someone there now who plays. How can I ask anything of you?'

'There's no one else.' An edge to his voice.

A pause.

'OK. Thank you. I'm sorry. I've no right to be possessive. Don't be annoyed.'

'I'm not.'

Another pause. Maria waits for his irritation to calm.

'I ask myself if you're happy,' Maria says.

'I'm not unhappy.'

'It's not the same thing.'

'No. It's not.'

The door opens down the corridor and Sergei beckons them in.

He hands Grigory the acetate sheet.

'A clean fracture on the metacarpal.'

Grigory holds it to the light to confirm, then brings it over to Yevgeni.

'Have a look.'

Yevgeni looks up at the sheet.

'That's my hand?'

'That's your hand. See the black line, at the bottom of your fourth finger?'

'Yes. The bone is broken then?'

'Don't worry. It'll be back to normal in a few weeks.'

Grigory sends Sergei off to get some painkillers, and they enter a treatment room. He takes a metal splint from one of the blue plastic boxes that sit on a rack in the corner. It looks like the tweezers Yevgeni sees in his mother's purse, except thicker. Grigory sits him down and slides it carefully over the finger, strapping it in place.

'No piano for you for a while.'

'I know.'

'Are you sad about that?'

'No,' he says. Then turns to check if his aunt will repeat this to his mother, but she's looking around the room pretending she hasn't heard.

Grigory hands the X-ray to the boy.

'Keep it. Put it up on your bedroom wall. Not many other boys have a photograph of their bones.'

Yevgeni smiles up at him.

'Thank you.'

Sergei returns with a small plastic container of pills, then leaves, winking at Yevgeni on his way out.

They say their goodbyes in the car park. Grigory has offered to walk them to the Metro but Maria refuses. He can tell by her voice that he shouldn't argue. Grigory shakes Yevgeni's good hand, tells him to be careful and to keep the dressing clean. He embraces Maria, her body so warm, slipping easily under his hands. They break, hesitantly, and Grigory reaches into his pocket for the plastic bottle and hands it over.

'Give him one if he can't sleep. The pain should pass in the next few days.'

'Thank you.'

'The piano. You know where to find me.'

'Yes.'

'Come and find me.'

Maria takes in his words and turns and walks into the evening. Yevgeni beside her, holding his hand up, inspecting the dressing.

A small alarm clock sits on a locker beside the boy's bed, but its bells will be silent, a silence that has carried through the past week. The boy wakes and stares at the longer hand, tracking its slow circle until the hour reaches five and grants him permission to peel off his blankets and enter the pre-dawn light.

The light is different this morning. A blend of mauves and yellows, ruby-rich colours that, upon the moment of his awakening, make him wonder if he has overslept: surely the dawn has already arrived. He feels an instant tightening, the sensation particular to this crime, familiar to him from those rare days when he has emerged late for school or for milking, the surge of panic that sweeps over the muscles when time has stolen precious minutes or hours from their hold. He sits up and looks at the small clock and his brain assures him back to a relaxed state. The clock is never wrong and, even if it were, surely his father would have come to place a hand on his ankle, waking him gently.

Artyom is thirteen; the age has finally come when he can rise with his father, when he can hold a gun and listen to how men talk when they are alone. He is not of the age when he can add to the conversation – he knows this – but someday, this too will come.

This hour is new to him, the pre-rising hour, the hour where nothing is required but thought. Before this spring, his life was comprised only of activity, by eating or preparing food, by walking the cows down the rutted lane, lining them up for milking, then walking them back once more. Endless days defined by school and work and sleep. Occasionally there would be a party, on V-Day or Labour Day, when they would walk to the Polovinkins' izba and join all the other families in the village. Where Anastasiya Ivanovna would play the balalaika and the men would sing army songs, solemn and low, until someone would turn the dial on the radio and they would spread into the lane and dance together, or if rain was falling, bump around on the porch and laugh. But this was a rare occasion, maybe three times a year, the whole village coming together, a village of twenty-five families.

On the first morning, on Monday, when he woke at four, the anticipation turning something inside him, he could think of nothing, but decided not to rise: his older sister, Sofya, slept six feet away and it would be wrong to wake her any earlier than necessary. Besides, his parents slept in the next room and his father would wake and dress and then be angry with him for adding another hour to his already long day. There was a possibility he would be denied the trip and would have to wait another year to shoot grouse with the men. One more year. He had pleaded with his father for so long now that another year would drain away the joy of anticipation, leave him murky and resentful.

And so, on that first morning, he simply lay in stillness and watched the rise and dip of the blankets that covered Sofya and the slow wash of light from a wakening sky, light that climbed the wooden walls and spilled over their neatly folded clothes resting on the two shelves of the opposite wall.

So curious, the colours he sees now, much different from the other mornings, seeping through the glass, making each aspect of the room seem precious, as though while sleeping they had been doused in wealth. His threadbare shirts seem gilded, the walls fashioned from a deep, exotic wood. He tries to think of a word with which to describe the sight to his mother when they sit over dinner this evening, but he doesn't know the word yet. When she says it to him later, he forms it on his lips, repeating it silently, 'luminous', the shape of the word causing his lips to move like those of a feeding fish.

He thinks of his babushka who died during the winter. His father took the door off its hinges and laid it out on her table and laid her on top of it. A simple ritual that lifted the weight Artyom had felt during those days. Seeing her presented like that, the moment wasn't as final as he'd expected it to be. Even though her skin had gained a greenish tinge, and her forehead was as cold as the stones they picked from the bare earth before ploughing. That night, when he took his turn to watch over the body, he spent his time staring at the candlelight dancing its way around the flaked paintwork on the boards, the gnarled iron of the latch. The light glowing then as it did now, softly vibrating around its edges.

When the hour hand finally nudges into position, Artyom rises and gathers his clothes and creeps into the kitchen. He pulls his pants over his underwear, laces his boots, drops some small logs into the stove, poking it back to life, and walks to the well outside.

Springtime. A freshness in the air. Everything growing, all around, everything feeling alive, blossoms and birdsong, all things paled in their coat of morning dew. He drops the bucket down and hauls it back up and cups the cold water under his armpits and over his chest, with its newly acquired trails of hair and, leaning over the well, pours the rest of it around the back of his neck, so that it parts over his head then joins upon itself once more, falling back to its origin in one sinuous length.

He stands and wipes the water from his eyes, smearing it

down his cheeks, and shakes out his head, the cold of the water charging through his skin.

He opens his eyes and the sky floods his retinas, a sky of the deepest crimson. It looks as if the earth's crust has been turned inside out, as if molten lava hangs weightless over the land. The boy looks into the depth of the sky, looking further than he ever has before, seeing through to the contours of the universe.

Artyom can hear muffled conversation from the pathway and sees steam rising over the hedgerows. He moves back inside to the kitchen, where his father laces his boots. The boy covers himself with a shirt and rubs it against his body, so it soaks up the remaining drops of water clinging to his skin. He slides into a woollen sweater and wraps himself in a coat and hat and folds his hands into a pair of fingerless gloves.

'Wait until you see the sky,' he says to his father. 'What a sky.'

'It's the same sky we've always lived under. It's just in a different mood.'

Artyom takes the large jug of milk from the fridge and pours it into two bottles, then seals and wraps them in wet rags before placing them in his satchel. His father hands him a box of cartridges and the shotgun, which he has already cracked open for safety, so that its two ends droop over his father's arm as if winded. His father gives him a nod, which is a silent reminder of the safety practices they have discussed: keep the gun open unless loaded; keep the cartridges dry and in their box; never point a loaded gun anywhere but at the sky or the target.

They join the men in silence, footsteps crunching across the packed earth. He has known these men all his life, known them at times to be loud and funny and full of song, but on these mornings they pay respect to the repose of the land, smoking in unison, opening their mouths only for a quiet greeting or a suggested change of direction or when a bird is spotted.

The boy walks a little further back from the men, trailing the huddled bulk of the group. He likes to open and close the gun, enjoying the reassuring *twock* that comes from the closure of finely engineered metal. He pushes aside the clasp and opens the shaft and closes it again, the sound of something fitting as it should. He's sure his father would look disapprovingly at such a habit and so he keeps his distance, keeps the pleasure his own.

They take the same route as other mornings, turning left past the Scherbak home, crossing a small stile over the drain and heading into the fields towards the pond where the grouse will have returned once more, having forgotten the deadly lesson of the previous morning.

His father had taught him to shoot only two weeks beforehand. It was a Tuesday evening when he brought the extra gun home. The boy knew he had received it from one of the other men in the kolkhoz – the collective farm – in exchange for covering some extra shifts; which in turn compelled Artyom to treat the gun with a reverence; the fact that his father was willing to work for it, for him. His father brought it home but gave no indication of his efforts. To an outsider, it might have seemed that his father merely found the object sticking out from a hedgerow at the end of the lane, that it was simply an advantageous quirk which interrupted an otherwise unremarkable day.

Artyom knew differently, though.

His father showed him how to line up the sights of the gun, demonstrated for him the different stances required when kneeling or standing, and when the boy was finally allowed to take his first shot at a depressed football they had hung from a branch, he was astonished at the power of the kickback from the weapon, causing him almost to lose his balance; despite the fact that he had anticipated it, been warned of it, had lodged the butt of the gun firmly into the notch between his shoulder and his collarbone. The compressed power of a weapon. This was what it was to hold power in your arms.

Crossing the second field, Artyom changes his path slightly, walking in an arched trajectory so he can approach some of the scattered bullocks chewing lazily in the morning air. He likes to rub his hand along them, the quivering life they hold underneath their hairy exteriors passing itself into his fingers. He likes the packed concentration of muscle beneath the beasts. When he was younger, he and his friends would punch the cattle hard, hoping for a response, but they never managed to provoke anything more than a disinterested look.

Artyom runs his hand over the head of the nearest one and feels the morning dew slicking his fingers, the heat emanating from its neck. The dew feels different than on previous occasions, as though it has the texture of fine material, and the boy looks at his fingers and finds them tipped with liquid. He scans the body and sees a channel of blood slowly pouring from the animal's ear, dripping to the grass below. He checks the next bullock, ten feet away, and finds precisely the same.

He deliberates whether to call his father, by now almost out of earshot, but the decision isn't a difficult one: cattle are important here; the difference between livelihood and starvation; he had known this even as a small child. His father hears the shout and stops, irritated, but then makes his way back to the boy. Andrei's son always displays good judgement: if he considers something worth stopping for, it is worth at least some consideration. The other men are as unhurried as the beasts; they rummage in their pockets and light another cigarette and watch and wait.

These cattle belong to Vitaly Scherbak. Though all the men work for the kolkhoz, each of them has an acre or two of his own upon which to keep a few thin animals. These cattle will spend next winter wrapped in old newspaper, sitting in stacked lumps in old fridges or packed underneath hard clay. For now, though, they stand, bemused, chewing their cud, looking at Andrei Yaroslavovych and his son walk amongst them, tilting their heads to the morning sun.

When Andrei returns he consults the group and they decide to let Vitaly sleep an extra hour. The beasts will need attention but they seem in no great distress and their neighbour could do with his rest. But the news brings some conversation to the remainder of their walk, murmurs of speculation as to what could possibly cause a whole herd to bleed in such a way. And Artyom is proud of this, he has gained further degrees of respect, a boy who could notice such things would soon no longer be a boy, could soon make jokes and observations and judgements of his own.

They nestle into the ditch and Artyom takes in the sky once more. The great, roiling sky, looming over the earth, drawing all things together in their relative insignificance.

The men load their guns and stabilize themselves with their legs. Each one focuses on a particular bird and readies himself to shoot. A single shot would scatter the flock and leave the rest of the men cursing their lost opportunities. They would shoot as a group, just as they worked as a group, drank as a group, lived as a group. This is Artyom's favourite part, the moment before the moment, when he can feel the concentration spread evenly amongst the men, the tufts of air from their morning breath spreading outwards simultaneously. Breathing together, being together. A hushed voice speaks out – 'Ready' – not as a question but a statement, a confirmation of their collective state, and the shots are released, two rounds each, noise obliterating the silence like a fist launched through a glass pane.

They are skilled shots, all having been through military service. All hit their prey, with the exception of the boy, who has yet to become as attuned to the sensitivities of the gun, the barrel bobbling slightly in front of him, tracing out a small, uneven circle. All is as it should be.

It's the following moments that mark the beginning of something distinctive, a tilt in the balance of the natural order, a moment they would relate in a thousand conversations that stalked their future lives.

Immediately after the first shot, the grouse flurry into the air, but when normally they would then glide in a smooth and rapid flight, low over the earth, today they rise and wobble back to the ground, or skim along for a few feet before crashing back to the grass, rolling in a drunken, graceless sprawl of floundering wings and buckling legs.

The men reload and shoot, but quickly stop, all of them feeling a strengthening unease at the absurd sight before them. They rise from the ditch and walk out into the field and flip the carcasses over with their toes, the remaining live birds still twisting in the grass, disorientated. Artyom pulls a sack from his satchel, collecting the game as he had done on other mornings, but his father tells him to put it away, these birds should not be eaten.

They have lived most of their lives on this small patch of earth. They know the tides of growth and season, the disposition of nature, its wonts and moods. They recognize a disharmony here, in the strange events of the morning. As they return to their homes, to sleeping families, they consider this strange morning, wondering if the strangeness would extend itself to them, to the humans who live in this place. And they know that this, as with all other things, would reveal itself with time.

In the Chernobyl nuclear-power plant, ten kilometres from the sleeping boy, as the hour hand on his small clock inched its way between the two and the three, flaming particles of graphite and lead, great molten wads of steel, spiralled through the night air, finding refuge in the roofs adjacent to Reactor No. 4. Fire spread fire spread fire, skimming over bitumen and concrete, boring itself down shafts, through ceilings, engulfing stairs, engulfing air. Elements blindly raging into the great surround: xenon and caesium, tellurium and iodine, plutonium and krypton. Set free unseen, accompanying the swathes of pirouetting sparks. Noble gases, expanding into the noble land. Neutrons and gamma rays streaming up and out, pulsing into the sky, over the earth, atoms careening into atoms, rippling through a continent.

In the control room, the operators watch the glass panel billow outward, testing its extremes, then retreating and attacking once more, sending particles into skin, into walls and floors, lodging itself into doors and keypads and necks and lips and palms. They see control rods launched vertically from the floor of the reactor hall; streaking upwards, dozens of weighted rods fleeing gravity and order, seizing their moment to soar above all they were made for, all they had known.

Steel girders buckle and twist. The baritone of wrenching metal thrumming with the steady bass vibrations of a blast.

Water everywhere: gushing through ventilation ducts, clambering over partition walls, racing down corridors. Steam filling the senses. A wall of steam, a chamber of steam, squirming its way into nostrils and earholes, seeping into eyes, down smoke-caked throats. They plunge their arms through steam, arms swimming while legs walk or buckle. Bulbs blown, the only light now from falling embers; blue flashes from electrical systems that spit out their protests.

The operators pick themselves up, dazed. There is a task, a function. What to do? Surely there's a button, a series of codes, a procedure, always a procedure. Miraculously they find the operating manual, damp but usable. They locate the section. There's a section. Ears numb from the piercing alarm. Eyes streaming. A section. Scanning through pages. A title: 'Operational Procedures in the Event of Reactor Meltdown'. A block of black ink, two pages, five pages, eight pages. All text has been wiped out, paragraphs hidden behind thick black lines. An event such as this cannot be tolerated, cannot be conceived, such a thing can never be planned for, as surely as it can never happen. The system will not fail, the system cannot fail, the system is the glorious motherland.

Workers burst out from the canteen and the locker rooms and run through waterlogged corridors, gas and dust whirling from the air vents. All is washed in the red glow from emergency lights. They wear white laboratory coats, white caps tied over their heads like kitchen porters. They are in a painting, a movie, a palate of red and black, light and shadow. They run into the bowels of the building finding stricken bodies: men foaming at the mouth, writhing listlessly on the floor. Radiation has already worked its way through their cells, their skin showing large, dark blotches mapping their bodies. The rescuers lift their fellow workers to standing, slipping hands underneath their armpits and heaving them upwards, their bodies limp as marionettes. They hoist these men over their backs and struggle down the stairwells.

One of them remembers the first-aid room in Sector 11,

three doors away from his former office. He reaches the room but the door is locked; it takes him several minutes to kick it open, several critical minutes. He knows that the radiation must be rising to deathly levels. Eventually the door plunges open and he staggers into a room lined with metal shelves, a gurney in its centre. There is nothing else. No iodine or medicine. No bandages. No cream for treating burns. Grey metal shelving and a steel gurney. Why stock a first-aid room in a building where no accident could ever occur?

Outside, the firemen arrive dressed in shirtsleeves. None of them thinks to bring radioactive protection. None of them has even heard of such a thing. Small fires are dotted everywhere, but they gaze at a single thick column of smoke rising thirty metres into the sky. Two of them walk to the roof adjoining the smokestack to assess the damage, their shoes lingering on the melting tar. They kick the lumps of burning graphite at their feet back into what remains of the reactor hall. Through the smoke they see the upper plate of the reactor's biological shield, a giant slab of concrete, a thousand tonnes in weight, shaped like a jam-jar lid. They see it resting casually against the rim of the chamber, lying askew, as if the owner had been distracted by a boiling kettle or a knock at the door and had neglected to replace it. They look at the span of the thing, the sheer bulk of the thing, and they feel smaller, weakened, standing there in their shirtsleeves, witnesses to the raw force of this mysterious energy.

When they return, they find the militia has arrived and are arranging the gathered firemen into groups. The men in uniform pass out some respiratory masks, made from thin, white cloth. These will last mere minutes before collapsing from heat and sweat and dust, and the men discard them mid-work so they can still be seen, several weeks later, cartwheeling around the complex or lingering guiltily on chain-link fences.

Hoses are hefted from their spools and carried through to the sites of ancillary fires. There are five fire trucks, and they travel back and forth to the Pripyat River, sucking thirstily at its waters. Men climb on to roofs with their ladders, traversing contorted iron and shattered concrete. They climb over withered pylons and steel joists that point aimlessly towards the heavens, stripped of their function. These men are efficient and brave, swiftly overcoming the smaller, scattered blazes. They return to the fire trucks and vomit. Vomiting men dot the scene, a choreography of retching; men doubled over, lab technicians and firemen and militiamen discharging the contents of their bodies on to the quivering landscape. A warm, metallic sheen lingers on their tongues, as if they have spent the evening sucking on coins. They lick their sleeves but the taste remains.

They feel so alone, individually, but collectively too. Here in this field, this nowhere, there are no panicked crowds to confirm their private fears, no mass concentration of shared terror, just a relentlessly churning sense of apprehension.

There are hundreds of men outside now, many standing furtively, wondering what to do. Nobody flees the scene. They stand in groups but do not speak. Conversation seems inappropriate. Someone comes down with a case of bottled water from one of the other reactors and the men take it and dispense it to those on the ground. They cradle their colleagues' heads and slowly pour water down their throats.

Some local doctors arrive, startled by what they observe, their training providing them with an intuitive appreciation of the consequences of such a morning. They set up improvised consultation tables around the perimeter of the plant and dispense whatever iodine is available, shine torchlight into pupils, check heart rates, spread gauze and ointment over rapidly angering burns. They order ambulances from every hospital within driving range, screaming of the urgency of the situation to impassive military orderlies.

Some men stand and smoke, despite the nausea, because really what else is there to do?

The firemen make their way to the roof adjacent to the central reactor hall – by now the only remaining fire. They are red-eyed and tear-dappled, their eyes streaming in silent protest at the cut and taint in the air. They feel unsteadied, disconcerted by the vomiting, but there is a job, they have been called upon, they work.

The military officials have finally recognized the risks of exposure and they adjust their procedures accordingly. The men are separated into five groups, with each group assigned to a hose. Two men stand at the front of the hose for no more than three minutes, then are relieved by their co-workers. Men sprint forward and back on the long roof, lungs bursting, attempting to hold back the impulse to gulp down great draughts of air as they reach their destination. Those that view them from a distance see the silhouettes of these men stretched against the dawn sky, moving with a regularity that is somehow comforting to observe, forward and back, merged together in the all-encompassing smoke, pushing on relentlessly, enduring.

Ambulances make multiple journeys, drivers setting out from Zhytomyr and Chernigov, from Kiev and Rechytsa and Mazyr and Gomel, and when they return, there are militiamen standing guard outside the hospitals, keeping all non-essential staff from the contaminated vehicles.

The constant drone of sirens, blending together with varied frequencies, their pitch rising and falling in accordance with movement and distance. Sirens droning on through the morning into the middle of the day.

Another interminable meeting. The sound of paper being shuffled. Monotone speeches. Grigory sits in a hospital committee room at the weekly gathering of department heads. They each have assigned chairs, all wearing the same suit they had worn the previous Saturday, and the one before that, and the one before that. He sits and listens and has no idea of the time. These meetings can take hours, speaker after speaker; the same statements being uttered; the same political posturing.

The only element of change with these sessions is the different seasons displaying themselves outside the window. Afterwards he usually drives to the allotment to sift soil through his hands. Today, he will tend to his potatoes, pile the ridges covering the sprouting tubers. A simple pleasure the spring delivers. April. A warm April Saturday. And he longs to be out there, with the drizzle and the birds, out where things are things, a growing potato, a gardening fork, rubber boots, where language is real – solid nouns: not contorted to ensure the pleasure of one's superior or one's superior's superior and so on and so on along the line of carefully manicured delusion.

Outside the window there's a small man-made pool with a single-tube fountain pockmarking the smooth glaze of resting water. He wonders if he should purchase a sprinkler for his tomato plants, if the summer would be a hot one. He has wondered this every week since February.

Zhykhov is summarizing; the meeting is nearly over. Grigory

could mouth the words in advance: 'All indices of work are good and we are accomplishing success in all the planned tasks.' A few months ago, over lunch, Vasily had composed a melody to accompany these words and, on hearing them, the tune plays in Grigory's head once more, an unconscious trigger that simply confirms his disdain for Zhykhov. Balance sheets taking precedence over patients, buying inferior equipment because it looks good, even if it brought with it tangible medical problems, the total subjugation of all their medical decisions to the whims and protocols of directives from the Secretariat.

As his colleagues gather their papers, standing them vertically on the table and banging them into a cohesive order, Slyunkov, the administrative secretary, hovers through the room and passes a note to Zhykhov, whispering as he does so. Zhykhov reads it to himself, then announces, 'We have received a communiqué from the Chairman of the Council of Ministers.' He reads it aloud.

'For your information, there has been a fire reported in Reactor 4 of the Ukrainian nuclear-power plant Chernobyl. The incident is under control but we have reports that the damage may be significant. However, I can reassure you that this incident will not stop the advance of nuclear energy.'

The last line is startling: it sits far outside the usual linguistic format of official communiqués. They are defending nuclear energy, as if anyone had questioned it, as if they were in the midst of a debate. Statements always come as unambiguous information. The Politburo communicates with orders or blank generalities. Grigory looks across the table at Vasily and can see he's sharing the same thought. *They're saying it to reassure themselves.* Something catastrophic must have occurred.

They all gather their papers and leave the meeting. Outside, amongst the department heads, there is some speculation as to what it might mean for them. This generalized discussion always happens afterwards, rival departments picking through the gossip, looking for ways to gain an advantage in their allocation of resources, awaiting talk of any unofficial developments.

Vasily and Grigory stand in the group and listen and offer a few opinions and then walk to a quiet corridor to talk freely. They decide to break with protocol and pay a visit to the administrative secretary. Ordinarily this would be perceived as an affront to Zhykhov, a subtle accusation that he didn't thoroughly cover an important issue in the meeting. But the news has just come in, and they could merely inquire as to any further developments.

When they push the door open, Slyunkov is sitting upright at his desk, typing. He is reluctant to give any information, but they both stand there in silence until Slyunkov can no longer bear the tension and informs them of the only extra details that he knows: that a state of emergency has been announced in the region; they've declared the disaster at 1-2-3-4, the same level as an all-out nuclear strike. The doctors are visibly shocked. They ask to speak to Zhykhov, to make any preparations that might be necessary, but are told that he is already on his way to the Kremlin: all the committee chairmen from the surrounding hospitals have been called for an emergency meeting.

There is nothing left for them to do but go home. It's not expected that they will be needed, but they'll be contacted if necessary.

Grigory drives Vasily to his apartment. They're mostly silent for the trip, too early to draw any conclusions. People are going about their weekends. They're almost all carrying something, preparing for something. Kids holding footballs, older women dragging shopping trolleys with leeks or carrots peeking out from the side panels. Grigory pulls up outside the block, his brakes letting out a moan. He's been meaning to have them looked at.

'You're sure you won't come in for some lunch?'

'Yes. But thanks. I want to go and get my hands dirty.'

'Margarita will take it as a slight on her cooking.'

'I've put away enough of her food to prove my devotion. But thank you. I just want to get some fresh air.'

'I know how you feel. Why not stop in for a drink on your way back.'

'Thanks, I'll think about it.'

In the allotment it begins to rain as he's kneeling, scooping the soil. The day is damp and sullen and he looks up and feels the drops break on his face and watches them transform the skin of the soil, black freckles appearing all around. He stands in the small wooden shed where he keeps his tools and listens to the staccato patter. There are a few families near the southern end of his section, and he can hear parents ordering their kids to shelter, some muffled screeches punctuated by their yelping dog.

He would like the chaos that children bring. He'd like crayon marks on his walls, stains on his rugs that are so ingrained that they're mistaken for part of the pattern. He'd like a child to push against him, force him to rethink what he knows, reshape his personality, something that other adults had long since stopped doing. He watches Vasily with his own kids sometimes, watches the way they casually hold his hand, sitting over lunch, the child like a smitten teenager. His meeting with Maria has stirred up layers of settled sediment but he doesn't want to think about it too much. He's reluctant to have expectations.

Grigory usually brings a flask of tea. Now would be the

time to drink it. But he's forgotten it, too busy thinking about this morning's news. Puddles form in the walkways between the plots. He'd like to indulge in the sheer pleasure of kicking into puddles, another reason to bring a child here; there are many things a grown adult needs permission to do.

The rain keeps coming. He should go, but he'll work on.

He returns to kneeling, progressing slowly along the rows, oblivious to the rest of the world. He becomes soaked but he doesn't notice this until he hears his name being called and watches Vasily striding towards him from the road and he wipes his hand on his sweater that now hangs heavy, filled with wet.

Grigory stands. It can only be something serious.

Vasily shouts to him before he comes within speaking range, clambering over a chicken-wire fence.

'Zhykhov called, looking for you.'

'I would have thought he has more important things to worry about.'

'Not really. We're pretty important right now.'

'What do you mean?'

'There's a committee flight leaving Zhukovsky airfield at 5.30. We're to be on it.'

'To go to the Ukraine? To . . . what is it called?'

'Chernobyl. Yes.'

Vasily reaches him now, talking at normal volume, panting slightly.

'But that's idiocy. What do we know about emergency medicine?'

'An endocrinologist and a cardiothoracic surgeon, it's not a bad place to start.'

'I mean, they surely have a team of experts for these situations.'

69

'For what situations, Grigory? When does something like this ever happen?'

'But surely they have plans in place.'

'Well, it looks like we're part of them.'

They both take this in.

'You have children, you can get out of it. I'm sure there's someone you can plead to.'

'It's a full-scale disaster. If I don't go I couldn't even apply for a box of pencils. My kids need to move schools next year, and Margarita's parents will retire in a few months. I can't turn this down. And, anyway, I'd prefer to be involved than to leave it to some back-slapping academic. At least we can be useful.'

'You hope.'

'Of course we can. We'll make sure whatever needs to be done is done.'

Grigory picks a sprouting tuber from the ground, shifting it from hand to hand.

'What else did they say?'

'That's it. They'll send a car for us at five. They'll give us the details at the airfield.'

Grigory throws the tuber into the next plot and gently sidefoots one of the ridges he's created, watching the soil collapse upon itself. So much for the work he's put in.

'Tell Margarita to come down here in a month or so. There'll be a plot of new potatoes waiting for her.'

'I will.'

In his bedroom, Grigory stuffs shirts into a sleek brown suitcase. An expensive purchase from two years ago, although apart from a couple of weekend conferences it has lain unused under his bed. He has no idea what to pack. What should one wear to a reactor meltdown? Socks lie scattered at random in his drawer and he selects several, balling them into pairs before firing them into the case.

A thought causes him to pause. A nuclear disaster. He could die in such a place.

Grigory looks at the striped socks in his drawer. He's walking into a poisonous lair and is packing shirts and socks. He sits on the bed and stares into the possibilities.

There were Saturdays, in his other life, when Maria would appear round the doorway carrying a bag of bread and a jar of chicken stock. Saturday lunches were a ritual for them, the time of the week when Grigory was at his most relaxed and they would relay news to each other, the small occurrences of the past days.

Grigory imagines the scene if she were here, seeing it as she would. Walking through the door to find her husband sitting frozen on their bed with a hastily packed suitcase. Of course she would think he was leaving her. So often she had asked him the question, usually after their lovemaking, when they were wrapped in each other, glistening from each other, 'You'll never leave me, will you?', and he would smile and reassure her, amused and astonished that this question could still be asked after all their time together, the infinite doubts in this woman's mind.

She would stand in the doorway, cradling a bag of bread, her mouth slightly open, framing itself in a question, waiting for voice and breath to complete the process. Her face with that lost look it could take on, like that of a child when it encounters something utterly beyond its experience, when it eats a fistful of sand or crashes into a pane of glass, that momentary suspension before the weeping begins in earnest.

Grigory would approach her, place his hands on her cheeks and kiss her, leaning in over the shopping.

'There's been an accident. A plant in the Ukraine. I have to leave in a couple of minutes.'

'How long will you be gone?'

'I don't know. A few days. No more than a week.'

He would underestimate their time apart, attemping re-assurance, but his voice would give him away, a vulnerability that only she could detect.

'It's serious?'

'Yes. But I'll be careful.'

She would step back and immerse herself in practicalities. She would instantly think through the clothes he would need and issue instructions for him to pick specific things out from the wardrobe and drawers as she grabbed toiletries from the bathroom shelves, towels from the airing cupboard. She'd lay them on the bed, folded and arranged, and he'd pack them with care.

A knock comes on the door.

He looks up, walks over. The driver stands there.

'Dr Brovkin?'

'Yes. I'm just finishing up. I'll meet you out front.'

'You must hurry. We can't be late for the flight. I would be in great trouble.'

'I understand. Just let me pick up a final few things.'

The driver walks down the stairs, looking back to check that Grigory understands the urgency.

He walks into his bedroom, opening drawers, grabbing bundles of clothes and stuffing them into his case. Who cares what he brings? No one will notice if the surgeon is wearing a shirt that clashes with his jacket. He grabs his keys from the kitchen counter and walks into the stairwell, places a hand on the doorknob and looks over his apartment. His furniture. His pictures. He turns the key in the lock and walks down the stairs and on the first landing he stops and knocks on the caretaker's door. No answer. He'll have Raisa give him a call, ask him to send on any post.

He hands his case to the driver, turns to his vacant window and realizes that he won't spend another night in that home. He'll sell the furniture, get a different place. The past has extracted its price. Whoever he was in those rooms, he won't be again.

At the airport, there are suitcases being loaded on to trolleys, some carpet bags. There are men standing, holding briefcases, looking for a connection, a familiar face. Grigory thinks he should have brought something to eat. He gets edgy, irritable, when he doesn't eat. This is not something he recognized in himself as a single man; another characteristic that emerged from his time with her. An attendant asks people their names, ticking off a list on a clipboard. Grigory scans the area, just as the others are doing. He doesn't see Vasily in the gathering. A man in a double-breasted grey suit approaches, offering his hand. Grigory shakes it.

'Dr Brovkin, thank you for coming.'

Of course. It's Vygovskiy, from the baths – the chief advisor to the Ministry of Fuel and Energy. Grigory can connect everything now. Zhykhov must be delighted to be close to the centre of such attention.

'I know very little of what's happening. Comrade Zhykhov read the communiqué at our departmental meeting.'

'He speaks highly of you.'

'So it seems.'

'You're wondering what you're doing here.'

'I'm here to help, comrade. Whatever you wish me to do. However I can be of service.'

'I have been appointed as chairman of the advisory commission. I have overall responsibility for the clean-up operation.'

'A daunting task.'

'Yes. But one in which I will be successful. We will all be successful. This is a tragedy, no doubt, but we have all dealt with tragedies.'

'And comrade Zhykhov suggested I may be useful.'

'No, actually. I requested for you to come.'

'You're placing a lot of weight on one brief meeting.'

'Dima is a good judge of talent. He didn't get to where he is without surrounding himself with people of great ability. And it's not just one brief meeting. I said my wife speaks highly of you, of your calmness under pressure. That's an instinct that never leaves. Look around this room, Grigory Ivanovich. I know only a few of these men. For most of them, I can't guarantee how they will respond under pressure. I know you have talent, have calm. Most importantly, I know you have integrity. You are not someone who merely carries out instructions, you'll bring a critical mind to the situation. I need people like you, Doctor.'

'I hope my opinion will be reliable.'

'It will. I have no doubt.'

They shake hands again, Vygovskiy looks him in the eye.

'We are the ones that must close the stable door.'

The aircraft is a troop carrier, all these suited men sitting in the slate-grey hulk of the plane. All of them thinking they could do with a drink. There is no insulation from the noise of the engine so they have to speak loudly to carry on a conversation.

Grigory boards with Vasily. There are no windows, just sloping walls. They could as easily be in an underground bunker.

When they settle, Vasily says, 'You know what's most surprising about this whole thing? That they've had nuclear power for this long without fucking it up.'

It was true. The same thought had struck Grigory. Any safety protocol he had tried to put in place in the hospital was always received as an implicit criticism of his predecessors. It had taken all his will and guile to set up a checklist of steps to make sure that standards of hygiene were up to scratch. Even three years previously, before the push for glasnost, such actions would have called into question his loyalty to the Party. If this was true for hospitals, why would a nuclear-power plant be any different? They need to take a hose to the whole Union, wash out everything that came before. Fire those in power. Promote talent. Listen to ideas. They need to do these things but never will. The system could never allow it.

In Kiev, they're met by every Ukrainian who has ever stamped a document. A long cavalcade of black governmental cars drapes itself outside the terminal, drivers standing to attention beside opened doors, indistinguishable from each other, same uniform, same stance, hands folded together in front, lined up along the stretch of concrete like an infinite mirror.

In the car Vasily chews on the arm of his glasses, a nervous habit that has resulted in the frames becoming puckered with toothmarks over time. A fact that is in keeping with his ragged appearance: hair receding, his collar hanging limp, a button missing halfway down his shirt. Vasily has always been like this, the sharpest brain in the room with the most crumpled suit.

Grigory sits and watches the landscape. Just distance out there. Unsorted thoughts, dim images running through him. Distance and sky and land. A horizon of no distinction.

It's early evening when the cavalcade reaches Pripyat – the feeder town to the power plant – snaking along the road like a funeral cortège, exuding gloom. There's nothing more serious than a procession of governmental cars: the vehicles seem coated with a patina of menace. They crest a small hill and can see the power plant in the distance. Grigory and Vasily press their faces to the glass, trying to get a decent view. A host of mottled colours still hangs over the plant, warping all perspective, so that the scene looks concave, the sky somehow curving around the facility, like a painted bowl. The smoke stretches up in a clearly defined column, fusing itself with the upper reaches of the sky. This is a sight that commands respect, Grigory thinks, a hushed awe.

The town is still going about its business. Grigory and Vasily cannot believe this. They pass a school playground where a football game is in full flow, men gesturing to each other with stiffened limbs, mouths opened wide, issuing mute shouts. Kids are still on the streets. Boys stop their bicycles on the roadside and enact strongman poses for the visitors, pushing their elbows wide, curling their fists towards their bodies. The braver ones cycle alongside, standing on the pedals but taking care to keep an appropriate distance.

A girl in purple trousers stands under an alcove, eating a chocolate bar. She can be no more than six or seven, a thin chocolate moustache running along the contours of her upper lip.

'All these children still on the streets. They need an immediate iodine prophylaxis. Why has no one seen to this?'

'Because no one sees to anything, Grigory. We'll have to clean this up with our own bare hands.'

There are no more words. Grigory thinks of Oppenheimer, tinkering with the atom in the deserts of New Mexico during the time of the Great Patriotic War: *I am become death, the destroyer of worlds*.

At Party headquarters, the room is large, but the delegation fills it. The groups are obviously more comfortable in this setting, speaking in clusters, renewing acquaintances, all of it so casual, suits at a conference. Grigory had expected that here, at least, under the shadow of this tragedy, the room would be filled with urgency. But it's all the same: back-slapping, clasped handshakes, introductions according to who attended what party, where one's dacha is located, their children's choice of university. Grigory hasn't had many professional arguments in his life, something he supposes has to do with his quiet bearing. But he can feel anger rising up his neck, pinpricks on his skin.

Some pretty blonde girls emerge from a back room carrying plates of food and glasses of vodka. Grigory grabs the nearest one by the elbow.

'Where did this come from?'

'Excuse me, comrade?'

'The food. Where did it come from?'

'The kitchen prepared it.'

'Did they? Where is your supervisor?'

She points to a balding man with a thin moustache standing at the back of the room, arms folded. Grigory drags the girl over, causing the conversation in the room to come to a staggered halt, a few lingering words in the silenced chatter.

Grigory snatches the tray of sandwiches from the girl's hand and thrusts it in the man's face.

'Where did you get this food?'

The supervisor is unnerved. He's a man who goes about

77

his life unseen, as innocuous as the tablecloths. A conversation like this is outside the narrow confines of his professional experience.

'Our kitchen staff prepared it.'

'And where did they get it?'

'That, comrade, is none of your concern. If you don't like it, don't eat it.'

Grigory releases his grip and the tray drops horizontally to the floor, the neat triangles of bread bouncing upwards in shock, the clang of metal ringing around the silenced room. He grabs the back of a nearby chair and turns it around to face him, then stands on it and addresses the gathering.

'For the rest of your time here, do not eat or drink anything unless it has been approved for consumption. Only pre-packaged items are safe to eat.'

The officials try to rid themselves of their sandwiches as subtly as they can, placing them on windowsills or on the catering table; some, to avoid embarrassment, stuffing them in their pockets – any strategy they can think of to avoid the tainted items coming in contact with their skin.

Anxious faces look Grigory's way, unsure if he is exaggerating. He faces them with a cold glare. Surely he can't be the only one present with enough expertise to understand the implications of what they are faced with.

A plant manager takes to the stage and outlines the events leading up to the accident, careful to phrase his remarks in such a way as to emphasize his own professionalism in responding to the event.

After the presentation, Vygovskiy approaches Grigory, motioning him towards two plastic chairs under a tall window.

'Thank you, comrade. I'm angry too. Everyone in this room should be angry.'

'I think they've forgotten how.'

Vygovskiy leans in towards Grigory. They speak shoulder to shoulder, looking like two old men on a park bench talking about the weather.

'I see this man on the stage and I feel guilt lying on me in layers. Three Mile Island – you know of this plant?'

'No,' Grigory says.

'It's a power station in America. They had an accident. Seven years ago, this was. Not a catastrophe, but a big problem, a serious incident. But the Americans learned from it. After the accident they put in place a safety system, one that would anticipate problems instead of just fixing things when they were already broken. I read of these changes, I studied their developments. I said to myself we need to do something like that here. I brought my proposals to the committee, but before I could present them formally, there were conversations in corridors, I was pulled into doorways. There was much talk about me, they said. They might decide to downgrade me, they said. Not outright threats – you know the way – just talk. So I did the smart thing, I withdrew my recommendations. I reworded my critique. I did as the entire nation has done. I stayed silent. I backed away. Because I did this, they made me chief advisor to the ministry.'

'We are all guilty, comrade.'

'When I was put in a position of power, I could have dusted off my proposal again. I could have said, "Here's an idea I'd forgotten about." But I didn't. The only thing we've learned from the past is how not to do it. I don't want people who'll keep their mouths shut.'

Vygovskiy leans closer, pats Grigory on the neck.

'I want you to take charge of the medical operations. This has been a shameful day for the Union. We will make this right.'

Vygovskiy stands and is immediately surrounded by a

circle of questions. He exits the room and the whole group follows, streaming into their separate offices.

And so the paperwork begins, the assorting and allotting, the segmentation into regions, the colour coding, the mountains of paperwork that spread exponentially from this point. They use the Party offices as an administrative headquarters and hang maps all over the walls, charting the affected regions, the anticipated radiation levels according to weather reports and probability analysis. Population estimates run vertically beside maps in various scales. They colour-code areas, they speculate upon water-table contamination and agricultural implications. They devise outrageous long-term solutions and then abandon these, or put them to the side, to be picked up at a later stage for reassessment. There are no definable models for this, no guidelines. There are only predictions and scant facts.

They call for serious military support and medical equipment. They discuss evacuation. Grigory agrees to remain patient until the proper transport can be arranged, so he appoints an evacuation committee to form a strategy and gives them strict deadlines. He orders iodine tablets to be dispensed amongst the population and is informed they have only one box. Grigory asks how many pills the box contains and the official replies casually that they are approximately one hundred. Grigory feels an urge to strike the man. One box, in a town of one hundred thousand, a town located next to, built for, a nuclear-power plant. Grigory says, 'I'm sure you looked after yourself, though,' and the man remains silent.

He drives to the plant with Vygovskiy and Vasily. They want to see it for themselves. Firemen are still working on the roof, dead on their feet, wild-eyed with exhaustion.

Vygovskiy orders them to cease their work. Now that the blaze has been dampened, their continuing to flood the reactor with water is counterproductive, resulting in nothing more than an increase in the level of water vapour, which floods into the other buildings.

Rubber facemasks have been delivered and Grigory orders everyone to wear them. They put them on and all traces of personality are erased: everyone now moves and walks with a sinister sameness, an inhuman mien. Hair becomes important for identification purposes. Vygovskiy recognizes people by remembering their hair; blond or black, crew-cut or curly. Voices filter through the masks as if disembodied.

They are still running the other reactors. Grigory hears a junior engineer mention this, then asks him to repeat it and he does so twice, only realizing the stupidity of this circumstance after repeating it the first time. Operators are still in their respective control rooms, going about their daily work, while ventilation systems pump contamination throughout the building. Vygovskiy grabs the man's lapels and pushes him backwards, and the man turns mid-stumble and runs in the direction of the reactors.

Local farmers arrive at the gate with food and drink. They're sent away. The farmers are confused, saying all their food is fresh; they state the fact that they're farmers, as if the soldiers guarding the gates are too blind to notice. The soldiers call Grigory over to confirm what they are saying and the farmers still protest, not understanding how their generosity could be taken as such an affront. The soldiers have to point their guns at them, and the locals back away, baffled and spiteful.

Grigory and Vasily sleep for a few hours in an apartment in the town. When Grigory enters the bedroom he throws his clothes into a waste bin beside the bed, tying a knot in the plastic bag and placing it in a cupboard in the hallway, which doesn't make them any safer but at least it's out of sight. He washes his hair with rubber gloves. He is hungry, he realizes he hasn't eaten since breakfast. In the kitchenette Vasily finds two cans of chopped tomatoes, he takes a tin opener and peels off the lids. Such a pitiful meal. They clink their cans with irony and gulp down the contents. Outside the window, some kids are drag-racing beat-up old cars. The two men know they could have them stopped or moved, but decide not to, the high pitch of the engines and the squeal of tyres are at one with the rip of thoughts through their heads, acting as a counterbalance, distracting them from what's happening all around. Grigory sleeps without rest, a shallow submission of the mind to his bodily needs.

Dawn rises over the plant and the familiar crimson sky reshapes itself. A squadron of helicopters thunder overhead and place themselves daintily on the surrounding country-side. Vygovskiy has decided to dampen the reactor core, using the helicopters to drop boron compounds, clay dolomite and lead into the site to stabilize the temperature. They are to be packaged and attached to small parachutes to avoid dispersion in the wind.

Nesterenko, the commanding officer, looks upwards towards the network of steel cables above the drop site, silently calculating the risks involved. He's come directly from Afghanistan. Twelve hours earlier he had been stationed in a battleground and it's obvious he would rather remain in a tangible conflict than be placed in this alien landscape battling chemical releases. The hazards would make each passing incredibly dangerous for his pilots: navigation through these wires would be intricate. Sheets of lead have been transported in and these will have to be secured to the underside of the helicopters to protect them from the powerful blasts of radiation. There can be no predicting what effect this would have on the stability of the craft. Had he designed the exercise to test the expertise of his men, he couldn't have devised anything more difficult.

Soldiers are spread wide across the next field attaching tiny parachutes to the cloth packages that will be dropped. Their uniforms are combat-worn, scuffed and ripped, details such as buttons or badges missing.

Grigory and Vasily ask to be included on one of the initial flights. They have been soldiers too; they know how these men think and they understand that having members of the official delegation on board will serve as an expression of solidarity with the troops, reassuring them and anchoring their leadership through more difficult times to come. The colonel advises against it, but they insist.

When the first helicopter is sent up, the whole field stops and stares, watching it thread its way through the smoke. A cheer rises up when the packages are dropped.

During the six months of their military service, the two friends spent countless nights on their own, supposedly learning battle-simulation tactics but in reality just being cold and wet and more than a little homesick. There were many days when they were sent from the base with a map and compass and a radio with a faulty connection to dig in for a few nights. Vasily called these the filler nights, when the commanding officers obviously hadn't planned any training activities, so they just sent the recruits out into the wilds to give themselves a break.

Grigory and Vasily carried their Ustavs, making sure the pages never got wet, and they set about memorizing every page, which was more an ideological ambition on the part of their commanding officers, but they were still young men, both eighteen, and they had a burning intention to do this well. They concentrated on the sections they were most often quizzed on: the sections on uniform and dress and appearance. They could both still quote copious amounts of the text: *The fly of the trousers shall hang at a perpendicular angle to the waistband. The teeth of the zip shall remain free of foreign bodies and should be attended to bi-weekly with a toothbrush. The crease of the trouser should begin at the midpoint of the thigh and not deviate in its line to the end of the leg* – and they indulged in this sometimes, on drunken evenings. Vasily's wife, Margarita, became so familiar with their incantations that when she heard the first words she'd lift the dishes from the table, carrying them to the sink as an amused rebuke.

When the friends met, they both had a year of medical school behind them and their brains had been attuned to learning difficult Latinate terms, so their Ustav was relatively straightforward by comparison. But all their learning never improved their situation. When they stood to attention, their sergeant would still find flaws or would invent some. And their knowledge, their readiness with an answer, often made them look arrogant, and so after they'd waded through the first sections they skimmed past the rest, happy with a more generalized knowledge, more knowing now, more aware of the absurdities of military practice and decorum. These were all the nuances they'd picked up before their training turned to hand-to-hand combat and this created a new phase of study where they'd test each other's technical accuracy by striking the poses captured by the line-drawing figures in the pages, imitating also their facial expressions, the nonchalant gaze or cold-blooded fury of these basic illustrations. Laughing at the earnestness of their former selves.

They were friends immediately. They spoke their first words to each other as they stood in line at the reception yard of the military base, while the attending sergeant shouted to all the newly disembarked recruits through a megaphone. They looked like all the others. They wore rags, just as their cousins and neighbours had told them to, knowing their clothes would be pitched away in a matter of hours, replaced by sharply pressed fatigues. Some men, the kolkhoz boys with their hoary farm-worn fingers, had traces of cow shit on theirs. Others were wearing woollen sweaters they had long outgrown, the material stretched across the camber of their overdeveloped chests.

'Were you warned about the shouting?' Vasily asked the man in front of him.

'Yes. I hear you get used to it, though,' Grigory replied.

'I think you probably just lose some hearing.'

The sergeants had boarded the buses and welcomed the men cordially, then screamed at them to get in formation behind the painted lines in the yard. Even though they had all been warned about this transformation, to see it in action was an incredible sight, a man switching effortlessly and immediately from a warm, friendly demeanour to a demonic intensity.

After Grigory and Vasily had collected their uniforms and boots they were posted together in the same barracks, where they eventually alighted upon the subject of medical school, a link between them that was both a surprise and a consolation, and later, when they realized they were both from Kostroma, their friendship was cemented.

There were many times during those months that Grigory suspected his lungs might explode from the intensity of the running. Times when his muscles couldn't lift his body to a full press-up position, hours when a small stone would scurry its way inside his boot and lie there, at the bottom of each stride, until his feet swelled up and it took all his strength not to scream out loud with the intensity of the pain.

Bodies were pushed in other ways; beatings were handed out, often in front of the whole battalion. A sergeant would pull someone from ranks, not even inventing a reason for his ire, and beat a man unconscious. It was not the sight of this that Grigory found disturbing – the men accepted their pummelings without complaint, so the sight lacked any pained drama. Even the officers, it was apparent, didn't have any particular taste for what they were doing. They had to work themselves into the fury. And afterwards, they walked away, no desire in them to bask in their positions of total dominance – it was the sound. The dull, weighty impact of flesh meeting flesh. He could still bring it to mind, years later, watching little girls playing their clapping games or listening to a barber apply alcohol to a freshly shaven face.

And still they ran, and swung and climbed and leaped.

So many of them talked to themselves. So many times Grigory had watched a man on the brink of collapse and witnessed a full and involved conversation being played out through the twitching of their lips, the physical battle taking on a dialogue of its own. He knew he did the same, in his own moments of desperation. A few cried uncontrollably. Others shut down completely, unable to focus their pupils upon whatever was placed in front of them. When a man was gripped with this kind of torpor, he was treated as though mentally diseased. Within a few days his mattress would be stolen and he would find himself sleeping in the corner of the dirt floor, swept there like the cigarette butts and the mashed leaves or bits of grass that were brought in by weary feet at dusk. If the recruit was unlucky enough to have his bunk within the small radius of heat given out by the stove in each cabin, they might only be allowed one night of weakness. Their nights would be spent lying in the corner until they cut themselves off completely from their billeting and ended up outside the barracks, frozen to death against the mess hall or hanging off the beams of the watertower, or from the sturdy boughs of the ash tree that stood at the entrance to the expanse of mud that was their recreation yard. The kolkhoz boys called them 'crows'. When Grigory asked why, they told him that at home they never used scarecrows to ward off threats to their harvest, they shot offending crows and tied them to poles, which they implanted throughout the crops. Once they did this, there were never any more problems.

Near the end of their training they were stationed in the Troitsko-Pechorsky region of Komi. It was late March and the land was deep in snow. Their platoon was camped in a forest, performing tactical manoeuvres. Each man had prominent cheekbones and swollen joints. Throughout the months, their will ebbed and flowed, there were periods of time when they could feel themselves growing harder, stronger, feel their bodies adapting to the demands being placed upon them. But they were at the end of that process, two weeks away from their leave, and they thought of nothing but rest and warmth. They wanted to be in a bed with Natalya or Nina, Irina or Dasha, Olga or Sveta.

They had dug into an ambush position waiting for a rival platoon to make its way into their lair and were under strict orders to keep movements to a minimum by order of their lieutenant, Bykov, a young, shrewd leader whose front teeth were missing, a trait which would have looked comical in other men, but in Bykov's case it seemed to demand more respect.

Sunlight twirled through the trees with the passing hours, frost blew in glassy sprays. A family of snow foxes lived about twenty metres north of their position and they became fascinating to the listless men; a set of binoculars would be passed around and they'd watch the cubs playing with each other, wrestling and leaping – enchanted by the distinct character of each animal – until their rations wore thin and they set out snares and caught and skinned them for food.

At night, they wore white sheets around their greatcoats, taken from a nearby village, for camouflage, and smoked in their foxholes and talked in hushed tones and improvised chess sets from cigarette packets and rationing tins and pebbles.

The lieutenant sent out regular patrols in anticipation of the progress of their rivals. Grigory and Vasily operated on different shifts, but one night Vasily's partner was struck down with bronchial coughing, and the lieutenant told Vasily to choose his partner, and he did, and the two men walked uphill through the trees, rifles ready, crunching gently through fresh snow. It took only five minutes of walking for the men to feel abandoned. Looking back to their encampment, there were no traces of life: even their footprints had lost definition and softened into a series of small, almost unrelated, indentations. They checked their maps once more and made certain of their grid references. Getting lost wouldn't be a total disaster as they knew the area well enough to find their bearings by daylight, but the embarrassment would follow them for the rest of their training: every comment from rifleman to cook would contain some kind of reference to their ineptitude. So they agreed on their position and buttoned their compasses into their breast pockets. Then, as instructed, they split up, approaching the crest of the hill from opposite sides, maximizing the range of their watch.

Grigory walked alone, peering into the night. A concentrated stillness all around. When he paused and listened, he could hear only the boughs of the pine trees adjusting themselves, nodding in repose.

He put some more distance between himself and the camp, then pulled out a cigarette and stepped out of the moonlight and lit up. He was careful to cup his hands around the tip, shielding what little light it gave off, and held the butt between his index finger and thumb. Bringing it deftly to his lips, he dragged deeply at the tobacco. It was good to be out here, to feel the sharp night air and stretch his legs, to do anything other than wait in a hole in the ground. He knew they were almost at the end. Lieutenant Bykov was beginning to get edgy, he couldn't justify staying put much longer, no matter how strategically smart their position. It was, after all, a training manoeuvre and perhaps the opposing side had already achieved their objective. Maybe they were all freezing their arses off while their comrades were partying a few kilometres away, drinking and packing their cases for home.

Grigory finished his smoke and started up again, walking through the trees, zig-zagging his way uphill. It took longer than he expected, almost three quarters of an hour. At the top he heard a movement to his left, and saw a swooping form, flowing close to the ground. Instinctively he raised his gun.

A whispered shout. 'Don't shoot, you bastard.'

'Vasily?'

'Yes.'

Vasily drew closer, the white sheet sweeping behind him like a cape. He held his hands up, mocking his friend.

'Where do you think we are, in a war?'

'You took me by surprise.'

Vasily laughed, a different kind of alertness about him, playful, overcoming his fatigue.

'I found something,' he said.

Grigory stood up, interested now.

'Really? What?'

'Come on, it's worth it.'

They descended the other side of the slope and passed through a valley, taking turns to lead the way through the trees, bending branches for the other, Vasily stopping occasionally to take out his map and torch and find their bearings.

Grigory wondered if they would be reprimanded when they returned, taking too long on their watch, but they could make some excuse, say they were following some figures in the trees but they turned out to be a couple of wandering wolves. And, besides, there was the thrill of doing something forbidden. It was nice to claim back a little autonomy after their months of blind obedience.

At the bottom of a short ridge Vasily told Grigory to drop his pack and rifle, slung the flashlight over his shoulder, tucked the map into his pocket and began the scramble upwards. It was not a difficult climb, but the ice and dark didn't help, so they were careful. Grigory wondered why they had chosen such a direct route and not wound their way up another hillside, until he got to the top and then understood. At the summit Vasily offered his hand and hauled up his friend and they sat on the snow and looked up at the great rock formations in front of them, the Manpupuner rocks: gigantic natural stone pillars, over thirty metres tall, standing wistfully on this windswept plateau, their outlines attracting the moonlight, instantly recognizable to the two men from their schoolbooks. Six geological wonders gathered in close formation as if in conversation and a seventh, the leader, looking out across the plains below.

'I had no idea,' said Grigory.

'Neither did I. As a kid, when we studied about the rocks, our teacher made us draw a map of the area. When I was waiting for you, I turned the map at an angle and recognized it. I could see it all in crayon again.'

All schoolchildren know the legend behind the forms.

The Samoyeds, the Siberian tribe, had sent giants to destroy the people of Vogulsky. But when the behemoths crossed this plain and took in the glorious beauty of the Vogulsky mountains, the shaman of the group dropped his drum in astonishment and the group froze into stone pillars, held there in their awe. The story, which held little interest for Grigory as a child, made sense here, now that he could see their configuration, all of them leaning into the wind, pushing forward with purposeful intent, and they bent and stooped as figures would, the axis of waist and shoulder line clearly discernible. Grigory looked out over the milk-white plains, out towards the mountains that were responsible for the giants' eternal torment, and he walked to the immense, unlikely rocks, the imprisoned figures, and placed a hand on the leader, reaching no higher than the top of the sole of his imaginary sandal, and thought what luck it was to come across such a thing, to have a childhood story made real and immediate, and he knew that this phase of his life was soon at an end, that in a couple of months they would be stationed in a military hospital, then university again, and his life in medicine would fully begin, and his thoughts turned to his former comrades, strung up on beams and boughs back in their camp, what glories they had missed, cutting short their young lives through desperation, and Grigory dissolved then into a river of tears, his body hunched against the stone figures, his head bent towards his waist, his arms crossed over his crown, and it was such a relief, finally, to feel the onrush of compassion, to confirm that his indifference to a hanging corpse was merely a method of self-protection he had to cultivate. And this realization caused him to break down even further, to flounder in a sea of emotion, understanding that the internal thrust of who he was would survive any conditioning, that as much as he might try to dull himself to the harshness, the indifference of the world, he would never be truly absolved.

Vasily hunkered beside him, a comforting hand on his back, not speaking, respecting equally the privacy of his friend and the sanctity of the setting.

Later, when the manoeuvres had ended and they drank by the fireside and celebrated their symbolic victory with their comrades, and Bykov walked around his men, congratulating them, praising their strength, Vasily and Grigory marked themselves with ravens, both of them heating a needle, burning through the skin and running ink into the crevices, remembering those who couldn't endure what they'd been through.

The intensity of military life eased for them then.

They bribed an administrator, who sent them together to a military hospital in eastern Siberia. They worked as nurses and porters and cooks, observing whatever medical procedures passed their way, and on summer weekends they lived out their fishing fantasies, hiring a small boat and heading out into the Velikaya estuary, where they spent whole days casting out into the crisp waters for pollack, caring but not caring if they caught anything, doing it for the pleasure of the task, languishing in the rhythmic lap of the water, casting their lines towards the horizon. There they caught snailfish sometimes, a strange gelatinous fish that had the texture and shape of a large roasted red pepper. The thing looked prehistoric, as if no one had told it about the requirements of natural selection, and they speculated intermittently as to the origin of its name, so that it became a running gag between them, to drop the question in at random moments, so that the very wording of the question became funny, then boring, then funny again, going through its own comedic evolution.

Sometimes beluga whales swept near their boat. Calm white presences, skimming through the water. From a distance, they would see the vertical spout of water from a blowhole and they would place their rods aside and watch. Occasionally an anchor-shaped tail would flip up and crash back on to the surface announcing a whale's presence. One simple action that never failed to be breathtaking.

In the shadow of the reactor Grigory looks over to Vasily. The helicopter is being readied, loaded for the drop.

'I'm thinking about the Manpupuner rocks. About that night.'

'Yes,' Vasily replies. 'I've thought about that too. There's something about the scale of this place.'

They turn their attention again to the column of smoke.

'And the whales at Anadyr.'

'Yes. We've seen some things.'

'Yes, we have.'

They're dressed in rubber suits, rubber boots, rubber gloves, gas masks, all in white. They're guided to the machine and strapped face down on the floor. They would view the reactor below from small holes in the lead sheeting. This has been decided as being the safest option. There's no readily available way of releasing themselves from the strapping and they wear no parachutes, the flight being too low for them to have any effect. They turn their faces to each other, fear drawing a taut line between the whites of their eyes, connecting them.

Two boys from Kostroma, how their lives had ushered them to this moment.

Then Vasily says, 'I feel like one of our fish, slapping around at the bottom of the boat.'

And Grigory smiles wryly at this, it's a good thing to say, here, right now, in the situation they've found themselves in, confirming their friendship, their history, providing reassurance to them both.

The engines kick in and every vibration from the machine passes straight into their bodies, boring into their core. After a couple of seconds of slow rising, they can make out the grass beneath them and then the surface blends into streaks as they ascend and spiral. The noise of the machine feels as though it originates inside their heads. There's no separation between themselves and noise; they are at one with the machine, as much a fixed addition to the thing as the steel bolts that stud its inside. They can make out the blur of concrete underneath them and then the craft steadies itself and the sight gradually fixes itself into focus. Another wonder that their eyes have set upon, another image to remind them of their insignificance, another marker in their friendship.

Below them they see the disfigured roof, a gaping mouth, its limits obscured by the fumes it exhales. They watch the parcels feather downwards, the packages of chemicals exploding into powder, chutes flaring into flame as they descend. The two friends lying prostrate before it. Such power. Radiation calcifying their bones.

The town of Pripyat unfurls, going slowly through its Sunday-morning motions. Almost nobody has to work today. Couples have blurry, half-awake sex, keeping it surreptitious, aware of their kids moving about, playing in adjoining rooms. Most have woken in the early morning to the throb of helicopters skimming above them; many had fallen back asleep. There is an awareness of the accident, mainly since yesterday evening. Everyone knows someone who has been sent to the hospital. There has been plenty of talk about the fire, people are unnerved by it, but of course it's under control, of course the management have plans to deal with these kinds of incidents.

May Day is next week and the schools have given the children weekend assignments, getting them to make bunting, to fold paper into shapes and chains, and on dozens of living-room floors, scattered throughout the apartment complexes, there are kids furiously working scissors, matting the carpet with runny glue. They talk about the situation, the couples in their beds, and the men who know something feign ignorance – what good could come from speculation? – and the men who know nothing wonder if they will get some paid leave, a chance to catch up and do things they often planned to do when not monopolized by the demands of work: paint the bathroom; put fresh shelves into the kitchen cupboards.

The early risers are walking their dogs, soaking in the morning sun and feeling fresh and healthy and energized and somewhat self-satisfied in their choice of Sunday-morning activity.

The town goes about the business of being the town but it's soon to become a memory of the town, a once-inhabited place, wistful, forlorn.

Paper starts falling.

Pastel-coloured paper falling from the sky.

Small sheets drop like giant confetti upon the landscape. It takes a moment for this to register. The dog-walkers notice it at eye level and are confused. The sound of a helicopter engine blares overhead and they fail to connect these two oddities and then they look up and see the deluge of coloured paper winding and twisting down towards them in the gentle breeze. A confection of colour. The sheer expanse of the sight makes it impossible to focus on a particular aspect: they take it all in at once in simple delight, the scene all the more pleasing in its unexpectedness. It occurs to several of them that this may be a practice run for the national celebrations. Perhaps they would be more outlandish this year.

A seven-year-old boy looks out from the window of his living room, pleased that his teacher has delivered the extra paper she had promised the class.

A man spoons yogurt into his mouth and freezes in his action, mouth open, spoon suspended.

Rectangles of colour on the pavement, a free-form cubist work. Green pages falling on the grass, each hue intensifying the other. Yellow pages on blue cars, blue pages on yellow cars. Paper catching on telephone wires, a kaleidoscopic clothes line. Kids streaming out of doorways now, rolling on the paper. One kid eating it because it looks so good. Dogs leaping and yelping, twisting on their hind legs, feeding off the excitement.

A woman in her fifties picks up a page. There is text in bold, clear letters. They have three hours to evacuate their homes. Each person can bring one case. Extra luggage will be confiscated. They are to position themselves outside their buildings at 12 p.m. They will receive further instructions at that time. Anyone not abiding by the guidelines will be separated from their families and arrested. She runs home to her husband, waving the paper in the air, shouting to all around that the pages are a directive. Her dog ambles after her, in charge of his own leash.

And word spreads quickly. Neighbours tell neighbours, who tell neighbours, the most ancient and reliable of communication systems.

The first helicopters to reach Artyom's village pass in the mid-morning. Artyom is on his way to his friend Iosif's to work on their motorbike. A few months ago one of the kolkhoz managers had come across them looking at a car manual, talking about horsepower and torque, and told them to come over to his place that evening, where his old Dnepr MT9 was lying in a shed around the back.

'It's a piece of shit. If you get it out of my way, you can have it.'

So they walked to the man's home, five kilometres away, and walked back, pushing it all the way. They stopped every few dozen metres to survey their new acquisition. Since then, every Sunday, they have been working on the machine. Neither of them knows what they are doing but they have taken apart every piece in turn and cleaned them all and put them back together again. They still don't have a manual, but from time to time one of their neighbours comes over and offers some advice and they do as suggested, but the thing still doesn't work. They don't care, though. It is their bike, their possession, and they both know it will break into a roar, someday.

Artyom hears a rumbling in the distance, getting louder, nearer, eventually surrounding him. The hedgerows are too high and thick for him to see over them, so he doesn't understand what's happening until the undercarriage of the aircraft passes over his head.

He stands amazed. The only loud sounds he has ever heard are from farm machinery, but they don't dominate the landscape like this, enveloping everything with their roar.

Artyom runs to his friend, the echo in his ears so strong that he can't hear his feet thudding on the earthen track. When he rounds the blackthorn bush at the end of Iosif's lane, he sees Iosif and his mother standing outside their gate, looking upwards. Nothing mechanical ever moves through this sky. They have never even seen a passenger plane up there. More helicopters. The leaves in nearby trees shudder with the shock.

They cup their hands over their ears.

'What's happening?' Artyom asks. But he realizes his voice is being consumed. A loose sheet of tin flaps on their roof.

Iosif's mother draws her boy to her. Iosif doesn't resist. Even though he's too old to accept such mothering, it seems irrelevant to wonder what his friend will think. When the aircraft have passed Iosif's mother asks, 'What are you doing here, Artyom?'

He's confused. He comes here every Sunday. He stutters his answer.

'The bike.'

He points towards the shed where they keep their chopped wood that doubles as the boys' workshop.

'To work on the bike.'

'Bashuk took it. Didn't your father tell you?'

Bashuk is Iosif's father.

Artyom wonders if maybe the helicopter has shuffled his

brain around. How could Iosif's father use it? It's broken. That's why they're always working on it. And how could his father not have told him?

Artyom looks at Iosif, not understanding. Iosif hunches his shoulders, displays his palms. Iosif's mother goes inside while Iosif explains.

'Your father came over yesterday. They both fixed it together. Apparently it was something pretty simple.'

He is almost shouting, even though the noise has passed.

'They were trying not to laugh in front of me. They knew what the problem was all along, they just wanted us to figure it out for ourselves.'

Artyom doesn't respond for a few moments. He knows that the men don't regard him as an equal, even if he's allowed to shoot with them. But it's a blow to realize that they still see him as a boy, someone to be toyed with.

They walk inside the house. Iosif's mother stands by their table, her palms spread flat on top of the wood, her shoulders hunched, the muscles in them so tight that it looks as though she is trying to push the legs through the wooden floor. She is breathing heavily. Iosif approaches her but doesn't know what to do. Sometimes his mother acts in ways he can't understand. Sometimes she cries while eating dinner but still pretends she's not crying. Sometimes his father hits her and, instead of hitting back, she does nothing, or says sorry, and Iosif doesn't know what to think. He hovers his hand over his mother and looks at Artyom and Artyom encourages him with a tilt of his head and so he places a hand on his mother's back and she softens, her elbows bend, she speaks breathlessly.

'I have some leftover martsovka. Would you boys like some?'

They sit quietly and she brings the food on two plates and

they eat. The sound of their forks tinkling against their plates. No one speaks for a few minutes. They don't ask questions, they wait to hear if Iosif's mother will offer some information. But, of course, she doesn't.

'How did they fix it?'

Iosif lifts his head and looks at Artyom.

'The bike. Did they say what was wrong with it?'

'They said it was the distributor. They said they'll show us when they get back.'

More silence. Iosif's mother is looking out of the window. The boys don't feel that they should stand up and leave yet. But it's difficult to sit still. Artyom straightens the fork on his plate.

'Something bad is happening.'

He says this as a statement, but it's a question too. A gentle request for Iosif's mother to reveal a little of what she knows.

'Yes.'

'Is it to do with yesterday morning?'

Iosif's mother turns sharply in his direction.

'What about yesterday morning?'

'Nothing.'

Artyom wants to ask Iosif's mother why the helicopters are passing. He wants to ask if there's a military base nearby that no one has told them about. He knows there's a Komsomol barracks in Mogilev; one of their classmates, Leonid, was invited there to receive a Young Pioneers award. But he knows never to ask about local history or geography. He can ask about far-off places. Any adult will talk to him about a trip to a city, their journey to Moscow or Leningrad many years before. In the school of two rooms that serves his and four other surrounding villages the teachers hold lessons on lakes and forests, the animals of the tundra, the feeding habits of a heron. He knows that the main industry of Togliatti is the Zhiguli car factory and Volgograd is a major centre of shipbuilding. He knows that during the tenth Five-Year Plan, 4 million square metres of housing were built in Minsk and that it was his fellow Belarusians that invented ice-cream (when peasants licked the frozen sap of the birch trees) and potash fertilizer. He knows that one quarter of all Belarusians died in the Great Patriotic War. He has begun to draw conclusions about how his village came into being, but there's nothing written about it in the four shelves of books that sit behind his teacher's desk and he knows not to ask.

The people here don't look the same as each other. Some are darker; others have the same wide faces as the Tartars he sees sometimes in copies of old newspapers. They don't speak about race or about the generations that preceded them. In this village, they're a collection of people from nowhere. They came here, one after another, when the war ended, when records were lost or destroyed and there were few facts floating above the ravaged plains for administrators to seize upon. In those few short years you could build a life for yourself that wasn't defined by fear. In other places they still sent people to the gulags for arriving to work two minutes late, for taking home a pencil in their breast pocket, for not having a particular stamp on a particular document on a particular day. But this didn't happen in communities the authorities didn't know existed.

When they came back from battle, the soldiers didn't return to their families or their loved ones: they knew there was nothing left. In their retreat from the Germans, four years before, they'd burned the villages of their relatives, eviscerating all life in the area, so that when the war turned and they crossed back into these places they were shocked at the extent of their own destruction: all these areas that meant so much to them were only recognizable by a stray sign or the black skeleton of a barn or grain silo. They knew the roads their trucks drove upon were made from the bones of their own people, that the bodies were so thick on the ground that the enemy hurled them together into long rows with great earth-moving machines, the battlefields long since stripped of trees.

These were roads they refused to walk on. They headed for fields, for areas of woodland, discernible in the distance. They simply walked away from their posts, ran away from documentation, from re-entry into the system. So when they reached an isolated spot and they stumbled across an iron stove, or the charred remains of a wall, they cut branches and started a fire and sheltered in the shadow of the stones. They burrowed into the ground for warmth while they built the more permanent shelters. Gradually they rebuilt the izbas, first with stone, then wood. They dug wells, drove cows and sheep from markets that were a two-day walk away. Women came and were welcomed and were never asked where they were from. They changed their names and never asked each other about the past. And they loved and bore children and when uniformed men arrived and insisted the burgeoning farms be formed once again into collectives, the men had their new documentation ready and agreed to what was required of them, but kept some extra land for their own use, a reward for their years of work. And no objections were raised.

They don't ask about soldiers here. They don't talk about the military here. Even those men who have just come back from service avoid the subject when they sit together in groups in the long evenings.

Iosif stands from the table and walks outside, and Artyom follows him.

Iosif's mother asks where they're going and Iosif tells her

that the sheeting on the roof needs to be fixed. He'll nail it down in case the helicopters pass again and it's ripped off. In the shelter, Iosif looks in the steel box under the workbench for a hammer and nails. There are only two walls to the shelter, facing north–south, made of thin lengths of wood, with the bark still on them. Logs are piled up against one of the walls and there's a small strip of earth where you can stand – the place where the boys kept their motorbike – which is spotted with blotches of oil from all their futile mechanical efforts.

'When did they leave?'

'Last night.'

'Last night? And they haven't come back yet?'

'No. Of course not. Did you not notice your father gone?'

Artyom didn't. His father often comes home when Artyom is asleep and leaves before he wakes. His father needs very little sleep. Sometimes Artyom wakes in the middle of the night and he can hear the wireless playing in the kitchen. There's candlelight and he knows his father is just sitting and listening. His father can sit for hours without distraction. When he was small, Artyom used to walk into the kitchen and ask his father why he was still awake, or sometimes he would say he was thirsty and his father would take the bottle of milk they kept sitting in a bucket of water – before they had a fridge – and let Artyom drink a mouthful, but no more than that. And he would sit in his father's lap and listen to the dancing violins and big thudding drums of the music that would remind him of fairy stories, of little elves and big, stomping ogres. The volume turned down so low that it seemed at odds with the drama of the music, as if someone was telling him an epic tale in snatched whispers. Artyom would lie like a sick calf in his arms, drinking in any warmth that came his way.

Iosif finds the hammer and rattles an old tin can full of nails, looking for ones that are strong enough for the job.

'Do you know where they've gone?'

'Pripyat. But you didn't hear it from me. If he comes home and Mother knows where he was, he'll hit us both with this.'

Iosif wields the hammer as he speaks, lets its weight drag his wrist wherever it wants to go.

'No, he won't.'

Artyom says this instinctively and they both look at the hammer that Iosif holds under his chin. Sometimes Artyom speaks with a definition that Iosif admires.

'Why did they go to Pripyat?'

'I don't know. What, you think I know everything? I don't know.'

Iosif finds the nails and puts them into his pocket and they climb on to the roof, pushing their legs off the side of the shelter to give them momentum. The structure wobbles when they put some force against it.

'I'm surprised the thing wasn't flattened when the helicopters went over.'

'I know. Me too.'

If they knew any specifics about the helicopters, what model or make they were, they would have used those terms, but they don't. They know every model of car ever produced in the Union. They know nothing about helicopters.

They walk along the roof, careful to stand only on the supporting beams, defined by the lines of nails; they don't want to fall through. Iosif kneels at the place where the tin sheeting has come loose, takes a nail into his mouth and holds it down. Artyom steps over him and weighs it down a little further along. This isn't really necessary, but he needs to make himself useful. Iosif decides to put new holes in the tin. If he just uses the old ones, it will be easy for them to be wrenched out.

Iosif bangs on the first nail and the sound of nail scratching the sheet makes Artyom want to bite down on his knuckles. He won't react though, he can't lose face in front of Iosif. He thinks that Iosif's mother must feel like she's in the centre of a tin drum. He expects her to come out and wait until they're finished, but she doesn't. Every sound is magnified against a tin roof. In their own house he often hears rats scuttling above them, a sound he has never become used to. He loves when it rains, especially when evening is closing in and he's doing his homework by the stove and the drops come down with a beautiful regularity, falling evenly over the whole roof, just gravity and water.

Iosif makes quick work of the hammering. Iosif does everything in short, sharp bursts. He's small but incredibly compact. His father has said he'll make a good boxer some day and Artyom doesn't doubt this, the way Iosif darts about. Even in school, when they have writing exercises to do, Iosif can't help but look about him, can't help but jitter his legs and elbows.

When he's finished, they sit and stare across the fields. Near the grain silo, there are two tractors tilling the soil. Both of them know how to drive a tractor, but the kolkhoz manager won't let them do any of the machine work. They only get the dull jobs, like feeding the pigs and milking the cattle. They've pleaded with him enough times, but he always says, 'And what if something happens, what then, you break a tractor, what then?'.

'I wonder what this all looks like from a helicopter,' Artyom says.

'I don't know.'

Iosif doesn't like to wonder. He likes to deal only with

things that are in front of him. Artyom can see him scanning already, looking for something else to do, now that their Sunday routine has been interrupted.

'We can probably go on the bike when they get back.'

Artyom lights up. Of course they can. How could he have forgotten?

'We can go places now.'

'I know.'

'We can ride to Pripyat, maybe even to Polesskoye.'

'We can ride to Minsk.'

They'd never been to Minsk. But they'd heard stories from their classmates.

'What about diesel?'

'We'll get some from the tank near the tractor shed. We won't need much. They won't miss it.'

Artyom nods. 'Of course.'

Iosif always knows where to get the things they need. He takes a handful of nails from his pocket and hands half the pile to Artyom and points to an empty paint tin near the gate and throws a nail at it. They're always throwing things at other things. The bucket is too small and the angle of the opening too narrow for them to have any real hope, but they like the challenge anyway.

'First one to land it gets first ride.'

'Deal.'

They fall into a rhythm, unspeaking, Iosif biting his tongue as he throws, and Artyom thinks again about what they look like from above. Two boys sitting on a weathered, green tin roof. He thinks that from up there everything must be broken into flat shapes. Great, square fields. Narrow, thin roads. The circular top of their grain silo. He wonders what the soldiers think of them. They must think these boys have nothing to do, they must think it's so far from any action. But Artyom and Iosif can throw nails at cans. They can make forts in trees. And now they can ride their motorbike through fields, hear it hum over muddy lanes.

Iosif nudges him and points to their right, another target for them. Artyom follows his finger and realizes he's hearing the bike, he's seeing their fathers trail along the road, stirring dust in their wake.

They fling the remaining nails into the bushes and lower themselves down off the roof. They push open the door to the kitchen and Iosif's mother is still where they left her. The plates sit on the table.

'They're coming back.'

'The helicopters?'

'No. Father.'

She rises, pushes her chair back and paces towards the door in one concise motion.

They wait in the laneway. When the men approach, Iosif's mother runs to meet them. The boys are tempted to run too, but they stay where they are. They don't want to seem too eager. And they both think that the bike looks like a smooth ride.

Iosif's father dismounts and talks animatedly with his mother. Artyom's father turns the throttle and stops alongside the boys.

'Let's go.'

He says this as an order. At first Artyom doesn't understand: surely his first time on their bike, the bike they've worked so hard on, should be a moment of pride, of celebration. Then he looks to his right and sees Iosif's father dragging his mother back to the house.

'Let's go.'

Artyom's father revs the engine violently and Artyom jumps on.

'Are you holding the side handles?'

'Yes.'

They move off so quickly that Artyom's head snaps back.

When they reach the house Artyom's father drives up to the porch and dismounts before the bike has fully stopped. Artyom gets off too and his father, holding the handlebars, lets the bike drop on to the grass and walks to their steps. Artyom tries to pick up the machine and put it on its kickstand but his father barks at him.

'Leave it. Inside now!'

His father rarely raises his voice. Artyom is old enough to resent his father giving him orders, but not old enough to disobey. He isn't certain if there is such an age.

Inside the house his mother is repairing his father's spare trousers. She works the needle with her sharp, precise hands, teasing the thread out at different angles. She has great skill as a dressmaker. Everything the family wears has in some way been reshaped and remodelled by her. Artyom wears his sister's old clothes but no one can tell – with the buttons swapped over and the shoulders recut – that they've ever been worn by a girl. In the evenings when he can't concentrate on his homework, he watches his mother's fingers. They function as indicators of her mood. He thinks of them as being like antennae, showing how much her senses are engaged.

'The military will be here any time,' says Artyom's father. 'They're putting people in trucks. Pack a bag, we'll need to sleep in the forest tonight.'

'What, the forest? What? I can't walk that far. The forest?'

'They're evacuating the area. There's been a fire in the power plant.'

'So they're evacuating the whole area?'

'Where's Sofya?'

He turns to Artyom.

'Where's Sofya?'

'I don't know.'

'I don't understand. Why don't they just put out the fire? It's not going to spread this far.'

'It's a nuclear plant. It's dangerous.'

'How is it dangerous? It's not as though there were bombs in there.'

'It's dangerous, that's all. Where's Sofya?'

'I don't know,' he says again.

Artyom's mother doesn't know how to react. She does what she always does when she's nervous, she busies herself. Artyom has seen it when people come over for dinner and she doesn't know how to talk to them. Or when his father compliments her figure in front of their friends. She carefully winds up her thread, and makes sure her needles are ordered in their pouch according to size. Then she pours herself a cup of water from the jug that's always on the counter. The one he has brought to and from the well a hundred thousand times.

'Go and find her,' his father says to him. 'And no fucking around with that bike. We need to leave right now.'

Artyom walks outside, glad to be away from the house. Sofya is a walker, so she could be anywhere. His father knows this. How the hell is he supposed to find her? She walks. She likes to look at birds. She hates that they go shooting grouse, but she knows better than to say anything about it. Their father doesn't have much time for himself outside of work. She doesn't want her disapproval to sully the pleasure of one of his rare pastimes. And, besides, she eats the meat, doesn't she?

Sofya was always the one who brought nature inside the izba. She collected beetles and birds' nests when she was young. She'd keep the beetles in jam jars under her bed. Artyom hated them but would look at them nonetheless, see them trying to clamber up the glass sides and fall on their backs and struggle to right themselves.

He runs. He can understand his mother's reaction. It's only a fire, after all. But all of it is tied. He thinks of yesterday morning, what they saw. He thinks of the helicopters overhead. Something huge is happening.

Sofya's not at their babushka's grave. Artyom pauses for a few minutes in front of it. He can't help looking around in case his father is watching, even though he's far from sight. The rushnik that's draped over the wooden cross is almost threadbare. The mound of earth is covered in green shoots. Soon it will be indistinguishable from the grass around it. One day the wooden cross will rot and crumble and people won't know there's a body underground, in a wooden box, his babushka. Already Artyom can't remember what she sounds like, what kind of things she'd say. He remembers what she looked like. But the rest of it, the sensations are as frayed as the material on the cross.

He runs to Sofya's tree: there's a tree with a wide horizontal branch that she lies on sometimes with a view to the shop in the village where she watches the comings and goings. She watches the village and Artyom watches her. She's only two years older than he is, but she knows so much more than him. Sometimes he says things and she just nods and smiles. The way his mother does.

He's sweating from the running. He's been running for half an hour. He calls into the Polovinkins to ask Nastya if she's seen Sofya but the place is empty. He runs to the back of their house and sees them, two fields away, driving their cattle towards the forest. Everyone is heading for the forest.

He returns home, panting, and walks through the front door, motions to put his hand on the handle, but realizes the door is lying on the table.

'I can't find her.'

Why is the door on the table? Instinctively he puts his hand on the frame to make sure it's empty.

His father is bundling their blankets into a sack.

'What?'

His father stops.

'Shit. Where can she be?'

'I don't know.'

'You looked at the grave?'

'Yes.'

'You asked Nastya?'

'They've headed for the forest, they're driving their cattle there. She isn't with them. Maybe she's already heard, maybe she's gone ahead.'

'No.' His mother is shouting from their room. 'She'd come back.'

His mother emerges from their bedroom, she runs her fingers through her hair, teasing the tangled strands out by jerking her fingers. An action that makes Artyom anxious just by looking at it.

'Andrei. You'll have to find her.'

'I know.'

His father strides out, calling back as he leaves. 'Do whatever your mother tells you. Make sure you don't leave her alone.'

The bike roars off and a great quiet descends. His mother walks towards him and holds him in her arms. Artyom can feel her hesitancy, she doesn't want to impose anything on him, she's aware that he needs to create his distance from her, the way he's stepping into manhood. But he accepts her embrace. Because she asks so rarely. He knows she needs a touch, a reassurance.

She steps away and picks up a potato sack from the corner.

'Pack your things. Bring something warm. And if there's anything really important to you, bring that too.'

'OK. Where did we get these sacks?'

She inclines her head towards the window.

'Your father emptied them out.'

Artyom looks outside. The lid of their wooden storage crate lies on the grass and their stock of potatoes has been spilled out in piles.

He turns again to his mother.

'We're not coming back, are we?'

She flattens her lips and shakes her head.

They pack and they wait. Each minute is stretched out. They sit and long for the return of half of their family.

They hear engines, coming from the direction of the village. It's not the bike, or helicopters. These sounds are mixed with dislocated speech. They walk outside. A mechanical voice carries through the air, words meshed into one another.

Military trucks with loudspeakers strapped to their frame can be seen over the hedgerows. As they near the village, the last ones in line stop and spread out into the various laneways.

'What do we do?'

'Let's go back inside. We're not leaving this house without them.'

A truck stops down the lane, probably outside the Scherbaks'. Footsteps walking towards them, voices getting louder.

Through the vacant doorframe, Artyom can see a soldier approach. He steps into the room.

'Into the truck. You are allowed one bag.'

He's not so much older than Artyom. Tall and gangly. He has a hand on the gun that's slung across his chest. Artyom could bundle him down the steps before he has time to point it anywhere. He looks over to his mother, anticipating a signal, but she has picked up her needle and is working on the trousers again, barely paying any attention to what's going on, as if this happens all the time.

'Into the truck. Let's go.'

The soldier is a little unsure. His order has now become a request.

Artyom's mother looks up from her stitches.

'My husband is out, looking for my daughter. They're coming back. But we're not leaving without them.'

'You can wait for them in the truck.'

His mother puts down her work.

'I see.'

She says this deadpan, diluting the soldier's order into merely one of a number of possibilities.

'We have orders to burn down the house of anyone who doesn't cooperate.'

'Fine. But we'll wait here while you do it.'

She provides no gestures or intonations that betray her fears. His mother has learned not to fear a pointed gun. This woman speaking is his mother. Yes, she has had a life before motherhood, before marriage, yet Artyom can't reconcile his scant knowledge of her past with what is happening right now, in front of him.

Confused, the soldier turns to the boy. Artyom wishes he had something with which he could occupy himself. He half wonders if he should pick up a needle and thread.

His mother points to the sacks that sit by the door, still no urgency in her voice.

'We're packed. We're leaving. But not without my husband and daughter.'

The soldier looks at the four sacks with clothes peeping out the top of them. He leaves. They wait. He comes back.

'OK. You can wait. But I am to stay with you. When the truck comes around again, you'll have to get on it. We can use force.'

'I'm sure you can.'

The soldier pulls a chair from the table, then decides he probably should stand. They wait. Artyom can't tell for how long. After some time the soldier sits. His mother keeps sewing.

Artyom walks to his room and the soldier follows. He takes a tractor manual from under the bed and returns to his chair and sits. The soldier does the same.

Eventually they hear an engine, a higher pitch than the trucks. The bike passes the doorframe, Sofya is behind his father, her arms across his chest. His mother stops her darning for the first time. They walk in and his mother engulfs his sister. Sofya lets out an even stream of breath, like a ball being deflated.

'They're here,' his father says.

His mother directs her eyes towards the kitchen table.

His father follows his mother's stare and turns to see the soldier. The soldier is embarrassed now, Artyom can tell. Time in the room has softened his resolve. He is occupying another man's home, sitting in front of his family with a gun across his lap.

His father approaches the soldier.

'Come with me, please.'

They walk outside and Artyom can see his father gesturing, pointing back towards the house.

'You think he'll let us stay?' Artyom says.

'That's not what he's asking,' his mother replies, seated again, still holding Sofya's hand.

His father walks back inside and takes some raw carrots from under the sink and hands them around. Then he takes some bread from the cupboard, breaks it into three chunks and gives it to them. Artyom moves the bread towards his mouth but his father stops him.

'Save it until you have to eat it. It might be a while before you get a meal.'

Artyom notices his father hasn't saved anything for himself.

The truck pulls up outside and they take their sacks, Artyom carries two of them, because he can. He throws the sacks inside the truck and climbs up, using the lip of the hanging backboard to give himself a boost.

He knows most of the people inside: the Gavrilenkos, the Litvins, the Volchocks. They live further out from the village. There are some that he doesn't recognize. He turns around to help his mother up, then Sofya. His father is standing by the truck, holding their door. Is he bringing the door? His father lifts it up to him and Artyom grabs it and places it face down and his father slides it to the back as people lift their feet, some complaining, and Artyom understands this. What is his father thinking, bringing their door?

'No talking,' the soldier barks out, his authority renewed.

His father climbs on board and sits beside his mother, not making eye contact with anyone. Artyom sees him grasp his mother's hand. Artyom has seen them do this countless times but he has the sense that something about the image is different, without quite locating what it is. The soldier closes the backboard, slides the pin into position and climbs aboard. No one helps him. A gold ring on the soldier's little finger clinks against the metal frame of the covering. Artyom realizes it as the truck moves off: his mother's wedding ring.

In Party headquarters Grigory listens to the presentation from the evacuation committee. He feels a thousand years old, the lack of sleep catching up with him, his body still carrying the vibrations from the helicopter. They've brought supplies during the night and so he sips tea from a polystyrene cup, the sugar and heat bringing some consolation.

They have mobilized any available buses within a ten-hour drive. Two thousand four hundred and thirty buses will stop at a meeting point sixteen kilometres from the town and then arrive in four separate convoys to facilitate crowd supervision. The town has been divided into four sectors, with the specific evacuation routes highlighted.

There will be dosimetric checkpoints in each sector to assess isotopic composition. People will be categorized according to risk and given medical papers to enable hospitals to process them efficiently. Five categories, stark in their naming: absolute risk, excessive relative risk, relative risk, additional risk, spontaneous risk. Anyone in the first two categories will be loaded into ambulances; the rest will be sent on buses. They anticipate that the dosimetric tests will take some time.

'Should I bother to ask?' says Grigory. 'Let me guess, we have fifty dosimeters.'

'No, sir, we have one hundred and fifty,' a junior assessor says, with a trace of pride.

Grigory pauses for a moment and takes a sip.

'That's approximately one per five hundred citizens.'

'Yes, sir.'

Grigory has the man removed from the room.

More military equipment arrives at the plant: Mi-2 fighter planes, Mi-24 fighter helicopters, instruments of battle. They send several robots designed by the Academy of Sciences for exploration on Mars. The lieutenant in charge of logistics has no idea where to park them.

At the evacuation site Grigory is astounded by the power of a crowd. The sheer weight and expanse of a gathered horde. The static hum of trepidation. Crying children: a small battalion of crying children. Mothers with worry streaking their faces; agitated men who find it impossible to still their hands rubbing their stubble, tousling their hair, clutching and unclutching their biceps. Thousands of hurriedly packed suitcases with sections of clothing peeking from their joins. Voluminous suitcases stuffed to an almost spherical state. Families caught caseless, using thick plastic bags with handles to transport the most necessary of their belongings, the bags leaking books and ceramic trinkets and suit jackets. Women with their meagre pieces of jewellery stuffed into their bras, which cause odd irregularities in their breast lines. Children wearing three layers of clothes, streaming sweat in the afternoon sunshine. Physical contact cascades throughout. Neighbours embracing. Couples holding hands, wives burrowing their heads into their husbands' chests, children on shoulders, in arms, hugging waistlines. Babies in slings. Teenage lovers kissing frantically, as they are wrenched apart, scrabbling for a final contact, clawing the space between them.

The soldiers carry megaphones and guns and arrange long, snaking lines according to the corresponding tower blocks, at the end of which are a doctor with a dosimeter and a trestle table with a lieutenant checking identity cards and stamping new medical papers. Those in the critical categories are hauled to the side, dragged behind a wall of soldiers and shunted into ambulances. They protest in a whole-bodied way, limbs churning, clothes falling loose around them, tearing in the struggle. Their families rush forward but are butted away, soldiers expertly dispatching blows to the lower neck, causing the injured person, children included, to crumple in slow motion from the knees. The space the crowd inhabits expands with their indignant rage, but they are kept at bay by the unyielding troops. These soldiers have seen battle and carry with them the resolute steeliness of experience.

When the buses arrive, the crowd surges forth, swarming round the vehicles, prising open windows, climbing on mudguards, bellying on to the roofs. Tear gas is released and the swarm retreats and the soldiers board the buses and drag out those inside, dispensing blows in full view of the crowd. Megaphones keep blaring instructions. Simple, clear sentences:

Return to your lines.

Do not attempt to board the vehicles without a medical certificate.

Anyone who attempts to do so will be severely punished.

Three lines repeated as a mantra, eventually restoring order. The crowd fatalistic and ultimately submissive.

The operation reports detail that animals are likely to be highly contaminative – radioactive matter would be soaked up through their coats – and so the troops shoot any animals on sight. Pets are wrenched from protective arms and shot in full view of their owners. Docile dogs looking innocently into gun barrels. The soldiers clench cats by the ridge of skin behind the neck and place a pistol under their squirming chins, blood exploding in all directions.

An elderly woman passes a large jar of milk around to her neighbours, hearing it aids with radiation poisoning. An official slaps the jar from her hand, yelling to her that it's probably contaminated, and the creamy liquid slopes in a single trail down the pavement, eventually combining with animal blood into a lurid, pink puddle. The woman remains still, helpless.

Grigory stands outside the operations centre – a hastily constructed tent on a slightly elevated point in the eastern sector of the town – and takes it all in. It's a military operation; there is nothing he can do to interfere. He watches the spreading chaos and feels impotent and alone.

To his right, slightly down the slope, Grigory sees a man attempting to carry a door on to the bus. The soldiers encircle him, all with their guns pointed, as if they're about to skewer the man. Grigory moves within earshot. The man stands with one arm around the vertical door, as if it's an old friend that he's introducing to a group of neighbours. He has a strong sweep of a chin, with short, grey stubble and a salesman's charisma. He's pointing to the intimate details of its surface. Grigory follows the man's fingers and sees some neat lines scored into the side of the panel at various heights, fractions beside them: $3\frac{1}{4}$, $5\frac{1}{2}$, $7\frac{1}{2}$. The man points upwards to a boy and girl, early to mid-teens, with the same definition to their faces, deep-set clear eyes. Grigory realizes the man is pointing out the measurements of their height as children, the markings of their growth. The man talks about the history of this object. The soldiers are intrigued by such ludicrous ambition, bringing such an unlikely object with him while everyone else is trying to smuggle on an extra bag or jacket.

Grigory hears the man had laid out his father on this door, ten years ago, then his mother last winter. After the wake, he had sat throughout the night holding her hand, the stiff body dressed in her best dress. He explains all this to the soldiers, he shows them the notches, the names, the tribal markings denoting the history of the thing, the only object he has ever cared for, a slab of grooved timber on which his own dead body will rest, until, mid-sentence, one of the soldiers steps up and stuns the butt of his gun into the man's nose.

Blood leaks down his face, glistening in his stubble, dripping from his chin. The door falls on to the concrete with a crash and the crowd panics, so tightly wound up they mistake it for a gunshot.

Some words still emerge from his lips: the momentum of the man's speech hasn't let him dry up completely. Then he stops talking and some other soldiers grab him, pull him forward and drag him away, pushing his family backwards. The door is consumed in the heave of the crowd. Grigory can see the family being pushed back in the surge, trying to swim against the tide of bodies, and the man is bundled into a troop carrier, where he covers his chin and mouth with his hand, and Grigory can't tell if this gesture is to stanch the flow of blood or to indicate his regret for his outlandish ambition.

Other soldiers are boarding trucks and Grigory finds out that they're ancillary squads, sent to search the town for anyone in hiding. He decides to join them, judging that a smaller group holds more opportunity to bring his calming influence to bear.

They drive to the western part of the town and walk through apartment blocks. Washing hangs on lines that stretch the width of each balcony. Fridges contain bottles of orange juice and lengths of butter on dishes. They find people behind shower curtains and wedged into airing cupboards. They find a pregnant girl lying in a hollowed-out sofa. Grigory stands on a balcony, glancing over the empty streets for signs of movement, and looks down and sees a pair of hands clutching the railings at his feet. He leans over the guard rail and finds a man hanging straight as an exclamation point, his gaze directed downwards, as if avoiding eye contact would keep him obscured from sight. A man hanging ten storeys up, his lean muscles taut with effort and desperation. In another apartment an old woman sits in her kitchen listening to the radio. When they enter in a clatter of heavy boots, she turns down the volume and looks peacefully at them, in total control of the situation. Before they have a chance to give the order, she refuses to leave. She invites them to beat her or shoot her if that is necessary, but she states that this is her home and she will die here. None of the soldiers has the appetite for this kind of violence, not here, not with this woman. They walk out and Grigory shakes his head and smiles in admiration and she raises her open palms to the ceiling, a silent gesture that says everything there is to say at this moment, in this room, in this town.

Many of the doors have notes pinned to them, to friends or relatives, stating a point of contact in the city. People have painted their family name on the door, an attempt to assert ownership. In dozens of apartments, they find tables fully laid for dinner.

They find a young couple sleeping in bed. They had been drinking for most of the night and lay there together under the sheets, oblivious to the commotion all around them. When the soldiers burst in, the man leaps from the bed in shock and then, realizing his nakedness, leaps back in again. The soldiers laugh and Grigory asks them to leave and then sits on the bed and explains the situation to the couple, staring into the dark eyes of the young woman, gaining her trust with the gentleness of his tone. They wait in the kitchen and when the couple emerge, dressed, carrying a few belongings, the soldiers clap and cheer and they smile shyly, and Grigory envies them their burgeoning love.

They put people in the truck and drive them to the relevant zones and then return and put more people in trucks. They pass a small graveyard and find a woman fisting soil from a grave – her parents' grave – into a jam-jar. She pleads to keep the jar but they take it from her and empty the soil back on to the ground. The woman has no energy to protest.

They hear a noise from a lift shaft and break through an iron grille and find a young boy, perhaps five years old, sitting on top of the lift, clasping his hands to his ears. One of the men climbs into the shaft and emerges a few minutes later with the boy bouncing on his shoulders, making horsey noises and steering the soldier by the ears.

They continue to shoot pets, despite Grigory's objections. Pets run from apartments and the soldiers fire their pistols at will and argue over kill numbers as if they were war heroes.

In the buses they don't talk. They are too shocked for words. Artyom sits with his mother and sister in a double seat, five rows from the back, each of them replaying the incident in their minds.

Artyom's mother watches the backs of heads bounce and nod and shake.

She didn't know the door mattered to him. He had never placed great importance on it and part of her wondered if he had tried to bring it with them as an absurd act of protest: 'How dare you try to take my home, watch me take a part of it with me.' Of course, the children were astonished. Of course, the listeners were intrigued. There were many angles to the man that were only revealed at intimate moments, in the smallest of ways. Oddly stubborn. Wildly stubborn. No one knew. The kids perhaps had a certain insight, but no one really knew the unfathomable depths of his stubbornness.

Andrei could slow everything down, all around her. He could bend time for her. When they made love in their bed, with his mother sleeping in the next room, a tough woman, full of harsh judgement, the slightest noise would bring tension – the old woman had sharp ears. So Andrei would be so careful, yet still so generous. They would make love while hardly moving. They would rock with mere whispers of motion, and she would bring him to release simply by the warmth of her breath on his neck.

'When we go I want to go first.' She had always told him this, when they were alone, and he would nod, agreeing, because they both knew that he was the one who would endure, that she was the one who would collapse, helpless, overwhelmed.

And now he is alone somewhere, in a truck or a cell, and she has two child adults to look after, to reassure and lead as best she can, though they're smarter, more aware than she is.

He will be sent along tomorrow. There can be no other possibility.

He will be sent along tomorrow.

Kids are moaning and shuffling. Artyom is sitting by the aisle, hanging off the side of the seat. There are families sitting on each other's laps, but Artyom doesn't want to suggest this to Sofya; the intimacy would be too strange.

The lights are on in the bus. They give substance to the cigarette smoke, a cloud of stained light hovering resolutely over them. Some children are sleeping, tired limbs slumped over the armrests, dangling over the passageway, heads lolling. A stream of whimpering trickles along the seats. There are intermittent rustling sounds, when people check which belongings they've forgotten, or dig into a plastic bag for an extra sweater. People are saying they're on their way to Minsk, but there has been no announcement. He's assuming there are some on the bus who recognize the route. Artyom looks around and realizes there aren't many men. Some old men, yes, but very few his father's age or younger. He didn't notice this while they were being shoved into the vehicles.

His limbs want to strike out, to destroy something, anything. There are enough nervous people around though, so instead he clamps his teeth around his cheek and bites down hard, feeling warm blood nestle around his teeth. He's never seen his father look bewildered, this man so durable, so assured, crushed by violence.

He'd like to look out of the windows, be distracted by the

unfamiliar sights, but he can't get a proper view past his mother and sister, through the smoke. Sofya takes a carrot from her pocket and eats it and Artyom does the same. They crunch on the tasteless lumps. Their jaws sore from a day of unwittingly grinding their teeth.

Artyom wakes. The bus has stopped and Sofya is punching his shoulder.

'We're getting off.'

It's night-time. The windows are matted with dull streaks of condensation. Artyom's brain feels the same way. He rubs his eyes with his fists, a gesture that reminds his mother of her boy at five years old, a naïve gesture that he will now surely carry through to adulthood. They gather their sacks, hug them to their chests, and wait until it's their turn to step into the aisle and out of the bus, spilling into the great pool of dislocated people.

Artyom looks to his left and sees that they're parked outside the train station. An abandoned car sits squat on its axle, people swarming around it, and Artyom walks over and stands on the bonnet to get a better view.

The main bulk of people are walking in a thick line away from the building, following hazard lights that have been laid like a trail.

Again he looks for men, fathers, but sees very few.

His mother has decided they'll go to her sister Lilya's apartment. She's not sure where it is but she'd recognize it on a map. So they need to get out of the crowd and find their bearings. Artyom turns back to the station. There are still a few lights on and a station guard leans against a column of the portico. Artyom signals to his mother and sister to meet him by the main entrance and, when he sees them making progress against the tide, he pushes forward himself and eventually emerges into empty space and approaches the guard.

'Is there anywhere to get a map?'

The guard busies himself and walks away, answering as he does so, reluctant to make eye contact.

'Try the concourse, there might be some on the information stand.'

Sofya and his mother walk towards him, looking around for possibilities.

His mother puts her hand in her pocket, brings out some roubles and puts them in his hand.

'See if you can find something hot.'

'To eat or to drink?'

'Either. I don't care.'

Artyom pushes open the main door of the station, steps on to the concourse. The place is deserted. Artyom is surprised that some of the crowd haven't filtered inside to get some respite from the chaos. He hears his footsteps reverberate around the empty space. It's an otherworldly sensation, to be alone in this grand expanse, a single figure under the great, arching roof of Minsk train station. The information booth is closed, but there's a map of the city on the wall, behind a plastic pane. He digs his fingers beneath the frame and slides out the map, rolls it up.

He steps inside an empty waiting room which houses a boy, asleep, alone, head on a table. The boy is almost embracing the tabletop, an empty packet of cigarettes beside his ear, a jar with some ash and old butts beside the empty packet. The boy's head resting on his hand, a grubby finger laid on his eyelid. Light filters through the discoloured plastic sheeting of the roof in a cool aqua-green. Artyom touches the tabletop and rubs some ash between his fingers.

Someone has a radio on in the distance. Folk music finds its way into his ears.

He finds an arcade where small stalls sell trinkets, all closed up. More people in this section, also searching for food. Station guards are silhouetted against the light, their caps flattening their profiles, giving them the grandeur of chess figures. There are old men hunched in corners, lying on plastic bags containing books and old coats.

In the station shop there are empty, square glass cabinets. A crowd is pressed against the counter. An old woman on the fringes eats a blini from wax paper. There is no anger in the queuing, no aggression in the gathering. People slope and drift. There is no more food to be had here, but they wait anyway, in hope.

He returns to the portico and shows his mother the map.

'Did you steal it?'

'Of course I stole it. You think there're shops selling maps for tourists?'

'I don't like you stealing.'

'Fine.' He walks towards the door. 'I'll leave it back.'

He has his own mind now. She can't scold him any more.

'No. You're right. It's fine.'

They've been fighting more in the past year. She can tell from his eyes that he's chalking up another victory. She'll win very few arguments from now on – not that she wants a competition, just a recognition that she still has some authority, that she knows things.

He lays the map on the ground in front of her.

'Her place is near the bus station. Get us to the bus station and I'll find it from there.'

Artyom runs his finger over the districts and finds it.

'OK. It's not far.'

'Did you get any food?' Sofya asks.

'No. All the shops have been cleared out. There were probably hundreds of buses before us. I'm sure people have stocked up.'

Artyom takes his mother's sack. Sofya can carry her own.

'How do we know when Father gets in?' Sofya asks.

'He'll find us at Lilya's.'

They head out into the road in single file, Artyom leading. He stays close to the walls. A man passes by with his head down, looking at his shoes. There are women and children sitting in the middle of the tarmac, quaking through tears. Artyom's mother approaches them and coaxes them into doorways, sheltering them from the pressing crowd. A woman in her forties walks backwards, screaming obscenities at the arrivals. She uses a term they don't understand: 'glow worms'.

They cross through the park, still keeping close. His arms are aching from the sacks, but he doesn't want this to be known, otherwise his mother will insist on carrying her own. Eventually, though, he stops, places them on the pathway and shakes out his shoulders.

His mother looks at him, concern weighing on her. Artyom sees her differently here, away from home, under the iron lamps of the pavement. She looks older than her age. The land, the work, has hardened her. Hardened her skin and face, but maybe also made her more determined. He thinks about how she works at harvest time, bent low over the straw, tying it together, gathering it into ricks. All day bent over, stopping only for the occasional drink of water. She's determined to get them where they need to go. A different strength to his father's.

'You're tired.'

'Yes.'

'Let me take them.'

He leaves the sacks on the ground and she heaves them over her shoulder and begins walking again. He'll take them back in a few minutes, when his shoulders have had a rest.

At the bus station there are more people, more chaos. The confusion is relentless but they are becoming accustomed to it. They move through the crowd more quickly now, spotting the gaps, less tentative in their steps. Artyom's mother doesn't hesitate in her direction and he and Sofya know that she recognizes where she is.

They reach a tree-lined street of apartment blocks. It's quieter here. They pass a group of men gathered around the opened bonnet of a car, drinking, one underneath with a torch, tinkering away. The men stare as they pass, carrying their belongings. The group don't say anything but Artyom can feel their eyes trailing him, aggression in their look. *So this is what Minsk is like*, he thinks.

'They don't like us here, do they, Mama?' Sofya says.

'No. I suppose they don't,' Artyom's mother replies.

They find the building and, pushing open the door to the entrance, they see the lift doors are wide open with the lights off and wires hanging out where the buttons should be. Artyom's mother lays the sacks on the ground and looks dolefully up the steps and arches her back, stretches her neck from side to side.

'What floor is she on?' Artyom asks.

'The eighth.'

'I'll take the bags from here.'

'Thank you, Artyom.'

The steps are crumbled at the edges, stones peeping through. So Artyom steps sideways, keeping the sacks at an even height to balance himself. There's a smell of piss in the enclosed space and it joins together with the scent of potatoes ingrained in the cloth which rises up as he swings the sacks. The walls are covered in writing. Names in huge black letters, connected in a fluid scrawl, a series of interlocked curls. On the fourth-floor landing there's a disembowelled teddy bear, its cotton insides greyed and trampled upon.

He pushes into the corridor and looks at his mother as she knocks on the fifth door down.

No answer. She waits and knocks again. No answer. She calls: 'Lilya. It's Tanya. We need your help.'

They wait. She looks at Sofya, who is staring at the ceiling, her fists curling around the opening of her sack. Sofya always looks upwards when she's angry. Artyom's mother leans against the wall and puts her ear to the door.

'You're in there. Your light was on. I can hear you. I have Artyom and Sofya. We need to come in. Please, Lilya.'

Artyom stays at the end of the corridor. He understands there's something private about the moment. He needs to let his mother go through this on her own.

His mother steps away from the door. Movement, a voice from inside.

'I can't help. It's too dangerous. You need to go to the shelter.'

His mother bangs on the door.

Some neighbours appear. Stripes of light cross the green tiled floor. A shirtless man stands in the corridor, his chest hair curled into dots. He fills the gap between the walls, hands on his hips, like a goalkeeper waiting for a penalty.

'Lilya. I'm your sister. Let us in.'

'You're poison, don't you know this? You can't stay around other people.'

Artyom's mother starts to cry. He hasn't seen his mother cry since he was a child. Sofya kicks the door but his mother brushes her aside. They both lean against the wall, hiding their faces.

The man with no shirt speaks.

'You heard. You're fucking poison. Get out of here.'

This half-naked bastard shouting at them. Artyom drops the bags and runs towards him, arms wide, a slur of dense breath in his throat, but the man sidesteps him easily and Artyom skids along the ground, tearing the knee of his trousers, skinning his flesh. The man steps into his doorway.

'If you're not gone in five minutes, I'll come out with my knife.'

He spits in Artyom's direction, the blob landing near Artyom's shoes.

'Five minutes.'

The man closes his door and the three of them bunch on the floor in individual piles, beaten. After a few moments, Artyom's mother walks over to him, cradles his neck in her hand and kisses the top of his head.

'Let's find a bed.'

They walk back towards the stairwell, their feet echoing in the corridor.

In Pripyat, night has drawn in and Grigory walks through the town alone. He passes a small carnival with a ferris wheel creaking in the breeze. The apartment blocks are dark, uninhabited now, looming.

Coloured paper still lies scattered around the town, mocking the tone of the day. Dead dogs littered everywhere, stagnant blood glistening through the darkness. Grigory occasionally catches the darting gait of wolves, drifted in from the forest, attracted by the scent of blood, courageous in the emptied streets.

He makes his way back to the operation headquarters in the main square, approaching from a side street, and as he enters the square he pauses in realization at the statue in the centre, the iron figure half kneeling, raising his open arms to the heavens, full of fury. He has passed it a dozen times in the last day, unaware of its subject: Prometheus, the Greek god who gave fire to the people.

This statue in this place.

Grigory slumps under the figure, spent. A young lieutenant approaches and sits beside him. He is also too tired to attend to his duties. He pulls out a cigarette and offers one to Grigory, who readily accepts, his first cigarette in ten years. And Grigory remembers how Prometheus was punished for his betrayal of godly secrets: Zeus had him chained to a rock and each day would begin with an eagle ripping his liver from his body, which grew back by evening, so that the suffering would be repeated to eternity.

They stay there, unspeaking, until Grigory says, 'I'm a surgeon. I never expected to live through a day like this.'

The soldier dabs a loose strand of tobacco off his tongue and spits.

'You remember, my friend, what comrade Lenin told us: "Every cook has to learn how to govern the state."'

They finish their cigarettes in silence.

November 1986

Sometimes Maria looks up and a day has passed, or longer, a month. Most evenings Alina, her sister, asks how her day was and she replies, 'Unremarkable'. And they add up, those unremarkable days. Days that, when you look back on them, even two weeks later, retain not a single distinctive moment. And if she's to admit the thing she fears most, it's this: the stealthy accumulation of unremarkable months, the rows and stacks of nothing, the unfilled columns when she sits down to account for her life.

She turns from her lathe and looks up at the small dust-caked clock that sits over the door to the locker room. It's quarter past four and Maria remembers her lunch – tea and herring and beetroot – remembers sitting with Anna and Nestor, but nothing else. How can the rest of it have escaped her? How can another day have almost ended?

In the past few years, life has become unrecognizable to her, existing somehow outside of her; in the passage of the seasons, in the momentum of a city.

'Maria Nikolaevna.'

Her line supervisor is standing behind her, clipboard, as ever, at the ready. He's a small man with a string around his glasses that he never uses, preferring instead to perch them on the top of his forehead.

'Are you with us?'

'Yes. Sorry, Mr Popov.'

'Mr Shalamov wants to see you.'

'Yes, sir. Should I go straight to see him or get cleaned up first?'

'Mr Shalamov doesn't like to be kept waiting.'

'Yes, sir.'

Mr Shalamov is their personnel officer. He oversees their initial training and that's the last most people see of him. Hearing his name puts Maria instantly on edge. She turns off her lathe and makes sure that the red emergency stop, the one at her knees, is also pressed. Two fragments of an unconscious routine, two more actions that add up to serious time, when you calculate the repetition.

He may not like to be kept waiting, but she'll step into the toilet nonetheless, put her hair back, wash her face. Because it's a universal law that the prettier you look, the more things will go your way. Sometimes she thinks her entire education was based on this. If she learned nothing else in school, it was how to prime yourself for passing men.

She stands over the washbasin, takes a nail scrub to her hands, scoops some water up and over her face and hears it shatter on the floor around her. Her hands are hard now, calloused, which is definitely an undesirable trait, but there's no way of avoiding it. They don't use gloves at the lathes, even though regulations require them to, because two years ago Polina Volkova, three workstations down, had the machine catch her glove, and her hand went with it. Half a second of gore, in which her hand went from being a hand to a shredded tangle of bone and ligament. So they wear gloves according to the regulations, but they don't wear gloves according to reality. It does mean, though, that her face is usually clean and clear, because her calloused hands have just the right texture to keep her skin invigorated. So there are compensations.

This job was not of her choosing and yet she's not necessarily ungrateful for it, knowing the alternatives.

She runs her fingers along the bases of her eye sockets, massaging them. Hazel eyes, as dark as her hair, full and alert. She pulls her lips over her gums and rubs a wet finger across her teeth. Strong, symmetrical teeth, a point of envy amongst her friends. Her gums a little more prominent than she would like, so that in photographs she's careful to contain the full breadth of her smile.

Grey hairs are multiplying across her head, with no discernible pattern. She thinks of Sunday mornings when Grigory would lie beside her and pick out the rogue strands like those gorillas on the nature programmes that forage through their mate for lice. When he couldn't isolate the single hair and plucked two or three at once, she would let out an involuntary whimper, which he found amusing. These sessions would end with him coaxing her back from her irritation, smoothing his hands over her. Lazy Sundays.

She ties her hair back and adjusts her fringe.

On her return to Moscow, not long after she and Grigory were married, she secured a job as a staff journalist at a notable newspaper, where she worked her way up to features writer. A position she held for several years until some underground articles she'd written came to light. What followed was a dangerous time for her. She had to realign all aspects of her personality, was forced to erase her outspoken nature; every word she spoke from that moment would be sifted through and interpreted.

She takes in the image in the glass. A certain slackening to her features now, a looseness, subtle but undeniable. Wrinkles like sketch marks smattered around her eyes. Fine details that perhaps she alone can see, but she can't stave off the thought that middle age is on its way. Three years of working here are beginning to take their toll. She wonders what she'll look like in another three.

And yes, it's true she's reconfigured herself to become what they've asked of her. She dresses anonymously, she nods her head in agreement with almost any statement floated in her direction. She has made it a point to avoid eye contact with everyone other than a few trusted friends, so she walks with her head bowed, a kind of self-containment, moving like a vessel, constant, never deviating from her course. But she's still here, surviving.

Maria takes off her package-brown workcoat, bangs the dust off it and then puts it on again. It drops shapelessly around her. She's lost weight in the past year. Her cheekbones protrude, her arms feel slightly insubstantial. There is only so much food that she and Alina can queue for, only so many hours in the day, although she's started to have decent meals in the canteen of the university – another reason to love the building.

She slaps her cheeks to give them some colour. She knows Mr Shalamov likes his employees to look vibrant, full of the joys, despite requiring them to spend all these dogged hours in this spartan shed. Should she leave the coat off or keep it on? She keeps it on. Mr Shalamov will surely mention its absence and it's not as if she has a tantalizing figure.

OK.

She glides out the door and moves hurriedly to the metal steps that lead to the management offices. Rough squares of brown carpet tiles. A secretary at the desk with a typewriter in front of her, a telephone and nothing else. The secretary looks at her with deadened eyes. Maria thinks that this is a woman whose days pass in staggered increments of time, her hours comprised of finely sliced segments. Answer a phone, five minutes pass. Type up dictation, fifteen minutes pass. No other workers to talk to. Managers who see her as barely human. Things could be worse. She could be this woman.

'I'm here to see Mr Shalamov.'

'Yes. He's been waiting.'

She says this with distaste. As if Maria should feel guilt at keeping the man from the reports he has to flick through, from the nap he has to take.

She makes a call and replaces the receiver. Maria stands in front of the desk. The woman types while Maria waits. A few minutes pass. The phone rings, she answers it.

'He'll see you now.'

'Thank you.'

Maria walks into his office with its large plate-glass windows that look out over the factory floor, so self-contained that Maria can hear her feet pad along the carpet. The silence makes what's happening out there seem like an intricate mime. Mr Shalamov is standing with his back to her, looking out over the waves of industry. He doesn't turn to acknowledge her. She doesn't speak. While she waits she looks down to her empty stool. Her comrades at her workstation going through the same motions, moving as fluidly as any of the larger machinery in the mid-ground, where aluminium panels and steel parts grind forward in endless sequences. A series of interlocking arcs and twirls. Nothing out of sync in this moving tableau.

On her first morning, having resigned herself to a future of repetition, she was surprised at the comfort that she was deriving from the crowd, the sense of common purpose, each individual working their way through a collective life.

The scale of it was astonishing, ten thousand employees. And there are other complexes nearby: an ammonia plant, a chemical-processing factory; a vast migratory movement makes its way from the city on buses and trolley cars and marshrutkas, and she is one of them, stepping in tandem with hordes of scarfed women and hooded men.

She wonders sometimes if perhaps she was born for this, that this life of hers was inevitable. Isn't this how people truly live: clocking in for work; whispered, surreptitious parties on a Friday night; duck-feeding on a Sunday?

The first sight of the factory made her pause in shock, made her realign her sense of scale. When she passed through the enormous, hulking doors, six times taller than a person, her superintendent met her and recited the facts: the assembly line a kilometre long, a new car produced every twenty-two seconds of every minute of every hour of every day. A sea of calibrated metal, waves of industry pushing onward with meticulously timed precision, a constellation of spinning parts.

The factory floor.

There was a grating whirr that vibrated into her feet and Maria knew she would become wedded to this sound. She knew instantly that she would carry this noise home, sleep with it for maybe years, perhaps until death. There was a timeline here that was permanent and previously alien. There was a time clock, a punch machine. Punch in and out. The superintendent gave her a card and let her know it was an imprisonable offence to cheat the clock. He had personally sent employees to prison. The machine punched perfectly symmetrical holes, exactly in the centre of the boxes.

There were time slots and days, printed in embossed type.

Her name in embossed type. Maria Nikolaevna Brovkina.

And she took this card five days a week, for the past three years. Punching in and out, marking her time.

Maria worked into the work, eventually finding comfort in camshafts. It had taken months for this to manifest itself – it was endless and repetitive and crushingly dull – but after a time the religious beauty of the task emerged. The detail, the exactitude required in working the lathe. How deep can an action go? How perfect can a human act be? Maria worked to a precision of thousandths of a millimetre. A micron, they call it. A micron.

And the repetition.

And the repetition.

And the repetition.

Guiding the mechanical arm as fluently as if it were her own.

Over time, Maria found her body easing into and around the action. Her body incorporated and enveloped it. Drinking water in the kitchen, a mid-night, mid-sleep drink and her arm would reach for the tap in the same flowing arc as the motion at her workbench. Her hand clutching the glass with a regularity only she knew.

Sometimes she works with her eyes closed. A dangerous act, dangerous machinery, but she can feel the precision of the task with a clarity that she still finds astounding.

Mr Shalamov turns and points to the chair in front.

'Please.'

She sits, resisting an urge to take out a handkerchief and place it down on the seat to gather any dust she's brought in.

'Mrs Brovkina. Thank you for coming to see me.'

Mrs Brovkina. It's still her name, of course, and she's seen it written down often enough. But no one uses her last name. It sounds odd still to be linked to Grigory and it saddens her to hear it, carrying as it does a residue of failure.

'Of course.'

'I've been looking at your file.'

She can't think of any recent discrepancies in her work, but of course that doesn't mean someone hasn't perceived, or even invented, any number of offences.

'Comrade Popov has been very complimentary. He says you're a very consistent worker. In fact, your production rates are in the higher percentiles.'

She feels no relief. The statement is a prelude. He's been through this process far more often than she.

'I try hard to contribute to the collective effort.'

'Of course. Just as we all do.'

She has spoken too early, singled herself out, made it sound like there are others who don't contribute. She could qualify her statement, but it's better to let it rest. Let him say what he has to say.

He lists off the major entries in her records. Dates of training. The promotion she was given last year. She can't help but think of Zhenya and Alina, can't help thinking about the size of their apartment. She doesn't think she could go home if she is dismissed from this job. She couldn't be any more of a burden than she is already.

He puts down the file.

'Tell me, what did you think of the lecture last month on the history of our automotive industry?'

So that's it.

'Unfortunately, Mr Shalamov, I was unable to attend.'

'Of course, yes. I see it now in our attendance records. Well then, what about the presentation on "Major Contributors to the Engineering Effort"?'

'I was also unable to attend that presentation.'

'I see. Of course. As a matter of personal interest, would you be able to name a major contributor to our cause in the field of engineering?'

The choice is to be arrogant or ignorant. It's not arrogance, though. It's knowledge. Why should she be afraid of such a thing?

'I know that Konstantin Khrenov was a pioneer of underwater welding.'

He sits back and nods, impressed. They both know that not many of his employees could pull a name like that just out of the air.

'He didn't feature in our lecture, Mrs Brovkina. That's very specific knowledge to have at your fingertips. I learned about Mr Khrenov's work in my second year of specialist study. Where was it that you heard about the man?'

They drag it out. This is what they do. Just ask a straight question. Just get to the point. It irritates her to have to dance through this minefield. She remembers to take a breath. There can't be any traces of frustration in her voice.

'In my previous work, I had some contact with under water welders. They spoke to me at length about their processes and history.'

'That sounds very interesting, Mrs Brovkina. This was in your work as a journalist.'

'Yes.'

'It sounds like you've cultivated an interest in engineering processes.'

'Yes, sir.'

'So why not attend our lectures? Do you feel your knowledge is too advanced?'

'No, sir. I had other commitments.'

'Oh, yes. I see this. Yes, right here. It says you're teaching English at the Lomonosov?'

'Yes, sir. Two nights a week.'

'A former journalist who spends two nights a week teaching English at the university. I read these facts side by side and they say something to me. Tell me, Mrs Brovkina, do you think this work is beneath you?'

'No, sir. Of course not. It's honourable work. I'm very proud of it.'

'Good. So why are you revisiting your former territories? Surely that life is past you now.'

She takes time to consider her answer; she can't leave herself vulnerable to the criticism that she's not placing enough emphasis on the progress of the plant.

'There is a shortage of English scholars. A former professor of mine requested that I help out in this area. I feel that it is my duty to aid our collective efforts in any way I can.'

'Mrs Brovkina, as I say, your work cannot be faulted. But there are some who would question your commitment to this particular field.'

She says nothing. She waits to hear his conclusions. She knows he can't ask her to revoke a job where they need her skills, even if it's only a couple of classes a week. The name of the Lomonosov carries some weight in higher circles. Mr Shalamov will no doubt be reluctant to get into an administrative spat with figures who may have more authority than he has.

'I have never asked about your activities previous to joining us here.'

The thing that every sanctimonious pen-pusher will always be able to hang over her.

'No, sir.'

'I would be wary, Mrs Brovkina. It may appear to some that you're treading old ground, reigniting old contacts. Some would say you're inclined to venture into areas you have been encouraged to ignore.'

'I wasn't aware of how it may appear, sir.'

'No. Of course. If you had given it some thought you would have refused their offer of work.'

'As I mentioned, sir, there is a shortage of specialists.'

'Did you know, Mrs Brovkina, that there's a shortage of highly skilled engineering instructors? Perhaps your time might be better served pursuing, say, a degree in precision engineering. I understand that you have scant family commitments.'

Scant? Yes. If you call queuing for food for four hours every weekend scant. If you call cleaning the communal bathroom or the stairwells or delivering laundry to Alina's clients scant. Then, yes, she doesn't have any commitments.

Don't argue, though. The way to deal with this is to agree and work out a strategy later.

'Yes. Mr Shalamov. These are possibilities I hadn't taken into account. Thank you for bringing them to my attention.'

His tone softens.

'Think of this as an opportunity, Maria Nikolaevna. A position as an engineering instructor is highly valued. In this plant we have a history of supporting those who have made mistakes in their past. They are often hungrier, more loyal. You are intelligent and possess an excellent work ethic. Perhaps it's time to ask yourself: "What are my ambitions?"'

She stays silent. It's already been decided. They'll take away the one thing in her life that provides any interest. The one activity that reminds her who she is. Next spring she'll be studying for an engineering degree, there'll be years of night classes ahead of her, dredging through stultifying textbooks.

He writes a note on a piece of paper, then very deliberately attaches it inside her file. He nods.

'Fine. You can return to your station.'

'Thank you, sir.'

At her workbench she releases the emergency stop, turns on the machine and switches her mind to neutral.

When she removes her glove to open the door, her hand always sticks. Just for the briefest of seconds. The heat leaves an imprint that recedes back into the brass.

Hunched men sit in the stairwells flipping cards into a bucket. They use an effeminate gesture, squeezing the card between two middle fingers then flicking the wrist outwards, displaying an open palm to the world. The cards twist in their high arcs, producing a crisply satisfying note on landing.

Maria opens the door to Alina's place.

'What is one hundred and fifty-three divided by seven?'

'Again?'

'What is one hundred and fifty-three divided by seven?'

She's been here for two years, even though it was supposed to be temporary, a couple of months to get herself settled after she split with Grigory. But she's still coming home to the folding bed in the living room, always attempting to inhabit as little space as possible, storing her few possessions in a cupboard under the window.

Yevgeni still considers her to be the origin of all knowledge.

'Well, let's find out. Give me your pencil.'

There's a communal toilet in the hallway, with mould slowly edging its way down from the corner of the ceiling and the tiles peeling off. The light flickers on when you twist the door lock.

What are my ambitions?

His question has played in her head all the way home. She's having difficulty reconciling herself to an honest answer and is glad of the consolation in her nephew's struggle with an abstract problem.

Yevgeni works the pencil round his copybook, numbers bursting from their appointed squares. His flaccid scrawl sinks diagonally down the page, rotating towards the end so the figures lie almost horizontally. 2 resting on its arched back. 7 leaning on its elbow, legs pointed outward.

She missed most of his early years, too busy travelling around the country reporting the small victories of working life, writing them up as though the workers were living sainted existences, achieving the greatest deeds, when all she saw was squalor and cynicism.

The newspaper sent her on journeys to far-away places, hidden corners of the Union where life continued in the most extraordinary circumstances, often barely any heat or light, toughened people who understood how to subsist with the most meagre of resources, reminding her of deep-sea urchins adapting to an almost extraterrestrial environment.

She had acted as a priest of sorts. There were times on those trips when people would tell her their most delicate intimacies, staring deep into the embers of a dying fire. Of course, they all thought initially that she was with the KGB, there to draw truths from them. But a few hours in her company and they realized she was too real to be truly invested in the system. She was too loose with her talk, too self-deprecating, telling little stories on herself, dropping small comments that could be interpreted as criticisms; though they would also hold up as factual statements if she was ever reported.

Salt miners in Solikamsk, grinding out a day's work in those crystalline tunnels. Or the sovkhoz – the state farms – in Uzbekistan, where the summer crops spread out past the curve of the earth, where she interviewed averagely built men with enormous, hoary hands, hands so roughened by the weather that the skin was separated into pads, like a dog's paw. The grain silos military in their bearing, gigantic cylindrical tanks from which biblical quantities of grain would pour into the bellies of vast trucks.

Everything enormous. That was the overriding sense that remained with her. The utter, mind-melting scale of the Union.

And how, in the wake of such experiences, could she not write of the reality of the lives she met? She sees now that she always knew, at least on some level, that such words would lead to a revoking of her privileges, a banishment from her profession.

Maria considers her nephew as he sits on her knee, warmth flowing from him, seeping through her overcoat, which she has not yet taken off.

His finger has healed, which is a relief to all. Though there's a swelling around the area of the fracture, like a huge, dormant boil. A physiotherapist in the next building showed them some finger-strengthening exercises, a series of bends and waggles which Yevgeni performed with religious devotion before bedtime.

They bought him a keyboard in the summer, one that sits on two metal trestles. A man that Alina does laundry for, a lorry driver, smuggled it back from Berlin. Alina gave him two months' free laundry for it, in addition to three months of Maria's wages, all she had saved up since she arrived. But when he brought it in the door and set it up and Yevgeni sat down to play for the three of them, Maria couldn't but feel a swelling pride, couldn't think of anything else she'd like to spend her money on, a satisfaction that lasted for perhaps five minutes until the neighbours started banging on the door, threatening to call the building superintendent, have them kicked out. It hasn't made a sound in four months. They tried various strategies to appease the neighbours. They brought vodka and sausages around to those closest, but when others heard about the windfall, they wanted their share. People at the far end of the building started to complain, even though they'd have to strain to hear even the faintest traces of a note. So they stopped giving out gifts. They would not be black-mailed. Such behaviour from grown adults.

So the genius plays with no sound, which, at first, she thought a picture of impotence. Now, even though it no doubt hinders his advancement, she thinks it's glorious. Sometimes Maria arrives home and sees him in the living room, her bed-room, and he's flowing to the music, doing all the dips and turns of head and drops of delicate hands that she sees in the concert pianists, and at first she thought he was copying them, emulating them in the same way that kids take on the celebra-tions of footballers. After watching him, though, on separate occasions, watching him when he doesn't know anybody is looking, she realizes he's doing it of his own accord, dancing internally as he presses down on the dull, plastic keys.

But all has not been so smooth recently. His tempo is beginning to drift. It's a slight quirk that seems to be growing exponentially. The auditions for the central school of the Conservatory are next April, and Yevgeni's training has come unstuck. There's a tautness in the household. Mr Leibniz has asserted that the boy would either grow out of his musical difficulties or fall deeply into the disordered void; there's no way to train it out of him: 'Music is a sensual medium,' he says, 'his style cannot be counted back to purity.' Maria passed the bathroom the other night and saw Alina gripping the taps, leaning back on her heels, head on the sink rim. Of course, if he doesn't get in the first time he can always reapply the next year, but the boy doesn't deal well with failure. Maria thinks that if he doesn't succeed initially, he won't get in. He has a fiery will. He blazes in his pursuit of the music. He's not one of those vapid automatons she sees when they go to a recital there, when they sit in that pale-green room and watch stooped men with silver-tipped canes greet each other and assess the performer's pedigree as if they were a racehorse. Afterwards each musician recieves their applause utterly devoid of appreciation, bending as though their body has finally refused to carry itself upright.

They look at their audience and see only judgement. They proclaim in silence to the room that they're talentless, worthless. *If only you knew the paltry depths of my ability. How painful it is even to stand here and receive such graciousness, how utterly unworthy I am.* So excruciating that they can barely keep their eyes open. It's all such bullshit. Every one of them has an ego the size of that barge of an instrument they play. Maria always feels the urge to walk up to the podium, grab them by the shoulders and shake them till their teeth rattle. Precious little orchids.

Her favourite thing about the Conservatory is to stand outside it, especially on weekdays – though she hasn't done this since she moved to the outskirts of the city – when the students are practising and the windows over the courtyard are all thrown open and a great clatter emerges. All these styles and tempos and tones competing with each other. All that sweat being expended. You feel as if you're standing in front of a great cauldron of creativity. All that discordance so full of life, so utterly at odds with the translucent figures that sit up on the rostrum at the recitals.

No, Yevgeni is definitely not of that mould and it's another thing she loves about him. There are tantrums. Sometimes after lessons he locks himself into the bathroom and refuses to come out. He throws things at walls. He bites his keyboard, bites his knuckles, pulls at his hair, kicks doorframes and lamp posts, a tumult of rage inside the kid.

And yet there's a joy to his playing; she delights in his fingers. Yevgeni has the lightest fingers. They skip along his knee while he watches TV. He often eats dinner with one hand, drumming into the tablecloth with the other. Sometimes they brush their teeth in the bathroom together and he hums scales as he does so. He jumps from foot to foot, singing each note in an almost perfect pitch, at least to Maria's untrained ears. Occasionally he even sits at her old typewriter, working the keys to a hammered frenzy, and she likes the sound of this too, the rhythm of who she used to be, given voice to the wider world once more.

Symphonies are running on the record player every waking moment. Debussy accompanies her as she clips her toenails, Mendelssohn guides the spoon as she heats beans.

There's a small tuxedo in Alina's closet and a bow tie with a tiny circumference. They attend competitions in regional halls in the sleet and hail, Mr Leibniz in the back row swaying his stick from side to side in a disciplined rhythm. The child at a piano bringing them there. A child in a mini-tuxedo.

Maria keeps him on her knee and guides his path through long division, adjusting his deviant numerals, reminding him how to fit the figures into their blue-ruled boxes. She lays out the numbers in neat columns and double rules the answer line at the bottom. She double rules it because this is what she's always done. An unthinking practice passed down through the generations.

Yevgeni has a jar of pencils on the table, which she finds immensely comforting. Bunched pencils bring reassurance. The rubber at the top is often bitten off. She can see where he has made indentations in the metal bracket with his teeth. He sits on her knee and finishes his homework and then Maria flicks his hair back from his forehead, kisses the peak of his skull, sends him to wash his teeth and looks at him as he goes out the door.

There was a child of her own once, or the early configuration of a child or a potential child. But she couldn't bring herself to have it. She didn't want it in this world. And its departure was followed a few months later by the departure of her husband.

After the procedure, Maria believed that, if they had taken an X-ray of her, there would be a single line denoting her outer shell, and nothing else. The doctors would see her as she was, just a thin film of skin, no organs or intestines or bloodflow, a single, contoured line. She often still thinks these thoughts, feels these feelings: her child's absence, her husband's absence. So many empty spaces in her life. And perhaps, she thinks, that's why she feels such delight when she watches Yevgeni sway along a soundless keyboard. It dignifies that which is not there. It reminds her that life can be experienced in ways that she has never contemplated.

Maria and Alina grew up in Togliatti, an industrial town in the Samara region, in an apartment similar to the one in which they live now. Her father worked the ticket booth in the train station, playing chess round the clock with a small cadre of friends who would drop by at appointed times. As she got older, she realized that when her father was referred to by people outside the family it was in a hushed, strained, maybe sour, way. Stray comments leaked through the cracks of winter-planed doors. People cast glances over downturned shoulders. She was exposed to it from the earliest age, and it took some time to realize – by watching how the same adults treated her few childhood friends – that this was not the norm.

He disappeared one day, a few months short of her twentieth birthday. It was Alina who finally told her that the notebook their father kept in his small booth didn't contain records of chess matches but a detailed account of the movements of the city. Who went where and when. Who bought what, talked to whom. What someone wore on a particular day, who they welcomed off the platform. Their father was the gatekeeper for the town, the all-seeing eye, passing the information along a chain of connections, resulting in actions which Maria couldn't help imagining.

Then he too disappeared and this was something they couldn't account for. There were no answers to this development. A Saturday afternoon when he went to the hippodrome to lay a little money on the horses and never returned. They questioned everyone. Everyone they asked gave no reply. She accompanied her mother to the buildings of the men he played chess with and they stood at their doors while a mother and wife broke down under the gaze of her daughters, physically knelt before these men, wrapping her arms around their legs in an action of abject desperation, and they looked into the mid-distance, viewing the ordinary motions of their street, her wretched family oblivious to them.

Alina is ironing shirts. Alina is always ironing.

'Now he's having trouble with his maths.'

'I know, I gave him some help.'

'First his timing goes. Now the little genius can't even count.'

'You can't worry it away. It's not like one of your creases.'

'Oh, and he's your child. You're right, of course. The past nine years I've been thinking he's mine.'

'Be sarcastic. I'm trying to be supportive.'

'The kid doesn't even listen to me, he listens to you. Since when did I become the enemy?'

'He doesn't want to disappoint you. Just give him some time.'

Maria folds some shirts. Alina sprays water from a plastic bottle and runs the iron over the damp patches, and steam expands into the room.

It's time for a drink.

It's a thing that has sneaked into her life: a drink or two and the evening counts its own way to its conclusion. And she's not ashamed. It's a fringe benefit of manual labour, no one questions your need to unwind. She stands on the balcony, glass in hand, with a clear bottle, its white label inscribed with one word in large black type: 'VODKA'. There is a pleasure, she finds, in its unadorned seriousness. The stark quality of the label eliminates the trivial drinker.

This is Maria's moment of quiet reflection.

What are my ambitions?

Sometimes she thinks into the middle of her unborn child's life. It's not a ghost that follows her around, she doesn't look at other kids and wonder what colour its eyes would be or if it would have difficulty tying its laces. But she sees imagined scenes. A daughter being fitted for a dress. Sitting for dinner in the apartment of a bright young couple, proud and radiant, though she doesn't know if her child is the man or the woman. Odd, imagined moments. Snatches of an alternative life.

When she had the procedure – as they kept referring to it – she didn't tell him beforehand. He is a doctor, he spends his life healing, repairing – there was no way he would allow her to go through with it. Instead she left a note in his jacket pocket. Just the facts, the decision, no pleading for understanding, no fleshing out of her thoughts.

Afterwards, when she had had a few hours' rest, she took a taxi home, bleeding and weak, and when she opened the door she saw him sitting on a wicker stool beside the stove. He held the note towards her, the scrawled lines she'd left to explain herself. Even in her weakened state she knew it was now a piece of evidence, and he held it up, not needing to voice the question, his eyes asking it for him: *Who are you?*

Of course, their marriage couldn't survive such a thing. That too was a calculation on her part. It was not only her actions that would hurt him, it was the independent nature of them, demolishing the closeness that had grown between them. Grigory is a man who listens, who speaks directly to the centre of things. This is why she fell in love with him. At parties he would stand in the corner and, inevitably, people would divulge their lives to him. Teary-eyed women returning from their conversations with him would clasp her forearm as they passed, making eye contact, thanking her, acknowledging her luck in finding such a partner, and her impulse would be to smash her glass into their teeth.

Sometimes, after work, she would visit him in the hospital, and he would be mid-surgery and she could look through the viewing window and watch the refined world in which he functioned, the ghostly lights and bodywear, the goggles and instruments, the small, highly skilled gathering focused upon a single point. She would stand beside the family of the patient as they held hands and wept, mumbling prayers under their breath, watching what she was watching, their loved one at the mercy of her loved one, and sometimes, from a distance, she would observe him –

unaware of her presence – speaking to the families in his white coat, and they would kiss his hand or fold into despair depending on his words, and how could she come home, after witnessing all this, and ask him to take on her worries? How could she do this when she wouldn't even allow herself to be irritated when he left empty containers in the fridge or stubble in the bathroom sink?

In their final weeks, they spoke to each other only through functions: 'Can you pick up some milk?'; 'The lightbulb in the bedroom needs changing'; 'Are there any clean towels?' There were times she felt close to him, reminded of what she once had, when a tremor of their intimacy would stir her into recognition. The scent of him. Or when he reached past her or stood near her, the disparity in their size, the natural protection he offered. In these times she wanted to reach out, place a hand on him, say a vulnerable word, knowing this was an impulse he shared. But they couldn't bridge that void, articulate what they needed to articulate. Their language had been unlearned and it had become too painful now to recall.

Now Maria has a folding bed that they keep behind the couch. Maria has two pairs of shoes, one of these so worn that water seeps through, and so they are only halfway practical for six months of the year. Maria has one pair of earrings and underwear so greyed it looks, and feels, as if it has been fashioned out of concrete. She has a faltering nephew and a long-suffering sister. She has a duty to them.

She doesn't have ambitions any more, she has responsibilities.

She flicks matches over the railing. They spit hot flame and twirl calmly to the ground, end over end, disappearing from sight after four floors. She'll run out of matches and look up, turn around, walk into the kitchen, and ten years will have elapsed. Already she's surrounded by the past. It seeps into every moment. Like the smallest things that remind her of her father. Someone cracking an egg. Someone sweeping snow from the bottom of their trousers. In the subsequent years there were no letters or postcards, no word sent back about him, and this leads her to believe that whatever happened had happened quickly. If he was locked away somewhere, they would eventually have heard about it. So there was no prison. They didn't even know if it was the KGB or someone whom her father had informed upon, some family whose lives he had ruined.

After the disappearance, their mother came to Moscow and joined the Lubyanka queue for information. The final refuge of the most desperate. Maria was already studying in the Lomonosov by then and Alina was married in the city, living south of the river. They took the queuing in shifts, Maria and Alina joining her when they could. They brought each other soup and warm blankets. A ten-day queue. The line snaking from Prospekt Christoprudny, all the way down to Nikolskaya Ulitsa, coming to an end at that small, brown door where they had a three-minute audience with a KGB officer who told them, 'No information, come back next week'; and people would walk from that door and return to the back of the line, beginning it all again.

Eventually, after a month of this, their mother crumbled. She lay in bed for weeks, wailing and sleeping. They fed her with whatever they could find, stewing old vegetables, leftovers from the market. Often her bed was soiled, and one sister would wash her down while the other scrubbed the mattress.

They placed her in a residential home and, to pay for it, Maria took work in Kursk as a cleaner in a hospital, moving from Moscow because any job that doesn't need a qualification is filled years in advance. So she went to Kursk and cleaned and saved and Alina stayed in the capital and did the same and they'd visit their mother on alternate months and look into her eyes and search for a gleam of life, hoping she would show some signs of progress.

Alina joins her.

'He's in bed?' Maria asks.

'Yes. He's tired. Have you some left?'

The bottle is passed. Alina takes a shot then smacks her lips, letting out a rasp.

'Look at us. Disappointed women firing down cheap vodka on a concrete balcony. My diagnosis is that we need men,' Maria says.

Alina smiles. 'Yes. Men. Remember what they were like.'

'I'm not fussy, you know, not now, I'll take any old thing: fat, missing teeth, hairy back. One who never remembers how to use a knife and fork. Even one who spits out his tobacco on the streets.'

'Ah. A man who spits. Is there anything sexier?'

'Nothing. Nothing that God has created in his blessed name can be sexier than my fat, hairy-backed, gap-toothed, tobacco-spitting man.'

'Don't forget the bad table manners.'

'Oh yes, a man who spits on the street and eats with his fingers.'

They shoot out a brief giggle and pass the bottle between them.

They once had men, both of them. They are attractive; Maria can view this objectively, or can at least try to. Perhaps it will happen again.

She phoned Grigory three times after their meeting this spring. Two calls to his apartment. Another to the hospital.

His secretary said he was away on business but she'd give him the message when he returned. Maria is half glad she didn't get through, though. Yes, it would be good to see him, to have him in her life once more. But what then? They couldn't go over old ground. She couldn't take him through all her reasons, all that happened around that time. It's not something she can burden him with.

And yet. Those few minutes in the hospital, when they waited for Zhenya's X-ray, were such a comfort. Simply to be in his presence was a recognition of the connection they had, a reminder that only the end of their marriage was fatally flawed.

Alina's husband was killed in Afghanistan. Serving the cause. Maria wasn't sorry and neither was Alina. He was violent and bigoted; brooded in the apartment; drank with his friends; drove military jeeps into walls just to see how sturdy they were. He cleaned his nails with his army knife, thought it gave him an edge, but it only served to intensify his pettiness, his military vanity. They never spoke of him but both frequently wondered how he had managed to produce Zhenya, the Mendelssohn-obsessed little lovable freak.

'He wants a pet.'

'Zhenya?'

'Of course Zhenya, who else do we talk about? He wants a parrot.'

'And? I would have thought it wasn't particularly strange for a nine-year-old boy.'

'Well, it's not, except for the fact that he is who he is and lives where he lives. But that's not why I brought it up. It's what he wants it for, that's the killer.'

'Well?'

Alina pauses. It's the privilege of the older sibling to tell a story with impeccable timing and poise. Her ability to hold Maria in thrall has never wavered since the two of them shared a bed as children and Alina told rambling, fantastical tales. Stories featuring villains with several limbs and princesses with secret, unattainable powers and lines that could cut you bare, faultless scalpel lines that described entire universes in an instant. She honed this gift to early teenhood, Alina the master storyteller, and they can both feel it rise up again, that authority she holds when she wants to titillate her little sister.

'He wants me to teach it to talk.'

She pauses. An exquisite pause.

'So he can still hear my voice if I die.'

And they look at each other, the pathos of the simple request working its way into the backs of their eyes, and then they buckle into laughter at precisely the same moment, tears streaming down, their lungs heaving with the gale of unfettered, unrelenting mirth, because they both know this child, both have an understanding of his kooky ways, the kid who spends entire days humming Mendelssohn but can't get his timing right, who can recite multiplication tables up to obscene numbers but can't handle long division, and they let all that has been pent up flow through their ribs and find its expression in full-mouthed hysterics.

After it breathes itself out they find themselves hunched against the wall. Maria lights a cigarette and they compose themselves under the bare bulb's light. And now they have two items to pass, the vodka and a cigarette.

Maria is the first to break the silence.

'Another city, where would you go?'

'East or west?'

'Whichever.'

'The big ones. The ones with good TV and plenty of hairspray. Paris, London, New York. Maybe Tokyo.'

'Tokyo?'

'Yes, the lights. I imagine they have a neon skyline. And the cramming of people in the underground train. And to be a foot taller than everyone else. To look down on everyone from a height. To be the queen of the rush hour.'

'Tokyo. But you'd have to bow fifty times a day.'

'Well, that would be another reason. The bowing, all these little people paying homage to me. And you?'

'A city with a white beach and women who drink from fancy glasses. A city with palm trees. I'll do what foreigners always do, open a bar on the beach. You can come and sit, wear large sunglasses, be mysterious, and Zhenya can play for tips, take requests from drunk honeymooners. Maybe even get a little action for himself.'

Alina palms her on the side of the head. More a sweep of the hair than an actual strike.

'What, the boy will never have sex?'

Alina scrunches her face and flails around Maria's head, both laughing again. With who else could they let their guard down like this, become schoolgirls again, enjoying surreptitious cigarettes and speculating about boys?

The moment passes and they take another drink.

'The hand exercises. You know about these?' Maria asks.

'Of course I know. The kid's obsessed. I come to wake him in the morning and he's lying there with his arms up towards the ceiling, bending those skinny wrists.'

'You know about the rose clippers?'

Alina stops laughing, alert now. She doesn't like it when Maria notices something about her boy before she does.

'What about them?'

'Nothing. A funny thing, that's all.'

An edge to her listening.

'So funny that you won't say what it is?'

'Well. It's nothing. I found him a couple of weeks ago, that's all. He was clenching and unclenching a pair of rose clippers.'

Maria does the action.

'Where did he get them?'

'Evgenia Ivanovich downstairs – you know how she likes her flowers. It's not important. Anyway, he's clenching and unclenching and I ask him what he's doing and of course he says, 'Nothing.' So I keep pushing and he says he's strengthening his hand. And I say, 'Why are you strengthening your hand, surely it's strong enough?' And he says, 'When I'm in the audition, and the other kids are there and we shake hands. I want to crush them. I want them to be scared of me.'

Maria tails off as soon as she's said this. When it comes out of the mouth of a nine-year-old, one as bedraggled as Zhenya, there's a ridiculousness in the schoolboy bravado. But the words coming cold, straight out of her own mouth, carry a supreme sadness. Even music, beautiful melodies, become an instrument of power here. The kid is constantly surrounded by forces that want to crush him to dust.

'I think he's still being bullied.'

'Don't worry. He's a stubborn kid, he's smarter than any of them. He'll do OK.'

'The other day, I get him to slice some carrots. I tell him to roll up his sleeves – why add to the laundry basket? – he refuses. I get suspicious. I walk over and pull up his sleeves and there's a red mark on his arm. He says they call it a Chinese burn. He says it's nothing, some game. Says it's just a thing they're doing.'

'It's a Chinese burn. This is what kids do.'

'Since when? It never happened when we were young.'

'It happened, it just never happened to us.'

'Meaning?'

Maria didn't mean to bring it up. The age-old argument leaking out again, slipping its way between sentences.

She sighs. 'Meaning what it means.'

Alina shakes her head in disbelief.

'And so it begins. Cling to it, dear sister, cling to your bitterness. What else do you have?'

Maria shrugs her shoulders. She didn't want to begin this but it's begun.

'It's not bitterness. I'm just willing to recognize him for what he was.'

'How do I spend my hours? In a hairnet pulling sheets from a line, feeding them through a mechanical roller. Ironing like a madwoman in the evenings. I have a mouth to feed; he had four. It was some extra money. A side job. People, the few who knew what he did, understand that. There are such things as shoes and bread and soup. I never saw you refuse them; our bones never jutted like some other children. Necessity. People understand, even now. Those who know.'

The tension rises, a particular tension for this particular subject.

'It was not laundry work. It was not even work. And people don't understand. And everybody knew, everyone knows. Name his friends – go ahead, count them. Who came to console us when he disappeared?'

'They were frightened. They didn't wish to be connected. They were all involved to some extent. He took no pleasure in it. How can you make this be anything else? We had dolls, we had books. Do you think you would have led the life you did if we had no books?'

'It was not just a side job.'

'Did he beat us? Did he make her life a misery? Not him. Be ashamed of those men instead. Set your life against those men. I say it again: you had dolls.'

'It was not a side job. The day that you realize it, that day will arrive.'

'Well, I'm not young and it has no marking on the calendar. I'm still waiting.'

Neither of them speaks. Maria goes back inside and places the pressed clothes into a delivery bag, one hand on top, one on the bottom. She puts a saucepan of water on to boil and spoons tea into the pot.

Their father went to the races on a Saturday afternoon and never returned. There were no explanations or justifications for his work; how he betrayed others, led them to a life of imaginable misery. They couldn't sit with him, understand him, listen to an old man's regrets. Only a void remains and it continues to wrap around their lives, tying them together in ignorance.

Maria sits listening to the water boil, currents of the past lapping inside her. The clank of a card hitting the metal bucket occasionally makes its way into the apartment. It's always like this. The recurring subject that dominates their lives. Every lengthy conversation comes around to it eventually, teasing out the intangibles, the unknowables. Because who really can have a clue as to why Nikolai Kovalev did what he did, pushing his little wood pieces, aligning all his forces. Maybe it was valour or self-sacrifice or vanity or greed. Maybe it was something he never thought about, just numbers on a sheet, little codes. Maybe he was more worried about his opponent's opening gambit or the exposed position of his rook.

Alina shuts the balcony door and places the near-empty

bottle on the kitchen counter. She wets the tea with the boiling water and waits for the leaves to settle into zavarka. Maria watches her by the reflection in the glass door.

Alina fills the pot and takes down two cups and puts them on the table, letting the tea stew again, then after a few minutes, pouring. It smells strong, relaxing. Maria thinks that she'd like to take a bath, but she'd have to clean off everyone else's scum first, not something she's prepared to do right now. Instead she tells Alina about the meeting.

'I know all the arguments. Of course you'll say it's a good opportunity, and it is. But I can't think about coming home, after my day, and opening that book and taking notes for hours on end. Three, four, five years of this. Already I can't face that thought.'

'But you said you never get to use your brain. You'd be pushing yourself, thinking in a new way. That's good, surely?'

'I don't have a natural aptitude for it. I could do it, but I'd have to grind it out. I'd have to study harder than most other people.'

'And there'd be classes. You enjoy classes. Other engineers with opinions, curiosity.'

'But I already have classes. They respect me in the Lomonosov. There's talk of giving me more hours – even a junior position. I was hoping that by next year they'd offer me some lectures, give me a research brief. You want to know about longer term, the Lomonosov is longer term. It holds more possibilities than being another clipboard holder in a factory. And it wouldn't take years of drudgery.'

'And now this.'

'And now this.'

'We can't do without your teaching money for a few years. There's only so much ironing that will fit in this place.'

They both look around. There are stacks of finely pressed sheets everywhere. They have to tiptoe around them. Shirts hang from a specially constructed rail, dozens of them. They sit in a sea of cotton and polyester.

'They're saying, *We own you, you can't do something else*.'

'Well, maybe show them your fidelity, prove your love to them, they might move on to someone else.'

'So I make a gesture?'

'Yes. Show how it benefits them to have you do other things. Show them you bring them something of benefit. You're cultured. They respect culture. Bring that to them in some way.'

'What about a recital? If they come and they like it, they donate. Use it to get Zhenya a rehearsal room. It might even brighten everyone up a bit.'

'So then. Zhenya will play.'

'You know how he is, though. Maybe he can't handle it.'

'It's for his aunt. If I asked, maybe not; but you, he'd learn to walk on his hands for you.'

They finish their tea and unfold Maria's bed and Alina helps her to change her sheets and pillowcase and they turn off the lights and settle down in their separate rooms and think about how they've survived together. No husbands or parents to rely on. If they disagree on their past, then they disagree on their past. It can't separate them. And each of them thinks how good it is to have a sister.

In the morning Maria walks across the courtyard and watches the watchers. Curtains flick overhead, figures stepping away from the glass. Nothing that happens in this stretch of land goes unseen. She steps over the kerbstones that are half painted, a job which the maintenance men occupied themselves with for a few days, before finding some other distraction.

She hasn't slept well, her mind ticking over after her conversation with Alina and then one thing leading to another, thoughts whirring uncontrollably in the dark. When this happens, which isn't often, she thinks of it as her mind unspooling, all those blank working hours being cast out, reclaiming their freedom.

She passes a car with brown tape in place of a back window. There are great mounds of uncollected rubbish around the pomojka. Plastic bags stacked upon black bags. The children use them as combat shelters for their snowball fights and she can conjure up the sour stench that will rise again when the snow melts and the air heats. The smell of a new spring.

Children adapt.

They take an untreated football pitch and use it as an obstacle course. They play volleyball with taped-up wads of newspaper. They don't have basketball hoops here, so they kick the seats out of old kitchen chairs and lash them to drainpipes. They spend their young lives inventing games with stratified, nuanced, ingenious rules and spend their adult lives resenting the constraints around them.

The bus steams up and bobbles to a stop.

Maria looks at bare branches set against the sky, lines running into one another, sturdy boughs tapering off into a fine filigree.

She wants to make love on a warm night with moonlight shimmering down rain-slicked streets.

When Mr Shalamov arrives Maria's waiting in the armchair outside his office. The secretary refuses to look at her, resenting her intrusion. A different species to the people that inhabit these rooms, with their well-cut suits. Even the secretary in a matching jacket and skirt. Maria wonders if the secretary changes into her work clothes, just like everyone else. Surely she can't wear a skirt like that outside in such cold, even with thick tights on. She can't have a locker room and Maria thinks of her changing in the management toilets, rising in status as soon as she slips on the soft material, and in the evening shedding that skin again, becoming just another nameless face, sneaking on to the bus home, averting her eyes, hoping that she won't see a worker she recognizes. Or more likely she feeds off the high-powered lives that surround her, massaging their bodies as well as their egos, sharing their beds.

Maria stands and speaks before the secretary has a chance to interject.

'Mr Shalamov.'

He stops and looks at her and then looks at the secretary.

'I'm sorry to intrude. I just wanted to continue our conversation from yesterday evening.'

A glaze in his eyes. She can tell he doesn't recognize her.

'We talked about the Lomonosov.'

He turns when recollection strikes him.

'Yes. We'll pick the matter up another time. Anya will set up an appointment. You'll be notified.'

His back is to her and he's moving towards his office door. She rattles off her prepared lines.

'I would like to make amends for my lack of participation in some of our previous cultural events, I have a suggestion for an event that would be good for morale.'

He stops and turns.

'Is there a problem with morale?'

His voice is icy. He's focusing intently on her. A cool, dispassionate glare.

Maria's nervousness melts away, instinct kicks in. She's faced a look like this dozens of times, someone uncertain about her intentions. She slows her pace, lifts her shoulders, talks to him clearly and warmly, like an equal.

'Let me begin again. My nephew is a talented pianist, a candidate for the Conservatory. I'd like to arrange a concert, in recognition of the abilities that are nurtured here. So many of our workers are gifted. Of course, you're in a better position than anybody to recognize this. I would like to arrange an evening in celebration of such great talents, an evening that honours the efforts of the simple worker, our ability to work in harmony. Perhaps some Prokofiev sonatas.'

He nods, taking in her words.

'A fine suggestion, Mrs . . .'

'Brovkina.'

'Mrs Brovkina, but perhaps now is not the right time.'

'I should mention that my nephew is nine years old. The evening could function as a symbol of our potential.'

'Nine years old. The child can play Prokofiev?'

'Yes, sir. He'll be auditioning for the Conservatory in the spring.'

He looks at the floor and looks up again.

'I'll think about it. As you say, such an event may contain a powerful symbolism. And we do our best to support talents, in whatever form they appear. I'll discuss it with our director of culture.'

'Thank you, sir.'

He turns into his office. The secretary looks at her. Maria smiles.

'Thank you for your patience.'

She walks down the metal steps and makes her way to her bench and her working day begins. She tells herself that this is a good morning. She'll keep telling herself this, even if she doesn't believe it.

Once again Grigory walks this flat landscape with the pale evening light drawing down, his only respite from the plain, hastily constructed buildings that are now his home. He came to this resettlement camp three months ago, when swathes of corn covered the fields and combine harvesters traced the land, supported by locals who tied the straw in bundles, standing it on end to dry and be taken home later for their horses. Rows and rows of them inching forwards, like a local mob whose intent was to beat the land into submission. A year before, this would have been a sight to take pleasure in, to watch a community reap their harvest, but Grigory has developed a suspicion of all types of agriculture, all signs of growth. He knows the dangers that lurk in the most innocuous things.

When he left Chernobyl they were harvesting too. Men from the clean villages on the outer rim of the exclusion zone would enter their neighbours' evacuated farms and pluck beets or potatoes from the earth. Often they'd take their children out of school, bring them along; their wives also. These were men who had always trusted the soil; it had never failed to provide for them. How could they believe the earth had betrayed them when vegetables were growing in front of their eyes? They would ask why they were allowed to work their own farms and yet their neighbours were forced to move because of some imaginary boundary. If their cattle needed feed, their neighbours wouldn't begrudge them. The feed sits in sacks – how can it be contaminated? Even the kolkhoz offices endorsed this view. They posted up signs saying it was permissible to eat salad vegetables: lettuce, onions, tomatoes, cucumbers. There were instructions for dealing with contaminated chickens. They advised people to wear protective gear and boil the chicken in salt water, to use the meat for pâté or salami and pour the water down the toilet.

In his final weeks there, when all of his authority had been stripped away, Grigory drove from farm to farm at the perimeter of the zone, showing his credentials, advising people of the dangers they were in. None of them believed him, until he took out the dosimeter and the machine beeped shrilly: 1,500, 2,000, 3,000 micro-roentgen per hour – hundreds of times the level of natural exposure. It was a method he'd adapted when it became apparent that all Vygovskiy's grand statements about a new beginning, about a thorough, methodical, clean-up, had been quashed by one phone call from the Kremlin.

The day after the evacuation, reports came in of a radioactive cloud that hung over Minsk. Grigory approached Vygovskiy about it. His superior nodded: 'I've been informed.'

'And they're evacuating?'

'They're doing everything they can.'

A few hours later he realized that supply trucks were still arriving from the city. Again he approached his superior.

'They haven't evacuated, we're still getting supplies from there.'

'They don't have the resources yet.'

'We have spare troops here, men sitting around waiting for instructions. What are they waiting for? We know every hour is crucial.'

Vygovskiy gestured towards the stacks of paperwork on his desk, the ringing phone.

'I have a power plant to clean up, Grigory. I have a team of nuclear engineers arriving any moment. There are men taking care of it.'

'What men?'

'Good men.'

Grigory returned to his office and called the General Secretary of the Central Committee of the Belarusian Party. They wouldn't connect him: the man was on another line. Grigory was incredulous. He waited five minutes and called again. He reminded them forcefully who he was, where he was calling from, under whose authority he worked. Still no connection. Eventually, after a half-hour, he got through.

When he mentioned the accident, the line went dead.

He walked into Vygovskiy's engineering briefing and gestured to speak to him outside. The group was arguing over procedure. Vygovskiy waved him away. Grigory remained until the group fell silent. Irritated, Vygovskiy followed him into the corridor, then indicated they should go to Grigory's office. Neither of them spoke until Vygovskiy closed the door.

'The KGB are suppressing our calls. I can't even speak with the Belarusian General Secretary.'

'Why are you speaking to the General Secretary?'

'Because there's a fucking radioactive cloud hanging over his capital.'

Vygovskiy spoke in a pointedly calm tone.

'They have orders to contain the information, in order to avoid a mass panic.'

'The KGB?'

'The KGB. The General Secretary. Everyone.'

'So there'll be no evacuation?'

'No. It's a direct order from the highest levels in the Kremlin.'

Grigory sat down at his desk. Vygovskiy remained standing in front of him, as though he were the inferior. He adjusted his tie.

'It's a direct order. What do you want me to do?'

Their voices rising in steady progression.

'I want us to do what we said we'd do. I want to deal with this situation openly, properly, with accountability. I'm getting reports that the city has background radiation of 28,000 micro-roentgen per hour.'

'That meeting in my office. The engineers are figuring out a way to get the water out from underneath the reactor. If uranium and graphite get in there, a critical mass will form and we might be dealing with an explosion of maybe three, four, even five megatons. If that happens you'll have to evacuate half of Europe. Should I get on the phone to the Polish premier, to Berlin? Fuck it, why not Paris?'

'Why not? They could help. There would be more resources, more expertise.'

'More hysteria. And that's not even taking into account what it would mean for our international profile.'

'You're talking like a politician, Vladimir.'

'This has international consequences. This is our most critical moment, politically, since the war. We both know this. Of course politics comes into it. Politics comes into everything. Now, if you'll excuse me, comrade. I'm getting things done.'

He strode out the door, slamming it after him.

Grigory picked up the receiver, then put it down again in its cradle.

He grabbed his jacket and a dosimeter and found Vasily in one of the medical tents, checking exposure rates amongst the soldiers.

'Come with me – that can wait.'

Grigory had one of the soldiers drive them to the apartment blocks. They walked up a staircase and into one of the apartments.

'Can you tell me what we're doing here?'

Grigory looked around and found the phone and carried it to the dining table, the cord straining to reach.

'There's a radioactive cloud over Minsk. We need to make some calls.'

He got on his knees and, dipping his head to search under the sofa, found what he was looking for. He dragged out a phone book.

'Who are we calling?'

Grigory threw the book towards the table. On landing it thudded and skidded along the vinyl covering.

'Everyone. Pick a letter and start from there. It's a lottery. See who lives according to their surname.'

Vasily placed his hand calmly on the book, flipping the corners of pages with his thumb, a rasping sound.

'This is ridiculous, Grigory. What are we doing here? Someone's apartment? You have an office and an administrative staff.'

'The KGB are monitoring our calls. I can't talk to anyone in the city or there'll be consequences. Not that I'm worried about that, but they'll cut us off immediately. We can't get anything done that way. I'll be next door, doing the same.'

Vasily slid the book away.

'We can't go against KGB diktats, Grigory. Who knows what will happen? It's the KGB.'

Grigory was halfway out the door. He stopped, turned, looked at his friend, twisted the door handle at his side.

He spoke quietly, all his momentum subdued.

'I hadn't expected it would be a problem.'

'It's the KGB.'

'There's an entire city blindly walking into an early grave.'

'I have a family.'

'So you keep saying.'

They were silent.

'Open a page,' Grigory said. 'There's a hundred families on each one; a hundred and fifty, who knows? What if it were a Moscow directory? What if we were to look under Simenov?'

Vasily stood up.

'I can't help you with this, Grigory. I'm sorry.'

Grigory stepped aside to let him pass.

When he called people he introduced himself as a doctor and explained what was happening. He told them to put their food in plastic, to put on rubber gloves and wipe everything down with a cloth, then put the rag in a bag and throw it away. If they had laundry drying outside, they should put it back in the wash. Put two drops of iodine in a glass of water and wash their hair with it. Dissolve four more drops and drink it, two for a child. He told them to get out of the city as soon as they could. Stay with a relative. Don't come back for at least a few weeks.

He made probably over sixty calls, until finally they cut him off. Sitting on a stranger's chair, pacing up and down someone's brown, patterned carpet.

Every reaction was the same. People were calm. They thanked him. They didn't question him or panic. Perhaps they didn't believe him or didn't understand the importance of what he was asking. Such simple things: wash your hair, wash your clothes, drink some iodine. It hardly seemed credible that these few actions could save your life.

That evening he went to his quarters to pack his bag and bedding and find another place to sleep. Vasily, lying in the next bunk, watched him place his belongings away.

'I'm not the enemy, Grigory. I'm not one of them.'

'Really? Then who are you?'

The next day he went to Minsk himself. Forced his way into the chairman's office, gaining access by holding the dosimeter up to people's necks, showing them the readings. They all had family here; they couldn't bring themselves to refuse him. The chairman told Grigory he could only spare five minutes.

'I've been on the phone this morning with the chairman of the Soviet Radiological Protection Board. He's assured me everything is normal, everything is under control.'

'Comrade, I am the deputy head of the clean-up commission. I'm telling you, you need to evacuate the city. You need to demand that military personnel come here at once.'

'They are already using vast numbers of troops at the accident site.'

'And I'm telling you to order more for yourself.'

'Doctor, there are only so many soldiers to go around.'

'We have the largest army on earth. Are we not always proclaiming the greatness, the scale of our forces? We need to get people out of here. This accident, believe me, will make Hiroshima look like an aberration.'

'You are exaggerating, Doctor.'

'I've personally taken background readings of 500 microroentgen per hour outside. There should be no one within a hundred kilometres of this city.'

The chairman stretched out his arms as if he were addressing a rally.

'I am a former director of a tractor factory. I do not understand such things. If comrade Platonov from the Radiological Protection Board tells me that things are fine, then what can

I tell him: he's lying? Please, of course not, they'd take my Party card.'

'Well, I'm a doctor, a surgeon, responsible for the clean-up. I've arrived here directly from the site and yet you're happy to tell me that I'm a fool.'

The chairman leaned forward, snarling.

'There will be no evacuation.'

'Where are your wife and children?'

'They are here, of course. How can I ask others to trust the system if I can't show them that my own family does the same?'

Grigory exhaled, shook his head.

'You're really that naïve.'

The chairman was unnerved by Grigory's tone. He spluttered out a response.

'The Party has made me what I am, made this country what it is. I have always trusted its judgement. A fire in a power plant won't change that.'

They argued for another half-hour until Grigory, defeated, picked up his bag and placed it on his lap.

'The city has iodine concentration in reserve – I know this is policy in case of a nuclear attack. At least put that in the water supply.'

'That, as you've mentioned, doctor, is for the purposes of nuclear attack.'

'So we'll protect our people from the Capitalist Imperialists, but not from each other?'

'Get out before I have you arrested for spreading anti-Soviet sentiment.'

'It's not only the air that's contaminated. It's your minds too.'

'Get out!'

*

181

Grigory stops his walk and takes a breath of the fresh evening air, savouring it.

The stars are coming out. He'll need to go back soon, do a final pass through the wards before bedtime. Through the gloom, he can make out the main road to Mogilev with the wedges of light from car headlamps moving in a steady trajectory. Remnants of corn stubble crunch under his feet, he can feel its stubbornness under his boots. In a couple of months they'll return with tractors and ploughs and turn the soil over upon itself once more, ready for sowing in the spring.

In the exclusion zone, there were great flaming pyres of cattle and sheep. They were folding the land inside out using diggers and tractors and shovels to make craters large enough to hold everything in sight: helicopters and troop wagons, shacks, trees, cars, motorcycles, pylons. They flattened homes by tying a huge chain around an izba, then hauling it forward with a giant digger so the izba would collapse on to itself, then they'd heave everything into a pit. They were cutting down forests and wrapping the trunks in plastic before laying them under the earth. He saw so much of this that when people tell him where they're from, when they mention the names of the surrounding villages and towns – Krasnopol, Chadyany, Malinovka, Bragin, Khoyniki, Narovlya – they bring to mind not only the landscape but what lies beneath it. He sees the places as a diagram, in cross-section, with figures working busily on top of the earth and other pockets underneath it, all neatly ordered: a section for helicopters, one for the izbas, another for diseased animals; which, of course, isn't the case. There is nothing neat about this tragedy.

He hears sounds from the road: a squeal of brakes and then glass shattering. Grigory looks in the direction of the noise and sees a sulphurous light, stalled. He runs towards it, the cold air inflaming his lungs.

As he nears he sees a man standing over a dog, waving his arms in the air, admonishing the felled animal.

The driver directs his invective at Grigory, but he ignores it and kneels over the dog. It's a German shepherd, young, less than a year old, Grigory estimates. The animal faces the front of the car with thick ribbons of blood around its hind-quarters and a web of drool laced around its mouth, its eyes turned upwards, their lids flickering in pain. Grigory rests a calming hand on its neck and the animal raises its head a few centimetres from the road and lunges forward, snapping its jaws. Grigory leans backwards, unafraid, and speaks softly to it, his tones reaching under those of the driver, who is still spitting out his complaints.

'Good boy. You still have some fight in you. Let's see what we can do.'

He reaches his hand towards the neck again, asking the animal's permission through the slow deliberation of his movement. He slides his fingers into its thick coat and moves downwards, feeling the strong pulsing of its heart, never taking his eyes from those of the dog, which are searching now, darting to various points in their circumference, show-ing tentative trust; it's placing its hopes in this stranger. Grigory moves his hands nearer the wound and the dog releases a moan, a sound as stark and elemental as its sur-roundings.

He looks up to the driver.

'Its pelvis is broken.'

'This is your dog? It's smashed my headlight, it's damaged my bumper. This fucking dog, coming out of nowhere. This is your dog? Someone will be paying, I assure you.'

'It's not my dog.'

'Of course you say that. "Not my dog." But you come and look after it. Why do you care? Coming out of nowhere. Of course it's your dog.'

'Please. It's in a lot of pain.'

'Who are you? A hero? A vet looking for animals to save?'

'I'm a surgeon.'

'Good. Then you can afford to pay for my headlight.'

Grigory stands and takes in the car, a black Riva. He walks nearer the man and looks him in the eye, a bullfrog wobble of skin under the man's chin.

'I don't know who owns the dog. I do know that it's in a lot of pain. I live in those buildings back there. If you take me home we can look after the animal and then ask around.'

The driver steps back, his gaze spiralling downwards in short, sharp bursts. His voice is now so muted that Grigory has to strain to hear him.

'I tell you what, you keep your dog. I'll pay for the damage myself.'

He steps into the car and drives off. There's a rattle from the front bumper as it drags along the ground.

Alone on the road with a shattered dog.

Grigory looks back to the settlement, the buildings taking on a deeper light by now, incandescent, then turns to the animal.

'You're a brave one, aren't you?'

He kneels once more and scoops the dog in his arms. The animal wails softly, but doesn't resist, recognizing the authority of his new master. Grigory walks back over the puffed snow, struggling under the dog's weight, its heart beating close to his.

Each night after his walk he enters once again into the few low rooms of the clinic. Returning to hear the breath of sleeping children, all of them waiting to pass under his knife. Grigory knows he has a weaker will than any of them and there are nights when he lies amongst them, hoping that their courage, their thirst for life, might pass into him, replenishing him.

Children who have already undergone thyroid operations and are regaining their strength sleep on thin mattresses laid out in rows along the floor. In the morning they rise and roll them into a wheel, tie them up with string and place them in the corner. There is a playground outside with a high net strung across it. They've received a batch of tennis balls as part of an aid consignment and the children invent complicated rhythmical games with them. In the breaks between surgery Grigory watches them and tries to decipher their rules, but they change daily, hourly, and so he pays attention only to the fluid motion of these children, identical scars running horizontally across the base of their necks. These are the healthier ones. The weaker ones lose consciousness while standing. They buckle to the ground, marionettes whose strings have been cut. Nosebleeds break out all the time. At any moment he can look across the yard and see half a dozen children pinching their noses, looking up to the sky, unperturbed by the spontaneous flow from their nostrils.

There are those for whom the sickness has spread to the lungs or pancreas or liver. They lie sweating in the few beds available. Many are placed back with their families in their accommodation, where they are guaranteed a resting place and a visit by a nurse. In the past few months, newborn infants have emerged from the womb with fused limbs, or weighed down with oversize tumours. There are children whose bodies have no sense of proportion, football-size growths on the back of their skull or legs as thick as small tree trunks, or one hand minuscule and the other swollen to grotesque dimensions. Others have hollowed-out eye sockets, lined with flat patches of skin: it looks as though the human eye is an organ that has yet to evolve. For many, there are tiny holes where the ear should sit. A child, a girl, was born two weeks ago with aplasia of the vagina. Grigory couldn't find any references to such a thing in his textbooks. He had to improvise by creating artificial holes in her urethra through which the nurses would squeeze out her urine.

During these nights, he gazes at them in their cots. Nothing is so unimaginable that it cannot be true. This is what he thinks. Beauty and ugliness resting within the single body of a diseased infant. The two faces of nature brought into stark relief.

No officials have made their way here, despite his daily entreaties. He wants them to walk into this room, a place where ideology, political systems, hierarchy, dogma, are relegated to mere words, belonging to files, banished to some dusty office. There is no system of belief that can account for this. The medical staff know that, in comparison, nothing that has gone before in their lives has any significance. There are only these months, these rooms, these people.

When they bury the dead, the corpses are wrapped in cellophane and placed inside a wooden coffin, which in turn is wrapped and placed inside a zinc casket and lowered into a concrete chamber. The families are never allowed to accompany their loved ones on this final journey. Instead they stand gravely by the door of the mortuary as the sealed van holding their dead disappears into the distance.

Grigory reaches his quarters, still carrying the injured dog, and lays him on the floor beside his single armchair, dark horsehair drooping from its seams, in the narrow space between his bed and the wall. His room has a single bed that dips heavily in the middle, a locker overrun with medical books and some detective novels that have long since out-lived their purpose of staving off the penetrative boredom. On the wall opposite the door are a small wardrobe and a washbasin. Grigory leaves the room and returns with a bowl, which he fills with water and places beside the animal's head. The dog is in too much pain to right himself in order to drink and so Grigory cradles its neck in his arms and brings him gently to a position where he can lap the water freely, his tongue folding around the liquid, gathering it. Grigory is coated in sweat from the journey and this is now turning cold, clinging to him, and as he peels the shirt from his body his own odour rises up strong and sour.

He wipes off the sweat with his bedsheet and puts the shirt back on – he hasn't any clean clothes at the moment, he finds he's never in the mood to do laundry – and he walks across the yard, which is silent now, an occasional TV set in the surround-ing windows throwing patches of throbbing blue light on to the ground. A boy stands at the gable end of one of the build-ings, bouncing a tennis ball between wall and ground, the bounce creating a pleasing double rhythm before the ball comes to rest in the boy's hand. Grigory walks to the supplies room of the clinic, gathering all he needs to treat the animal, and on his return, he pauses to watch.

The boy changes hands as he throws and catches. A quick snap from either wrist before he releases the ball, alternating the surfaces, so the ball hits the pavement first and on the next throw strikes the wall first, the flight switching between languorous arches and rapid straight lines.

A solid boy who is almost a man, wide-shouldered, drift-ing his hips from one side to the other, as if caught by a gentle breeze. This boy too has a scar across his neck. So they have met before, Grigory observes, although he doesn't recall the boy's face.

'Do you remember me?'

'Yes. You were the doctor who worked on my neck.'

'That's right. How are you feeling?'

'A little better, stronger. It doesn't scratch as much when I eat.'

'Good, that's a good sign.'

Their voices linger in the air, so few other sounds present.

'What's your name?'

'Artyom Andreiovich.'

'Artyom. That's a man's name.'

The boy smiles.

'I'm glad to see you up and about. It's a happy ending to my day.'

He lifts an open hand in goodbye and then pauses, leaving the hand in the air momentarily, as though he is stopping traffic.

'Are you afraid of dogs?'

'No.'

'OK. Follow me then.'

Grigory turns and can hear the boy's footsteps in pursuit, bouncing the ball by his side as he goes, never breaking stride. In the room, the boy kneels over the dog, stroking the side of its head. He hasn't had an exchange with an animal since he left Gomel and he feels this lack intensely, a farmboy surrounded only by people, forced to live in a warren of indistinct, prefabricated huts.

Grigory unwraps a fresh needle and twists it on to an old syringe and then slips it into the rubber cap at the top of the benzodiazepine vial and pulls back the plunger, so the liquid runs fast and pure into the body of the instrument. The boy watches with interest, seeing a man with skill and knowledge perform his routine up close. Grigory pushes the plunger upwards and a straight jet of liquid catches in the bulb light, breaking into droplets as it descends in a perfect parabola. He tells the boy to hold the dog's head and to be careful in case it reacts badly. He slides the needle into its hindquarters and the boy can hear the palpatory suck of punctured skin and watches the liquid drain from the syringe. He can feel the dog's head vibrate in reaction to the pain, and keeps his hands soft yet firm. The animal moans but accepts his treatment.

They wait for the anaesthetic to take effect and the boy looks around the room. His eyes settle on a page, torn from a magazine, which Grigory has pinned on the wall to the side of his bed. A small, imperfect moon hanging over a low mountain range, barns and shacks in the foreground, barely perceptible in the scale of the image.

'The place in this photograph. Is it near here?'

'No. It's in America.'

'You have been there?'

'No.'

'Then why do you have it?'

Grigory looks at the image again. It has become so fused with the features of the room that he has almost forgotten it, a last remnant of a previous passion, the moon hanging serenely in a clear sky, all features of the landscape below placed in relation to its delicate curve.

Grigory's first camera, at fourteen, marked the end of childhood. He divided his youth by this distinction: pre-camera/post-camera. At fifteen, an elderly man in their building donated some darkroom chemicals to further Grigory's passion and, in retrospect, this marked another stage in his maturity. He acquired some black foil at a market and set up his darkroom in the communal bathroom. A tiny room, seven feet by four feet, and traced a line of foam sealant around its perimeter, keeping out the slivers of light that would otherwise stream upwards from the irregular meeting points of the ancient wall and floor.

The room became a womb to him. Grigory would work in the middle of the night, when no one would be knocking on the door, the perfect darkness more enveloping than the sleep from which he had emerged. He knows the contours of that space more intimately than those of a lover, the positioning of the bathtub and sink, the small medicine cabinet with its mirror, the equipment tray he would carry from his room, rattling gently with bottles and beakers, placing it in exactly the same position each evening, so he could find the necessary materials in the darkness.

At the end of their street was a park with a copse of beech trees which taught him about colour. So many images of the beech trees piled high under his bed, separated by thin sheets of cardboard. The depth and range and personality of colour. Day after day, throughout the summer and winter, he would take his camera to the trees and observe, over the passing weeks and months, how their colour adjusted according to time and light and weather, how purples would transform themselves to scarlet and orange, yellow and off-white, and the thousands of gradients between each shade.

Grigory looks at this American landscape now, frayed around the edges, a crease line from the magazine's spine bisecting the mountains, and turns to the boy and feels envious, despite the tragedy of his life, of the boy's ability to view the world through inexperienced eyes.

'I brought it from home. I don't know why I have it. Perhaps it reminds me that I have a small life. Does that make sense to you?'

The boy nods. 'Yes.'

'I used to take photographs. When I lived back in Moscow. They were all of buildings and people. Full streets. At night the sky was orange. I like the deep, black sky in this photograph. In my apartment, I would look at it and feel like making a campfire in the middle of my living room.'

Artyom looks at the picture again and wonders what a photograph of their home would look like now. He knows all the stories. His father, while he could still speak, told him that everything around their home had turned white. Not as in winter with snow covering all things, but in summer, with the grass high, leaves quivering in the breeze, flowers blooming in their fullness, but everything drained of colour.

If this same photographer had wandered into their homeland, would there be anything left to photograph? Only two shades left in that place. The dark sky and the white land, white as the clouds that streamed over this landscape in America. Artyom thinks of the tyre hanging from the oak tree outside their house, swinging lonely. Every part of his home, everything he touched, saw, put his weight upon, is underground. But he can't imagine this: his mind isn't able to erase all that he has known. When he finally goes back he knows he'll feel like a cosmonaut walking on the moon.

In Minsk, when they left his aunt Lilya's building, they had no energy or desire to walk to the bus station, to wait in line and sign forms and be directed to a shelter which, they knew from the direction of the walking crowds, was at the other side of the city. Standing outside the apartment block, they could hear chaos still hanging in the air. Artyom's mother walked as if carrying a weight – the way she clung to Sofya – and all three of them wanted, to their core, a place to lie down, somewhere they could close their eyes. They could face whatever would come tomorrow. They just couldn't face it at that moment.

The weather was warm enough to sleep outdoors but they would be exposed to whoever passed by. Artyom decided it would be too much of a risk and, besides, his mother needed some privacy, needed some time to take in her rejection.

Opposite them was a long row of metal shelters, low sheds made of the same tin sheeting as the roof of their izba. Each shelter was sealed with a padlock and some had pieces of furniture outside them or other cast-offs: a wing mirror from a truck, a bicycle seat with a bent shaft. Artyom looked around to see if anyone was watching and then walked the whole line of them, pulling at each lock, until finally, after covering fifty metres, finding one that wasn't closed properly, he pulled open the door, hunched over and walked inside, bumping into unknown objects. He stretched up until his fingers located the cable, which he traced to a switch at knee level just inside the door. He flicked it on.

There was a line of old paint pots sitting along the tin wall and, now that he could see them, he could also smell their biting chemicals. In the centre, there was a space large enough for them to lie down and he could make out thick rolls of dense grey material, stiffer than cloth, which stood on end, dry to touch. It would be enough.

He stepped outside and beckoned his mother and sister and when he saw Sofya wave back he ventured inside again and set about laying the material down on the metal floor.

When his mother arrived, she said the material was 'under-carpet' and Artyom didn't know what this was and when she explained Artyom found such a thing hard to understand, people who were rich enough to put carpet under more carpet.

He took a jacket from the door and put it on his mother. She tried to refuse, to give it back to him to wear instead, but Artyom and Sofya insisted and his mother didn't have enough will to resist. They cleared their pockets of whatever food they had left – a few carrots and some ends of bread – and they ate quietly, a grim picnic, until Sofya said, 'What is that smell?' and they scrunched their noses up and, it was true, there was a sickly-sour smell. Like meat gone bad. Artyom's mother lifted her armpits and smelled underneath them and folded her mouth in disgust and Artyom couldn't help but laugh at this, his mother was always so insistent on cleanliness, there were so many nights after pig-feeding that he came home and she sent him to the well and supervised from the window as he scrubbed himself. He laughed and Sofya laughed too, and leaned into their mother and sniffed her armpits, like a runt looking for a nipple, exaggerating the action, and Artyom did the same and his mother laughed then too, and she wrapped her stinking arms around them, pressing their faces to her, and they giggled some more and then relaxed into her, disregarding the smell, feeling protected. Sleep came quickly.

When Artyom woke, the light was off and the door open, allowing in a vertical stripe of grey light from the morning sky. He saw a figure standing there and sat up suddenly and shook his mother, and the figure said, 'Hello.'

His mother sat up too and the figure said, 'I'm going to turn on the light. Don't be shocked.'

Sofya woke with the light, pushing herself upwards un-steadily by her arms, the way Artyom had seen newborn calves assert themselves into the world.

It was a man older than his father, but not quite elderly. A comfortable, lined face, grey hair streaming from under a knitted, black hat.

'You came on the buses last night?'

Artyom made to reply but held himself back, left space for his mother.

'Yes,' she said.

The man picked up two shovels near the door, put on a pair of gloves that hung by the hook.

'You'll need to get food. There's a truck coming to pick me up. I know where the shelter is.'

They stood and dusted themselves off. Sofya slapped her face to wake herself.

'I'm Maksim Vissarionovich.'

'Tatiana Aleksandrovna. These are my children, Artyom and Sofya.'

'Were you cold?'

'No. Yes. We used some things. I hope it's OK.'

Artyom's mother realized she was wearing the man's coat. She began to take it off.

'Please. It stinks, I'm sorry. The sun hasn't come up yet. Wear it until you get there.'

'Thank you, Maksim Vissarionovich.'

'Just Maksim. You slept in my coat, you know me well enough.'

The man had great, sweeping eyebrows as unruly as his hair.

'Then please call me Tanya.'

'Of course.'

Artyom rolled up the undercarpet and Maksim pointed to their sacks of belongings.

'These are yours?'

'Yes,' Artyom replied, and Maksim grabbed all three in one hand and dipped and hefted them over his shoulder with a neat turn, and Artyom noticed the man's wrists, the impressive width of them.

Artyom placed the undercarpet back with the other rolls.

'No, bring it.'

Artyom pointed to the roll, questioning, and Maksim repeated himself.

'Bring it. You might need it.'

A truck pulled up outside, a shrill whistle beckoning them out. A flatbed truck carrying five men, a shallow metal tub in their centre in which a fire burned, with logs sticking out and sparks crackling.

'We've a stop to make first,' Maksim said to the men, and then climbed in front with the driver, an anonymous figure hunched over the wheel.

Another vehicle. Another journey to somewhere. Artyom spread his hands in front of the fire and warmed them. The morning wasn't so cold and he suspected the men kept the fire out of habit, a luxury they afforded themselves to compensate for the early rise.

'You're from the buses,' one of the men said.

'Yes,' Artyom's mother replied.

'Have you come far?'

'From Gomel.'

'Far enough then.'

'Yes. I suppose.'

As the wood burned, lit splinters and sparks caught the trailing air and tailed behind them, darting and crackling in their wake.

Artyom could see his mother was running questions through her head. She looked upwards and chewed the inside of her lip, then addressed the men.

'People were wary of us last night. Can you tell us what you've heard?'

The one who replied had a face of dark stubble with a dusting of white tracing the line of his chin.

'I hear there's militia guarding the hospitals.'

'Why would they do that?'

'They say that people are coming to the hospitals poisoned. They're worried about it spreading.'

'Like a plague?'

'It's just loose talk.'

'Are you not worried to have us share your truck with you?'

He looked around to his comrades. They were men of understatement. They pressed their bottom lips upwards, shaking their heads. One of the men spat into the fire, but the gob didn't reach, hitting the side of the tub, where it sizzled and collapsed into a drip of brown sap. The man with the white chin had a bunch of keys, which he turned on his finger, the metal ringing as they flopped forwards and back.

'If you're poisonous, why do they bring you to the city? To all of us? If you're poisonous, they'd keep you out there, where there's no people. You don't look poisonous to me. You just look lost.'

'We feel lost.'

He directed his look to Artyom.

'You know what we do?'

Artyom couldn't answer. He had just accepted the fact that they were on their way to work.

'You collect rubbish,' Sofya piped in.

'That's right.'

He turned and directed his conversation to her.

'You'd be surprised the things we pick up. Last week Pyotr here found a radio. You can't tune it in but it crackles. So he brought it home and played it for the mice. They haven't come back yet. That right, Pyotr?'

Pyotr smiled a mangled grin at Sofya.

'I'll keep it till someone throws out a cat.'

Sofya smiled back, equal to the man's warmth.

'People get rid of things they don't need. It doesn't mean that they don't have value, though. You just need to adapt them to a different use.'

He stopped twirling the keys and poked one of the logs further into the fire, causing a brief blaze of sparks that disappeared into their clothing.

'You'll be fine. You'll go home or you'll adapt.'

'Thank you,' Artyom's mother said.

'I'm just saying what I know.'

A pause.

'Where do you take it all?' Artyom asked. They didn't have anyone to collect their rubbish at home. If they didn't need something they burned it. There must be a big fire somewhere.

'To the dump.'

'You don't burn it?'

The man looked surprised.

'No. We don't burn it. We pile it up.'

'And then what do you do?'

The rest of the men laughed at the question but the man with the milky chin took it in and thought about it.

'We put more on top of it.'

'So it's where things end up?'

'Yes. I suppose so.'

Another man said, 'It's where we've ended up,' and they laughed again.

They arrived at a warehouse on the outskirts of the city, a long, squat building surrounded by other long, squat buildings. The men helped them disembark, carrying the sacks and the roll of undercarpet. Artyom's mother took off Maksim's jacket and handed it to him, and he refused it but she was insistent, an immovable stubbornness in her voice, so he took it and she shook his hand and they called out their thanks to the men on the truck, each of whom responded with an open hand, covered by a ragged glove, and the truck disappeared into the morning, the suspension wheezing in the distance.

On the ground were the imprints of thousands of feet, leading from everywhere, merging into a muddy route to the entrance.

Artyom's mother announced their arrival to the guards and they asked where she was from and heard their names, but they were just obeying routine, they had no lists to cross off and just nodded towards the door.

There were no queues in the warehouse; everyone had been registered during the night. All they could see were people laid out in their minute homes. Every family had a couple of square metres of carpet, cordoned off by drooping pieces of cardboard that had been taped to the floor. Thousands of small lives compacted together. Artyom recalled lifting a large stone and seeing a swarm of insects crawling underneath. This was what a city would look like if you took away all the walls and furniture.

Everyone was sleeping. There were only a few people moving about; so few that it seemed odd to look at a vertical figure, someone standing or walking: seeing this many people stretched out gave the illusion that humans were built to exist on a horizontal plane. Odd, too, to see so many people exist in silence after the chaotic noise of the previous day.

Pigeons flapped overhead, darting their heads to take in every aspect of the place.

A woman wearing a yellow sash approached them. They

could tell from her face that the smell from Maksim's jacket still lingered. The woman spoke to them with distaste.

'Your cards.'

'I'm sorry?'

'The cards.'

Artyom's mother stalled, not understanding; surely they wouldn't refuse them entry.

Artyom leaned in towards his mother. 'She's asking for the cards they gave us before we boarded the buses. When they scanned us with their meters.'

'Of course.' She directed her reply to the woman, and patted her body and pulled out a small purse from under her sweater with some roubles and three categorization cards.

The woman looked at them and asked Artyom's mother to confirm their full names and dates of birth, which she did. The woman nodded towards Artyom and Sofya.

'You can't hold their cards for them. They'll need to show them any time they're asked.'

'Of course.'

'Come with me.'

She led them to a door with a series of locks and took out a set of keys and turned the bolts one by one and told them to wait there. Artyom peeked inside, saw piles of green blankets set on top of desks, and he guessed that this room was originally the office area of whatever it was this warehouse stored. The woman returned holding a small stack.

She handed the blankets to Sofya, gave Artyom's mother an improvised map, hand drawn, showed them how the area had been divided into sections and told them that they would collect their food once a day from the provisions area in the far corner of the building. Their section would be called over the loudspeakers and they would present their cards and get their food and bring it back to their living quarters. She said 'living quarters' without a trace of irony, as if they should be grateful to inhabit a strip of carpet.

She pointed out their section and turned over to the back of the map, which revealed the number of their area. Artyom's mother asked where the toilets were and the woman pointed to a sign with an arrow halfway down the left-hand wall.

Artyom's mother asked if there were showers.

'There are no showers.'

'What about washing?'

'Let's hope it rains every few days.'

Artyom's mother took in this information without surprise.

'My husband is missing. Where can I find out about his arrival?'

The woman snorted through her nostrils.

'Look around. Everyone's husband is missing.'

They looked and could see very few men.

'A representative from the secretariat will visit this after-noon. We will know more then. Food will be handed out mid-morning. Have your cards with you at all times. If you cannot present your card, we will confiscate your food. That is all.'

'One last thing.'

The woman paused, resenting the time that was being demanded of her.

'Do you know how long we'll be here?'

'As long as you're told.'

She turned away and sat by a chair against the wall and picked up a magazine.

They walked through the maze of carpet and cardboard and sprawled limbs, finally finding their area, a space just big enough for the three of them to lie side by side. At the farm, whenever a cow was sick, they would section it off in its own pen until it recovered. That pen was bigger than their area. Probably more comfortable too, Artyom thought, if the straw was fresh.

Sofya sat on the roll of undercarpet, and said, 'So this is home.'

Artyom's mother chewed her gums and nodded, not looking at them.

Artyom walked outside. He could hear his mother calling instructions to him in frustrated whispers, but he didn't care. He needed to be alone. At least he could take in the peace of the morning. Everything that his eyes set upon was made of steel and concrete. A line of pylons stretched out with corkscrew endings, which balanced a series of buzzing wires. Trucks passed on the roadside so fast and heavy that he could feel the concrete bounce under his feet.

Not a blade of grass to be seen.

Nothing breathing, not even himself.

All that had come before erased in a single day.

'He's asleep now. We can get to work.'

Grigory's voice brings Artyom back to the room. It takes a moment for him to readjust, to concentrate on the job at hand. He looks down and sees the dog at rest, a comical leer on its lips, his molars showing. He puts his hand in its coat. It's good to touch the hair of an animal, coarse and alive.

Grigory says something and Artyom turns around, not comprehending. Grigory repeats the word: 'Ready?'

Gently, they turn the dog on to its back and Grigory clips its hindquarters, then shaves it with a razor, so that eventually the dog looks like a creature of two halves: hair and skin. Artyom can't help but smile at how strange it looks, can't help but think that if a dog has such a thing as vanity, it's in for quite a surprise. Grigory instructs Artyom to hold its hindquarters off the floor, and he does so and is surprised at the weight of the animal. Grigory wraps plaster of Paris around its pelvis, dipping the swatches in the bowl of water before he does so, then has Artyom help him fold the dog's legs into his body, so it can drag itself along while it recovers. They both take pleasure in their actions: healing something that contains no mystery; a broken bone that would be fixed, that is definable, a medical problem that has a resolution. And they both quietly look forward to the day when they will cut the bandage away from this animal and see it walk, unsteadily, across the yard, its trauma behind it.

Artyom is surprised at how quickly the bandages dry and, when the cast is set, they lay a blanket over its hunched form and Artyom looks at Grigory, a shine in his eyes.

'It's yours now. You can take care of it.'

'We can't move it. It's asleep.'

'Of course not, but when it wakes.'

Artyom shakes his head sadly. 'I can't, my mother wouldn't allow it into our quarters. Besides, what could I feed it? We barely have enough food already.'

'Well, let's keep it here then. He's your dog, but it lives here. I'll have a word with the supplies secretary, see if we can get some scraps.'

Artyom smiles wide and bright and Grigory takes this as a gift for carrying the animal here, tending to it, a reward that makes it all more than worthwhile. They shake hands, an exchange that has a strange solemnity to it. The boy has an aura of experience, of gravitas, any youthful naïvety long since departed.

'Batyr. I'm naming him Batyr.'

Artyom nods, taking in the fact with eagerness, the anticipation of a new parent stirring within him.

He repeats the name before he exits. 'Batyr.' It's the first good thing he's done in months.

Maria is three hours into her shift when it happens. The commotion comes from above them, the metal stairway to the management offices. Shouting. A scuffle. At first they think it might be an argument between two senior managers, which would be a juicy piece of gossip in itself, but it's a woman's voice. There are no women on the management committee. Maria's comrades stop and look up. They all instinctively press the suspension buttons on their machines before turning around. The whole place, powering down momentarily, the sound of forces slowing, cooling. Maria looks around and can see others looking around, captivated as the great beast to which they have chained themselves quietens its roar.

The void is replaced by a murmur. More shouts from the stairway. Those who can see spread word to those who can't. It's Zinaida Volkova. They can't believe this. They ask those nearest to confirm and see a bundle of black cloth being ushered by three officials through the doors that lead to the reception area.

In the forty years Zinaida Volkova has worked in the plant, she has never been known to raise her voice.

Zinaida is a senior committee member of the workers' union. Everyone knows her, knows her story. After the war, at twenty-four, she had become a member of the Zoya Kosmodemyanskaya work brigade. A welder with two Hero of Labour medals. Zinaida is who you go to if you have a personal problem. She organized extended maternity leave, secured concessions in working hours for those who had obligations to a sick relative. Half of the factory have stood before her at some stage, had her listen to them with that alert stare of hers, twitching like a bird, doling out advice and reassurance.

Even the line supervisors are in shock. They can't treat a Hero of Labour this way.

When Zinaida's protests fade, a menacing silence takes over. Some machines tick in their state of rest, parts cooling and contracting. Nobody moves. They see a man in a grey suit walk hurriedly along the metal walkway in front of the plate-glass windows. Mr Shalamov.

The line managers look down at the floor, or stroll as casually as possible to the toilets.

The plant chairman, Mr Rybak, emerges from the glass door of his office.

'Start your machines.'

Silence.

'Who here can do without their job? Put your hand up.'

Silence.

'I will stand here with a clipboard ticking off names if I have to. Ask yourselves if you want to go home to your families and tell them why you will be standing at some other gate to some other factory tomorrow morning. Stomping your feet in the freezing cold. Turn on your machines or explain it to them.'

A slight shuffling across the building, like a breeze has floated through.

A machine purrs, revving up.

The line managers return to the floor. They say nothing, just stare at the workers. The sound spreads, flywheels gaining speed, moulding machines reaching full pressure and, in Maria's section, router blades becoming invisible as they turn. Industry washes forward once more and everybody is filled with self-loathing.

At lunch Maria sits, as usual, with Anna and Nestor, her strongest friends in the factory. Anna has a two-year-old daughter, so feels particular loyalty to Zinaida. The extra maternity leave was a godsend.

'So,' Nestor says.

Nestor is a construction draughtsman and so has direct contact with different processing areas. He has a wan thin face, his jawline meeting at a dimpled chin.

'She's been trying to set up an independent union. Apparently, the last wage cut sent her over the edge.'

Their wages have been decreased three times over the past six months. The union barely raising an objection, the officials getting backhanders from the management. Everybody knows this. But they aren't in a position to object.

As wages come down, food prices have been rising. Sugar has doubled in price in the past eighteen months. Bread and milk have risen by sixty per cent, meat by seventy. All of them know how to readjust a household budget, to cut corners an extra millimetre or two, to scale back and scale back. You still need to eat something, though. Some of the older workers have been fainting at their stations. People have been getting ill with much greater frequency and Maria has noticed other, more subtle, changes that the body takes on. She notices how Nestor's gums have receded. He has three children. He takes on the majority of the sacrifices. People's skin has greyed, their hair has dried, become fragile. Each evening, on the bus home, she notices strands of dislodged hair resting on the shoulders of their dark jackets.

Nestor lowers his voice. 'She might get her wish now. I can't see people continuing to be represented by the rest of that gang.'

'It's not as easy as you think, Nestor. An independent union is quite a fight.'

'Other places have got concessions. The dockers in Vladi-vostok. The railway workers in Leningrad,' Anna says.

'Only because they had to – they are crucial industries. The authorities are getting a lot more hard-line about this. They don't want protests like that to spread. One place gets concessions, they come down even harder someplace else. Why else would they fire Zinaida?'

Nestor looks at his lunch distastefully and lights a cigarette instead.

'Zinaida gave the union credibility. It'll be hard for them to carry on without her. There'll be a petition started by the end of the week, mark my words.'

Maria snorts. 'Names on a page. What good does that do?'

'It's a start.'

'It's not anything.'

Anna looks at Maria.

'I didn't see you walk away in protest.'

A sharpness in her voice.

'No, you didn't,' Maria says. 'I'm thinking of my wage, same as everyone else, pitiful as it is.'

'Maria Nikolaevna Brovkina.'

Mr Popov is standing at the entrance to the canteen. It's so rare for a line manager to come here, among the workers, that a silence descends.

'Mr Shalamov would like to speak with you.'

She murmurs to the other two, 'I'll tell you later,' and walks through the door, whispers trailing in her wake.

This time, when she enters his office Mr Shalamov stands and shakes her hand. She sits in the same chair as before.

Mr Shalamov leans forward, elbows on the desk, adjusts his glasses, smiles, leans back in his chair, smiles again.

'I would like to speak, Maria Nikolaevna, about your suggestion. You mentioned it would be good for morale. I think perhaps you are right. Let's celebrate the talents of our workers.'

They're watching her, of course, from the floor. Everyone sitting over lunch, clear to all of them that the management is trying to co-opt her. It's her own fault for opening up the discussion in the first place, showing a willingness to play along.

'My nephew won't be able to take on the extra rehearsals. My apologies. I approached you without fully checking through his commitments.'

Shalamov coasts on without missing a beat.

'I've done some asking around. He's a very talented boy.'

'He's been having trouble recently. His teacher is worried about his sense of timing, says he needs to go back to the basics. He wouldn't be able to fit in any performances.'

'I know almost nothing about music. Is that serious?'

'It could be. His teacher says he is at a delicate stage, he's not old enough to have mastered the necessary tempos. It can only be done by repetition. After some time it should come naturally.'

'Well, that is a shame.'

'Yes.'

'Who is his teacher?'

Maria shifts in her chair.

'I can't remember his name. My sister takes care of his tuition.'

'I see.'

He nods. Silence.

A child with skewed timing is not a sufficient excuse. They both know it.

He smiles.

'I do have some friends involved in music. Perhaps we could get the boy another teacher.'

'That's very kind, but he's happy with the man he has. It seems he's making good progress.'

'On the contrary, it sounds like he's doing very badly indeed.'

A pause.

'My friend's name is Yakov Sidorenko. Do you know of him?'

She exhales.

'Yes. Of course.'

'Yakov Mikhailovich is a generous artist, a true friend to the worker and to youth. He's offered to accompany your nephew in a recital in our own house of culture. Such a modest man, Yakov. You would never hear him speak about his achievements.'

Maria hates the patronizing tone. There's no avoiding it now. She'll be seen to take their side.

'I'll have to consult my sister, and of course my nephew.'

'I would have assumed, Maria Nikolaevna, that you would have done this already before approaching me.'

He takes a pen from his jacket pocket and starts looking over some paperwork. Maria waits for permission to leave.

'If you decide that your nephew is not up to it, if you were overstating his talents, then you may of course refuse. I wouldn't wish to stand in the way of a boy's development. But may I remind you that Yakov Mikhailovich is a professor in the Conservatory, not someone you would wish to insult. On the contrary, if your nephew is as talented as they say, I would consider it an incredible opportunity for him. Also, to refuse would greatly disappoint Mr Rybak. He has invited along a committee member from the Ministry of Automobile and Agricultural Machinery.'

He points his pen in her direction.

'Now would not be a good time to disappoint the chairman, believe me.'

'Yes, sir.' She says this without looking at him.

He nods and stands and offers his hand.

'You said it yourself: we have talented people here, why not celebrate our talents? I encourage you to think of this as a good opportunity for both of us, as well as for your nephew.'

She turns without acknowledging him – she doesn't need to pander any more. She'll have a couple of minutes in the lobby to gather her thoughts, decide what or what not to tell them all. Perhaps the truth might be the best option. Though, in her experience, that is rarely the case.

No talking.

You form the line and when in the line you do not deviate from the line.

You stand an arm's length behind the boy in front. You place your hand on his shoulder to judge the space between you and then you release your arm and take a half-step backwards.

When the gym master blows his whistle you begin the exercise. When he blows it again you stop. You count out loud to eight when performing the exercise. When not performing the exercise you count to yourself. When counting out loud, you do not mumble, you shout it clear and crisp, separating the numbers: one . . . two . . . three . . . four . . . five . . . six . . . seven . . . eight.

You start with star jumps, then tuck jumps, to warm the body. Then you do press-ups, sit-ups and squats. Then you repeat them all again.

Yevgeni has a slit on the side of his shorts – not a large rip, but a worrying one, worrying because it's growing exponentially. He has a choice to make. When doing the star jump he can extend his legs to full width and risk tearing them more, or he can keep his legs in a little but risk the gym master making him run laps for the next half-hour. He has only one pair of shorts; there used to be another pair but he's grown out of them, they rode up his thighs like a pair of swimming pants. The other boys laughed at him so he had thrown them out. This was six weeks ago. His mother had promised to take him shopping for a new pair – but she never did. He asked her to give him the money and he could get them himself, but she never had it on her. He suspected that she didn't want to give it to him, that maybe he would spend it on something stupid, or he would meet Ivan or whoever and they would force him to hand it over. He reminded his mother after the last gym class, told her he had a rip in the side of his shorts, and she got angry and said he could mend it himself. But he didn't know how to sew, and, anyway, men don't sew, even he knew this. She was sorry for being angry and promised she would get him a new pair before the next class. Well, the next class is this class.

He should have asked his aunt. She's always good with anything to do with school. She helps him cover his copybooks with old wallpaper and sometimes when he opens his lunchbox he'll find a square of chocolate inside. When this happens he has to stuff it in his mouth at once, in case any of the other kids see it and take it. Six months ago a kid called Lev saw him put the square in his mouth and ran over to him and jammed his fingers in the joint where Yevgeni's jaws meet, and his mouth opened before he had time to swallow and Lev picked the square out, nearly dissolved, drenched in saliva, and ate it. Then he punched Yevgeni in the stomach for being so greedy.

Everyone has the same gym uniform. Red shorts and a white singlet. Some of the older kids have hair under their arms and Yevgeni thinks it a strange place to have hair.

He listens to each popped stitch during the warm-up. Every time he does a squat he can feel the strain on the material. Maybe it would be better just to be obvious, just run the laps, but he's been doing it a lot recently and it's embarrassing. When he runs along the wall behind where they do their press-ups, the kids in the back row always stick out their feet to trip him. Yevgeni knows the gym master sees this, the gym master sees everything, but he doesn't say anything. It's an extra, unspoken, part of the punishment.

They finish the warm-up and then form lines behind the gym mat. When you do your floor routine, you stand totally straight and raise an outstretched arm to the master, to let him know you're about to begin. This is how they do it in competitions. This is how they do it in the Olympics. Everyone says the gym master was in the Olympics when he was younger. Yevgeni told his mother this, but she laughed: she knew the gym master when he was younger, when the Olympics were held here. 'He was at the Olympics all right. He won the bronze medal for sweeping floors.' Yevgeni has never breathed a word and still the gym master doesn't like him.

It's his turn for the floor routine. The kid behind shoves him forward.

He pulls his shoulders back and raises his arm to the gym master, nice and straight. First is a forward roll. He likes these. The secret, he has found, is to bend your knees really low and to look straight ahead. He rolls to the end of the mat, feeling the particular kind of head rush that comes from turning your brain upside down, over and over, the cool, white swirl that spirals down from the top of his skull.

Now a backward roll. He has never quite understood the moment when you have to lever your bum over your head. Sometimes, when he's getting frustrated with it, he'll tuck his bum over his shoulder rather than his head. It means he'll be crooked when going backwards, but it's always quicker. Sometimes the gym master gives out to him for it, and sometimes not. Yevgeni senses that the gym master doesn't really care what he does any more.

Yevgeni makes it to the end of the mat, and the next kid

stands up. He makes his way to the back of the line. He really needs a drink of water, but they aren't allowed to bring water into the gym. They can have water after the session, but there's always a long line to the fountain and by the time he gets a drink he's already late for the next class.

Yevgeni scratches his bum and, as he does so, he realizes that one side of his shorts, the side with the bad rip, flips up behind him. He looks down and realizes just how serious the situation is. Now, they're torn almost all the way to the top. He looks at the clock on the wall. There are only ten minutes left of class. If he times it properly, he can tie the laces on his gym shoes and move straight away to the back of the line and then take his chances with the warm-down exercises. He'll have to untie his shoes without anyone noticing and then tie them again. He might still have to run laps, but the situation is getting desperate. Why does he have to do gym if he hates it so much? Adults don't have to do gym. His mother isn't forced to go on the vaulting horse or the trampoline, although he has to admit that it might actually do her some good.

A blast of the whistle.

'Line up before the ropes.'

He hates the ropes. The ropes are the worst thing he could be asked to do, in his current predicament. There are five ropes hanging in a line and there's usually a race between five pupils at a time. Yevgeni isn't very strong, so he usually loses. Everyone sprints towards the ropes and the gym master looks at him. He can't fake the shoelace trick now.

'Yevgeni, go to the front of the line. You can give us a demonstration on how it's done.'

A titter around the class. If you're in charge, you're always funny. The gym master could give them a lecture on how to manufacture a gym mat and everyone would still laugh.

Yevgeni wishes he could refuse, wishes he could run out of the door, but he isn't suicidal. He'd prefer the class to see his raggedy underwear than face the gym master after an episode like that.

He walks towards the front of the nearest line, his lips pursed in defiance.

'No walking,' the gym master shouts.

As he reaches the front, Yevgeni is struck with a moment of genius. He'll run to the other side of the rope and climb up facing the queue. This way the tear in his shorts will be nearest the wall, the opposite side to the gym master.

Why has his mother not bought him a new pair? He has asked her. She said she would. And he knows that when he goes home and tells her what happened she'll scold him for not reminding her. 'I can't be expected to remember every tiny thing,' this is what she'll say. But gym shorts aren't a tiny thing. They're important. They're life or death.

The gym master blows his whistle and Yevgeni sprints forward. He reaches the rope, runs around the other side of it and begins climbing. Already the other kids are laughing at him, but it can't be helped. What he's done is still the best option.

The gym master looks at the queue of kids and tells them to be quiet and, while he does so, the bottom falls out of Yevgeni's world. The worst thing that can possibly happen happens. Arkady Nikitin, the sweatiest boy in the class, is climbing beside Yevgeni and is even lower down the rope – due to his sweaty hands – and so he sees the tear in Yevgeni's shorts and sees the gym master looking away, and so he tugs hard at the shorts and Yevgeni hears the rip and looks down to see his shorts floating down to the ground away from him, taking his scraggy underpants with them. And then the whole class sees this. They look up and see Yevgeni stopped in shock, almost at the top, his grey underpants lying sprawled on the floor in full view of everyone, like a rat that has lain in the middle of the road for weeks, entrails spread out in opposite directions.

A gale of laughter, the whole class dissolving, and Yevgeni can see the gym master laugh too, briefly, and then he starts to shout at Yevgeni to get down at once.

The gym master has a bald spot which can be seen clearly from up here. Yevgeni stays frozen, clutching the rope, and the longer he holds on, the more irate his gym master becomes. He can see the man's face turning red. Yevgeni clamps his feet around the rope, the way they've been taught, and closes his eyes. There's no way he can come down now and face the embarrassment, the rage. He seals his lids shut and hums the beginning of Chopin's 'Raindrop Prelude', the notes dropping their peace on him. The sound of rain ticking on a glass windowpane; leaves rustling with falling water. The notes caressing him, refreshing him, sweet Chopin drenching him. He can feel the rope swaying wildly: the gym master is trying to shake him down. But Yevgeni isn't moving – if he wants him to come down, he'll have to climb up to get him. Yevgeni clings on for his life, ten metres in the air, the rope burning his fingers, chord sequences pattering along his shoulders.

Two hours later Maria leaves the principal's office. She walks past Yevgeni as he slumps on a chair outside and when she passes he picks up his bag and scurries after her. She moves quickly when she's annoyed. So he can tell she's annoyed.

'I'm sorry.'

'I don't want to hear it.'

'I didn't mean to cause trouble.'

'Well, you've caused it. You had me leave work early. I do this two times a year, maybe it's OK. How many times is this?'

'I don't know.'

'I know. It's four. I'll be lucky if I'm not fired.'

'I'm sorry.'

'You're not sorry. This is not good, Zhenya, especially not now.'

It isn't fair to blame the child for her problems at work. But still, he did call *her*. He could have called his mother. So maybe he deserves it.

'You could have called your mother.'

She realizes he's not responding. She looks to her side, but he's not there. He's stopped. She's the one walking quickly. She's the one who's angry. He's the one who should be keeping up. She stops and looks back. He's standing there with his bag around his ankles. They're in the playground by now, in full view of how many hundreds, if not thousands, of kids, and yet Zhenya has no qualms in putting down his bag, causing a scene, his hands clamped to his head, holding clumps of hair in his fists. No wonder they pick on him – the child is a gaping wound. Maybe this is to do with not having a father, or with too much mothering, with the women being too indulgent because of his talent. Who knows? Let Alina deal with it. He's not her child, after all, and she's not in the mood for it today.

She paces back to him and grabs his arm and drags him back into motion, and he's as raggedly obedient as a stitched doll.

This child needs to learn some things.

They get on the Metro and talk it out. Yevgeni explains what happened and Maria can see a kind of logic behind it. The things you can't do as a kid, the actions you can't take, how the smallest things become magnified, reaching crisis point.

She stops him mid-sentence.

'Show me your arm.'

'What?'

'Show me your arm.'

Yevgeni pulls his sweater back. Nothing. He knows what she's looking for already, trying to look casual. Nothing escapes this kid.

'The other one.'

'No.'

'Why not?'

'OK, it's there, you don't need proof, Mam has seen it already.'

'It's a Chinese burn then.'

'Yes.'

'Do we need to be worried?'

'No.'

'Zhenya?'

'No.'

'Are there a lot of other kids getting them? Be honest now.'

'Yes. Loads.'

'You're not the only one.'

'No. We do it all the time.'

Taunts, name-calling, ear-smacking, spitting, kicking, teachers handing out beatings, snot-flicking, note-passing. Thank Christ she isn't still in school.

She'll let the subject rest, but she can't guarantee that she won't come back to it. It's a fine balance, being a live-in aunt. She wants him to confide in her, but she feels many of the maternal responsibilities, the same irrational fears, as Alina does.

'I have a question,' Maria says. 'Do you know any Prokofiev?'

'Eh' – he thinks for a minute – 'no.'

'Do you know who Prokofiev is?'

He looks at her, eyebrows raised. Of course he knows who Prokofiev is. That's like asking who Lenin is.

'My manager at work is asking about a recital. If you played for them it would be a big help to me.'

But he doesn't know any Prokofiev.

'But I don't know any Prokofiev. Do I have to play Prokofiev?'

'I don't know. Maybe not. I'm just asking, in theory, if you had to. It might not happen.'

He says 'yes'. He says 'of course'. But he hunches in on himself in a way Maria knows. He doesn't want to do it. He's worried about his timing. He's worried about everything.

The train pulls to their stop and they get out, the platform so empty, everybody still at work, and Maria feels an urge to get back on the train and make the most of the afternoon, take him to Red Square, have him walk around the shops in TsUM, let him smell real food, perfume; touch fur. The child has never experienced what it's like to run your hand along a shining pelt. Or they could have tea in the Metropol, have waiters bow to them, hear the clink of teacups, go to a show in the Bolshoi, put his hand on the appliqué wallpaper. Be other people for an afternoon.

But, they can't afford such things, and he has laundry to deliver and she has a class to teach. And, besides, Alina would kill her.

They walk up the steps into the sunlight. The market is here, as always. Vegetables. Military wear. Re-soled boots. Sunglasses for the November glare. You could probably get yourself some nuclear warheads here, if you had the money. There's a container of figs with the lid off on one of the tables. It's maybe ten years since she's tasted one.

She moves on. She'll buy something, an indulgence to make sure there's no hard feelings. She's said her piece. The boy has had quite an afternoon: it can't be easy being a prodigy.

They stop at a blini stall and Yevgeni orders one with ham and egg and Maria says, 'What? Everything I touch turns to gold? Come on now. Be reasonable.' And he smiles guiltily and orders one with red cabbage and sausage. Little runt, he knows the limits. The woman pours the mixture on to her round hotplate and then swirls it with the long, flat knife so it runs to the edge but doesn't overspill.

Nearing the towers, the drunks have colonized the play-grounds, sitting on swings, glugging from bottles. One is lying flat on the merry-go-round, his head extending out one end, legs the other, a bottle of antifreeze lying on his chest, staring up at the photos of soldiers on the windows above him; memorials to family members who have died in service. All of them in their full dress, caps tilted high. The standard shots from academy graduation, faded with the weather. At night, when the lights are on, they cast a ghostly pallor over the place, giving a fleeting impression of stained glass. Maria knows that most of these soldiers were as stupid as tree trunks, fired up on their own testosterone, but she likes their glowing presence, a reminder that a home isn't just comprised of furniture and electricity and plumbing. She understands why the babushkas can't walk past one without blessing themselves.

Maria and Yevgeni climb the stairs – the lift is still out – and Maria turns the key and Yevgeni puts the greaseproof paper into the bin and lets out a belch.

'Don't push it, Zhenya, just because your mother's not here.'

'Sorry.'

'Wash your hands. We'll get started. I'll help you.'

His day is getting better.

It's a Wednesday, which is the end of Alina's laundry week, the day when the piles of freshly pressed sheets reach their peak, covering every available surface. Maria opens the door to the living room and steps into a tundra landscape. The place is so stark and pristine she can almost hear the Siberian winds whipping through the room.

Alina has pinned a tag on each stack with the owner's name and address and Maria begins to line up the piles in order of delivery. A stack has tipped over near the windowsill and Maria picks it up and shakes out the sheets for refolding. She hands two corners to Yevgeni, and they automatically go through the process. The ritual is not without its satisfactions. Maria loves the sensation of snapping the corners of a freshly dried sheet, yanking it tight between her and Yevgeni, the clean, sharp lines that emerge when they each pull tight, stepping forward and back, as though they were in the middle of a formal dance.

They pack up and start their deliveries in the falling snow.

They knock on doors in dimly lit passageways. Hand the bags over to people whose hands are dappled with liver spots, with raised veins. They smell smells they don't want to think about, and hear rubbish flowing down the chutes around them set into the walls, arteries of waste running inside the building. They shoulder open doors of broken glass and doors where the glass has been replaced by wood or cardboard or not replaced at all, and with these ones, with the panels absent, they step through them, but first they place their hands forward, fingers splayed, feeling for what may or may not be there, like a blind man entering an unfamiliar room.

They go back to their apartment and restock and then head out once more, doing this systematically, building by building.

They walk up stairways with kids sprawled all over them. Kids not much older than Yevgeni, a bottle of glue in front of them, and Maria doesn't have to tell Yevgeni to be careful because the child already knows. How can he not, the synthetic leer on their faces?

They deliver a bag to a man with no hands, just bandaged stumps, and Maria walks inside and puts his laundry in the cupboard. The place is immaculately tidy and he explains that the woman next door comes around all the time to make sure he's OK, and Maria feels good about this; it's not all despair or spirit-stripping cynicism.

They see a birdcage that contains a cardboard bird, coloured in with crayon.

They see a red-candle waxwork of Lenin, burned down a little way so that he looks as if he's had a lobotomy.

They see a medical skeleton, standing in the corner of a room, wearing a broad-brimmed black felt hat.

Their last call is Valentina Savinkova, a friend whose husband works with Alina, and she doesn't need to get her laundry done, but she wants to help out. Alina is a little embarrassed by her custom, but of course they're not in a position to turn it down.

'You don't need to have us do this.'

'Of course I do. I don't want to be washing my sheets. Think of the time it saves me.'

'You have the time.'

'I have the time, but I don't want to be wasting it on ironing, washing. It's not charity, believe me. I let Varlam think it's charity, otherwise he wouldn't agree to it, but all that walking up and down to the basement. All those dull conversations I'd have to get into. Please' – she swats an open hand past her ear – 'your sister is doing me the favour.'

She pours vodka into three glasses and Yevgeni laughs. She looks up.

'Zhenya, of course.' It's her turn to laugh. 'I have some kvas.'

She goes out and comes back in with a large glass, a handle on the side.

'Here. You can pretend it's real beer.'

Yevgeni doesn't much like kvas but he drinks a slug and pats his tongue off the roof of his mouth, the tartness of the drink drawing his cheeks together.

Valentina looks around the room.

'I should have cleaned.'

'You've just talked about how you couldn't be bothered doing laundry and now you're saying you should have cleaned.'

'What, you're the KGB now? I'm contradicting myself. Fine. Is this a crime now too? You send this beautiful child over as a spy. Yes, you, Zhenya, you're a beautiful child. I'd come over and mush your cheeks, but I'm drinking my tea and you'd probably disappear into the couch in shame.'

Yevgeni doesn't know how to respond to this.

'So why are you here too, Maria? Did you think your little spy needs some supervision?'

'No, just help. It's a lot of work for a kid and I had an afternoon off.'

'An afternoon off? Sounds mysterious.'

'It's not. I had a meeting in his school. Alina couldn't make it.'

'And so you're seeing what the child gets up to on his rounds, extorting food from vulnerable, lonely women.'

'I'm thinking maybe he shouldn't be doing this alone. Those kids on the stairs.'

'I know. The corners are darker lately. I know.'

'It's not a good place.'

'It's fine. There'll always be a few. It's fine. It's not like Zhenya will be getting caught up in all that. Besides, I hear you're bound for the Conservatory, Zhenya.'

'Not exactly.'

'That's not what I hear. All the practising is going well?'

He's silent. He doesn't like it when adults get together and then include him. He's just not one of them. Why pretend otherwise?

'We got some fish. In the bedroom. Go and have a look.'

Yevgeni bounds off the couch. Maria waits until he closes the door.

'I'm worried about him. We still haven't found a place for him to rehearse. An audition for the Conservatory in the spring – there's also the possibility of a recital at my work – and the child practises on a keyboard with the volume turned down.'

'He can't practise at his music teacher's?'

'The man's old, his wife is senile, we can't ask more of him than we already do. You don't happen to know of anyone with a piano?'

'Of course not. What kind of circles do you think we move in?'

Maria lowers her eyes. Valentina softens her tone, refills Maria's glass.

'I'll ask Varlam to keep an ear out.'

'Thanks. I'm sorry. I don't mean to bring my problems here.'

'Don't worry. I need something to keep my mind occupied. It's a relief to hear about something practical. I've been worrying about the strangest things lately.'

'What type of things?'

'I don't know. Just things. I've too much time on my hands.'

Maria waits patiently. This is always the nature of conversation with Valentina: she approaches the topic in waves, the tide of information coming gradually. Maria, being Maria, listens while someone talks themselves into understanding, or revelation.

'I don't know. I'm forgetting things. My keys. My purse. I forgot my coat a few weeks ago. I was at a play in the Hermitage, on my own, and, afterwards, I walked for twenty minutes in the pounding snow before realizing I had left my coat behind.'

'Must have been a good play.'

'I'd tell you, but of course I can't remember.'

'Are you worried? Do you need to see someone?'

'I don't know. I don't know. There are people who'd kill to be in my position, you know. Just forgetting. Having no memory makes you innocent. You can't obscure things.'

'Has something happened that's made you want to forget?'

'Maybe. I don't know.'

Silence.

'There's something. What is it?'

'I saw something the other day – a few weeks ago, actually. The strangest thing.'

More silence. 'Well, I don't know how to put it. The strangest thing. I was in the Lefortovo – you know how sometimes it's good for meat, the lines that sometimes spring up.'

'Yes.'

'It was Varlam's birthday and I wanted to cook him something special, some pork maybe, and I hung around,

225

went to the places where I had queued before, and eventually I came across a line and I got a shoulder of pork, a beautiful slab, let me tell you.'

Valentina is slightly bug-eyed, with hair chopped under her ears, which further emphasizes the oval shape of her face. Maria could see her standing at the door of the memory, wondering if she should step inside it, wondering if this was doing any good.

'Then I walked back to Kurskaya station. I was really pleased with myself. He works so hard, Varlam. You know how it is, Alina works hard too. I wanted to make him a meal to celebrate him. I know Varlam hasn't done amazing things in his life. He's feeling, at the moment . . . what's the word? . . . unaccomplished. So I wanted to cook him a meal that recognizes what he means to me. A meal fit for a good man.'

She swats the air again, scattering away irrelevant information.

'Anyway, with this package of meat in my bag, I'm proud of myself. I'm a good wife. And I'm walking those backstreets – you know where I'm talking about, there's a steelworks building and it's near all those railway lines.'

Maria nods. 'Yes.'

'The evening is coming down and I feel like the only person in the city – there's no-one else around, not even any footsteps to be heard – and I turn a corner and see something hanging from a lamp post.'

She pauses, looking up, and her voice turns lighter.

'And right away I feel like it's going to be something strange. I don't know why. The weight of it maybe, the way it swung on its own weight. And I look up and it's a dead cat, hanging from a short piece of rope, its eyes gleaming from the streetlight. And I feel it's looking right at me.'

'My God.'

'I know. Its mouth is open, fangs bared, snarling, spitting, the way cats do. I tell myself I need to get out of there, so I start to walk faster – I'm nearly running, in fact. My shoes have a thick heel, so I'm staggering and I slip but regain my footing and look up, and there's another one. I kept my head down all the way back to the station, but I could still tell, from the corner of my eye, that there were more – maybe twenty. I don't know. I was so worried someone would come around the corner, some militia guys, and I'd be the only one around with these fucking animals strung up, and they'd start asking me questions.'

'Of course.'

'I couldn't even cook that dinner later. I just couldn't bear the sight of raw meat. I had to dump the package near the station. The blood was leaking through the paper and getting on my hands. I wanted to puke.'

'I'm not surprised.'

'I haven't been sleeping well since.'

'I can imagine.'

'I've been forgetting things.'

'Yes.'

'So I'm glad you came today. I would have called over anyway. I wanted to ask if you'd heard anything like this before. When you wrote for the newspaper, maybe people talked about such things.'

'No. I'm sorry. They didn't.'

'I'm sitting here wondering why cats are hanging from lamp posts.'

'I don't know. It seems like a statement of some kind.'

'Who would make a statement there? In Lefortovo?'

'I know. But what else could it be?'

'You don't know. I don't know. Such an odd fucking thing.'

Yevgeni pushes open the door again. It's a little too

neatly timed for comfort. Maria hopes he's just bored with the fish.

'Did you see them?'

'Yes.'

'What did you think?'

'Their colours are beautiful.'

'Varlam loves them. He wakes sometimes in the middle of the night and he says that, if he just watches the fish, he falls asleep again.'

'He can see them in the dark?'

'The bottom of the tank lights up.'

Yevgeni definitely wants one now.

They say their goodbyes and Maria hugs Valentina, offering reassurance, and Valentina mimes that she doesn't want what she's said to fall on other ears, and Maria nods and Valentina knows she can trust Maria. This is a woman who's never in her life passed on a secret.

They carry the empty laundry bags and feel the release of the weight.

'Thanks for helping me.'

'It's fine, Zhenya. You're good to do it all on your own.'

They walk, listening to the sound of their own footsteps.

'I suppose you want some fish now.'

He shrugs his shoulders, 'No, not really.'

'Did you hear what we were talking about?'

'No.'

A pause.

'What were you talking about?'

'Nothing.'

Maria is leaning against the perimeter wall at the viewing point for Lenin Hills: the Moscow river below; a ski-jump and slalom course to her right; the star of the main Lomonosov tower raised high into the night sky behind her.

This same location was a favoured meeting place in her student days, with its beautiful view over the city. Men would wait here for her and take her ski-jumping, a tactic, she now suspects, to get her adrenaline running, her blood pumping, desires racing. She hasn't stood here in years. It's the opposite side of the university from the Metro stop and there's always somewhere else she needs to be, even tonight. She's resolved to make her way to Grigory's later, a relatively short walk by the river. She needs to ask about a rehearsal place for Yevgeni. Although his offer of a piano had been several months ago, Grigory is not the type to go back on his word. He might even be agreeable to letting the boy come over a few days a week, even if he has ignored her phone calls.

She's waiting for Pavel – an old friend, or teacher, or lover: whichever traditionally comes first in the list of distinctions. Before her classes, she slid a note under his door, asking to meet up, something she's done every three or four months since their reacquaintance at a party last year. They rarely meet casually, even in the corridors of the faculty, but she finds it a relief to have a long-standing friend come back into her life, someone, independent of Alina, who knows her well enough to enable her to think things through. She wants to clear her mind before she meets Grigory, wants to dispel the possibility of unburdening herself upon him. She'll ask for a favour for the boy, nothing else.

She's been waiting for Pavel for half an hour, watching the skaters on the river below her, lit up from the Central Lenin Stadium. Her gloves are thin and her fingertips feel dumb and immobile. She's never become used to the snapping cold of the dark season. She's never known any other kind, and yet the deep winter always finds ways to surprise her, wrapping itself around her skin, biting at her exposed extremities. She's reminded here, though, in this spot, with couples walking past, skates slung over their shoulders, that she loves the peacefulness that descends at this time. People speaking as they dress, in muffled, layered solitude. Condensed steam everywhere, moisture-laden breath. Winter always assumes a certain otherworldly gait. It has a texture and speech all of its own, a written language, snow nestling itself in lucid patterns, iced windowpanes pleading to be deciphered, skaters cutting swirls into the frozen river.

'It's beautiful, isn't it?'

Pavel has placed himself soundlessly beside her, an old habit which makes her jump out of her skin.

'You startled me.'

Pavel smiles. There's a childish edge to his humour, always seeking an opportunity to irritate, to tease – an aspect so at odds with his status as a professor of literature. People revere him. He repeats his question.

'It's beautiful, isn't it?'

'Yes. And so quiet. I feel like I can hear every sound on the river.'

'Do you skate? I can't remember.'

'I could skate in a straight line, I just could never turn.'

'That's a problem.'

'I think it was something to do with relying on only one

foot. I stopped trying just before I hit my teens. It was probably a wise decision, looking back.'

'I skate from time to time.'

'Of course you do. The man of five hundred talents.'

'If you start complimenting me it might be the end of our friendship.'

She smiles and they embrace, warmly.

When Maria was a student, his lectures were eagerly awaited events not just within the department but throughout the entire university. The hall would be crowded with engineers, medical students and marine biologists. They'd fill the steps, squeezing in three wide, the crowd clustering at the doorways and spilling out into the lobby, listening intently, laughing with their fellow students inside – those lucky enough to get a seat. Professor Levytsky drew effortlessly on the classics, embellishing his points with stories from the writers' lives, their sexual proclivities, anecdotes of everyday embarrassments. He could hold a room with magnificent power, using silence as a way to taunt his audience, to stir them into their own internal opinions. From his mouth, poetry became a fine meal, each distinct word gaining its own flavour when issued from his lips.

'You got my note?'

'Of course, I read it with pleasure. You've always written a good note, Maria.'

'I'm sure I've had many successors.'

As an undergraduate in her first year, Maria had pursued him with zeal. In her first two months she wrote five love letters, slipping them under his office door in the late evenings. The letters themselves were a sexual awakening to her; she was surprised at her ability to write such sensual prose, surprised that she knew what she knew, experiencing the bodily tremors while she wrote, becoming heated as she lay her longings down in ink. And, in later weeks, when they lay in bed, him asleep, she would trace her finger along the lines on his fine-boned face, following the progress of those early words that were etched now into his crow's feet, chiselled into the grooves of his forehead.

'No. Notes like you wrote take real daring. There aren't many out there with your courage. At least that's what I'm telling myself. I'm claiming it's them and not me. I'm telling myself I still inspire the same yearnings.'

'Of course you do.'

'Please. Look at me. I'm an old man. I have tufts of hair growing from my ears. It's a definite old-man symptom.'

Maria cranes her head back.

'I see no ear hair.'

'I clip it. They can take a lot but I'm keeping my vanity.'

'It's a good thing to keep.'

'It's the best thing.'

Pavel ended it after six months, sitting over morning coffee, while she was making out her list of errands for the day. He said he was preventing her from making her own discoveries. She remembered the words distinctly, remembered her confusion that an errand list and a lover's rejection – her first great rejection – should occupy the same space. A break-up like this should be done in a romantic place, with tears and rain. This is what she thought then, a girl of nineteen. She needed to make her own decisions, he said, discover her own opinions, not sit under the weight of his experience. She had no idea what that meant at the time. She spat curses at him, called at his apartment in the middle of the night, attempting to catch him with a new lover, which she never did. In the end it mattered little; she was obliged to abandon her studies anyway, move to Kursk. When she returned to the city with Grigory she was a few years older; married, wiser, carrying her own bank of experiences. Had they met on the street she would perhaps have thanked him, told him she realized the unselfishness behind the statements, the accuracy of them.

A pause.

'You wanted to talk to me.'

'Yes. I don't know why.' She hesitates. 'I do know why, it's just difficult to articulate.'

'I'm in no hurry. Talk to me.'

Maria notices that Pavel's eyes are still the same shade of milky green. She wonders if our eyes change colour as we age.

'I'm worried that something is happening, something I should be aware of.'

'I don't understand.'

'I've been hearing things. Odd things, from various sources.'

'What sources?'

'Neighbours, people at work, remarks in the class. They . . .' She hesitates again.

'Yes?'

'Have you heard about the *Shining Solidarity* phenomenon in Poland?'

'No. I don't think so.'

'When the Solidarity movement had to go underground, they developed techniques to keep up morale. They had help, of course. The Americans would send in aid shipments through Sweden, mostly communications equipment.'

'What kind of equipment?'

'Basic stuff. Books. Printing machines. Unregistered typewriters. Photocopiers. But the CIA gave them one impressive toy. A machine that transmitted a beam which overpowered the state-broadcast signals. Every few months on millions of TV sets the Solidarity logo would appear, with a recorded message announcing that the movement lived and the resistance would triumph.'

'It sounds like science fiction.'

'But it happened. It kept the movement going when people thought it had been extinguished. Viewers were asked to turn their lights on and off if they'd seen the logo. When this happened, a glittering lightshow would sweep through the suburbs. Such a show of strength. The whole city glinting like a piece of foil in the wind.'

The sound of skates cutting into ice.

She continues. 'Things are coming my way. I don't know. Worrying things. A neighbour of mine has seen cats strung up from lamp posts. They mean something. I know it. There are kids in the Tishinski market on Sundays buying up old military uniforms, cutting them up, making fashion statements. Other things too. I hear of clubs where women dance with replicas of red star medals over their nipples.'

'And you disapprove?'

'Of course I don't disapprove – let them jerk off over the whole army. But I need to know I'm not wrong. Something is happening. I can feel it.'

'You're worried?'

'No. I don't know what I am. Restless, maybe.'

'You're thinking maybe you want to get involved.'

'That's not it. I have responsibilities. I have people who rely on me. I'm just barely clawing my way back from the wilderness.'

Pavel doesn't speak for a while, simply blows on his gloved hands, rubs them together. The length of their friendship apparent in the silences.

'There are so many nights when I'm in a reception room in the faculty, sharing a drink with former students, and I don't know who I am. I'm droning on, making witty remarks, droll observations, to people who are no better than reptiles, men whose job it is to do obscene things.'

He turns to her, and Maria notes to herself that he's more reticent than before, another way the years have taken hold. She couldn't imagine hauling him through a blazing row any longer; a sombre weight to his words now.

Their relationship was largely built upon ideological arguments. She was constantly questioning, reviewing, surmising, churning all her newly gained knowledge through the prism of her personality. She'd argue with him anywhere. So many times their lovemaking was abandoned because of a throwaway comment from him. Or she would storm into his office, not bothering to check if there was a colleague inside, and bombard him with her fusillade of newly researched facts, slinging in an occasional well-chosen quote to underline her point. On one occasion, she exploded into a barber's while he was in the chair getting a shave, picking up an argument in which he had silenced her, one day before, with his experience of debate and with the tapestry of facts that were always within his reach. A narrow, smoke-filled room with two barber's chairs, one empty, and a row of waiting men, condensation clinging to the glass mirrors. She pushed open the door and cleared the barber away as he held his blade aloft, astonished, looking to his customers for support, but they were as shocked as he. Pavel's rebuttals came so rapidly, with such force, that the front of her coat was dotted with flecks of shaving cream. Pavel remembers that he wiped himself with a cloth, put on his jacket, paid and left, with a stubble-mottled face, all without breaking the flow of the argument, countering her well-prepared perspectives, loving every moment of it, loving the intellectual stretch she provided, loving how it was intertwined with her naïvety, so that often she would be unable to recognize the limits of her argument, blowing everything out of proportion, and in these moments he would pause, would cease his replies, and Maria would realize her error and he would spend the next couple of hours trying to coax her back from her disappointment in herself. Trying to make her see that it was her commitment to her subject, her righteous fury, that made her so attractive.

'You've heard the joke about the chicken farmer?' he asks Maria.

'I don't think I have.'

'A chicken farmer wakes one morning and goes into the yard to feed his brood. He finds ten of them dead. There is no reason for this. They were healthy, some of his best birds, so he is confused. He is worried the rest of the brood may be similarly affected so he decides to ask comrade Gorbachev for help. "Give them aspirin," the premier says. The farmer does this, and ten more die that night. This time the premier suggests castor oil. The farmer does as suggested and ten more are dead the next day. He goes back to Gorbachev and is told to give them penicillin. He does this and, the next morning, all the chickens have died. The farmer is distraught. "Comrade Gorbachev," the farmer says, "all my chickens are dead." "What a pity," Gorbachev replies. "I had so many more remedies to try."'

Maria smiles at him. He's always had a beguiling mouth, shape-shifting, simultaneously knowing and innocent.

'And this is funny?'

'She comes to me for help and ridicules me. It's fine. Funny isn't the point. The joke is the point. The weakness is the point. The fact that they are telling this joke on production lines, at football matches, in taxis, this is the point. Where we've come to. This is the point. I haven't written a line of poetry in nearly twenty years. Not since the crackdown after the Prague Spring. I took my reputable job and taught the books they wanted me to teach, stayed away from saying anything controversial by telling little smutty stories about the writers' lives.'

Absently, he packs some snow between his gloves, forming a concave disc.

'So many of my friends kept writing. Even in the camps they wrote. Even when they got to their lowest point.' He is very still, then continues. 'They're dead or hobbled now, and I'm still eating professorial lunches. You know how they got their writing out of the prisons?'

'I've heard a few different ways.'

'They swallowed it and shat it. Or rolled it on their tongue and exchanged it in a visitor's kiss. Women secreted it inside themselves and let the guards pretend to attempt to pick it out. Can you imagine the humiliation? They did what they felt necessary.'

'How many times did we talk about this, even back then? Go and ask one of your friends – the ones who are still alive – if you should have kept writing.'

'They can absolve me precisely because they've been through it. I can't absolve myself.'

A ski-jumper misjudges his flight, coming down in a flurry of light snow.

'I can feel it too, a moment opening up. They see their flaws, they are aware of the need to modernize. Gorbachev looks at those leaders before him – Chernenko, a senile old cripple with emphysema; Andropov, a man who had to have dialysis twice a week, who was so sick that everyone suspected the General Secretary was in fact dead – and he is pushing for change but doesn't know how to modulate it. We are making jokes about the man's indecision. He is no longer a figure of fear. People are hungry for more. I know you see this too. But there is only confusion now; no idea where to push, who to ask.'

Maria nods. 'Sometimes I hear these words, "glasnost", "perestroika", and they sound to me like the final breaths of an empire.'

Pavel throws the disc of snow towards the trees, they watch it disassemble in the air.

'There are some people I want you to meet.'

'People?'

'Yes, people. People I respect. Not windbags or idealists. Serious people. People who are talking of serious things, about access to markets, a maximization of resources.'

'I'm not asking for a way in, Pavel. I just want to be ready.'

'Have you thought about the possibilities of us going back to where we were? They may close ranks again soon. It can't happen on its own, you know. In the fifties, I drank for three days straight when word trickled out about Khrushchev's secret speech. The end of Stalinism, the end of fear. We were expecting an era of prosperity. We listened for a great chorus of contradictory opinions. But it didn't come. So we went back to doing what we do so well: watching, deluding ourselves with fragile hopes, with an occasional moment of grace or luck; holding on to these things as omens. Hoping ourselves into inaction. Perhaps in a year we'll be shot for daring to tell a stupid chicken-farmer joke.'

'Perhaps.'

'You'll think about what I said.'

'Perhaps.'

'I'll let you know about our next gathering. If you decide to stay at home, I'll understand.'

She nods. 'I know.'

When they part she walks down through the pathways between the slalom run, skiers dipping and rising from the undulations of the trail, many of them hunkered down, elbows and head tucked in, trying to extract the maximum speed from such a short, shallow course.

She reaches the pathway by the river and looks up. Pavel is still there, his face cupped in one hand, his gaze resting on the river, on the skaters swooping languidly in the still night. She stays and watches him until he moves off. A man who is used to his own company. A couple stand and kiss right beside him, too close for comfort, but he doesn't react, following the thread of his thoughts to completion before moving away.

Her walk takes her past the Vorobyovy Gory station, set inside a great glass bridge that funnels the Metro trains from the south to the centre of the city, its struts and girders slicing the ice of the river below into a latticework of shadow.

It's her favourite part of the city, this walkway. Tree-laden hills curve down into the river. There are no grand statements here, no monolithic towers, no gesticulating statues. The Central Lenin complex is spread out on the opposite side of the river, but the buildings maintain a degree of modesty, their design quietened by the sweep of nature around them.

Nearing Grigory's apartment, she sees his window on the top floor of a staggered block, in line with the upper reaches of the Andreevsky bridge. The light is off. It's ten o'clock, too early for him to be in bed. Such a thing would be contrary to his sense of order. He's out. Maria knows she can't let the moment go by without some sort of contact: if she passes without leaving a note, she may not have the courage to return.

She stands on the slope in front of the gatepost, looking at the uninhabited apartment, and this is an experience that is not unfamiliar to her: looking at her home and feeling like a stranger. The same anxieties descend. She dreads the possibility of meeting anyone. She smoothes her way into the shadows.

At the door she presses his bell to confirm he's not there. No answer. She punches in the code on the lock and finds the combination is still the same; the door pops open instantly for her. It's a short hallway, but wide and well lit. She hasn't been here since the day she took the last of her belongings, closed the door of the apartment, stumbled down these steps. She can still see the way he stood in their small vestibule, between the large mirror on the wall and the small oval one on the coat stand. Both mirrors bounced his reflection between them, so that before closing the door for the last time, Maria found herself leaving not just him but an endless multitude of him. Standing there, his shoulders wrapped in heartbreak.

The memory overwhelms Maria and she leans against the rows of brass letterboxes and stares down at the chessboard tiles. She runs her hand along the nameplates under each slot and finally comes to his: Grigory Ivanovich Brovkin. She'd hoped that maybe both their names would still be there, but of course hers had been removed: wouldn't she do the same in his position? Why keep a daily reminder of your loss, your great disappointment, your great failure?

It wasn't his failure, though, it was hers. She hopes that time has allowed him to relinquish all self-recrimination, releasing him from the wreckage she brought upon him.

Maria takes a notebook and pen from her bag. She leans the pages on her thigh and begins to write. After the first few sentences she hears footsteps on the stairs and looks up to see the caretaker descend towards her.

She nods in greeting.

'Good evening, Dmitri Sergeevich.'

He pauses, surprised.

'Maria.'

He doesn't say her patronymic name. She presumes it would imply too much respect. He has passed her on these stairs before; on a few occasions, walking with a man who was not her husband, making her way to their darkened apartment. Each time, Dmitri Sergeevich had not attempted to hide his distaste at her betrayals. Maria remembers how, on passing him on those occasions, she had wanted to melt into liquid, to trickle down the steps, to flow down the hill and join with the river, where she would become indistinguishable and irrelevant, shapeless and free.

On those two or three occasions he had seen her eyes hollowed with dread and mistaken it for guilt. He had seen her grapple for her keys, attempt to slide one of them into the lock, while enduring the full glow of his judgement. He had seen her do this while battling through tears of anger and fear and mistaken them for tears of shame.

She had hated him then, not for his spite, but for his inaction. A moment of discretion, a few words to Grigory in a darkened corner under the stairs, was all it would have taken for her to be released from her torment. Instead, he despised her silently and kept his distance from her husband. He watched her life crumble before him and didn't have the wit to join together the events. He couldn't read what she was saying to him with her trembling hands, with her smudged eyeshadow, with her faltering steps.

He stands at the bottom of the stairs now, unshaven, his clothes rumpled, a radically different figure from the neat, well-groomed man she remembers. She looks at him with the stains on his cardigan, his greasy hair, and is surprised to feel no anger. The man was simply going about his business. He wasn't responsible for the cruelties of her situation. And, for her part, she is relieved no longer to experience the humiliation that a glance from him would evoke.

In the past few years she has replayed her actions countless times while sitting at her workbench, her limbs functioning independently, her mind back here, and has long since reassured herself of her fidelity, if not in body then in everything else; everything that remained her own, at least, remained his.

'Why are you here, Maria?'

A softness in his voice.

'I'm looking to leave a note for Grigory.' She lifts up her notebook. 'I'll finish and slip it into his letterbox. Can you tell him I called?'

He approaches her, and she flattens the notebook against her chest, instinctively protective. Her humiliation, his hold over her, hasn't, it seems, entirely passed. He doesn't reach for the notebook, though; he gently takes her hand. She is too surprised to resist.

'Please, Maria, come and sit.'

'I'd rather not. I was just passing. I hadn't intended to stay. It's late and I need to get home.'

'Please, Maria.'

She sits, unnerved.

'Would you like some water?'

'No, thank you.'

Perhaps Dmitri Sergeevich's opportunities for company have become rare. Perhaps his isolation is causing him to look upon her as an old friend.

'How is your wife, Dmitri Sergeevich? I apologize, I can't seem to remember her name.'

He waves away her question.

'Grigory isn't just out for the evening. He's been gone for months now, Maria.'

'Oh. I see.' She tucks her hair behind her ears. 'I didn't know. But his name is still on the letterbox.'

'Yes. He still lives here officially, he just hasn't been home in a long time.'

'He never sent word to me, but then, I suppose, why would he?'

'He left quickly. He didn't have a chance to inform anybody. I myself got a call from his secretary.'

'Did she say where he went?'

Maria is aware that her voice is rising. It's not like Grigory to act spontaneously.

'She didn't say exactly. She simply mentioned that there had been an accident in the Ukraine and his skills were needed.'

'She didn't say *exactly*. But you know where he is.'

He takes a breath, twists a button on his cardigan.

'The news reports of Chernobyl started appearing a couple of days later. I paid close attention. He left the same day they became aware of the accident.'

'Chernobyl is in the Ukraine?'

'Yes.'

A moment of blankness. She stares at Grigory's name on the letterbox.

'I would have been in touch with you, but I had no idea how to reach you. Grigory Ivanovich hasn't had any friends drop by looking for him. You're the first one to visit.'

She has no idea what to do. She finds herself saying this out loud. To Dmitri Sergeevich, of all people. She realizes she doesn't even know his last name.

'I have no idea what to do.'

'Call the hospital – I've been sending his mail there. They'll be able to help.'

Maria doesn't take in anything else he says. She knows she

thanked the man but doesn't become aware of leaving the building until she is walking down the slope to the steps by the bridge.

How could they have sent him there? How could he still be there?

She stops and looks around. She's passed through the innards of the bridge and out on to the viewing platform that sweeps down to Leninsky Prospekt. The Academy of Sciences is to her right, glowing amber and grey. An intricate building that calls to mind the workings of an old watch, as if its outer panels have blown off to reveal the refined minds inside it, grappling with problems far beyond the realm of the humble citizen. To her left, Gorky Park stretches out, unlit, a reservoir of darkness in the vast expanse of the city.

He has already been through so much. She has put him through so much. All of it beginning here, in this very spot.

It was here that Mr Kuznetsov had first approached her. Even after he had lain naked in her bed, inched his way inside her, she had continued calling him Mr Kuznetsov, not wanting him to mistake their relations for intimacy. After the first few occasions, she knew that he had grown to find a sexual charge in her formal address, but it was too late then for her to relent.

That night, the first night, she had received a call from one of the sub-editors at the paper. A story was breaking which they needed her to cover. *Could you come to the office?* Looking back, his reluctance to outline what was happening should have raised her suspicions, but she felt such a surge of relief that it overpowered her sense of caution. The call meant she was being invited back to the fold, they were telling her they would forgive her indiscretions. That previous afternoon she had stood before the editor's desk and watched him hold up her offending article, a short piece, no more than a hundred words, the headline legible from where she stood:

200,000 ATTEND FUNERAL OF
WARSAW PRIEST

She was hardly surprised. She had known the article would stir up difficulties; in fact, she had done her best to slip it past the editor's attention, handing it, casually, at the last minute, to the most junior sub-editor, apologizing for overrunning her deadline.

It wasn't an ordinary funeral and it wasn't an ordinary death. Five days beforehand, two police divers had pulled Father Popiełuszko's body from a reservoir near the town of Włocławek, an hour's drive west of Warsaw. The priest's face was collapsed, beaten, his body bloated. Despite this, when the divers pulled him up, they recognized him immediately. Father Popiełuszko had been more popular even than the Solidarity leader, Lech Wałesa, because he had the extra authority that a collar and cassock bestow. His Sunday sermons had attendances of forty thousand and upwards. They came to hear him talk about the injustices imposed upon the working man. He stood and reminded them through soaring rhetoric that the child Jesus was born into the family of a carpenter, not of an apparatchik. They came and listened and walked back to their homes, the surge of his speech patterns lengthening their stride.

Father Popiełuszko had had the eyes of the regime firmly fixed upon him. It was well known that he stored funds and passed them on to the Solidarity groups in Warsaw. When his body was identified, such a public rage swept through the city that the authorities immediately identified and arrested the three agents of the secret police who were responsible for his death. It was an unprecedented act for a ruling authority to give up its own agents, but it calmed the situation enough for the funeral to pass off peacefully.

Maria was careful not to write about the background. She detailed the ceremony and included some pointed quotes from the eulogy. She indicated with skilfully selected words that the death was not from natural causes, but, otherwise, she kept to the ritual itself and let the readers draw their own inferences.

The editor held up the piece. He accused her of expressing anti-Soviet sentiment, of encouraging dissent. She had her rebuttals prepared. How could this be anti-Soviet matter when the authorities themselves had made publicly known that the perpetrators were SB police? She was reporting on a funeral; it had nothing to do with politics. Maria had no doubt she was on steady ground. She could defend every sentence against accusations.

Her editor listened and nodded and then produced several pages of pink carbon paper, covered in her familiar scrawl. Pages she'd written for a samizdat, which had been typed and copied and typed and copied until her words had been thumbed through by several hundred pairs of hands.

The editor displayed each set of pages and listed off the headlines:

GDANSK ACCORDS ENABLE POLISH WORKERS TO ELECT UNION REPRESENTATIVES

SOVIET FORCES ACCIDENTALLY SHOOT DOWN KOREAN AIRLINER

MASSIVE OVERPRODUCTION OF ARMAMENTS CLAIMS CHIEF KREMLIN ADVISOR

Maria couldn't believe it. The samizdat went to incredible lengths to make sure authors would be untraceable.

'I've never seen these before.'

'Fine. In that case, I can hand them to the KGB to conduct some handwriting analyses.'

She placed her face in her hands.

'Writing inflammatory articles for a ragged underground paper is one thing. But now you are trying to bring us into disrepute. I'm obliged by law to report you.'

There was nothing to do but wait for it all to unfold.

Maria spent the day pacing the apartment, waiting for the knock on her door, thinking about the interrogation room she would soon find herself in, the sleep deprivation and starvation, the days of endlessly repetitive questioning.

She couldn't even bring herself to let Grigory know what had happened, telling herself there was no point in burdening him with the same sense of dread. So when she received the call that evening, she was swept away with the relief. She grabbed her coat, made her way to the Metro stop, taking the same route she's just walked. When she reached the viewing platform, Mr Kuznetsov was standing there, looking at the traffic below.

Mr Kuznetsov, her editor. A stale man, desiccated skin, flat, unresponsive eyes.

She stopped, recognizing him straight away; it was clear to her at once that his being here, intercepting her journey, was no coincidence. Immediately, all that would transpire unfolded in her mind. It was all set up to play out beautifully for him. He would remind her that, due to his discretion, she still had a job. He would remind her that the KGB would be very interested in her dissenting view. She even predicted that he would use the word 'implications', use it to promise the destruction of her husband's career.

'And there are other implications,' he proceeded to say.

The words still ring out to her, even now, with a terrible clarity. Her life imploding with that single sentence.

If she had had more time, if the conversation had taken place in his office, perhaps she would have fled, found Grigory, told him everything. He would, of course, have confronted Kuznetsov, paying no attention to how well-connected the man was. It would have meant the destruction of a fine career, another skilled doctor disregarded. Grigory would have been deprived of the very thing that defined him.

But, of course, Kuznetsov knew that too. His standing there, so close to her apartment, meant that she couldn't defer the decision. And once that determination was made, she couldn't turn back. As she lay with Grigory later that night, afterwards, her deception expanded into the millimetres that separated their bodies. Lying there on the freshly changed sheets, another man's body heat still contained in the core of their mattress.

The only influence she could bring to bear was her lack of willingness. When Kuznetsov prised her apart, her body proved itself resistant to his touch. The lips of her opening as stiff and dry as cardboard, causing them both to burn as he propelled himself into his rhythm.

She looks away from the spot where Kuznetsov once stood, his presence still palpable, and gazes down into the cold heart of the city. Leninsky Prospekt is straddled by neon-lit billboards, all of them proclaiming the superstitions of her leaders. Their weaknesses, the tensions, the conflicts, the secrets that give the Party a reason to exist, the fears that make their hearts flurry in the quiet of the night:

- 'The Communist Party is the Glory of the Mother-land.'
- 'The Ideas of Lenin Live and Conquer.'
- 'The Soviet Union is the Source of Peace.'

Sentences swathed in vanity. This rhetoric surging through their institutions and overflowing into the minds and actions of individuals. Surging through Kuznetsov as he surged into her: creating, eventually, her unwanted child, her unwanted life.

And when she rid herself of the child, it compounded her guilt. All she wanted then was to turn away from the world, from Grigory. Not revealing it all to him then – now that she can reflect upon that time – was a wilful act of self-destruction. When it was all over with Kuznetsov and he reported her anyway, she was glad. She welcomed the punishment, she told herself she deserved to toil away at a job she hated. To lose herself in menial tasks, to shut down her mind, close off her personality.

She makes a pact with herself as she walks down the broad avenue, traffic whipping past as she disappears into the pavement underneath Gagarin's steel monument, as she descends on the narrow escalator: she will no longer be just another shadowed form in this city built on whispers.

The snow is coming in force now, these past two weeks, dropping its full weight from the sky. Huge, feathery flakes clump on Artyom's lashes, small drifts gather in the nape of his hood. All around, the resettlement camp is silent, not much moving other than the trucks that come and go.

The snow sits evenly both on the ground and on the flat roofs of all the prefabricated huts, so they look as if they've been driven upwards from the earth, their yellow walls the only colour for kilometres around, a colour that was probably intended to elicit cheer but instead serves only to emphasize the cheap, inhospitable nature of the constructions. They would look cartoonish but for their dilapidated state. Already, in many, windows have fallen from their frames and the residents have taped up cardboard or nailed up the doors ripped from their kitchen presses to keep the wind out.

In every hut there's a fuel-burning stove. So much of the day spent poking and prodding. They get their fuel allowance from the supplies store: a wheelbarrow of logs for each home, delivered by a young soldier with red-raw features and a permanently runny nose.

Batyr is improving. After three weeks, Artyom can see how his coat is beginning to regain its lustre; he's starting to put on weight. Artyom visits him at mealtimes and, more recently, takes him for walks. He's built a small cart for the dog, big enough to rest his haunches on it but small enough so that he can put his front legs on the ground. There's a handle on the back of the cart that Artyom uses to push him forward, and Artyon is aware that it must look strange, but there are many stranger sights here.

He gives Batyr food which he scavenges from the sacks of waste piled up at the back of the storehouse. There are always soldiers guarding the building, but Artyom made a point of introducing them to his two-legged friend. They knelt and rubbed Batyr behind the ears, patted him, ran their hands vigorously up and down his flanks, and when they did this he saw a brightness in their eyes, the animal taking them away from routine, and he saw them then as brothers and sons, laughing at the dinner table, feeding scraps to their own dog as it looked at them pitifully with its head on their knee, imploring them. Now they let Artyom poke away at the rubbish, as long as he promises he'll tie the bags up afterwards, they need to keep the rats away.

At first he was feeding Batyr from the clinic's leftovers – the doctor arranged it that way – but after about a week the kitchen staff told him to look somewhere else. He could have gone back to the doctor, but the man is busy, he has more on his mind than where to get scraps for a dog.

Because Sofya is sick, she has a room to herself. Artyom sleeps in the same bed as his mother. His mother changes in this room, so he sees her naked from behind. Neither of them cares. What was important before is no longer important here. They sleep side by side and his mother rises three or four times in the night to check on Sofya.

There are some mornings he wakes to find his mother has curled into him in her sleep. Such a thing doesn't feel unnatural to him. He understands how the body seeks reassurance; he doesn't resist because he needs it too.

Their hut doesn't leak like a lot of the others. The adults

hardly talk about anything else, a constant exchange and comparison of the physical status of their homes. Artyom thinks that this is maybe because they can do something about it, do some repairs; the huts can be fixed, the sickness can't. Artyom's thankful that their place doesn't leak, at least not yet. If Sofya had to lie there in the cold, it would be worse.

Every hut has a kitchen-cum-living room and two bedrooms. There is no toilet or running water of any kind. They have an electric hob and the stove and an electric radiator in each bedroom. Some people have TVs or radio sets; their relatives have dropped them off at the reception hut, leaving nothing else but their names. No note. No one enters further than the reception hut. Artyom understands why.

Artyom is one of the oldest boys in the settlement. He's seen a couple of others his age, but they were weaker than he is and who knows what kind of state they're in now. He feels strong. His mother keeps asking if he's getting enough rest, but he likes the air, he needs to be outside. It gives him a purpose.

He walks to the woods almost every day collecting wood, handing it around to their new neighbours. He never expects anything for it – it didn't cost him anything anyway – and from time to time his mother receives a kindness in recognition for his help. Last week a woman in sector 3A gave her a pair of her son's boots for Artyom's walks. The boy had died a few months before. And so now Artyom finds himself trudging along between the trees in a dead boy's boots. But it doesn't concern him in any way.

'I'm lucky to have a son like you, Artyom.'

'You're not lucky, Mama.'

'There are people worse off.'

'That may be true, but not much. We're not lucky.'

'No. You're right. We're not.'

Grigory sits on some outside furniture, leaning on a metal table, dabbing his fingers in a pool of condensation at its lip. A spider dangles below, twirling languorously. He will soon begin surgical prep, inside for the rest of the day, so he takes in cool breaths while he can; watching water twist along the tendrils of ice that hang from the roof of the clinic, the one solid building in the whole settlement. Brick walls half a metre thick that mercifully retain heat. They speculated as to its use before they came here, an old barracks perhaps. A stubborn musty scent in the operating theatre despite the plastering, the painting and the daily scrubbing.

People here waiting, solemnly waiting. He watches them walk laps around the recreational area in the middle of the settlement. Walking and waiting.

An elderly man sits on a nearby bench, hands clamped under his armpits. Grigory feels no impulse to speak to him, nor to his own colleagues when he twists open the handle of the common room, puts his shoulder to the expanded door. Even in his breaktimes he is unaccompanied, slow to welcome any intrusion into his guarded world. Four tables in the room and still he manages to stake out a private territory. He tells himself, has hinted to others, that his mind needs to recuperate, so many hours spent in total concentration – and this is true; sometimes it's beyond him to make the few simple choices demanded of him in their small canteen. When they ask – tea or coffee? rice or potatoes? – he shifts listlessly, unable to mouth the correct words.

He can also recognize, when he has a will to, that these are the strategies of an only child: to create a world impervious to others, your passions sealed off, as contained as the canisters of oxygen the anaesthetist carts into the building. This is his ease.

How different would it be, he wonders as he pushes wearily off the chair, with Vasily here?

Out in the fields the snow is so deep that Artyom has to wade through it. He keeps his pelvis lower to the ground and leans into his steps. It takes so much effort that he doesn't feel the cold. He reaches the first trees of the forest and trudges inside. These trees mark a border; time slows as you pass through the line of branchless trunks. The light that comes down has air inside, as if it's been passed through a tea strainer, and the rays split into strands of drops as they fall on to the forest floor, landing silently like dancers, turning as they descend.

The sound of his own breath. Trickles from hidden streams. A branch struggling under its load. The air, too, somehow distilled. Smoky air. Strong air.

Tall trunks with no branches. A stoat slithers up one, twenty metres away, a white blur ascending.

Artyom walks and sits and walks again, looking for fallen branches. When he is thirsty he scoops snow into his mouth and looks up at the canopy far above him.

It was a forest, back there, that claimed his father, and in the silence Artyom can feel a connection amongst these tall trees, as if they are drawing him here. They sway nervously, confessing their remorse, creaking like a door forced open in the wind.

Back in Minsk, they had been in the emergency shelter for a month before they found his father. New people kept arriving.

At the end of the first week, their floor space was cut in half, so they no longer had room to lie down flat. They were forced to sleep in shifts, there were so many of them bunched in under that roof. The whole place stank of sweat. People complained continuously of the smell. Babies were getting rashes from not being cleaned. Eventually, the militia set up a line of hoses at the back of the warehouse to deal with the problem. Everyone was given a plastic bag, and you queued up at the back door, and once you stepped outside you had to strip naked and put your clothes into the bag. You had to tie a knot in the bag and then, still holding your clothes, you'd stand in front of the wall, near a drain, and the militia would hose you down. Afterwards, you used your own clothes to dry yourself off, then put them back on and re-entered the warehouse, with small puddles between your toes, your shirt and underwear sticking to you. For the first few days the militia guys would rate the women. The women would stand in a line, naked, holding their plastic bags in front of their genitals, and the guards would shout out a score between one and ten. If any woman complained, her bag would be sprayed until it was torn and her clothes soaked through, so she would have to walk back inside naked or sodden, the material sticking to her skin, under the watchful eyes of a thousand people.

Sofya would always come back crying. His mother always came back quiet and stayed quiet for most of the day.

There was a place to wash babies. Gas rings were laid out on the ground with metal buckets of water resting on top of them. Another bucket of cold water would be placed on the ground beside each one, so the mothers could balance the temperature of the water and then scoop and pour it over the babies. Artyom saw one mother accidentally touch her child's foot on the metal rim of a hot bucket, burning it. The infant wailed, bellowing with such desperation that a crowd of people came outside to see what was wrong.

There was no information about his father. Not the first week. Not the first month.

People talked in the beginning about how they got here, what they were doing before the call to evacuation. They went through their whole routines: who said what, who did what. People speculated. Many thought it was the capitalists that had sabotaged the plant, infiltrated it somehow over a long period of time and caused this chaos. The capitalists were intimidated by the progress of Soviet energy, they were becoming desperate in their scheming. People didn't stray into wider subjects, though, they didn't talk about where they came from, what paths their lives had taken and – as Artyom came to notice – after the first week, they almost stopped talking altogether.

Nobody knew anything about what had happened to their loved ones. A great blanket of longing descended upon the building. There were guards stationed along the perimeter fence, no one could pass without bribing one of them. Some gave away all they had in the first few days and walked to the hospitals or the other shelters, but they couldn't find any information there either and were forced to return for the food and shelter offered to them, poorer than before, no chance of release until they were told they could go – if they would ever be told they could go.

Arguments broke out over floor space. Every centimetre was a precious commodity. Some people would try to adjust the makeshift walls of their allocation, and those who had been cheated would return and scream and tussle, and Artyom saw how petty people could become when desperate.

They had been there almost a month when Artyom's mother woke him in the middle of the night.

'Artyom,' she whispered.

He woke easily. He couldn't sleep soundly in this place, his body so confined, the constant shuffling noise, snores, sleepy mumbles, infants taking it in turns to wail their complaints.

'Yes?'

'There's something I need you to do.'

She pulled out a small package from the folds of her clothes, a piece of soft cloth, wrapped very tightly with some elastic cord. She unwound the cord and displayed three gold nuggets. Artyom couldn't see them very well in such weak light, so it was only when he touched them that he realized they were teeth.

He pulled his hand back, startled.

'Where did you get them?'

'It's not important.'

'It is important. Where did you get them?'

'I didn't steal them.'

'Well, they're not yours. You don't have any gold teeth.'

She was quiet; she let him realize it himself.

'They're Grandmama's.'

'Yes. I'm sorry. Plenty of people do it. Before she died, your grandmother made us promise we wouldn't bury her with them.'

Artyom was quiet for a few moments.

'Are you angry?' she asked.

'No. I just didn't know.'

'I'm sorry, Artyom.'

She didn't speak until she could see he was ready to continue.

'I need to find your father. Things are getting desperate. We can't stay here for ever.'

'OK.'

'These are the only things of value that we own. You'll

need one to bribe the guard. After that, only use them if you have to. I want you to find Maksim Vissarionovich, the man who brought us here. He'll be kind to us. See if he knows someone – a nurse, a Party official. Anyone.'

'Where will I find him?'

'Look for rubbish bins on the street. Ask any rubbish collectors you come across. If you still can't find him, go back to Lilya's building and wait for him at his lock-up.'

'OK. Do we know his last name?'

'No. I never asked.'

She shook her head as she said this, regretting her stupidity. She was close to him; Artyom could smell her sour breath. She took his face in her hands.

'You know not to use any of the gold unless you have to.'

'Yes.'

She kissed him on the forehead.

'Thank you, Artyushka. And remember to come back. If you went missing too, I couldn't bear it.'

'I should go now, shouldn't I? Maksim will be working soon.'

'Yes, you should.'

Artyom knew she was watching him as he walked softly to the door, stepping over limbs that spilled into the passageway.

At the gate, when he had given one of the pieces of gold to the guards, he asked them to point him in the direction of the city centre, but they just shrugged; they weren't from here.

So Artyom walked through the industrial wasteland, his first time alone in the city. He saw some crows gathered around a stray rubbish bag and kicked out at them, announcing his presence on the streets, and they exploded upwards, the group splintering as it gained height. He saw the smear of streetlights ahead and made his way in their direction, passing a textile factory and a car scrapyard. When he reached the main road he followed the flow of the traffic, reasoning that, at this time of the morning, they would be heading towards the city. He walked for an hour, the pavement narrowing, trees becoming more prominent, grass aisles in the middle of the road. He looked everywhere, drank it all in. There were old houses made of stone, with stone-roofed porches. The buildings here were solid, were made to last.

Artyom found himself touching everything. Now that he could see it in daylight, had time to reflect on it, the city was different in every sensory way. Even the space of the city was completely unlike the spaces he was used to, with the rectangles of sky between buildings. The sweeping streets. Statues and chiselled lintels. Gateposts. The lines in the road, the big, green lane where the officials drove. The kerbstones. The railings. All of this not alien, but odd, unlike anything he was used to.

His father was safe. He had to be. He was somewhere else in the city, confined in a different area. Looking for them, just as they were looking for him.

Eventually, he stopped at a crossroads and saw a street with full rubbish bins taking up half the pavement outside the houses. Artyom stopped a passer-by, a man with a long, grey coat, his top button dangling from a thread. He asked if the rubbish would be collected this morning, and the man opened his eyes wide, held his arm out and pivoted around, displaying the rubbish bins in answer, and walked on.

Artyom sat at a bus stop and waited. Every ten minutes or so a bus would pull up and the driver would open the door for him, then shake his head in irritation when Artyom waved him onwards. There were so many cars on the street: Moskviches, Volgas, Russo-balts, Vazes, Zaporozhets. He was in awe of the lines and colour of them, listening to the roar of their engines. All of these, having come alive from the pages of the manuals, there in actuality, speeding along the road in front of him. He approached some of the parked cars and ran his hand along their contours, but a woman in the row of houses opposite shouted at him, told him to mind his business.

If Iosif was here they'd probably find a way to pop the bonnet on some of them and slaver over the engines. Iosif was so much more adventurous than him. Artyom thinks he remembers Iosif saying he had an aunt in the city, so he's probably being well looked after. He's probably watching television at night and eating tinned peaches straight from the can. Although, maybe not. Things don't always work out the way you expect. After all, Artyom had an aunt in the city too, so Iosif could be saying the same about him.

He was hungry. In the shelter they'd be handing round breakfast by now. There were so many people there at this stage that there were no more queues; the militia came around delivering bags with packages of food for each meal, collecting the bags when everyone had eaten. Artyom hoped his mother would save something for him. But of course she would, she was his mother.

He waited for a while and then approached one of the bins and rummaged around. Nothing. He dug through a few more. Near the end of the street he found the carcass of a chicken, some tea leaves stuck to it, bits of newspaper, but nothing he couldn't pick off. He ran his fingers in the spaces between the legs and the body, scooped up slivers of white meat from between its ribs. Real meat. Now that he had a taste for it, he wanted to stuff the entire thing into his mouth, wanted to crunch on the bones until there was nothing left. He raised the carcass up and licked it, taking in some tea leaves but mostly enjoying the grease on his tongue.

'Hey. Get away from there.'

The rubbish collectors had rounded the corner. They hung from the truck in their bright-orange jackets, staring at him. One of them stepped down.

'What are you doing? Get away, you fucking rat.'

Artyom wiped the grease from his mouth with his sleeve.

'I'm sorry. I was waiting for you. I'm looking for Maksim Vissarionovich. He collects rubbish.'

'I think you're looking for fucking dysentery. That's what I think.'

Artyom didn't know what dysentery was.

'I need to speak to Maksim Vissarionovich. Do you know him?'

'No. And I don't care. Go and root through some other rubbish. Just do it in another area of town.'

The man was standing close to his face, all aggression. Artyom stepped out of his way and the men emptied the bins into the back of the truck and clattered them on the pavement. Artyom was fascinated. He'd never seen a vehicle like this one. It had an internal arm that crushed the rubbish down and drew it inside. He stood and watched as they passed. But they didn't go very far. The truck cut out and when they tried starting it again the engine just made a dull, straining sound. They popped the bonnet and rummaged around for five minutes with the same result. Artyom knew that sound. He stepped forward and approached the engine and grabbed the ignition coil with such assurance that the men let him carry on. He unbolted the coil, cleaned the contact points with his shirt, then replaced it back in its slot and tightened the bolts. He gave a thumbs-up to the driver, who turned over the ignition, and they listened to it moan and gurn until it spluttered into life.

The man who had spoken to him smiled wryly, calmer now.

'What's this guy's name again?'

'Maksim Vissarionovich. I don't know his last name. He lives near the bus station.'

'Anyone know him?' he asked his workmates.

Shakes of the head.

'OK. We'll find you someone who does.'

He indicated for Artyom to sit in the cab, and the rest of the men returned to their platforms and grabbed their respective handles. They drove through the streets, low-hanging branches scraping the windshield. The driver had a knob on the steering wheel which he used to drive the thing one-handed, grinding it around corners, driving so close to lamp posts and walls that Artyom was sure they were going to crash, until he flicked the wheel in the right direction and the truck spun around miraculously on its own axis.

They left the city and, after a few minutes, turned off into a narrow side road arched with trees. They stopped at a barrier, where the driver flashed a card to a man in the booth, and they edged down a slope and on to a concrete platform.

Gulls dropped down from the sky and skimmed over a vast synthetic territory, a seascape that was entirely comprised of things discarded. Bulbous plastic bags, strings of electrical cable and soggy cardboard were congealed into a single, amorphous mass. Bulldozers surfed the waves of slosh, surging uncertainly against the semi-solid waste. They looked as if they could tip over at any moment, but they climbed steadfastly, before plunging back once more into the expanse.

The man from the back of the truck walked forward to a tin shed twenty metres away. Artyom sat in silence in the cab, the driver barely looking at him – not out of spite or revulsion, Artyom sensed, he was just a man who didn't feel a need to make a connection, who was happy in his own thoughts. The man emerged from the shed and beckoned him with a wave and Artyom opened the cab door and the air slithered into his nostrils, leaving a filmy residue against the back of his throat. He had never smelled anything like it. He clasped his hand to his nose and breathed only into the cupped space of his palm. As he stepped out on to the ground, a grey, cloacal muck encased his shoes. It was a struggle even to walk in this place.

'I asked around. He's due back in a couple of minutes. You can wait here.'

'Thanks.'

'And you. Thanks for your help.'

They shook hands and the man climbed back on the truck. Artyom watched as it rounded one of the mounds and backed up against a low, concrete wall and spat out its chewed-up contents. The men stood around and shared a cigarette and talked amongst themselves, and when their truck was emptied they stood at their positions once more and drove up the laneway, back into the morning, into fresh air.

Artyom stood and watched, captivated, his hand still in front of his face, and took shallow breaths through his mouth. The graveyard of all that was once useful. It was all a kind of greyish brown, an anonymous sight. After a few minutes of looking, he was shocked to realize that there were some people moving through the rubbish, covered in this sludge barely distinguishable from their surroundings. They walked with sacks slung over their shoulders and picked things up and examined them, turning them over in their hands. What a way of life. Rising every morning to scavenge around this hollow, barren terrain. This was not a place he could ever have imagined; a place so man-made. He looked out at these people wading through filth, letting out a bleat of delight if they salvaged something they could sell, finding small traces of encouragement buried in all the desolation, their comrades running towards them to share in the excitement. And Artyom would return frequently to this moment, in the following weeks, when he watched sickness engulf his father, when blood seeped out through the pores of his father's skin, when he began to realize that he could never understand or predict the pathways that someone's life could take; that the will of a desperate person was stronger than anything he knew and that fate unspools in its own stubborn way, beyond influence or rationale.

Maksim arrived and greeted him, full of consideration, and fed him and took him back to the shelter, returning three days later, having located his father in one of the hospitals. Maksim waited at the gate while they washed as well as they could and dressed in the best clothes they had brought with them. As they got in the car, she looked at her children and said, 'Don't we look well?' and smiled. It had been a month since Artyom had seen his mother smile. He found the sight so reassuring, as comforting as a fire on a winter's afternoon.

At the front door of the hospital they used the last gold tooth to bribe their way into the building.

There was nobody else there. The place was wrapped in silence. The only sounds were the echoes of footsteps that rang through the corridors. It was disconcerting to see a public building so empty. A shrill silence, their ears attuned to the constant turmoil of the shelter. Sofya said, 'I think my ears are going to crack,' and Artyom knew what she meant.

Once the attendant had given assurances that he would take them through to Artyom's father, Maksim said his good-byes and wished them luck. He slipped some money into Artyom's mother's hand, but she refused to take it. They struggled for a few moments, grasping each other's wrists, and Maksim kept saying, 'Please,' even though he was the one leaving the money and, eventually, Artyom's mother relented. He left them his phone number. 'Please. You've no one to look after you. If you need help, I'll help,' and walked out the door. Each one of them called out their thanks, but he batted it away, kept his head down.

In the corridor on the third floor the attendant introduced them to the nurse. She took Artyom's mother aside and spoke to her quietly. As their conversation continued, Artyom watched his mother edge away from her, palms raised, as if she had just walked into the cage of a wild animal.

He heard the woman say, 'His skull is compromised.'

He heard the woman say, 'His central nervous system is compromised.'

Sofya heard it too.

Artyom asked Sofya, 'Compromised from what?'

Sofya wouldn't reply.

'Compromise'. Isn't that something you do when you can't agree? How can a skull be compromised?

They walked into the room, and everything was much better than Artyom expected it to be. His father was sitting on the bed, playing cards with men they knew: some of their neigh-bours – Yuri Polovinkin, Gennady Karbalevich, Eduard Demenev. It was surreal to see them all sitting here, as if they were at home, chatting after a meal, whiling away the hours before sleep.

Artyom's father looked up and saw them enter, and Artyom noticed his eyes flare, his pupils expand. He thought his father might drop the cards in his hand, his muscles going slack with surprise.

He turned to the other men.

'I'm in trouble now.'

The men laughed.

He embraced each of them, wrapping his arms around them, pressing their bodies into his. And even though the nurse advised against it, they didn't hesitate to touch him. How could they? And Artyom's mother didn't scold. But when they turned around and faced the other men, there was an odd force in the air, a wariness. They didn't volunteer to come forward, they just nodded. The men, for their part, stayed withdrawn.

Artyom's father was wearing pyjamas that were too small for him; they rode up his arms and legs, clung to his chest. It made him look like a small boy who had grown magically overnight.

In the sterilizing room, Grigory stands in front of the sink; surgical hat tied in a knot at the back of his head, goggles and thyroid collar on, and cleans under his nails with a plastic, disposable pick. He has long, deft fingers, disproportionate to his short palm. When he's satisfied, he takes the scrub to his hands, lather forming around his knuckles. Five, six operations a day and still he feels the absence of his wedding ring, nothing to place on the steel shelf in front of him; instead it lies abandoned, in the upper drawer of his bedside locker, back there in his city. He works the tap with his elbows and rinses his hands, seeing the skin emerge sleek from under the foam and backs into the operating room, holding his hands up, palms facing him, the nurse helping him to slip on the gown and gloves.

His team is already gathered around the bed. An infant, three weeks old, lies on the operating table, dwarfed under a surgical blanket.

Grigory looks at the tiny girl, her eyes peacefully closed, her neck hardly bigger than his wrist. A human life in its most vulnerable state: a shallow-breathing infant resting on a narrow ledge between the twin precipices of birth and death. An urge rises in him to touch the child in reassurance, let her feel the warm hand under his glove, but he looks away from the peaceful face, from the flickering eyelids, turns his concentration to her beating chest.

The child has a congenital heart disease, truncus arteriosus – rare everywhere but here – her aorta and coronary and pulmonary arteries all emerging from a single stalk. A complicated operation; one that will take hours. He'll have to separate the pulmonary arteries from the aortic trunk and patch any defects that emerge, then close two ventricular septal defects, holes in the walls between the two lower chambers of the heart. Lastly he will place a connection between the right ventricle and the pulmonary arteries.

They have a single cardiopulmonary bypass machine in the clinic – continuously in use due to the sheer numbers of surgeries they are required to perform – into which they will divert her blood.

He takes the scalpel and rotates the handle in his fingers, readying himself. He presses into and pierces the small chest, feeling the skin give way. He holds back the fragile ribs with a clamp, then inserts a thin tube into the femoral vein to withdraw blood from the body, passing it through the machine to be filtered, cooled, oxygenated and returned again by way of the artery. Through the magnifying lenses that sit on top of his goggles, he can see her quivering heart, light purple, carrying on in its dutiful rhythm. So tiny, half the size of his fist.

They work at a pace now, other hands contributing, entering and exiting his line of sight. Grigory hears no sound, not the bleep of the CBM nor the mutterings of his team, the hoovering of the suction of the vacuum pump that the junior registrar uses to keep the area clean. This is the stage when he functions only by vision and touch. These are the moments for which he is respected, for which all his silences, his distance, are forgiven by his subordinates. They too understand the demands of the work, many of them running on false energy, anything to get them through. Grigory has noticed an attendant or a nurse move swiftly the few times he's entered the storage room they use as a dispensary. He is beyond asking questions. Medical supplies are one of the few things they have in sufficient quantity and his theatre runs flawlessly. Everything else is outside of his concern.

If the team need to communicate with him they wave a finger in the periphery of his visual field and, on the few occasions they do this, he looks up, taking a brief moment to locate himself in his surroundings, sound streaming back in, a sensation that reminds him of emerging from the swimming pool. He stops only to drink from a straw that the nurse holds close, attuned to his signals, or to communicate with his staff, no more than a few fragmented sentences. He works steadily throughout, neither too confident nor overly tentative. He has to feel his way through, let his thoughts merely drift along the surface of his mind. Hours in this state of intensity.

Sweat trails down the ridge of his skewed spine. He hasn't

had a swim in six months and this is taking its toll, his scoliosis asserting its grip on him in the hours before bed, so that most nights he can be found lying twisted on the floor of his room, contorting his body at various angles, breathing deeply, waiting for his muscles to relent. Quick spasms dart their way up his back, but he ignores them. The pain can come later.

Nearing the end, he sews Gore-Tex patches into the septum holes, secreting them inside the lining of the heart, where they will expand as the organ grows, if it does grow.

When he is finished, he can put down his instruments and look at her again. Perhaps she will live, he thinks. Perhaps there is no radiation stealthily making its way through the long grass of her metabolism. These infants, to him, are flickering flames in the midst of so much darkness, so much extinguished hope. He wants to cup his hands around them, protect them from the pervading winds.

His junior closes up and Grigory walks into the afternoon sunlight, discarding his surgical wear into the appointed basket as he goes. Outside, he bends over, hands on his knees, and takes in great gulps of fresh air, free now of responsibility, however temporarily.

Day after day like this.

He can feel himself becoming less distinct, over time, becoming like a photograph left out in the sun, curling at the edges.

He lets out another breath.

'You're just out of surgery.' A woman's voice. A nurse he can't place.

'Yes,' he says. 'I'll be ready again in a few minutes.'

She puts a warm hand on his shoulder. Grigory wishes the heat would move down to his coccyx; it might provide

269

some relief. He opens his eyes, unfolds with difficulty. She isn't a nurse. It's a woman, her face lean, cheekbones that direct his glance towards her eyes. A stranger. He would like to make an effort, but he turns away, too tired to affect politeness.

'I wanted to thank you.'

He moves to the door. 'Don't mention it.'

'He loves that dog, it's given him a new lease of life.'

Grigory pauses.

'I thought it was the operation that left him weak, but he needed a companion. You understood this. I, his own mother, didn't.'

He turns back, his mind spooling through the previous weeks.

'Your son . . .' He clicks his fingers, trying to spark his memory.

'Artyom.'

'Of course, yes.'

'He's doing well?'

'Very well. He's coming back to himself again. The dog, I don't know what . . . it took away his anger.'

Her pupils wide and dark, soaking in the daylight.

'I'm glad.' Grigory hesitates. 'More than glad. But I didn't understand anything. The dog needed help. Artyom is a good helper.'

She nods, smiling to herself, then looks up. The man before her has a kind of frantic weariness to him, as though he is skimming across the surface of his days. She can tell he will lose momentum soon, plunge into deep waters. He runs a hand across his face and she senses that he too is aware of this.

'We all need a good helper,' she says.

Now a nurse arrives, stands at the doorway, looks at her

watch without speaking, reluctant to draw him back to the theatre.

'They need you again so soon?'

'I'm sorry.'

The woman takes his hand. The sensation so foreign to Grigory. He is the one whose job is to touch; prodding, pinching with his fingers. Her skin has the consistency of thick cream.

'You understand more than you think, Doctor. You already know that medicine isn't magic. Most of us still believe that everything can be healed with a swipe of your scalpel.'

He pats her hand and withdraws.

'It was good to meet you,' he says.

'Yes.'

The nurse holds the door for him and he walks inside, passes the viewing window for the theatre, another young life laid there in readiness.

An elk bolts into the depths of the wood, surging into the dark with a burst of rolling muscle. Artyom is shocked into stillness, then curious. He turns and follows steadily, carrying the kindling which he has tied in a sling behind his back. The prints of the animal sit clear and fresh on the snow. If he's lucky, he'll catch sight of it again when it pauses, calms its fears. He treads as quietly as possible, spreading his weight from heel to toe. The snow shallower as the trees pack closer. He hears a scream and freezes. His first instinct, a girl in trouble. Artyom drops the kindling to the ground and dips out from under the sling. He runs forward twenty steps and then sees the elk again, its head raised to the treetops, its vast antlers tilted downwards. A beautiful beast, pushing out this shrill noise, at odds with its bulk. A plaintive cry, a keening. Then it quietens, raises its head and disappears once more.

It took Artyom's father fourteen days to die.

His face was swollen and, when the shock of seeing him had faded and Artyom looked closer, he noticed that the glands under his father's ears were sticking out like small, round pebbles. When they came back the next day, these were the size of eggs. The day after that, he was alone. Each man had been placed in a separate room. They were banned from going into the corridor, talking to each other. So they communicated by a series of knocks. Dash-dot, dot-dot. Remembering the code from their military training.

Artyom, Sofya and his mother stayed in the nurses' quarters behind the hospital. On their first night in the hospital, the attendants tried to remove them from the common room where they were settling down to sleep. But they saw the steely determination in Artyom's mother's eyes. These people wouldn't be moved.

The nurses' apartment was a small room with a double bed, a gas ring for cooking, a fridge in the corner and a shower room. They were almost alone in this building too. Now all the nurses lived on the bottom floor; the rest had moved out.

A few days later there were no nurses at all; it was the militia that cleaned the bedpans, changed sheets, administered medicines. Artyom asked one of them where the nurses had gone and was told that they had refused to do the work. It was too dangerous.

How sick do you have to be to frighten a nurse?

Small, black lesions developed on his father's tongue. A

day later, black spots appeared all over his body, each the size of a five-kopeck coin.

After that, Artyom and Sofya weren't allowed into the hospital.

Artyom pieced together what had happened. His father told him some things. Yuri talked to him too. Sofya sometimes answered his questions. And, after his father died, his mother opened up a little. There was no longer any reason to protect him.

In Pripyat, when everyone was being evacuated, some officers gathered the men together, told them it was their duty to make their homes safe again. It was up to them to clear the damage. No one objected, glad of the opportunity to help.

Artyom's father was assigned to work on clearing the forests. The other men asked to join him. They drew attention to their experience of working together in the kolkhoz and managed to get official approval.

They lived in tents in the forest; Yuri said they felt like partisans during the war. Soon the forest turned red, all the leaves a bright shade of crimson. Yuri remembered Artyom's father picking up the red leaves on the forest floor, saying: 'Mother Nature is bleeding.' There were tiny holes in them, as though caterpillars had run amok. They were given dosimeters but threw them away.

'*Either we do the work, or we don't do the work, and we've decided to do the work.*'

This is what they said.

They chopped the trees. Cut them down with chainsaws. They sliced them into metre-and-a-half pieces and packed them in cellophane and buried them in the earth. At night they drank; they had been told vodka helped with the radiation. 'Vodka,' they laughed, 'helps with everything.'

The troops flew a flag over the reactor: two days after the accident they put it there as a symbol of pride, endurance. Five days later it hung ragged, eaten by the air. A day after that, a new flag, turning in the breeze. A week after that one, another new flag. Everyone tried to avoid looking at the flag. The flag was disconcerting.

They worked on.

One by one the chainsaws died. Nobody could understand why; they were in pristine condition, their mechanisms just wouldn't respond. They were all replaced. Each man worked with a new chainsaw. These died too. Eventually, they took axes to the tree trunks, and at night they needed to drink even more to dull the pain of their raw shoulders. 'Back-breaking work, chopping down tree after tree by hand,' this is what Yuri said, and Artyom didn't doubt it.

They shot animals they came across in the forest and roasted them over a spit and ate them. Supplies were readily available, but they grew tired of tinned food after the first week. Roasting an animal on a spit lends itself to conversation. After a few weeks someone noticed that he couldn't smell the meat roasting on the spit and the other men realized that they couldn't smell it either. Nobody slept well that night.

The forest turned orange and they said to each other, 'Maybe Mother Nature's blood is crusting over?'

One day they realized that the straw in their tents came from stacks near the reactor. They decided to clear out their tents, but after three nights sleeping on the bare ground, they brought it back in. Yuri said he made a joke, 'Better to die of radiation than pneumonia,' but nobody laughed. They stopped laughing after the first few weeks, after the chainsaws broke down again.

One night it rained and in the morning the water in the puddles was green and yellow, like mercury.

All around them, soldiers and men like themselves were burying everything. Gennady Karbalevich came up with a slogan: '*Fight the atom with a shovel.*' They said this to each other sometimes as encouragement. They said it ironically, bitterly, but also with defiance: let nature come and fight them; they each had an axe.

Artyom's father told him he thought about him all the time. There were sparrows everywhere, littered dead on the ground. You couldn't help standing on them, he said. They were covered in autumn leaves, even though it was still May. When he felt them underfoot he thought about that morning, out shooting. He prayed that Artyom was somewhere safe, somewhere clean, untouched by all this perversion of nature.

Artyom didn't get to see his father when the tumours metastasized, not within his body, but instead crawling to its surface, till they clasped his face, trailing his features like poison ivy. He didn't get to see him when he was producing a stool thirty times a day, comprised mainly of blood and mucus. When his skin started cracking on his arms and legs. When every evening his sheet would be covered in blood and Artyom's mother would give the soldiers' directions as to how to move him, and make sure her husband had fresh bedding for the night.

Artyom stayed with Sofya in the nurses' quarters and roamed the city for fresh food, which they paid for with Maksim's roubles and which they would bring back and make into soup, which their mother would take down when she came back to sleep for a few hours. She came back to sleep and to lie to her children; to pretend that their father wasn't in any pain, just resting.

At the end she couldn't lie any more, not when his tongue

fell out. Not when she'd hold a bedpan at the side of his bed to catch the blood which ran in rivulets from no particular place in his body. Not when he would cough and spit up pieces of his lungs, his liver, choking on his internal organs. She would never tell them that she'd look at him and see him crying out to her as though from the end of a long corridor. His eyes wailing their pain, like an infant when it can't express its need, can't make itself be understood. She couldn't lie and couldn't face her children, so she stayed there beside him, slept on the chair next to him, unable to touch him because it would bring too much pain. Her children brought the soup to the attendant at the reception desk, who would deliver it to a table at the entrance to the ward. They never asked to see their father. He belonged to their mother now.

In the clearing Artyom waits for the air to return to stillness, leaves vibrating from the thudding hooves. Around him, the bushes are dappled in red. Kalyna berries.

Those nights by the wireless, when the music had quietened and they watched shadows from the candlelight wrap around the plates and saucepans, his father would tell him stories. In one that they returned to often, the living and the dead were connected by bridges made from Kalyna wood. They crossed easily from one side to the other, doing this so readily that after some time they could no longer distinguish between the two realms.

Particles skimming through the air. Underneath what he sees and smells and hears. Snowflakes concealing their star-tipped patterns. Animals curled up under the ground seeing out the winter, their hearts beating with only the faintest of rhythms. His father is here: a shadow dancing, merged into the life around him. Inhabiting the cells of these things, just as radiation, displaced atoms, inhabited his own living cells, changing him.

He would listen to his father's tales, drinking his glass of milk, resting like a sick calf in his father's arms.

A slight buzz bores through the air. If you look across Red Square at this particular moment, you can see several people twist their heads in sync, turning their faces towards the noise. A small white plane edges its way under the clouds, emerging strange and determined. A ripple of awareness, people nudging each other at the sight, anticipation building as the sound gains clarity, closing in on them. The plane banks and sweeps its way towards St Basil's cathedral, looking like a fixed-winged gnat in contrast to the grandeur of the iconic, bulbous domes. Everyone gazes at the same point. Hands are raised, the scattered gathering pointing at the sight, following its direction, the plane travelling along the flight path of their fingers as if they are guiding it downward, the autonomy of the small craft abandoned to the will of the collective. The plane circles once more, lower now, the propeller hum dominating everything until it dips from sight. Those closest can hear the short screech of a landing and a rattle of wheels on the cobbles along Vasilevsky Spusk, the plane bouncing and jolting as it taxis along parallel to the Kremlin walls and emerges into the expanse of Red Square. The crowds stream towards it, waiting for the solid figure of Gorbachev to emerge, the premier descending from on high, landing just outside his office, but the plane contains only a lone pilot, a tall, skinny, dark-haired young man wearing sunglasses and a red aviator's suit.

They encircle him, curious. Tourists thrust notebooks

towards him, asking for an autograph. Others place bread into his hands and he chews it sidemouth and nonchalantly takes the pens and signs his name. Mathias Rust. Alighting from the heavens with a twenty-page plan to end the Cold War.

The bus stops in the Arbat, and Margarita, Vasily's wife, gets off and takes two steps and feels a hand on the small of her back. She turns, quickly, ready to strike, then stops, shocked.

'Come with me.'

Maria guides her through an alleyway crammed with street vendors selling nuts and dried fruit, and there's a smell of spices in the air, mixed together, indistinct, and they take several turns left and right, slipping through the crowd, and end up in the Mololodjosh Café on Gorky Ulitsa. It's a Saturday afternoon, which means there's a jazz band playing. They sit side by side in the back, in the dark.

'I'm sorry for all this,' Maria says. 'I called to your apartment this morning, but there was a white Volga parked outside with a good view of your window. I wasn't sure if you were aware.'

'Don't worry. I'm aware.' Margarita repeated the words, ruefully this time, letting her spite roll over the syllables, 'I'm aware.'

Maria waited for her to continue.

'I don't know why they've decided to pitch up on my doorstep. This is the worst of it. If there was something I could do or stop doing, it would be so much easier. Some kind of solution to this. But there isn't. I've gone weeks without sleep, thinking over the possibilities. I'm sick with fear. What would the girls do without me?'

The waiter brings water and a glass of cognac for each of them.

Maria says, 'I'm sorry. I don't want to make things worse. I felt I had no choice but to follow you. I haven't had any word. I just need to know something. The hospital won't help. There's no one else to turn to.'

'You look as tired as I do,' Margarita says. 'How long is it since you've heard from him?'

'I haven't. I only found out just over a week ago, from the doorman in his building. If I think of all that he's been through all this time. I didn't even get to say goodbye, not that a goodbye would have been any help.'

'I barely did myself – say goodbye – it happened so quickly. He was here, at home, then he wasn't. No warning of what it would be. I had no idea of the seriousness.'

'Did he?'

'Yes, although he didn't let on. But when I think back, the way he played with the kids, I could tell. Lifting them up, turning them upside down. Things he hadn't done since they were much smaller. A need to touch them. I should have known then. But we find ways, don't we, to deny what's in front of us.'

Maria nods. Margarita checks her watch.

'I can't stay too long. I came to town to get a break, leave it all behind for an hour. But now that I'm here, I feel I should be back there. I don't want them to wonder about me.'

'The girls?'

'No, the girls know where I am. I mean the watchers. I can't even tell how many of them – maybe just four, taking it in shifts. If I think about them filing their reports . . . How do you wake up in the morning and go to a job like that?'

'They enjoy it.'

'Of course they do. My Sasha waves at them on the way to school. They wave back, all smiles, shameless. I told her they're friends of Vasily's, told her they miss him as much as she does.

Told her they'd get upset if she ever talked about her father to them, they'd start to cry. I don't know if she believes me or if she's just putting on a show. I find such things hard to distinguish now. She never asks about her father. Maybe because she knows I won't tell her anything. But it's also possible she knows more than I do. Not a single question in the past two or three months. As if we're living in totally normal circumstances.'

'Have you talked to him?'

'If you can call it that. I can hardly recognize it's him. He's developed this mechanical way of speaking to me. I know he does this to let me know he's not keeping things from me on purpose, to remind me that they're listening, but it feels like having a conversation with the memory of your husband. It's only at the end, when we talk about my day, when he asks about the girls, says his goodbyes, it's only then his voice warms. It's only then I get a little of him down the line.'

'So you know nothing either?'

'Not anything more than we see on TV. "You don't need to worry," he says. "We're making a lot of progress here," he says. "The men are very committed," he says. So, I worry.'

'This is what we do.'

'This is what we do. You haven't been together for years, but of course you worry. How can you not?'

'Has he mentioned Grigory?'

'No. I've asked him, certainly. But whenever I ask, he says he has a meeting to go to. He obviously says this when there's something he can't discuss. I ask him why they're having meetings at night. Can they not plan their days a little better? He doesn't even laugh.'

Maria rakes her fingers across her forehead.

Margarita continues, 'Don't read too much into it – or maybe do, I don't know. He can't talk about anything, believe me. He can only tell me about such mundane things. If he could talk about it, at least then I'd feel I'm helping. A voice he can turn to.'

'He hears your voice. I'm sure it's helping more than you know.'

'At least they have each other, going through what they're going through.'

'We can't imagine.'

'You, maybe. You've been out there, seen the country. Me, I even forget what the Arbat looks like.' Margarita looks around. 'It must be six months since I've been down here. My own city.'

A trumpet player blasts out a solo and they wait for him to finish. Margarita puts her fingers in her ears, attracting looks of scorn. The piano temporarily takes over and the trumpeter twists the mouthpiece off his instrument, jabs the corner of his shirt in there, whirls it around, dumps spit out from the body of the thing, buying time. He waits again for his moment, like a schoolboy with his hand up, eager to show off his abilities. When he finishes there's a ripple of applause and Maria leans in close again.

'I've been to the hospital every day. They pass me from one desk to another. Nothing.'

'The hospital, please. Vasily hasn't been paid in months. They're refusing to look into it; apparently it's not their responsibility. I took Sasha into them, got her to pull up her shirt, show off her ribs. I thought I could guilt them into handing over something. But no, the woman didn't even flinch. Now they just direct me to the Ministry. So much paperwork. Pink and blue and yellow forms. Still no payment. I tell Vasily this when we speak; he says he's made calls, he's had senior people approach the Ministry. He says they're snowed under with administrative matters. There's a lot to deal with, he says.'

'Meanwhile . . .'

'Exactly. Meanwhile.'

A few couples get up to dance and the women watch them turn and sway.

Margarita speaks softly now, not taking her eyes off the floor. 'Vera had a headache the other night so I sent her to bed early. Maybe it's worry – who knows? I don't want to think about it. You remember Vera?'

'Of course.'

'Anyway, she sleeps through the night and in the morning she doesn't have time to do her homework. So I give her a note. She's a good girl, Vera, she doesn't want to get in trouble, already has her mind set on university, wants to wear a white coat like her father.'

A woman in grey rests her head on her husband's chest, closes her eyes, rubs her hand along the back of his shoulders as they move.

'She comes home shaking. I'm wondering if it's a fever, but there's no temperature. Finally I get it out of her. Two men stop her on the way back, ask for the note. How they even know she has one is beyond me.'

'Maybe she was reading it on the street.'

'This is what I asked her, but no. She's certain about it, and I don't doubt her. She's smart enough not to attract attention. But they stop her and they let her know they're around, tell her if there are any other notes they'd like to see them.'

'She's not so old.'

'And I have to ask myself.'

'That's frightening for a kid.'

'I have to ask myself: why, if Vasily is doing their work, are they watching, listening, denying his family a decent meal? I mean, is this what it means to be a good citizen? I mean, we're hardly a threat. I just don't understand why they're giving us all this attention.'

Margarita shakes her head, looks at her watch again.

Maria says, 'I have a little money saved – very little – but I want you to have it.'

'Of course I can't do this, you have your own struggles.'

'Grigory would want me to.'

'You have no responsibility towards us.'

'I do. We are responsible for each other now.'

Margarita holds the sides of her chair, closes her eyes.

'You coming out of nowhere. You don't know what this means.'

After a moment Maria stands and says, 'Please, it's nothing. This is for me. If I can't help Grigory, I can at least help you.'

Margarita rises too, takes her hand, kisses her cheek. 'Be careful.'

'I will. You too. I'll be in touch.'

'I'll try to send word, let Grigory know you're thinking of him.'

Maria doesn't know what to do with her hands. She places them to her face, to her forehead, then takes them away. Hearing her say his name.

'Thank you. I didn't want to ask. You have enough worries. Yes. Thank you.'

'Be careful. I mean it.'

'Yes. Of course, yes.'

They leave in separate directions and spend their return journeys looking around them, scrutinizing every face.

Yevgeni is coming back from rehearsal and he makes his way home through the yards. Everything here is at a loss, all of it clapped out or cracked or just plain ugly.

The carcasses of car seats, and a one-wheeled cart, and old speakers with their cone-shaped diaphragms dragged out and mattresses with their springs shot through, and plastic crates, and the only cars are burnt-out shells with no doors or wheels or fittings of any kind, just the pure black skeleton.

Everything of local lore happens here. Shooting games and card games, human fights and dog fights.

He doesn't quite walk through it, more around it, skirting the periphery, sidling alongside its hazards, because he likes to look; there is always something to look at. The days here are not made up of the usual things. No homework or dinner or laundry or shoe polishing or pictures of Lenin. Different rules apply here. You can spit on the pavement, for one. You can put your hand down your pants, for another. There are always guys talking in groups with their belts slung low and a hand down their front, guys with scars and shaved heads. You walk in a slow drawl here, you drag your feet, scuff your sole off the concrete. Yevgeni doesn't do this. He's a kid. He doesn't have the requisite experience to carry it off. Some things he isn't so clever about, but this is something he knows.

If you look hard and are lucky, there's the possibility of seeing sex in progress, the actual act. Two kids from his class once saw a couple doing it against the wall, trousers around their ankles. Yevgeni couldn't understand why they didn't just take their pants off, but this was another element of the great secret that everybody talked about but no one really understood. But the validity of these claims is not in doubt, because everybody who has passed through – and all those who claim to have passed through – have seen the shrivelled-up condoms lying in the afternoon light, spent balloons, which, if you looked hard enough, or went close enough, had clear jism weighing down their ends, and careful if you inspect one of these with another kid, because the custom is to pick it up and slug the other guy over the face, and there are stories, too, of kids running home with matted hair. And the joke is that you'd never go bald. And the prospect of seeing the act in action, seeing a man and a woman enacting the thing, intrigues Yevgeni, intrigues him and disturbs him in equal measure, because this place has the lure of these kinds of possibilities, but he also knows that if he actually witnessed something like that he'd run home terrified.

He hasn't come here to see sex. He hasn't even really come here to see anything. He just wants to be on his own, out of the reach of neighbours and his mother's spies. He wants to be somewhere where nobody is watching.

The recital is a month away now. He's been asked to play Prokofiev's 'Tarantella' from *Music for Children*. A folk dance. A kiddie tune. How cute.

The evening has been explained to him. Yakov Sidorenko will play Prokofiev's first three piano sonatas. Then Yevgeni follows with the 'Tarantella'. The 'Tarentella' is for spoilt brats whose parents trot them out when they have guests over. Look how well my Leonid or Yasha plays. He's said this to his aunt Maria, but she told him he has no choice. Her boss has decided, and that's what he needs to do. Yevgeni could tell she felt bad about it, though. Her voice drops off at the end of her sentences when she's feeling guilty.

Yakov Sidorenko won't respect him if he just plays some kiddie tune. Yakov Sidorenko knows music. Yevgeni went last year with Maria to see him play a Liszt sonata in the Tchaikovsky Hall. Sidorenko tiptoed through the notes, then he leaned back and played as if he were just hanging on, as if the music were a train that would come off its tracks at any moment, until, at the end, he crushed the keyboard, the music curled up into a corner, took its last breaths and died all around them.

And they want him to play a kiddie tune in front of this man.

There are tables stacked on tables, great pyramids of them, and trolleys with wheels hanging in the air which turn merrily to a gust of wind. There's grass coming up through the concrete, patches of it all around, and there's a basketball hoop nailed to a wall through which many things are thrown but never a basketball; bottles and newspaper, cans and rocks, everyone at some point needing to test themselves against the challenge of the circle.

Yevgeni walks and looks and doesn't stop and tries not to look like he's looking.

A group of guys in fake leather jackets roast potatoes over a fire in an oil drum. There's always an oil-drum fire going. Some of the older kids from school are there, the ones who don't go to class but just walk in laps around the playground, or who smoke in the toilets. There's one guy, Iakov, who plays in a rock band, so it is said, and he must be sixteen or seventeen, wise to so many things that Yevgeni can't articulate or even imagine.

The barrel has burn holes in the side which set free irregular bursts of sparks, but these never cause the guys to flinch. Even when a spark catches their jacket they just nonchalantly sweep it away with an open hand.

Iakov raises his head and spots Yevgeni, who has paused, staring at them, and Iakov slaps his friend on the arm and waves Yevgeni towards them, and Yevgeni puts his head down and keeps walking, even though they've probably seen him – of course they've seen him – but maybe there's a chance that they'll let it pass. Actually entering into the centre of things is not what he intended. He hears a whistle, shrill and piercing, which echoes around the buildings. There's no way of ignoring it, a whistle means that you've been noticed, and don't even think about running. He can whistle through the gap in his front teeth, a reedy sound, but this one is like the blast of a militia siren, two fingers wedged under the tongue. How they do it is beyond him. All those hours running arpeggios up and down the keyboard and still he can't make the one sound that really matters. Get Mr Leibniz to teach him this instead.

He looks up towards Iakov and looks behind him and points to himself, *You're calling me?*, a dumb cover, and Yevgeni knows it and Iakov knows it, but he has to do something; he couldn't just be open about the fact that he'd brazenly ignored him.

The only way to get through this is to show abject deference.

Iakov waves him over again and they all turn to look, everyone giving a skulking look, a look that growls, and he runs towards them, his arms pumping, constricted by the straps of his schoolbag so that he can only really move his forearms up and down, which he knows makes him look ridiculous but better that than keep them waiting.

Iakov throws an arm around his shoulder and bends him forwards, rubbing his knuckles off Yevgeni's head.

'This is the kid.'

'Which kid?'

He takes his arm from around Yevgeni's head and stands him up, displaying him. Yevgeni's face is by now the colour of the fire, a result of the run and the embarrassment and the jostling, all tinged with the element of dread.

'The gym kid.'

'Gym kid? What gym kid? He does cartwheels on top of moving buses?'

'Little fucking tomato muscles. Big fucking deal. He's got superpowers or what?'

'Hey kid, show us a handstand on this barrel.'

A quick wave of stunted laughter.

The guys are all older than Iakov. Even Yevgeni can see that Iakov is struggling in their company. They have bicycle spokes shoved into their potatoes and they hold on to the end of the rod and slowly turn the potatoes over the flame, taking them off every now and again for inspection or to blow off any embers that look as if they have potential. Yevgeni can smell burnt oil and metal and rubber or whatever they are using for fuel, and a faint tint of crispy potato skin dancing over the stench.

'How many times do I need to tell you this story? Hanging on to the gym rope, his cock dangling in the wind, and Sukhanov down below with that crazy worm vein on the side of his head practically exploding he was so fucking mad.'

Illumination all round, rods going vertical so they can turn and get a look at him.

'Hey, you're the kid.'

A few cuffs around the head, loose-wristed though, friendly.

'That Sukhanov used to make me sweat out the contents of my ball sack.'

'Sukhanov would make his own mother bleed.'

'Up there for three hours, I hear,' Iakov says.

Yevgeni knows he can't have been up there for more than five minutes, but he lets the story develop its own pathways, lets them stretch it whatever way they want: it's their story now, not his. He looks down and smiles. You don't smile in front of them. Be respectful. Know your place. You're only a hero so long as you don't know it.

'Hey kid, this one's done. Take it.'

They flick him a potato, a short backhanded whip that makes it twirl through the air towards him. Yevgeni palms it and then bats it between hands, tapping and blowing, way too hot to hold.

Iakov gives Yevgeni a wink and a sideways nod: show's over, time to go home.

Yevgeni walks off, still blowing the potato, scuffing his soles off the concrete, because he's done good, kept his mouth shut, stuck one to the man.

'Fucking Sukhanov. Let him come round here, I'll show him a fucking headstand.'

Pavel calls and invites her to a party, and Maria finds herself standing in an old bakery, with iron window frames divided into squares of frosted glass and the night outside coming through in a lustrous wash. Above her, on shelves and ledges, dozens of candles sit on cracked dishes, flames wavering, shadows running up the walls, sculpting the darkness of the high wooden roof.

She is one of the early ones and she curses herself for looking too eager, and she's borrowed a dress from Alina – nothing striking, a plain black cotton dress with a dark felt shawl – but she looks as if she was born in another century from the people milling around the room, in their torn jeans and denim jackets, and the click of her heels pierces the conversations and she is nervous of slipping on the tiled floor. The feeling dissolves eventually as others arrive, and after some staggered conversation and a barrage of compliments she relaxes. She is who she is, and not being dressed like everyone else is not exactly a situation she is unused to.

One of the old bread ovens still works, and they've turned

it on and left the door open to heat the space and everyone gathers on the other side of the room to avoid the blast of arid air, and they press close and talk easily, shedding layers of reserve, the conversation becoming less sporadic, words flowing easily, stories and darting wit and a studious consideration in many faces.

Everyone talks about the pilot. The whole city is talking about the pilot.

The facts are consistent. He's nineteen. He's a West German. He was wearing a red flight suit. This is what made the news. This one had to make the news – half the city saw him land. The West German government has already appealed for clemency.

They stand and talk. The talk is that the air defence command were afraid to take him out of the sky: three years ago they shot down a Korean civilian airliner that had drifted into Soviet airspace. They thought it was a spy plane. An international embarrassment of incredible magnitude.

So, the talk is that no one was prepared to give the order.

A few in the room are saying he's a genuine emissary, sent from the West, a modern-day Messiah. Already they are being mocked.

The official line was that the Moscow radar was down due to routine maintenance work.

Maria wonders where the hell Pavel is. She talks to a tall, slim guy in a black sweater with holes where the shoulders should be. He's a botanist, mid-twenties, with deep-set eyes, and he talks without expecting a response, and she sips her vodka, half interested, and tries not to look at the door.

'We took him to be a weather balloon.'

Some people in a circle in the corner are doing impressions of the generals readying their excuses for Gorbachev.

'There was impenetrable, low-hanging cloud.'

Each one elicits a round of laughter, and Maria smiles wryly. Their intonation is pitch perfect: they slur their words, speaking like Neanderthals, and a couple of them take on the persona of gorillas, chewing their knuckles, wrists bent, scratching themselves, elbows at unlikely angles.

'His flight pattern replicated low-flying geese.'

The laughter builds with each enactment.

There's a box in the basement of their apartment block, stacked together with Alina's husband's belongings. Letters, photographs, a restaurant bill, cinema stubs: all the detritus of her marriage that she couldn't bring herself to throw away. It's too difficult, too obscure, to think of Grigory out there; she has no reference points, no landscape to imagine. And she hasn't told Alina what she knows. Her sister would respond with practicalities, tell her glibly that she's loading herself with unnecessary worries, try to reassure her with all those bullshit news reports. So, instead of dwelling on the possibilities, she thinks of the box instead, fills it with all the unspoken words which they've yet to exchange.

A man wearing a dark cap arrives to ironic cheers, and he carries with him a large bag. Some of the group huddle around him and help him unpack, and they join metal pieces together until Maria realizes it's a movie projector that he's been carrying, and he displays the tin can containing the reel to everyone as if it were a bottle of fine wine, and there's a hushed murmur of approval and Maria is annoyed that Pavel never mentioned that a film would be the focal point of the evening, and where the hell is he? An hour late is too much, even for him.

The movie is *Solaris* by Tarkovsky. They sit on whatever is available and lean against the far wall, and the botanist has managed to manoeuvre himself beside her, but he's timid enough to keep his hands to himself and Maria isn't anticipating any problems. They have to aim the image over the ovens and because of this the picture is elongated as if the figures in the film are in a hall of distorting mirrors. Maria kind of likes this element, the way the mouths and noses stretch out in close-ups, which makes her consider what an odd thing the human face is in its configuration, how strange in its regularity, all the billions resembling each other.

They stop the reel, and there is some mumbling and fiddling with the projector and the man in the dark cap announces that his speakers are blown so there won't be any accompanying sound, and there are boos and hisses amongst the crowd, who are getting into the crowd spirit, but Maria can tell nobody really cares, they've all probably seen it anyway and know the plot, and the lack of sound somehow enhances the stretched-out picture, makes it all the more curious, and the heat is still blasting from the oven and the industrial taint of the noise it makes is oddly appropriate to the images. They watch people speaking with no sound and Maria finds herself considering the tongue action and lip movements, and it can't be denied that it provides a faintly erotic twist.

Scenes pass and nobody moves, everyone as entranced by the spectacle as she is. Maria looks around at the group, bundled together under the blue light that flares and deepens as the camera changes its viewpoint. There doesn't seem to be that many of them, now that she can see everyone gathered together, a small crew of drifting souls, all reaching to gain purchase on something solid and worthwhile, and the thought strikes her that if a fire consumed the building and they were all trapped inside, would anyone actually notice? Everyone here claiming they were in fact somewhere else.

The film as she remembered it is an intense psychological

drama set in a space station, but viewing it here elicits ripples of laughter throughout its small audience. The flimsy and narrow spaceship tunnels, the claustrophobia and intense desire for privacy, the reassuring fantasies the characters cling to, the great, looming, all-controlling planet outside, all so close to their own experience that they have no option but to titter in recognition. Take the sound away and political allegory becomes satire.

Maria allows herself to be swept along by the motion and rhythm of the camera. She's never done this before, too distracted by the narrative, but now she pays attention to the cutting pattern, the length of a shot, and she looks at the outside of the frame, rejecting where the director wants you to look, seeing instead a blurry stair rail or desk lamp; the smudged, unfocused items on the periphery that hold their own quiet captivations. Watching it is like reading a child's picture book: no words to pay attention to, just the language of images.

They take a break at the end of the first reel and people spill into the corridor, smoking and talking, and there's a queue for the toilet and Maria sees Pavel hovering around the door.

'You look lovely.'

'Thanks. You look late.'

'I know, I'm sorry.'

Pavel holds up a bottle he's brought and pours a swig into Maria's glass, locates one for himself and blows the dust out of it. He pours and puts the cap back on and lays the bottle on the floor, clamping it between his feet, and they clink glasses and sip and Pavel looks around the room and Maria looks into her glass, swirling the liquid around.

'How long is it since we've done this?' he asks.

'Done what?'

'Shared a drink.'

Maria pauses, thrown slightly off kilter.

'I don't know. Maybe five years?'

She could have come to him. When the trouble started with the newspaper. Pavel would have given advice. She could trust him. Why didn't she lay more faith in others? Pride maybe, she thinks. She doesn't like to show her weaknesses. Pavel has always been loyal to her, even if they let a long time pass without seeing each other. She didn't ask him to dig out a teaching role for her; he was aware of her situation and just called her up one day. At first she wondered if his kindness had a motive to it, if he was perhaps trying to rekindle things, but no, there's never been an underlying edge to their conversations.

She draws him into a corner.

'What do you know about Chernobyl?'

'Why?'

'It's begun to interest me. What have you heard?'

'Probably the same as you. Of course, I don't directly know anyone who has been there. It's all hearsay. But, yes, there's been talk.'

'Such as?'

'I don't know. Wild tales, odd tales. The animals have been affected, rabid wolves are populating the forests, two-headed calves being born in the local farms. Fairy-tale stuff.'

'So you don't think there's any truth in them?'

'I really don't know. A West German kid lands a plane in Red Square – who would have believed that one if there weren't so many around to see it?'

'Anything else?'

'A colleague of mine, his cousin works as a night porter in one of the hospitals in Kiev. They've been bringing the clean-up workers there. There are sections of the hospital that even the doctors refuse to enter.'

'And? A porter has more than one story.'

'Well, he talked about a girl in Belarus who was brushing her hair. Eleven years old with beautiful, long pigtails, and she's preparing for bed, running a wide brush through her hair, holding it with one hand and brushing with the other, and the whole handful just dislodges from her head. She's bald within thirty seconds. This is what they're saying.'

Pavel raises his eyebrows in conclusion, takes another drink.

'But if you ask me, a porter is a job with plenty of gossip time.'

Maria transfers her glass to her other hand.

'Grigory's there.'

Pavel's eyes widen.

'Are you sure?'

'Yes.'

'How do you know?'

'I called on him after we met at Lenin Hills. I hadn't seen him in months. He was gone.'

'Have you talked to him?'

'No. I can't find out where he is. I've spoken to anyone who might know. Nothing.'

She says this and her face buckles.

Pavel draws her to his shoulder. She stays there, forehead pressed against his collarbone. Breathing deeply.

'I'm sorry,' he says. 'I'll ask around, I have some medical friends who have sway in the Ministry of Health. I'll get them to find some details.'

Maria steps back. Nothing to wipe her eyes with, so she uses her hands.

'Be careful about it. I don't want anyone to draw attention to him.'

'OK. I will.'

The crowd clusters in again and the second reel of the

film is loaded and plays, but Maria can't pay attention any more. Her eyes stray from the screen. Instead she looks at the beam coming from the projector, dust swirling through it, the past floating everywhere.

When the film finishes, people stand and stretch, unrolling their vertebrae, cigarettes still dangling from their lips. Maria's eyes itch from the smoke.

Pavel takes her elbow.

'There's someone I want you to meet. If you're up to it?'

She nods.

They enter a room further down the corridor. This one is filled with portable steel racks, about two metres high, presumably the cooling room for the baked bread.

A man in his early forties is standing alone, inspecting the employee notices, still pinned to the walls.

He turns. His clothes are well-cut, hair swept back from his forehead, an impressive bearing, a firm handshake.

'Danil is a lawyer who looks for honest ways of practising the law. If a writer needs to arrange an exit visa or begin the rehabilitation process to get his name cleared, Danil is the one we turn to for advice.'

'I see.'

Danil has assured, intelligent eyes.

'I'm presuming you're not here for the film, Danil.'

'No, I'm not.'

He draws a flyer from his pocket, a small white rectangle of paper, clumsy block print.

Maria reads it. It's a strike-appeal leaflet for the plant Maria works in, requesting that workers meet at the main gates in ten days' time just before the morning shift begins. They intend to march through the factory and on to the main road, which they'll follow all the way into the city.

Maria has seen hundreds of these already. They've been

leaving them on trams and trains on the way into the plant. Workers pass them around on their walk home. Nestor, in particular, is very excited. He's expecting that at the very least the factory board will appoint a new set of union officials. He claims they may even reinstate Zinaida Volkova. Maria has stopped arguing with him.

'What do you think?' Danil asks.

Maria looks at Pavel, asking if she can trust this man. Pavel nods.

'If they want to strike, then let them,' she says.

'Is there much support among the workers?'

'Yes. I think so. People seem enthusiastic about it.'

'But you aren't.'

'No.'

'Because you think it's futile.'

She answers reluctantly. 'Yes.'

'You think it's futile because you have background knowledge. You've studied the developments in Poland. You know that the strikes there were toothless until Solidarity came up with a new tactic.'

Maria stays silent.

This was true. Maria had a source in Poland who reported developments to her of a strike in the shipyards of Gdansk six years ago. A few hundred workers entrenched themselves inside a factory. They held the machinery hostage and the factory chairman could no longer bring in unemployed workers. It was a much different prospect for the militia, they couldn't just chop down the strikers on the streets. To clear them from the factory would need a full-blooded military operation, and the chairman didn't have the stomach for that. It had the added advantage of holding their morale together, reminding each other that they had a claim on their own workplace.

The tactic spread like wildfire. Most of the other factories in the region did the same thing within a day. The authorities cut the phone lines so word wouldn't spread, but of course it did. Within a day or two, half the country knew what was going on. But not here. The Russian press didn't cover it. Maria wrote some samizdat articles, tried to get the word out any way she could, but, in retrospect, the conditions probably weren't right for people to listen. Brezhnev was still in power and he commanded a vast amount of authority. People lived in too much fear to contemplate such actions.

Maria still stays silent.

'I know about the recital at the end of the month. It would be quite a statement of intent to keep a high-ranking member of the ministry from leaving the building. That's not even taking Yakov Sidorenko into account. Holding a world-renowned pianist would draw immense international interest. It has the potential to be a very significant moment.'

Maria doesn't respond; she remains very calm. Eventually, she says, 'I don't know what you're talking about.'

Again, Danil nods his head.

'I understand. Go away and check out my credentials with whoever you need to talk to. Once you find out I can be trusted, have a think about it. This is an incredible opportunity. Pavel has told me about your leadership qualities. But I won't put the boy in that situation without your permission. I will leave that decision up to you. All I ask is that you decide soon.'

Maria shakes his hand and leaves. Pavel stands to follow her, but she stops him. She wants to be alone.

Alina stands abreast of the ironing board, taking shirts from the basket, shaking them out, using an old bottle of window-cleaner to spray water on the particularly creased areas.

She's listening to the radio. It's a documentary on the flora and fauna of the Arkhangelsk Oblast. It's the only thing on besides music and politics, and she's had enough of both of those for the moment. The rural accents are a pleasant change, she finds she likes hearing the background noises, birds and wind. The sense of space they carry somehow expanding the dimensions of her home.

It's a lovely evening, despite the cold. The sun spreads its colour over the canvas of the city, the white and grey walls soak in its warm hues, and she shakes out the shirts and hangs them on the backs of her kitchen chairs and the traffic weaves reassuringly below, cars and buses criss-crossing at a constant pace, and she feels contented, in her own way. Maybe it's the gentle sway of the evening, but she can't deny that something seems to be coming to an end. The forces that have pushed against her for so long are beginning to relent.

The iron has a compartment for water, but the nozzle has rusted and it sprays a russet-coloured residue on to the material, so she's taken to using the plastic bottle. She needs a new iron, but this is not something to think about, not right now, not when they let her off from work early, told her to take an evening for herself, to go home and relax – not that this is a possibility. How little they know about her.

She irons and listens and follows the progress of the evening light smoothing itself slowly across the room. This, she supposes, is her own rehearsal of sorts. Soon the apartment will be empty. Not for a couple of years yet, but it's coming. Zhenya, when he's old enough, will have a live-in scholarship. Maria will find a man or will be able to put aside enough to bribe someone for a place of her own. Maria will always be OK. People are drawn to her. She has that gift.

Alina thinks it won't be too much of a shock when it comes. It will take adjustment, but it's not as if the place was filled with a bustling family, the neighbours' kids crashing through the door, chasing each other around the table. Maria is gone all the time, anyway, especially in the past few weeks – often to teach, often she doesn't say – and Zhenya, of course, is practising.

She spreads out the collar and irons the back and then the front, pressing down hard on the corners.

A recital with Yakov Sidorenko.

She had to sit down when Maria told her. Zhenya's talent has never worried her – his temperament certainly, but never his talent. What really concerned her was the opportunity. It's all very well being a genius, but people need to realize it too. *People like us don't get those opportunities*, she's often told herself and this has always been her secret dread, that she wouldn't be wealthy enough or connected enough to lay out a real opportunity for her child. That in twenty years he'd be working at some menial job and spend his cigarette breaks thinking of what he could have been and resenting her, what she couldn't provide.

And so, even before the event, she can claim a certain degree of parental accomplishment. She has brought him to the cusp of achievement. She is the one who found him a mentor, paid for his lessons, demanded diligence. If the worst should happen, if the boy crumbles under the pressure, or they've overestimated his promise, well, such regrets are a burden she won't have to bear alone. No one can point a finger at her, tell her she didn't love enough, encourage enough, provide enough.

Shirts of beautiful light cotton, cross-stitched, double cuffs, sharp collars. People in their own building, living the same lives as they are. She would like to ask them some day where they get the money for such things, but that would probably mean they'd get their shirts laundered somewhere else, and it's not as if she doesn't need the business. Money is still, as she so often says, life and death.

The programme is comparing the feeding habits of rose-finches to rufous-tailed robins. They tweet freely in the background, uninterrupted for long stretches, and it's not hard to think they could be sitting just outside on her balcony, talking their talk. When Zhenya goes to the Conservatory, things will open up for her; she may finally have some time for herself. The possibility unnerves her a little. She has no idea what her interests are, no idea what she'd do besides work. Perhaps she'll get Maria to recommend a few books for her, expose herself to other lives. She'd like to make an effort to see more wildlife, to go and stand on the top of a mountain, sleep in a tent, turn her soon-to-be solitary life to her advantage. She's been to the park, what, once a year, since Kirill died? This is a disgrace, obviously, but parks are for those who can afford the time.

She's never had money, even when she was married. Kirill never had the kind of sly intellect that she sees in some of the men who come to the laundry, the casually indifferent way in which they sign their names on the return slip, slide over their roubles, the way they exude assurance, how apparent it is that they flow through life unobstructed by petty concerns.

Kirill was a different type of man, possessing a more temporary kind of effectiveness, a blunt simplicity in how he dealt with things, with people, never backing down, always ready to pounce on weakness, and of course this nature of his provided a shelter for her younger self. Beside him she was no longer the put-upon, the victim. Such a contrast to her father: his enclosed ways, his secrecies, the weight they all carried around with them, Maria too, wary of how people saw them – which was, of course, the point. There was also an attraction for her – this can't be denied – in the threat he posed to other men, their hesitancy in his presence, how they could sense the force of his will. On the bus, all it needed was a stare from Kirill and other men would rise, offer their seats, stumbling out of her way, embarrassed, almost hypnotized, and she would feel a surge of power too, by association, by osmosis. This was a man who could take anything he wanted, including her, who was always ready to sweep aside anything in his way.

But her older self knows that such a nature is death to a marriage. A man who can think only of the immediate, whose range of needs is essentially the same as a dog's – his fixation with dinner, those endlessly repetitive questions, not to mention his sniffing around other women – such stupidity on her part. Power is not about dominance. She really only realized it when she gave birth. Holding that helpless child in her arms. Strength is not as straightforward as she had thought. Of course, he wasn't there to witness it, to stand by her bedside, he was off on a weekend hunt, his pregnant wife cooking her own dinners, barely able to move. Her giving birth while he killed something. A telling symmetry there, now that she can look at it afresh. And see what she produced. Yes, Zhenya shares his extraordinary stubbornness, but otherwise is unlike him in every possible way. They would have hated each other. Maybe not yet, but five years from now, without a doubt.

Yet Maria never judged, never criticized her in retrospect. For that she is grateful. Had it been the other way around, she knows she wouldn't have been so lenient.

When Alina received word that her husband had been killed, there were no tears: a vague sadness, yes, but no more than that. By then she hadn't seen him in eighteen months. And she wasn't even surprised. Of course his macho vanity would get him killed. Of course showing his comrades how courageous he was would be more important than coming back to his wife and child. It's easy to be courageous in a war. See what it's like to work a seventy-hour week, see what kind of self-sacrifice that takes.

Flatten the sleeve out from the seams. Run the iron forward and back.

She doesn't miss him, but she often misses the idea of him. Feels the absence of someone to fill that role. Someone to talk to Zhenya in the way that men do, that understanding they have. She's a poor replacement, despite all her efforts.

Someone to fill that role for her too. A man to hand over a small stack of notes, let her do what she wants with them. Play money. He used to do this, on occasion, if he was feeling magnanimous. 'Go and play,' he'd tell her. It wasn't much, but the change was so satisfying: money being freed of necessity, becoming a thing of pleasure. She'd come home with a slightly damaged housecoat, or a hat that just needed a little stitching, or a pair of silky-smooth tights, and feel as fresh as a sixteen-year-old, and Kirill would smile that possessive grin of his that she couldn't resist and say, 'I should give you this present more often.' Such are the small things that linger.

Finish with the cuffs.

She hangs the pressed shirts on the top of the door, the tips on the metal hangers digging into the wood. Even though she's long since tired of ironing, she still finds pleasure in the smell, a richly satisfying odour, as comforting on the nostrils as baked bread.

She and Maria make two salaries, and she has this laundry money on the side, and Maria contributes with her teaching money, and still it's not enough. It's not as if they gamble it all away, or drink it all, or buy expensive creams and perfumes. They barely have enough to clothe and feed themselves. Nearly half their food they buy under the counter, because they have to; otherwise, they'd starve. She should open a shop, provide a service people really need, become a butcher.

Maria's salary helps. The salary, if she's honest, surprises her. Alina never thought her little sister would be able to stay with a dull job. She always lacked that kind of consistency. Things have always come so easy for her. Yes, her looks play a part, but she has a way, a kind of grace. Barriers open for Maria in a way that they don't for her. Even now. Look at the teaching thing, dropping out of the blue. People would kill for that kind of work. It's why she can be so fucking righteous about their father. She doesn't know what it's like to have to weigh up the options that are available. Maria has always had another way out. People, their father included, don't compromise because they want to, they just run out of choices. What was he to do? Tell them no? Tell the KGB he considered them to be morally flawed? Please. The man had a family. Have a child, then she'll understand.

Alina irons a shirt with yellowed stains at the armpits. She's become used to these sights, she's seen far worse. Don't even get her started on underwear.

But yes, Maria's recent consistency is impressive, and she's wonderful with Zhenya and she's her sister. Maria has helped bring them to this point, Zhenya's future laid out in front of him. And Alina can take a satisfaction in knowing that all her struggles have, in the end, been worthwhile. She has a son and a sister, and the marriage at least brought them the apartment. This she regards as Kirill's legacy, not Zhenya; the boy is all hers – laying him in a laundry basket for the first two years of his life, sleeping in the same bed as him all those years when she couldn't afford an extra mattress, an abundance of reasons for her to lay full claim on the child – but his military service made their home possible. Without it, she can't begin to imagine what they'd do.

A key rattles in the door.

She puts down the iron. Her arm hairs riffle with suspicion, a mother's instinct. It's Yevgeni. She hears him hanging up his jacket, the rasp of synthetic material, and this confirms it: Maria wears a good woollen coat that Grigory bought her years ago. She puts down the water squirter and takes a breath. She puts her hand on top of the iron. There might be a rational explanation for this.

He freezes at the open door, no idea she'd be here. He steps aside, a frantic rustle. Something different about him; she can't place it. She's left the ironing board, pacing towards the door, and he passes again, down the corridor to his bedroom. It strikes her then: only socks on his feet. He came in wearing a pair of running shoes, expensive, from the West.

'Zhenya!'

He makes a burst for his room; she follows, gaining; the boy disappears inside, slams his door. All of this taking maybe half a second.

'Zhenya!'

She works the handle. Locked, obviously. She's been meaning to take the bolt out, he's getting to that age.

She bangs her fist against it.

'Open this door at once. Why aren't you at rehearsal? I have a right to know.'

'I didn't go.'

If Kirill were here, as he should be, being a father, he'd break the door down. Another reason not to be a hero. She thinks about doing the same. It's a flimsy door, it wouldn't be difficult. But there's something unsightly about a woman putting her shoulder to a door, even if it is her own son's, even if he deserves it. She knows it would lessen her authority, in a way she couldn't explain.

She paces back up the corridor. Reaches up to the shelf over the coats for the running shoes, takes them down. Light blue. Soft on the insides, lightweight, well stitched, a logo on the sides. She carries the evidence back to his door.

'I'm holding them in my hands, Zhenya. Tell me right now.'

Silence.

'The last thing . . .' She's so angry she can barely get the words out. 'Believe me, the last thing we need . . .'

Silence.

She bangs again.

'I won't have this conversation from behind a door.'

'Fine. I don't want to talk about it.'

'I am your mother. This isn't a hotel.'

'I know. If it was they'd leave me alone.'

'He decides to be funny. He decides he's a big enough man to be smart. Be smart, see where it gets you. Be smart, your recital two weeks away. You don't know this yet, but believe me when I say – I am your mother, believe me – "There's nothing in life . . ."'

'". . . so tragic as a wasted talent."' His voice is muffled behind the door, but she can tell he's saying it as if he's reciting a nursery rhyme, a mockingly sing-song tone to his voice.

Her will beginning to break. 'Zhenya, please. I only want what's best for you. Open the door.' Her voice wavering.

Neighbours knocking on the wall. The superintendent will be up again. He spoke to them when all the arguments were happening over Zhenya's new keyboard. He won't be pleased. She can't, on top of everything, afford to get an official warning. It won't help anything if they're homeless.

Nothing.

'Fine. You'll have to come out, to eat, to pee. I'll be waiting.'

She leans her back against the door, then slides down. This is just the beginning. Everything coming undone. It had to happen. She expected it, deep down. She starts to cry. Hopefully, he'll hear her. She flings the running shoes down the corridor and they bounce off the walls, bounding into the kitchen, their energy somehow igniting hers again.

'They're going out the window,' she calls back as she stands up and follows them, makes a point of sliding open the balcony door as loudly as possible in protest. Holds them in her hand, dangling them from their laces, pulls back her arm. But of course she can't follow through. Who knows where he might have got them? They could belong to someone else and, besides, good footwear can't be wasted. They're well made, they'll last. They're not a family that can throw good clothes away, even those of dubious origin. She looks at them, hanging from her fist, turning slowly in unison, joined in their fate, and she remembers she's left the iron on.

She moves to unplug it, does so and leans against the counter. A shirtsleeve lifts in a stream of breeze, and she turns to the freshly pressed shirts lined up on their hangers, and reaches over and drags them all down, dropping with them. She grabs the whole bunch of them and wrings them into a bundle and bites them, bites down hard, stifling a scream, and they lie there, twisted, until Maria comes home.

Mr Leibniz lives in an old apartment in the Tverskoy district, in the same rooms where he spent his childhood. The walls are wood-panelled, faded and warped now, with intricately moulded covings and large double windows that open out on to the street. The building is four storeys high, weathered turquoise, with the brickwork showing in large, damp patches at street level, varnish peeling off the windows.

Maria has only been here in summertime, to watch Yevgeni play. She likes coming here; it has the same old-world look as their street in Togliatti. Approaching it alone, through narrow, cobbled streets and courtyards, allows her to relive some of her childhood, to gaze up at the high windows smattered with men in ushankas looking down upon her. Walking through the place allows the everyday to slip, momentarily, into the background. The stairway of the old house has an ancient smell, a nutty mustiness. She walks past the first landing, where Mr Leibniz's neighbour peeks his stubbled face out of his door, noting her arrival. Up two more flights. On each one, the steps are coloured with a mosaic of light from the small stained-glass window above the landing, each window cracked in its own distinctive way, a triangular notch missing from the first, the second with a hairline fracture that runs diagonally along its length which someone taped up years ago, so that now the tape has its own particular antiquity, parched and glossy, delicate to the touch.

The steps have an endearing groan. Maria imagines they've been consistent in their complaints throughout the years, never failing to let out a bleat of misery when pressed upon. An impulse with which she can empathize. She walks the steps with trepidation, the weight of all these developments resting upon her. She's put so much on the boy. This is no situation for him to become involved in. She's tried to put aside the thought that she's endangering his future prospects, but such a thing is impossible.

She stands on the mat at the door and kicks the skirting board to dislodge the snow in her soles, cursing herself for not doing this on the way into the building. A small stack of snow is deposited on the mat, its surface sculpted with the pattern of her soles. She knocks on his door and hears him respond and she turns the handle and walks inside, saying, 'Hello,' softly as her head rounds the door.

Mr Leibniz stands behind his wife, cutting and shaping her hair, a sheet draped around her body. They're framed in the large window, almost two-dimensional, his wife sitting benignly in profile, wet hair sticking to the sides of her face, and Mr Leibniz behind her, trapping hair between his fingers and chopping with the scissors. Mr Leibniz waves a hand in greeting and smiles but stays at his post.

'Sorry. She was getting restless, so I've decided to give her a trim. It calms her down. Please, come in.'

Maria had picked some snowdrops from the nearby gardens and she holds them forward uncertainly, feeling like a schoolgirl.

'Thank you. They're beautiful. You'll find something in the kitchen. Would you mind?'

'Of course not.'

She emerges a couple of minutes later with the flowers standing in a jug half filled with water. She walks towards the table and places the flowers down beside Mr Leibniz's wife, just out of her reach, and she smiles at them, a beautiful, clear smile, then looks at Maria and confusion sweeps its way across her eyes, needing a cue, aware that she knows the face.

'This is Zhenya's aunt. Maria Nikolaevna. You remember Zhenya?'

The smile unrelenting. Maria can tell she holds the smile as a way of staving off the confusion. Her look contains something else now, a shadow of distress, on some level an awareness that she should know this name, this woman, and a panic there too, the instinct of a child when they are caught doing something outside the ordinary, eating oranges in bed or lathering their face with shaving cream, unsure how to gauge the seriousness of their crime.

Mr Leibniz leans over and takes his wife's hand, running his thumb over the topography of soft veins. He introduces her again.

'It's Zhenya's aunt, Maria Nikolaevna. Don't worry if you don't recognize her. She's only been here a few times.'

'Ah, good. Maria Nikolaevna. Come and sit. The bus will be along at any moment.'

Maria smiles and nods.

'Of course. I'll wait with you.'

They sit in silence for a few minutes. Maria finds this unnerving at first, but then realizes that Mr Leibniz wants his wife to become used to her presence, to relax with a stranger in the room, and once she understands this, Maria too relaxes and just watches him at work, watches him combing and cutting, her own thoughts falling in tandem with the fine, white hair that laces together on the floor around the chair. He clips methodically. He combs the hair, then pinches it with his fingers, then clips. Maria is impressed at the fluency with which he transfers the comb and scissors, the comb almost sidestepping the scissors, slotting automatically between his fingers. Every few minutes he steps back and brings his eye line level with his wife's shoulders and pulls the strands of her hair downwards on both sides simultaneously, ensuring symmetry. His wife sits with the sheet tied up around her neck, hands underneath, formless, just the bright, calm face, looking out of the window. After a few minutes of this he begins to talk.

'She's always been proud of her hair. There are so many evenings I would come home to her hunched over the bath wearing one of my vests, pouring beer over her head or cracking an egg on it. Always these strange-smelling potions over the sink, oddly shaped bottles. She used to have such lovely, dark, healthy hair. She'd love it when I would run my fingers through it. It would lighten her mood instantly.'

Mr Leibniz takes a step back and bounces her hair in his hands and looks critically at his work, then to Maria.

'What do you think?'

'I think I should get you to cut my hair.'

'I'm a butcher. But I try my best. Wait till it dries out – you won't be inviting me anywhere near your head then.'

'You're being modest, you're not just cutting and slashing. I can see you have experience.'

'I had four younger sisters. I learned to cut hair quickly. And also the war. When I was in recovery in the military hospital I became an unofficial hairdresser to the nurses. They were all preoccupied with looking good. They see all that blood, they want a haircut. It was their way of escape.'

'I'm sure you capitalized on your vital role.'

He points the scissors at her in delight.

'I was ruthless.'

Mr Leibniz brushes the hair from his wife's shoulders, then unties the cloth around her neck. He goes to the kitchen to fetch a sweeping brush and Maria looks at the woman and feels an impulse to wave a finger in front of her face, to see if her eyes will follow, a small test of how responsive she is, but of course she suppresses this, keeps her hands folded together on her lap.

When he's finished sweeping he asks Maria if she'd like anything, a drink maybe, and she declines and he brings the dustpan and brush back into the kitchen. Maria can hear a rustling at the bin and a trickle from the sink as he washes his hands, and when he comes back he takes a towel from a cupboard and dries his wife, dropping the towel over her head and mussing her hair, and she doesn't object, remains totally still, and he drapes the towel over her shoulders to catch any remaining drops and runs a brush through the strands, smoothing the hair back with his free hand, and after that's done he sits on the divan beside Maria, and they both look at her sitting there, glowing like a spring morning, and Maria shares his sense of satisfaction, even though she's done nothing to earn it.

'How long has she been like this?'

'It's hard to say really. It's been two or three years since we've had a completely rational conversation. It sneaked up gradually.'

He pauses to see if she is just asking the question to be polite but he can tell by her attentiveness that she's interested, and so he continues.

'Katya was always busy – needlework or visits to elderly neighbours – she was always interested in things going on in the outside world. She was the one who kept us informed. I've only ever really cared about music, some literature maybe. She clipped things out of newspapers, old photographs and suchlike, and kept them in a scrapbook. Every few months she'd take out an old scrapbook from a previous year and look through it. I think it was her way of marking time.'

Maria nods.

'Anyway, one day I looked in one of her most recent books and the first few pages had neatly clipped articles, carefully spaced out, and then as the pages went on it was a paragraph or two, chopped off with ragged edges, and as the pages moved on they had less and less coherence, until at the end there were only blocks of colour or text, plastered on top of one another, like a collage.'

He looks out of the window.

'All her forgetfulness and unfinished sentences were probably what led me to take down the book in the first place, but it wasn't till I looked at the pages that I put it all together.'

'Did you ask her about it?'

'Yes. She was as shocked as I. She couldn't remember sticking them in. That was almost four years ago.'

'I'm sorry.'

'No. It's not so bad. She has times where she's lucid, and I'm grateful for them, and there's often a strange pleasure when she experiences the past. She looks at me sometimes like she did when we first met – the awe of first love. It has many unexpected blessings.'

'Alina said she was a teacher.'

'Yes. They let her keep her job when I was arrested. Her father was part of the nomenklatura. She cut off all contact with him, but he obviously couldn't bring himself to let her starve or have her taken.'

He has an angled nose, broken at some point, a shoulder that drops away, disproportionate to the other. But he sits with beautiful poise, direct and upright, despite the natural inclination of his body. His voice has an unusual richness to it, a honeyed rasp.

Maria is tempted to ask him more, but she's here for a reason. She shifts position.

'Zhenya.'

'Yes.'

'What's the problem?'

'There's not an easy answer to that. I don't presume to know the child, I just teach him piano.'

'He says he's not happy with having to play the "Tarantella". He says he doesn't want to play *Music for Children* – he thinks it's patronizing. It's a very proud child you have there, a very stubborn child.'

'Try living with him. Does he want to choose another piece?'

'He's nine years old. He doesn't have the first idea what he wants.'

A raise of her eyebrows, a downturn of her mouth.

'My manager is very set upon the selection. I'm not sure we could get permission to change it regardless. He likes the image. In his mind, I think, even if Zhenya isn't all we say he is, he doesn't lose too much face. Prokofiev wrote it for children, it's not supposed to be perfect – this is his attitude, or at least that's what I imagine it to be.'

'It sounds as though you don't have full confidence in the child either.'

She shrugs, no need for pretence; this man has done some serious living.

'I feel as though I've placed him in a difficult situation against his will. But I know you think we smother him.'

'I think a musician plays because they need to play. They don't whine because the lighting is bad or the room is too cold or they're not ready. A natural musician attacks the keyboard, tames it. They're willing to fight, no matter the circumstance.'

Mr Leibniz's tone changes, a more formal diction. Maria feels like a student herself.

'So his sense of timing?'

'His sense of timing, nothing. He practises what, four days a week, a few hours each time. This is completely ridiculous. He still believes he can just think the music into being. He hasn't spent enough time immersed in the notes, he doesn't know how to read the flow of a piece. His instincts are fine. The boy has incredible natural musicality. But music is a demanding mistress. It requires total commitment. He has to understand it before he can charm it or beat it into submission.'

'He's only nine years old. It's a little too young for a death sentence.'

'You know what Prokofiev was doing at Zhenya's age?'

'I don't think I want to.'

'Writing operas, that's what. And the boy complains because he has to play a piece with a prissy name.'

'Do you think he'll make an impression on Sidorenko? Tell me honestly.'

'It depends on Sidorenko. Most of the graduates of the Conservatory come out with incredible technique and very little appreciation for natural musicality. They play like our footballers, all coaching and drills and tactics, very little individual skill. Zhenya is blessed with a musical language that's all his own, but right now he's too caught up in right and wrong, in technicalities. But you can't learn what the boy has. Maybe Sidorenko understands enough about music to recognize this. On the other hand, maybe he doesn't know how to listen.'

'What if we skipped the concert, just let him audition?'

'An audition will be more difficult. The committee will judge his schooling, his technique, they'll want to see he's the right kind of candidate, that he'll uphold their reputation.'

'And you don't think they will?'

'Do you? I say it again, the child doesn't even have a piano in his home.'

A movement from the corner. Mr Leibniz's wife raises her right arm. Mr Leibniz stands and guides the arm back down to her lap, but she raises it again, her head lolling, puppet-like, listening, tuning into whatever silent impulses are surrounding her.

'Under the desks, under the desks.'

She calls this out in a warbled voice, no strength in the breath, but Maria recognizes something in the words, the force of intent there. This phrase formed a routine that cut through her schooldays too.

Flakes of snow ruffle against the window, and the old woman turns her attention to these and Mr Leibniz shows confusion, his eyes questioning. Maria realizes that his education took place at an earlier time.

'It was a school exercise. In case of nuclear attack.'

'Ah yes. Of course I've heard about them.' He sits beside his wife, holds her hand. 'They must have been terrifying.'

'Actually, I loved them. I remember very little of school. But I remember the nuclear drills. I remember how we'd do them sometimes on rainy days, straight after assembly, when everyone's clothes were still wet, and we'd crouch under the tables and I'd smell the damp and steam and feel close to everyone.'

'People talked of nothing else. There were plenty of grand statements about our absolute power, but the fear was so immediate, naturally. Those missiles sitting in Italy and Turkey, pointing straight at us. I'm sure you felt it too as a child, probably more so.'

'I remember raising my head during one of the drills – we were under strict orders to lie still – and looking around and thinking that this is what it would look like if a bomb actually hit. All of my friends crumpled on the floor, only the teacher still standing.'

She laughs at this detail.

'At that age you think teachers are indestructible.'

Mr Leibniz pats his wife's clenched hand.

'If only that were so.'

After a silence he says, 'Katya brings the past in here, she guides my memories, makes me relive the things that departed from me as a young man or things which I chose to ignore.'

'Are there particular years that she remembers more clearly?'

'Yes. Sometimes in the middle of the night, she sits up in bed, listening, hearing things. She has an incredible sensitivity to noises in the night. I know she's reliving the Stalin years, the months before I was taken away. We had so many nights when we were waiting for a knock on the door.'

'It must have been terrible when it finally came.'

'Not so terrible. There was actually a great sense of relief. I stood in this room in my robe and slippers, and they pushed through from the corridor, surrounding me, and told me to get dressed, and I remember an odd sense of justification, that at least I hadn't made the whole thing up in my mind. Waiting in dread is an incredible strain.'

'How long were you in the gulags?'

'Ten years. Then they closed them and I came home and stayed out of sight. I tuned pianos and walked in the park.'

Maria rises and steps to the piano near the door, taking it in; it strikes her as being much bigger than the proportions of the room would seem to allow.

'It was a gift. It belonged to an engineer, a lonely man, very respected. When he died, it was passed to me under his wishes.'

'It's beautiful.'

'Do you ever play?'

'No. I don't have that kind of patience. My husband used to, occasionally.'

'Used to?'

'Yes.'

Mr Leibniz doesn't press.

She runs her hands along the marquetry designs on the side, takes pleasure in the feel of the curve; like a hip bone.

'Would you have done things differently, before you were arrested, if you could have those years back?' she asks.

'What could I have done?'

'I don't know. Surely people put up some kind of resistance.'

'There was no resistance. Resist what? There were no rights or wrongs, no grey areas, there was just the system. I did all I could do, I survived. I've lived long enough to take care of my wife. That was my only ambition.'

It's time to go home. Alina is working late and Maria will need to cook. She takes Mr Leibniz's hand. His wife is elsewhere.

'Thank you for speaking with me. I'll make sure Zhenya doesn't miss any more practice.'

He senses a change in her, a doubt in her grip. He dips his head, seeking eye contact.

'I speak to you as a man surrounded by forgotten years. The only change for my wife and I will be death. Resistance is for the young. And you, whether you realize it or not, are still young.'

Maria smiles and squeezes his hand, a flush of deference in her cheeks.

In the corridor she looks down at the pools swelling around the mat, solid snow transformed into liquid, trickling down into the stairwell. On the floor below she hears movement and the groan of the irritable step. It fires an image in her mind and she continues the sound in her imagination, boots trampling up the stairs, the arrogant strides of authority pacing their way to this landing, knocking on this door, standing where she is standing. Soldiers filling up the corridor. Mr Leibniz in his robe, dream-muddled. That feeling of utter helplessness, not a single person to speak out for you, a feeling so strong she could reach out and touch it with her hand.

At half past ten Grigory finishes his shift and makes his way to the cafeteria. The place will be closed, but he has a key. If he hasn't eaten, they leave a meal for him in the fridge. A tub of mackerel with beetroot and mayonnaise, or sometimes cow's tongue and roasted turnips. He hardly tastes it, eats it cold. Often he has to concentrate just to lift the fork to his mouth. He rarely uses a knife; the instrument has shed its innocence for him.

First he sees the strip of light below the door. As he nears, he can take in the smell. He recognizes it instantly: zharkoye. One of the other surgeons must have finished as late as he; the nurses and attendants rotate surgeries so their meals are earlier in the evening. He pauses, thinks about turning back for his room; conversation is inevitable. But the smell of onion proves irresistible, the thought of a warm meal so comforting.

He opens the door and sees a woman standing over the cooker. The mother of the boy.

She turns, smiles.

'They said you were almost finished. It's ready for you.'

The surprise makes him wary.

'How did you get in?'

'One of the nurses.'

'She should have asked permission.'

'From who? No one's going to deny you a decent meal. They practically kissed my feet when I suggested it.'

'I'm not your responsibility.' He says this and then regrets his words. He can leave his authority back in the surgical ward.

She slides the wooden spoon back into the pot, leans against the counter facing him. She speaks slowly, gently, aware of his tiredness. Perhaps it's the light, but he seems even paler than those few days before.

'I understand. I'm not here to mother you. I'm here to thank you. It's a celebratory meal.'

'What are we celebrating?'

'My Sofya is getting better. She has been in bed with a temperature, diarrhoea, having trouble holding down food. Of course I thought the worst. But they did some tests and she's a lot healthier, eating her food, colour back in her cheeks again. It turns out it was only an intestinal infection. It feels as if she has been brought back to life.'

Grigory runs his hand through his hair. He's still not sure he wants to discuss someone else's life. Even if they have good news.

'And we're celebrating the return of my Artyom. That dog has brought him back to me again. He's talking again, telling me things. That crippled dog has helped more than you know.'

Grigory nods, relenting, and slumps into a chair.

She serves him and they eat without speaking. The beef and garlic steams up into his face and he drags down the smell and eats heartily. When he finishes she fills his plate again. She waves her finger before he can refuse. 'We have enough. It's a celebration, remember.' She watches him eat, a satisfied smile on her face.

Now that he can look at her, properly consider her, he sees lines of worry etched into her forehead and around her mouth. But her smile is a flare of crooked teeth, a burst of energy and light.

When he finishes she pushes aside the plate, takes a bottle from one of the cupboards and fills his glass.

'I shouldn't.'

'None of us should.'

She dips a finger in her glass, then kisses her fingers and flicks a few drops of vodka on the floor. They drink and crack their glasses down.

She puts an elbow on the table and rests her chin on her palm.

'Tell me why you are here.'

This woman can change the tone of the room in an instant. Her manner is both open and direct. Not aggressive, simply without triviality. He puts his two hands flat on the tabletop, tucks his thumbs underneath and settles himself, and thinks about his reply.

'Well, my superior at the hospital recommended me to an advisor at the Ministry of Fuel and Energy. I was sent to Chernobyl and then they transferred me to a resettlement camp.'

'That's not *why*, that's *how*, but no matter, we'll get to it.'

'What about you? Did you come from Pripyat?'

'We lived in the Gomel region. A small village near the plant, obviously. But I'm from Moscow originally, like you.'

'Artyom told you?'

'Don't worry, we all know about you. Silence is no defence around here.'

He doesn't test her statement, doesn't want to know. Grigory takes the bottle and pours both of them another glass.

'How did you end up in Gomel?'

'I fell in love.'

A meandering smile on her mouth.

'Did he . . . your husband . . .'

The words came stuttering out of his mouth. Without his white coat, he is lost with such a topic. He has no idea how to discuss such things outside the realm of professional expertise.

'Yes. He died before they moved us to this camp. He worked as a liquidator for the plant. They gave him the job of cutting down the neighbouring forests.'

'I'm sorry.'

A pause.

'Thank you.'

He knows by her silence that she doesn't want to be the next to speak. He considers changing the subject, but there is no other subject here.

'How did you meet him?'

She thinks about her reply. She'd like to describe it all to someone. Why not this doctor? She hasn't had a chance to relive it in a story.

The day Andrei walked into the tailor's workshop near Izmaylovsky park and was introduced to the assistant, who was chalking up some suit material for cutting. Pins clamped in her teeth, her jaw clenched in concentration. She looked up at him in acknowledgement, and immediately his blue eyes were the only colour in the room, eyes as resonant as a lingering piano note. She stopped what she was doing to look, and he looked back at her. She took in the way he stood, feet planted to the floor, shoulders back, a man who knew the world, who was equal to its vigour. She slid the pins from her mouth and had to make her apologies and leave, confused. She walked for hours that afternoon, trying to locate the sensation within herself, but she couldn't read her own feelings, they were new to her, and it was only later that she realized it was the elusive sensation of love that had crept up on her unawares, a sensation for which she had no reference point. And when the thought began to develop into realization, her inclination was to dismiss it: such things are the preserve of adolescents, not someone as old as she. She told herself she is someone who knows the hardness of the world, who understands that to survive is to nurture the practical, to keep steady and quiet and choose things based upon their value.

A week later, he was there again, as she had hoped, modesty and confidence combined in his honest face, back for his second fitting. When the tailor left the room for more pins, Andrei stood there, wearing the frayed material, unable to move, a living dummy, and she approached and put her hand to his waist, folding the swatches for a better fit, and adjusted the angle of his lapels, her breath rippling over his chest as she did so, and he gathered her neck in his hand and they kissed briefly, in the moment. When he returned, the tailor tweaked and tucked the material while they stole glances at each other, the gorgeous pain of anticipation.

Later still, when the streetlights had come on and the tailor had walked away in his hat and coat and she had locked the door, she saw Andrei silhouetted in an alcove, and she unlocked the door again and his shoes clicked against the wet cobblestones and she let him into a darkened corner of the vestibule under the stairs. He bunched her hair in his right hand and placed his left flat and vertical on the downward valley of her smooth stomach, and they kissed a kiss that was a language unto itself, a kiss that was a separate country, until she pulled away from him and smoothed her hair behind her ear, and he saw her flat lobe with two elliptical holes and a small crescent-shaped scar just under it, the healed skin whiter than the rest of her. She, in turn, rotated his face into the light and traced a finger along his jawline. Not speaking, just watching, each of them observing the other.

On the stairs they were all decorum again, playfully affecting nonchalance, both understanding that once through the door there would be a torrent of hands and tongue and want, and she even made a little game with the keys, as though she couldn't quite remember which was the right one for the workshop, playing with him, drawing the tension out, until it seemed that Andrei was likely to put his shoulder to the door and pop it off its hinges, and then she did a double-take with him. She looked at him casually and put the key in the slot, then paused and turned and looked into his eyes, serious as fire, then turned the key fully and pushed her way in, and his hair was on the cusp of her neckline, his hands on her upper arms, before they even managed to close the door.

She understood the word *belonging* then. Inside herself she was honed and made real and cast around his form, morphing into the same shape, and there were heat and lust and strands of thread in her hair, and a pincushion by her right ear and the dummy looming over them, sides filleted out, and she was there but not there, experiencing everything in the moment, consuming every detail of the experience but also outside herself, fragments of her past blurring through her mind, and he smiled reflectively in the middle of it, their thoughts linked, and they broke somehow into giddy trills of laughter, almost losing the moment and then serious again with a twist of his pelvis and a tightening of her mouth.

Tanya would like to explain some of this to the tired surgeon. She would like to talk about love once more, to share her experiences, but the wounds are still too raw.

She answers his question.

'I worked as a tailor's assistant and he came in one day to get a suit adjusted.'

'And you moved soon after.'

'A while after. He was doing his military service. When it

finished, then I became a farmer's wife. A life, I'm surprised to admit, I loved. Feeding chickens. Milking cows. Who knew a city girl like me would adapt so well?'

Tanya rises quickly and takes their empty plates and places them in a plastic container. She'll wash them later. When she returns Grigory offers her a glass and they drink and he waits for her to continue.

'Sometimes on TV they show things from the area. One night they showed people swimming in Pripyat River, people tanning themselves by the banks. The reactor in the background, smoke still coming from it. They get an old lady to milk a cow, she pours the milk into the bucket and a man comes over with a military dosimeter and measures the radiation level, and it's normal. Then they measure some fish on a plate. It's normal. Everything is fine, says the commentator, life is going on as normal. In the shelter, after we were evacuated, some of the other women would get letters from their husbands at the plant. Same thing. Life is returning to normal. Everything normal.'

There is a box of matches on the next table. Grigory reaches over for it, takes one from the box, lights it and watches it burn down to a stub in his fingers. He lights another. Then he speaks.

'I had a contact in Minsk. A surgeon also. In the earliest days I approached the hospital to tell them what was happening. There was a radioactive cloud hanging over the city. We were forbidden to speak officially of this. So, I spread the word any way I could, talked to people who were in contact with large groups.'

She sits back in her chair, folds her arms, listening intently.

'I talked to my colleague and he was already aware of the situation. Nobody was coming in yet with radiation poisoning; that would happen in the following weeks. But there were plenty of people, many of them prominent Party members, who needed to get their stomachs pumped after overdosing on iodine tablets. So the medical staff naturally drew their own conclusions. But then he said something else. He said his friend was a librarian and that, the day after the explosion, four KGB guys came into the library and confiscated any relevant books they could find. Anything on nuclear war, radiography – even basic science primers, books to get kids excited about physics. They went to such lengths, of course people believe the propaganda.'

Tanya shakes her head.

'Did you meet any liquidators?'

He's unsure if she wants an answer. He looks up to see how he should reply and she stares back calmly, waiting for a response.

'A lot of people volunteered. Thousands, not just locals like your husband. That first week they brought in busloads of factory workers, students. They were throwing people at the problem, offering them three, four times the average wage. Not everyone came for the money, though. Some were just put on a bus. They thought they were coming for just a weekend, a reward for their productivity. I saw people taking photographs of each other in front of the reactor, to prove they were there, as if it were a tourist stop.'

He runs a match through his fingers. He would like a cigarette.

'At first they treated it like a holiday camp. They worked, of course, shovelled topsoil, dug drains, and in the evening they'd get smashed. There was plenty of vodka to go around. Although eventually that ran out and they started drinking anything they could get their hands on: cologne, nailpolish remover, glass cleaner. By then they were drinking to blank out their days, to forget what they'd seen.'

'Why weren't they replaced? Why were they made to stay for so long?'

'At first they were supposed to be there for two weeks. The initial guidelines made sense – I myself demanded many of them – but they quickly became compromised because of budgetary restrictions, or stubbornness from some senior official. Every man had a radiation meter around his neck. No one was supposed to be exposed to more than 25 micro-roentgen, the maximum dose the body can withstand. We gave each of them three sets of protective outfits. But my superior revoked his decision to supply washing machines; he wanted to save whatever clean-water sources we had left. So the men had no way of washing their gear. After the third day, they were constantly wearing radioactive clothes. After those initial two weeks, they decided not to replace the liquidators, not to sacrifice others. In the morning planning meetings they would calculate how many lives they'd use up on a particular task. Two lives for this job, four for this. It was like a war cabinet, men playing God. Worst of all, it did no good. Those people were replaced anyway, they became too sick to work.'

'That was when you left?'

'No, even then I stayed for another few weeks. I thought I could be useful as the voice of reason, as someone who would defend the workers. Then I found out that the Party had organized protected farms near Mogilev. They were growing their own vegetables, scrutinizing the water supply. Everything was being overseen by experts, the very people who were needed on the ground, in the local villages. They had their own herds of cattle; each bullock had a number and was routinely tested. They had cows which they were certain gave out fresh milk. Meanwhile, in the stores around the exclusion zone, they were selling condensed and powdered milk from the Rogachev factory – the same stuff we were using in induction lectures as an example of a standard radiation source. That was when they had to get rid of me. I went back to Minsk and talked to Aleksei Filin, the writer. Told him everything I knew. He spoke out during a live TV interview, some literary programme. It was brave of him, he was arrested over it. He's still in confinement, I haven't been able to trace where they put him.'

'Why weren't you arrested?'

'They threatened it. I was prepared to go. They were going to put me in an insane asylum. They whispered that if that didn't suit I could find myself in a tragic accident. "Look around," I told them. "You're too late." But irony is something the KGB can't quite grasp.'

He looks out of the window, running a finger along the rim of his glass.

'Ultimately, they need surgeons, and I'm more useful working here than sitting in a padded cell.'

They're silent for a few moments.

'You must worry about your own health,' Tanya says.

A blank stare.

'No.'

'But you were there.'

'And I was one of the few there who knew what he was getting into. If I was going to worry about myself, I should have done it before I arrived.'

They're silent for a few minutes. Each with their own resentments. Tanya is the first to speak.

'Andrei told me a joke, before he died, one that was going around the site.' Grigory realizes she's looking for his assent to tell it, and he nods and she continues. 'The Americans fly over a robot to help with the clean-up. So the supervising officer sends it to the roof of the reactor but, after five minutes, it breaks down. The Japanese have also donated one, so the officer sends that one up to replace the American robot but, after ten minutes, word comes back that it can't withstand the conditions either. By now the officer is angry, he's cursing their shoddy foreign technology. He shouts at his subordinate, "Send one of the Russian robots back up, they're the only reliable machinery we have around here." His subordinate salutes and turns to go. As he's leaving, the officer barks after him, "And tell Private Ivanov we've lost a lot of time, he has to stay up there for at least two hours before he gets his cigarette break.""

Tanya smiles at the memory of Andrei telling it, his caustic humour, lips curling around his teeth, his words a combination of defiance and regret. She begins to weep.

Grigory waits until her tears lose their force, then takes her hand.

'I've just realized you've never told me your name.'

'Tanya.'

'I'm sorry, Tanya.'

'Thank you.'

She wipes away her tears with the base of her palm.

'Enough. This is a celebration, and I'm under orders.'

He sits up, his shoulders pushed back.

'Orders?'

'Of course. There's endless speculation. They want me to find out something. You think a disaster like this is enough to keep us from gossiping? We embrace any distractions.'

He smiles.

'What kind of speculation?'

'The only kind there is.'

'You want to know if there's someone back home?'

'Well, there's no one here – look at yourself, that's obvious.

I'm asking the *why*. You came here to help, I know this, we all appreciate it. But there's always something else.'

He cradles his glass, eyes downturned.

'I don't mean to pry.' A mother's voice, soft with concern. 'It's just harmless chatter.'

There was the vase exploding against the wall. There were the remains of their kitchen chair, a pathetic desultory thing that lay beaten beside his legs as he sat near the stove. Walking in, she already knew – of course she did; she had placed the note that morning. Not seeing anything – not noticing the wreckage of their home – other than his look, the rage in his eyes.

He thinks of their relationship as one comprised mostly of afternoons. Work consuming both of them; he arriving at the hospital in the early evening, attending patients into midmorning; she leaving the apartment early, writing her articles before the offices filled up with talk and distraction, before editorial meetings devoured her time.

But there were afternoons. Late breakfasts on their days off. Waking to the midday sunlight, sheets contorted around them. Her smell at its fullest at this time. He would run his neck and face along her glistening body, harvesting the glorious odour of her sweat. He would lift her arm upwards, pressing her wrist against the headboard, and linger in the warm nest of her smell, first running the tip of his tongue along the shy stubble, then lapping up the fullness of her in long, wide strokes, repeating it all again below her waist.

Afternoons wandering through bookshops, her giving him a guided tour of the printed word. Then reading in the hours before supper as he lay with his head on the centre of her, her leg draped over his shoulder, claiming him.

The afternoons changed then, out of nowhere.

Afternoons when the weather was too harsh to leave the apartment and they would swap rooms, avoiding each other. He would move into the bedroom, she would move into the living room. He would shave at the sink and exit as she entered for her bath.

When she became pregnant, he thought it would be a new beginning, would cast away the gloom that had settled over them. Instead she sank further into herself.

Then came the afternoons when she covered herself in the protective wall of a book and he would snatch it from her hands and throw it against the wall, shouting, 'Talk to me! Look at me! I'm standing here. Don't treat me like a fucking ghost!', and she would rise from her chair and gather the book from the corner and select her page again and sit as though she had dozed off for a minute and lost her place.

Afternoons when they would walk through the streets in a rage and then dampen down in tea rooms, where the presence of others would force them into civility, and he would tell a joke or a story from his childhood and a smile would skim across her face, a sunburst over a dreary, grey sea, and then pass again, serving only to taunt him with what they had once had.

The afternoon of irreparable damage. A lunch in the Yar – a rare thing, no alcohol, obviously, but a good steak with Fyodor Yuriyevich, then chief of surgery. Comrades dropping by to slap him on the arm. Horse talk, football talk, advice on which seminars to attend, which periodicals to submit work to. Questions about his paper on cardiomyopathy. A refrain from Fyodor on what it must be like to be young. Working, publishing, so much to come, family and all that entails. A new premier elected. A strong, vital man. Charismatic. A man who would renew the Union, usher it into the modern age. So much to

334

look forward to, Grigory. Praise on his technique. Fyodor had scrubbed in on a recent case, a crash victim, not an easy procedure, not by any means.

'But you handled it well, Grigory. Your surgical team never exchanged a glance. Total calm, that's all you need. Hands of ice. Never rush. Although you could bring your times down. What's your best time on an endotracheal intubation?'

'Never as quick as you, sir.'

'Damn right. Beat me on that and I'll transfer you to Primorye.'

Winking at Grigory, friendly but not without challenge, half meaning the threat, which obviously was the best compliment of all.

And after Fyodor had left and no one approached the table any more, Grigory reached into his jacket to pay the bill and pulled out an envelope. High-grade paper. No handwriting or address. A promotion? A bonus? A proclamation of love from some junior nurse? He unfolded it there on the table and recognized her handwriting and felt a rush of hope: finally, some clarity; all that she couldn't say wrapped into a letter. Of course this was how she would communicate. She would explain it all, lay it all out on rich paper, put it all between the margins: her perspective, the inner workings of her mind, her apology, her thirst to renew herself once more, the consolation she felt in him.

The letter contained none of these. The language was formal, businesslike, as though she were apologizing for turning down a job offer or cancelling the rental contract on their television set. So clear and brief that he didn't need to read it again. A delineation of facts. She had decided not to keep the child. No emotion, no regret, no apology or explanation.

Grigory left without paying. The waiter followed him into the street, calling after him, and Grigory turned and pulled out whatever notes were in his pocket, stuffed them into the waiter's fist and walked north. He walked and turned corners and walked again, often returning to his own footprints, and he stopped and considered them, then headed in the opposite direction.

At home, washing his face in the bathroom, he looked down at the plughole, a small, dark circle surrounded by white porcelain. That first night together, their meeting at the lake, the white plateau stretched before them in endless, flawless possibility. Now their relationship resembled that environment: cold and hard; whatever life existed lurked only in the dark waters below. He would gladly smash the surface and plunge himself into the depths, drag her to warmth, but all she would allow him was a thin line of connection, and he waited in vain hope, stooped above it, dependent on her to show the merest flicker of need.

Grigory hears the closing of a door, transporting him back from his thoughts.

Tanya has called next door to the nurses' quarters and convinced them to part with another bottle. She pours, and they drink and open out the plains of their life to each other, speaking of their pasts.

When the conversation eventually comes to a pause, she sits up suddenly.

'I almost forgot.'

She walks to a press near the cooker and returns holding something wrapped in sackcloth. She lays it on the table between them.

'It's a gift.'

Grigory stiffens. 'That's very kind of you but, for professional reasons, I can't accept gifts.'

'You gave my son a dog. I'm just returning the gesture.'

'I kept the dog. Your son merely looks after him.'

'Well, then, I'm giving you something to look after. I can't work it myself. I don't know how to take care of it.'

A short, exhaled laugh.

'Now I'm worried. You're not giving me another damn pet to be responsible for?'

'Open it. And of course I'm embarrassed about the packaging. They don't seem to prioritize wrapping paper in their supplies.'

He looks at her once more in order to give himself permission. He drags the package over and puts his hand in and pulls out a camera, a Zorki, a few years old, but in good shape. He detaches the lens and takes off the cap and holds it to the light, checking the surface for scratches, like a wine connoisseur sniffing the first glass from a new bottle.

'Artyom told me you liked photography. I mentioned it to a few people. We wanted to give you something, to show our gratitude. It wasn't too difficult. Someone always has a cousin. There's not much film, I'm afraid, so you'll have to do some wangling of your own.'

He holds the gift and looks at his hands. He has done nothing other than his duty, his professional obligation. Even the acts of these people's most intimate love will be tainted, their offspring inheriting their tragedy. This is what distresses him most. Nothing but bleakness ahead. How can he hold their gift in his hands? He lays it on the table before him.

Tanya leans over and clasps both her hands over his.

'You have done so much good here.'

'What good have I done? Look at the sickness around you.'

'This is a place where we have come to endure. You have

helped to make it endurable. You have brought care into our lives. You cannot know how important this is.'

She takes the camera and places it in his hands.

'Now you can do something for me. I want to be photographed. I want something I can save for my children.'

He runs his fingers over the dials, his natural fluency returning in an instant.

He raises it to his eye and focuses on her.

She is confident, gazing straight into the lens, her pupils reflecting in the gentle light. She resists the urge to pose, and stays with her body open and unconsidered and, even before she does this, Grigory knew this would be the case, a quality that so few people have. She simply sits on her chair and talks to him as he makes his first steps back to a past life.

He begins to move as he shoots, opening the aperture and changing shutter speed on instinct, attuned to the light of the room. He varies his angles and positioning and occasionally the shutters pause, taking a full second between their opening and release, and she holds her breath in these moments, the anticipation gathering everything in its stillness.

She speaks again.

'Look at me.'

She says this as he is pointing the lens right at her.

'Look at me.'

He narrows the focus so that her eyes fill the frame.

'You're not listening. Look at me.'

He takes away the camera and looks at her, and she approaches and kisses him on the forehead and draws back and puts her gaze in his and clamps her hands around his face.

'You need to go back to her.'

He opens his mouth to say something, but she shakes her head, blanking out his impulse.

'This is not some kind of martyrdom. They'll find another surgeon. You have done all you can do. Staying here any longer will break you. I have to be here. You don't. You need to go back now.'

She kisses him on the lips. She kisses him tenderly but with nothing else behind it, no underlying want. An asexual kiss. Years since he has felt the touch of a woman's lips.

Maria and Alina sit at the table, pushing around some pork and cabbage with their forks. They sit and stare at the empty place. A plate in the oven. Yevgeni's tuxedo washed and ironed and starched, hanging on the door. His shoes polished. They are showered. They have done each other's hair. Their clothes are laid out also, in Alina's room, all they need to do is put them on. This is supposed to happen after dinner. Alina has secretly been looking forward to dressing with her sister. It's been maybe ten years since they dressed up together, shared lipstick, consulted on fittings, applied eyeliner, the whole point of being a sister brought together in this ritual.

In forty-five minutes an official car will pick them up. They'll drive on the green strip of the Chaika lane, passing all civilian traffic, which Alina has mentioned repeatedly to everyone at work, a thrill almost on a par with watching her son perform. They'll pick up Mr Leibniz and drive to the factory. Alina wanted to ride in the same car as Yakov Sidorenko; it would give them an opportunity to press Yevgeni's case. She also just wanted to be in his presence, to sit with a man of such civility, maybe learn something from him, even smell him, the refinement of his cologne. Maria wouldn't allow it, though, said it would place too much pressure upon Yevgeni, would fill him with dread. Mr Leibniz concurred. So Alina accepted the situation and they will travel separately.

If they travel at all. All this is what they have planned, but they're supposed to leave in forty-five minutes and Yevgeni isn't home yet.

Yevgeni left Mr Leibniz's two and a half hours ago. He was due to be home ninety minutes ago at the latest. They push their cabbage around and listen for the key slotting into the door and a mass of apologies. Their gaze drifts towards the window, but it's already too dark to see much. A son and nephew, wandering out there somewhere.

Other plans have been put in motion, plans that only Maria and a few select people are aware of.

Pavel had been right about his friend Danil. The man knows how to put things together. Her meetings with him took place in nondescript offices. The two of them alone. There are others in the planning group but Danil meets them individually, so their plans aren't compromised. Each time, he arrived and talked through her instructions and listened to any insights or worries she may have had and addressed them then; or, if not immediately, certainly at their next meeting. Maria was worried about food and water supplies, Danil has arranged that there are enough canned goods and bottled water in the stock rooms to last the entire factory a month. When she asked what would happen when they cut the heating, Danil told her that they'd managed to smuggle in two generators for electricity and enough gas canisters and heaters to see them through the first few weeks. If things become entrenched, they can ration the hours they use the heaters, and all the protective clothing in the factory will provide decent warmth.

When Yakov Sidorenko is playing, Zinaida Volkova will take to the stage and announce the strike, reading out a list of their demands. They have men assigned to block the door and take care of Sidorenko, the ministerial consort and the factory management. Any workers will be free to leave but it will be made clear to them that they can't return.

At that point they'll take Alina and Yevgeni from the building.

The two sisters have called Yevgeni's schoolfriends and knocked on the doors of some boys in the building that he knows. Nothing. Nobody knows where he could be. Mr Leibniz says he wasn't worried or distressed, that when he left he seemed ready, normal, cocky. This worries them both even more.

Maria asks herself if he could have been picked up. Does anyone else know about this? No. Danil is too good at what he does. She did as he said and asked around. His reputation didn't fit that of a KGB mole; he has had too much success in agitation and he doesn't display the particular brand of dumb curiosity that they project, always asking questions, always interested in what's going on. Danil knows not to inquire about things that don't concern him. And he is trusted by the right people. For Maria's first meeting, Danil arrived with Zinaida Volkova, and Maria knew that, from then on, she would be prepared to do whatever was necessary. Zinaida is a unifying figure who the entire factory will get behind. She also knows how to work the corridors of power. Her successes in previous negotiations, gaining concessions for the workers without any real strength behind her, show that she is capable of so much more. Most importantly though, her credibility is beyond doubt. The workforce knows she's not there to line her own pockets. And she'll be effective. She'll make a formidable leader and a strong adversary in negotiations. Danil left them alone and Maria spent a couple of hours talking to her, impressed by the clarity of thought the old woman displayed, the directness of her language, the simplicity of her goals. She was looking for an independent trade union, voted for by the workforce in open elections. They would be free to hold open meetings and free to strike. 'Everything will come from this,' Zinaida said, and Maria doesn't doubt that these two demands are enough to open up a whole range of possibilities. She does doubt that they can gain these kinds of concessions: what they are asking for is a shift in ideology, an opening of previously closed doors. For all the talk of restructuring and openness, they'll soon find out how far the programmes of glasnost and perestroika will stretch.

And still he's not home.

She should call Danil. He's left a number to contact him on if anything unexpected comes up.

The ticking of the clock above the kitchen door resounds off all surfaces. A few ants walk determinedly along the floor, moving parallel to the kickboards at the bottom of their kitchen cabinets, then slipping away in a crevice at the corner. The cabinets are fronted with orange plastic. It gives the kitchen an oppressive air, makes the room feel even smaller. They've talked about this, talked through every aspect of this apartment, Alina always longing for better, Maria just wishing that every day would come to a close. Alina stands and starts opening the cupboards purposefully, and Maria doesn't ask what she's looking for, just watches her. She finds a long, white, plastic cylinder with a picture of a black ant on the front. She kneels down and pours a smooth, white line of the stuff into the seam between the floor and the kickboard.

Alina puts the cylinder back, sits down at the table again and puffs out her cheeks.

'I'm past being annoyed. I'm worried now. Is he staying away or is he in trouble? Would he put his mother through this if he didn't have to? That's the question I'm asking myself.'

'I know.'

'It could be one or the other.'

343

'I know.'

Maria stands, goes into the hallway to grab her coat and hat, scarf and gloves.

She comes back in, wrapped up.

'I'm going to look for him.'

'I'll stay here and wait.'

'I'll be back in half an hour. If he comes home, get ready. I'll change in five minutes.'

'OK.'

The door closes. Alina stands and clears their plates, scraping food into the bin. She washes them, puts them on the draining board and sits. This is an essential part of motherhood, the ability to sit and wait. Her life tied inextricably with that of her child.

She sits and waits. Then she stands and grabs a dishcloth and dries the two dishes.

Yevgeni reaches the barber's house, and the light is off, which is to be expected. He knocks on the door, a patterned knock with a 6/8 tempo that Iakov has taught him. There's no answer but Yevgeni perseveres and after a few minutes he can hear a shuffling and a little man with a sunken face opens the door and raises his eyebrows at the kid, asking Yevgeni what he wants without even having to speak.

The man's name is Anatoly Ivanovich Nikolaenko, a permanent fixture of the district, who knows everything there ever was and anyone who ever could have been. Yevgeni always sees him on the street, walking that little mutt of his, which looks like half its parentage comes from rats. Yevgeni thinks the man might actually be three hundred years old, his face lined like bark.

Anatoly stands there in the doorway with his arms folded.

'I have a message for Iakov.'

Anatoly whistles inside and calls Iakov's name. He does this with a turn of the head and a slight arch backwards but otherwise doesn't move, remains standing there with arms folded, both of them waiting, Yevgeni wanting to break the silence, Anatoly looking as if he had been born in this position.

Iakov emerges from the corridor and Anatoly departs into the gloom.

'Come in,' Iakov says. He closes the door.

Yevgeni takes an envelope out of his jacket and hands it to Iakov.

'You're a good one, Zhenya. You're gonna grow up smart.'

Iakov puts an arm around Yevgeni, a fraternal gesture, but Yevgeni doesn't like this, it feels unnatural, a gesture that he considers to be outside of his upbringing. Besides, Iakov's not old enough himself to patronize him so much.

Yevgeni has been running packages for Iakov since their meeting in the yards. Some gambling thing he has going, Yevgeni knows better than to ask what. The job is totally uncomplicated. He knocks on a door, says Iakov sent him, and whoever is inside hands him a brown envelope which he then delivers to Iakov. He never looks in the envelopes, but he knows there isn't so much money in them: Iakov is too young to be allowed to run any kind of substantial operation. There are older men in the yards who would have control over these kinds of activities. Yevgeni knows all this; he knew it before he'd even been there. It's the kind of common knowledge that floats about, one of those topics that cause adults to change their tone. Still, Iakov is good to Yevgeni, rewards him well, tells him to look after his mother.

Yevgeni hasn't properly put it all to use yet. All he has bought are two pairs of gym shorts and, of course, the running shoes. Stupid idea. He thought he was being careful,

345

staying within the limits of what's acceptable, but he can't blame himself for getting caught. It was just dumb luck that his mother happened to be home that evening. He panicked, he knows it. If he'd been more casual, said a couple of words, made nice, thought of a decent excuse for being back – it doesn't exactly require genius: Mrs Leibniz being sick, for example – then went to his room, it wouldn't have been a problem. But he panicked. Understandable, though: I mean, when is she ever home?

He's storing up the money. It's not so much yet, but it will be, it's steady, it's growing. His bedside lamp has a hollow base, so he rolls up the money and hides it in there. He'll probably soon have more saved than his mother does, which only goes to show how shit-poor her wages are. All that sweat over wrinkled clothes. It won't be him. Already he's got rid of the laundry run, fixed it so Ivan Egorov will do it for him instead, and the sweet justice of this situation causes a warm rush in his chest every time he thinks about it. He approached Ivan in the schoolyard, made him an offer. Ivan, of course, already knew about Yevgeni's new contacts. He asked about his finger, mumbled his apology, which Yevgeni pretended not to hear, which Ivan then had to repeat, louder, more clearly. The most satisfying sentence Yevgeni has ever heard anyone speak. This is what Iakov means when he talks about influence.

Of course, his mother will find out that her boy is no longer delivering her laundry, but he's prepared for this even-tuality, he'll pass it off as a favour: Ivan wants him to do well, they've become friends – this is what he'll say, not that she'll be convinced. But she'll be fine. He'll play the kiddie piece tonight and then have free rein to do what he wants. She'll have even less reason to object when she finds out about the money. The Conservatory will probably mean more expenses.

So, not much will be said, she'll ask her questions because she feels she has to and he won't answer because he doesn't have to, and she'll take the money, take his help. Tonight will make everything all right. He's been practising hard. He knows the piece backwards. He's not even really nervous, though that might change in front of all those people.

'Come on inside.'

'I can't,' Yevgeni says. 'There's somewhere I have to be.'

'What? You're such a busy man that you can't spare five minutes? Come on, say hello to a few friends of mine. It'll do you good.'

'I really can't. It's important.'

'Don't insult me, "It's important." This is important too. These are people it will do you good to know. If they get to know your name, that's a good thing, Zhenya. It'll be a help to your mother, believe me.'

Iakov leads him through a corridor to a lighted doorway at the end. To the right of the door sits a two-tone barber's chair, white and beige. A framed photograph of Yuri Gagarin hangs over one of the mirrors; over the other is a black-and-white photo of some Spartak footballer. In the corner there are some fake plants, stooping down due to the weight of the dust that's layered their leaves. To the left of the door there's a table surrounded by seven men, some similar to Anatoly with the same withered features, and a couple of others Yevgeni recognizes as the men who were roasting potatoes that time Iakov had called him over.

There's a poker game going on, and when they see Yevgeni the men kick up.

'Hey, what is this?'

'No cartoons in here, Iakov. Get the fucking kid out.'

'He's a kid, it's fine.'

'You're a fucking kid – this one here, he's barely out of

nappies. I don't want him squealing and bitching in my ear. Put him back in his playpen.'

'He's a kid, he's quiet.'

'I swear I never want another one in my sight. Fucking screaming at three in the morning. How many mornings was I woken up by bawling?'

'Too many.'

The men all nod in consent.

'Come on,' Iakov reasons. 'He's been walking around for me for the last few hours. Let him stay long enough to warm up his bones.'

Anatoly stands up, pointing towards Iakov.

'I know this boy since he was four years old. Before he had that girl's haircut, which, by the way, I have offered three thousand times.'

'No cutting my hair, Anatoly. Forget it. It's where I draw my great strength.'

He flexes a nascent bicep.

A round of guffaws.

Anatoly takes Iakov by the shoulders, pushes him into a chair and nods towards Yevgeni.

'Your child can stay, but if I hear a fucking squeak.'

'He won't say anything.'

'A single fucking squeak, so help me.'

Anatoly looks at Yevgeni, winks and points to the barber's chair. Yevgeni sits down to watch.

Silence sweeps through the room and they get down to the serious business of the game. One of the men whips the cards around the table, and they don't take them up and look at them, as Yevgeni has always done the few times they played at home, instead they keep them flat, taking only a brief peek at the corners. They don't use roubles to bet but various mechanical materials, a combination of nails and bolts and screws and nuts. There's a mound of these in the middle of the table and various-sized clumps in front of the men. Yevgeni knows he should go. His mother and aunt and Mr Leibniz will be waiting. But twenty minutes more. He has twenty minutes before he really needs to leave. He can make up some time by running. He watches and keeps his mouth shut and the game expands into sequences, ranging from the tense and perfunctory – where everyone is concentrated on the other, throwing little sidelong looks, one of them massaging some small bolts in his hands as though he is rolling a cigarette – to a more expansive mode, where they drink and laugh and talk of obscure things, of women and former jobs. And occasionally there's an eruption, when someone takes a hand unexpectedly, when they brandish their cards, laying them out like a fan, wrists up, and there follows an outburst from the others, an intestinal moaning, hands slung towards the ceiling in frustration at the vagaries of the game. Yevgeni has never actually seen grown men play a game up close before. How odd it seems that, even at their age, they are caught up in the same dilemmas as he sees in his schoolyard, the laws of luck and skill.

Yevgeni can't make out who's winning. Each pile of chips seems to be roughly the same shape and size, with the exception of Anatoly's, whose resources are quickly depleting, forcing him to play more erratically, until finally a hand comes down to Anatoly and another man. Anatoly has no more nails or screws in front of him; everything has been pushed to the centre of the table. Iakov drums the table lightly to ratchet up the tension and Anatoly looks at him as if he might reach forward and pull Iakov's fingers from their sockets, and so he stops, looking a little sheepish.

Anatoly lays his cards forward. Yevgeni can tell it's an impressive hand by their expressions, the downturned mouths and tucked chins and faint nods. The man opposite takes a moment to display his own cards, enjoying the moment of strike, looking at Anatoly with a predatory eye. Yevgeni can tell by this look, even before the man shows his hand, that Anatoly has been defeated. Anatoly knows it too, a small death occurring throughout his features, the faint glaze of hope and expectation extinguished, and his face becomes even more shrunken, looking as though it might be swallowed by his shoulders at any moment.

He shakes hands reluctantly with the other man and walks from the table in disgust, sitting on the arm of the barber's chair, suffering the ultimate cardplayer's indignity, unable to participate in a game in his own home.

He sits beside Yevgeni, and Yevgeni folds his arms, an action that seems to age the boy by fifty years, drawing him into the bitter circumference of the luckless gambler. They watch a few hands, and then Anatoly leans in closer.

'You hungry? You want something to eat?'

'No, I'm fine, thank you.'

'I'm hungry. I have some ham blinchiki in the fridge. You want some?'

'OK then. Thank you.'

'OK then.'

Anatoly puts a hand on Yevgeni's head to punctuate the end of their exchange. He leaves the room, and a couple of minutes later the lights go out. The men at the table curse and someone flicks a cigarette lighter and they are caught in tiny intimacy, the flame dancing shadows around the room. They call to Anatoly for some candles, and he calls back that he's looking already and emerges a few minutes later holding a plate of steaming blinchiki in one hand and a candle in the other. He offers the plate to Yevgeni, who takes one of the blinchiki in his hands, and then Anatoly places the plate on the table and rummages in his pockets, drawing out some extra candles, and the men murmur their gratitude and continue their game as if nothing has happened. Anatoly, still holding his own candle, tilts his head to Yevgeni, gesturing towards the corridor.

'Come with me.'

Yevgeni follows him, touching the walls to guide himself, until Anatoly opens the door on to the street, where the city is shrouded in black, hiding from itself, betraying nothing. There's a rich, syrupy darkness. A car turns a corner and its lights reveal corners of buildings, stalks of lamp posts, as though the street is being rediscovered, someone stumbling upon it after many years, blowing away the dust, smelling the musty air. The darkness turns all sound to a whisper. And then a floop and crackle. Yevgeni thinks for a fleeting second that the city is cracking, breaking into fragments, but there is colour now, a flash of blue coming from his left, and he turns to see blue bursts of fireworks light up the dark velvet air. He's seen fireworks before, of course, but not without any surrounding light. Not when they're the only colour to be seen in the whole city. There's a line of people leaning against the opposing walls and the blue wash clings to their features, a look of delight flaring across their faces. As his eyes adjust, Yevgeni can see others walking now, coming from the cusp of the hill, heads bobbing in the slope of their walk, edging slowly along the pavement, all points of orientation obliterated. Others in doorways become defined, old men on canes and women with mufflers and buckled boots watch the night. Gaze up and down the street and sometimes bend over to take it in from other angles. A large bird beats its wings above them and Yevgeni looks up to see it gliding over, its span almost connecting the rooftops.

He feels a shove from behind. The men from the poker game pour on to the street, full of hurried purpose. Iakov grabs Yevgeni's neck and steers him in their direction.

'Come on.'

'Where are you going?'

'We have some things to do.'

'I need to go home. I said I'd be home soon. My mother will be worried.'

Iakov stops, looks at him. Slaps him on the back.

'Of course. We'll give you a ride. Besides, it's too dangerous to walk.'

A swell of blue light propels them forwards.

Maria bolts down the stairs, two at a time, feeding the banister rail through her right hand. She'll find a phone box, maybe down near the Metro stop. She doesn't want to call from too near her building in case they trace it back. She may trust Danil by now, but she doesn't know how prominent he is, how much attention he attracts.

She's careful where she steps. Can't take a tumble now. Watch out for needles, broken glass. There's a wad of toilet paper here and there, and she doesn't want to know.

Mr Leibniz was right, they've mollycoddled the boy. Apart from everything else, this is his moment. Where is his ambition? Does he want to be like all the other kids? Does he see the lives around him and think he wants one of those, wants to dull his imagination, spend all his evenings watching TV, or drinking and talking about inanities with no end in sight? All these weeks she'd been thinking that he didn't like the pressure, but maybe it was the possibility of success that scared him, that he may have to stand apart in this world. Be something other than average. She knows that if she sees him outside she'll grab him by the shoulders and shake him. Tell him there are only so many opportunities in life, even fewer if you come from where he comes from.

She bounds down the last flight and comes to a stop beside the lifts. She needs to hurry but not look as if she's hurried. She doesn't want people asking why she's running to a phone box. Word will get back to Alina, or others. She'll be asked why she didn't make the call from home.

She hands around some cigarettes, asks the men drinking meths if they've seen a boy wandering around. They look at her, trying to figure out what she wants to hear before answering. She doesn't wait to listen to their replies: she should know better than to ask.

The faces of dead soldiers leer down at her, the pages almost transparent with the lights on behind them, phantoms all of them.

She finds herself scanning cars, trying to make out if there are figures in the front seats waiting for her to pass, whispering into radios while heaters on the dashboard trickle out streams of warm air. She heads towards the phone box near the school. She waits at the traffic lights, and ranks of cars pass slowly by, ploughing through black sludge, causing it to fan out from their tyres.

They'd be leaving now, Anna and Nestor and the rest of her colleagues, no doubt resenting her, having to give up their evenings to hear some spoiled brat. The lights turn red but she doesn't cross. She wonders what happens if tonight doesn't go ahead. Will she need to flee? Word will surely get out. You can't have a plan as extensive as theirs and keep it a secret for too long. The supplies alone will give them away. Danil may have been able to get them into the building without any fuss, but try getting them out again. Her fate is being played out without her. She has no control over the next few hours. Why did she not pick Zhenya up herself? Too much faith, that's why. All of this turning on the fulcrum of a nine-year-old boy. Of course it was bound to go wrong. She crosses the road at the next opportunity and passes the school, graffiti tainting the lower part of its façade, crawling up past the window ledges, coming to an abrupt end at the height of an outstretched arm. People pass, returning late from their shifts, many with dust or dirt on their shoes and jackets, determined to get home, their bellies cavernous. A twist of her shoulders to avoid a collision. It's not just manual workers, though, unskilled production drudges like herself; men walk by in suits as rumpled and baggy as their skin, looking downwards, too weary to face the horizon, their only wish to be alone.

She reaches the phone box, saying a silent prayer that the thing still works. She doesn't grab the handset, she clutches the cord instead, pulls on it, and it doesn't come away in her hand. Miracle of miracles. She pushes some kopecks into the slot, takes the number from her pocket and dials. Even in this, a phone call, she's taking an enormous risk, the possibility of a recorder automatically spooling in some dark room, her voice transferred to tape. The call connects and she hears a single beep, a machine; it could be Danil's, it could be someone else's. There should be a code, she thinks, some prearranged ambiguous phrase, but there isn't one. She thinks quickly and says enough to get the message across: 'He isn't back. We can't go ahead,' and then hangs up.

She puts the handset down and walks hurriedly away. The pace is probably unnecessary, they can easily find her if they are in fact looking. She should go home and pack a bag, get a train somewhere, try to mitigate the risks for Alina and Zhenya. She can be out of the city in an hour or two.

Everything goes dark.
Light no longer exists.

Maria stops in terror. Her long-held fear has come to pass:

blindness has come upon her. She used to wake in the middle of the night and wonder if she had lost her sight. The fear is still so present that she insists on keeping the hall light on, so when she wakes in this state she can look at the glowing seam under the door and reassure herself. She never thought it would happen while she was still awake.

But no, there are shapes, a moon, cars cresting the hill. Her panic releases. The power is out. She starts to run. Alina will be in a state. If she had managed to stave off fearing the worst, she will no longer be able to do so. Her child is out there, in the black. Her worst fears will be unleashed.

Maria runs for a few minutes, then stops, no idea where to turn off for home. She crosses the road and then crosses back. All the shadows the same, all the buildings indistinguishable without their surface features visible. She needs to find the school, a different building from the rest. She can navigate her way from there.

She slows and passes two men and sees their attention fixed on a point behind her, hands held in the air bearing witness, and so she turns, looks where they are looking. Fireworks blossom over the city, umbrellas of bright-blue sparks burst open, distributing delight, a gasp of wonder from unseen figures nearby.

She walks steadily now, her heart rate returning to normal, and she finds the school and turns and traces her way home by instinct. She moves in the opposite direction to everyone else, people emerging from the buildings to stand in the road and stare, people coming together to stand and gaze and murmur speculation with strangers and friends alike. They yearn for surprise, a moment of wonder, which they'll chew over and savour and return to in the months ahead.

Maria finds the multilayered voices calming. Her childhood fear has abated now. Lights will return – already she feels certain of this – bringing Zhenya with them. She'll pack a bag and be gone from their lives before morning. The unknown holds no fear for her; she's spent enough years swaddled in ignorance. At this very moment, on the other side of her country, the sun is rising. So much out there for her. She sees the horizon pushing out like an old carpet being unrolled.

She cups her hands to her cheeks to warm them and realizes she is sweating, despite the cold. She turns into the courtyard, flat, grey shapes all around. Anyone who has felt the urge to do so has left home already, so she is alone down here, figures bobbing on balconies above her. Alina is one of them, no doubt.

She finds her building and traces her hand across the number on the porch just to make sure. She yanks open the door and can feel the concrete under her feet, markedly different from the snow and gravel. The crimson tip of a cigarette whirls in the air at waist level. Someone is sitting there.

'Hello?' A man's voice, vulnerable, unsure.

She pauses.

'Hello. Is there someone there, please?'

She should walk on. This is not a place to speak to an unknown man, unprotected. But there's something in the voice. She stops.

'What do you want?'

She can hear a shuffling, the crimson tip rises, he is standing; the flare of a match, a jawline, is revealed for a fleeting moment. The light compresses and the flame is drawn nearer a face, a nose, an eye. His eye.

'Grigory?'

His upper lip stretches into a smile, a row of teeth.

'Maria? Is it you?'

She replies breathlessly, 'Yes. Is it you?'

'Yes.'

The cigarette is discarded, the match goes out. He lights another one, closer to his face this time, leaner than she has known, shadow-sculpted, hollowed-out eyes. An aged face. He steps closer, brings the match to her. She can feel the lick of its heat. He reaches out in the dark, finding her, both of them trembling from the cold of the night, from the warmth of their touch.

They've been walking for five minutes. The fireworks still flare, but there are longer pauses between them now. Rubbish bins are being set alight. Yevgeni sees bursts of fire whenever they emerge from the alleyways to cross a main street. He's stopped believing there's a car, but what is he to do? He can't just run off, wander alone through the streets. He has no idea where he is, for one thing. His toes are cold, his shoes too flimsy to offer any decent protection from the snow. He should have bought boots instead of running shoes. A pair of boots and his mother wouldn't have asked questions, just accepted whatever he said, so relieved that he had a new pair.

He tells Iakov his feet are cold, careful to keep his tone steady: he doesn't want to moan. Iakov keeps walking but looks at him, punches him on the shoulder and hands over a small bottle that he takes from his jacket pocket, telling him to drink.

Yevgeni has never dared to taste vodka till now, but Iakov is looking at him, measuring him up, and there is no choice involved in this: he is here with these men, under their protection. He can't risk being abandoned.

The bottle isn't much bigger than his hand and has a curved body that fits snugly in the palm, and Yevgeni takes a deep breath and downs a mouthful, and coughs as the liquid sears the inside of his throat. Iakov laughs and the three men in front look back and laugh too. 'Don't worry,' one of them says, 'you'll get better at it.' And they laugh again. Yevgeni can feel a surge of vomit reach the back of his tongue, but he manages to quell it. He takes another breath and lets the sensation subside. The men don't wait for him and he has to run to catch up, their strides are so long, eating up the ground in front of them.

A figure walks down the alleyway in the opposite direction, a rectangular shape crossing his chest, and, as they near, Yevgeni can make out that the shape is a TV. The group of four, Iakov included, stop in front, blocking the man's way. Yevgeni hangs back a few paces, wary.

'You moving house?'

The man looks from side to side and considers turning around, but there are four of them and one of him and, besides, he's carrying a TV. Really, how far can he run?

'Something like that.'

'It's a good idea. No traffic at this time. No one to bother you.'

'Except of course you ran into us. Are we bothering you?'

The man stays admirably nonchalant in the circumstances. 'No. No bother.'

Yevgeni can make out that the rabbit ears for the TV are slung around the man's neck and resting on his chest, the two metal prongs sticking outwards making it look as if his chest has been pierced from behind by an archer.

The oldest of the men, the one who was winning at cards, is the one who leads the exchange. Iakov and the others take their cues from him.

'It's better at night, you know, because if people see you, they can get the wrong idea.'

The guy with the TV grins dumbly, no idea how to stack the odds in his favour.

The oldest guy looks to Iakov, who is standing to his right, then back to their temporary prisoner.

'Drop the TV,' says Iakov.

'What?'

Iakov takes a step forward and punches him on the head, a hard, short hit on the temple as the man tries to duck. The TV bounces to the ground, its screen imploding with the impact.

The older guy takes the cord for the rabbit ears and wraps it around the man's neck, and they plant punches on his face, his head bobbling from side to side, at the mercy of their blows.

The sound of effort, heavy breathing, pleasure mixed in, delight, thrill. The men are enjoying their work. Yevgeni can hear a strangled noise coming from the man's mouth and can see blood and saliva dripping, and he takes another swig of vodka to numb the shock, and Iakov approaches him and grabs him and pushes him forward in front of the man, who is kneeling on the ground by now, beside the shattered TV, arms covering his head.

This is what men do too, Yevgeni thinks. Even as they get older, this is what they do. He didn't know such a thing. How could he? What men does he know apart from Mr Leibniz and a couple of male teachers; the gym instructor? He has no recollections of being in the company of grown men. He has never been taken anywhere by his father: no films or pool rooms, no games of football in the park. No one has ever shown him that this is what it is to be grown up, hanging around poker tables and burning barrels, fighting and drinking. There are things his aunt and mother couldn't provide. Maybe he has been raised as a little girl all along. He needs to accept this opportunity.

He stands there looking at the man, cowering. They shove him forward. He can hear Iakov say, 'Kick him in the head.' It sounds to Yevgeni like he's calling it out from a hundred metres away.

The other men snicker.

'*Do* it.'

This is what men do. This is what it means to be one of them. Yevgeni lets fly a kick into the man's neck and there follows a rumbling cheer from the others, and he swings out again and again, the man's neck soft and doughy at his foot, and the man looks up at him, eyes burning in indignity, and Yevgeni draws back and makes contact with the man's chin, which sends him sprawling backwards. The contact feels as solid as kicking a wall, something dense, not muscle and fat, hard bone. His foot is ringing with the impact. One more into the body of the man. Another one. He's not the helpless one any more, the one with dainty fingers. It's his fists and his feet that will carry him through.

He stops, panting, satiated.

The others walk on and Yevgeni stays and looks at what he's done.

The man groans in a basso rumble and takes on the same form as the TV: shattered, slumped.

Yevgeni runs to catch up.

Chaos is building. Crowds are tearing through the streets now, cars parked at any angle, dumped in the middle of the road. People are running in all directions. A line of militia vans snakes its way towards them, their roof lights pulsing colour into the air. They cross the road and wait for the militia to pass, and the oldest of the men approaches a car. He pierces the driver's window with his elbow, and unlocks all the doors, and they pile inside, Yevgeni squeezes into the middle of the back seat, his shoulders almost around his ears. The man in front takes a screwdriver from his pocket and jams it into the ignition and the car stammers into life and the back wheels screech, and they pull out into the road, the back end fishtailing from side to side, and Yevgeni can feel the heat of the two men pressed beside him, Iakov in the front seat whooping with excitement, and where the hell are they going, taking up the middle of the road, fireworks in front of them, still blossoming blue.

They gather speed, careening through the streets. Yevgeni has to lean forward and clutch the headrests of the seats in front in order to avoid being shaken around. The men beside him list from side to side as though caught in the midst of a powerful sea storm. If they crash head on into something, Yevgeni knows he would be flung through the windscreen. Air whips through the car from the broken window, fragments of glass shuffle across the dashboard.

They brake suddenly and a woman sprawls over the bonnet but rolls off sideways and continues into the street. Yevgeni can't believe that the driver can anticipate anything, considering the speed at which they're travelling.

The driver constantly combines the handbrake and accelerator, so that the car bolts and buckles with a stubborn will and Yevgeni's shoulders keep connecting with the seats in front. He has to concentrate intently to avoid ramming his head into the hard frames underneath the upholstery.

They drive for ten minutes maybe, the driver relaxing – less to contend with as they move to the outskirts of the city. Yevgeni is glad, after all, that they're not bringing him home, he's not ready to face his mother and aunt, not after what just happened. And he doesn't even want to think about playing the fucking kiddie tune.

They screech sideways and come to a halt. He hears doors

click open one after another, and the men jump out. He stays where he is for a moment, disoriented, nauseous.

He hears Iakov shouting after him and gathers himself and steps out of the car. They are far away from anywhere, some industrial area. The place is lit only by car headlights; they aren't the only ones who have decided to come here, wherever 'here' is. Gigantic light posts, like tree trunks in the gloom. People running, carrying large boxes with their lids torn off, dumping them inside the cars and then running back for more. Some people, his mother's age, older, are pushing and dragging caged carts, the kind you see being hauled out of delivery vans, stacked with boxes upon boxes. The boxes spill out their contents as they're being bumped along. A packet of biscuits rolls end over end towards a drain, scuttling away from the madness. A can of sardines comes to a stop against a lamp post.

Kids a few years younger than him are smashing windscreens with wheel wrenches. The glass sounds like crashing waves and the panes fold in a way he wouldn't have predicted, a tapestry of cracked glass that curls up like burnt paper. Near the steel roll-up door at the entrance to the nearest warehouse a young woman is pouring honey into her mouth, and it spills along her neck and slowly makes its way down her T-shirt, though not spilling exactly, he thinks, rolling, turning over upon itself.

Inside, people have paraffin lamps and candles and torches for guidance and they crash their carts into one another's and scream and yell.

Boxes stacked upon boxes, wide aisles of thick steel shelving. People crawling up them, ripping and tearing with glee, feeding on their contents, dropping them from a height to their partners on the floor down below. People throwing jars against the concrete floor just to watch them explode.

Yevgeni stays near the walls, crouching out of sight, retreating into the darkness. At the end of a centre aisle, four boys stand and tear the tops off cardboard packets of washing powder and shake them out, and the white particles drift down in a foggy haze, settling in piles, sticking to the thin metal filaments of the shelving units so, at a glance, they seem like small, snow-laden trees in what looks like a minute winter garden, a place of quietude amid all the chaos. Yevgeni hunkers down in an empty space under the shelves and tucks his legs up, wrapping his arms around them, and watches the soap dust linger on its way down and smells the soft chemical smell, and thinks of his aunt and his mother standing on their balcony at home, wearing the borrowed dresses, their hair pinned up, staring at the fireworks, wondering where he could be, their hands knitted in worry, starch under his mother's nails.

But his mother stands alone, watching, wearing her housecoat, a scarf wrapped around her pinned-up hair, looking out for her boy, trying to make out his form in the moving shadows. Maria is inside, at the table, clasping Grigory's hand, two steaming glasses of tea in front of them. They don't speak. Now is not the time. Now is only the time to sit and be free from explanations. Grigory removes his hand from hers and clasps her shoulder, her upper arm, her wrist, examining each part of her by touch, turning them over in his skilled hands, naming her bones once more, claiming them, 'Manubrium. Ulna. Radius. Scapula.'

Alina turns towards the door and watches. She can't go inside to break their reunion. She can't go to bed alone, imagining her boy out there. She can only stand here, on this balcony, waiting dutifully.

Sunlight has persuaded the city to return to itself once more. Yevgeni steps into the morning. It's time to go home. He passes a construction site and stops and walks in, wary of guard dogs, and opens the cab of a digger and finds what he had hoped, a workman's jacket, heavy and black with a luminous strip around the waist. He takes it, resolving to bring it back in a couple of days. Someone will arrive at work and have to make do with a thin coat, and there are many things in life that aren't fair but this is one he can do something about.

He walks through the still streets, windows smashed and cracked; on the pavement a baby's bottle and a bicycle tyre, broken glass and food containers encrusted with ice. A bread van passes him, the driver looking casually amused at the obstacles to his regular route, one hand out of the window pinching a cigarette, swerving gently every now and then to avoid the smouldering piles left over from improvised fires.

Snow sponges up the wash from the streetlights, which burn again, as though nothing had happened. Morning in Moscow: the city timid and languorous and his. In these hours he owns both the city and the day. He feels different, feels that he knows the character of things in a way that he didn't before last night.

Yevgeni walks for a half-hour, and the buildings become older, more solid, and he arrives at a great square and looks at the trees, their branches snapped, with twigs and large splinters bobbing in the fountains, and realizes where he is:

the statue of Pushkin looking down on him, the Rossiya cinema to his right, the great plate-glass frontage smashed to such an extent that the place looks skeletal, half finished. Even the huge movie posters at the front have been taken. It becomes obvious to him now where he is headed. It's probably no accident that he's ended up in this district; his legs know the route well enough to carry him here unthinkingly.

He walks through alleyways, litter spreading from overturned bins. He passes a house with emaciated plants dangling over the porch and a sundial on the patch of lawn to the side that has been reappropriated as a bird table with a netful of nuts hanging from one corner. Another corner, another street, walking until he reaches the turquoise building. In the morning sun it looks as though someone has slugged it in the stomach. Its roof sags, concave but valiant, a patchwork of replacement tiles fixed at irregular angles so that streams of air filter through the house.

Yevgeni pushes the door open and walks up the steps that wake with a moan and greets a cat patrolling the corridor with a waggle of his finger under its chin. It smoothes itself against his hand, shunting his arm with its head. He opens a door gingerly and steps into a wood-panelled room and sits at its dominant feature, a baby grand that takes over about a third of the floor space and is turned at an angle so that there is room for the door to open fully. Yevgeni looks at it in the sallow light and wonders for the first time – it had never occurred to him before – how the hell they managed to get it in here, the windows and stairwell so incredibly narrow.

He runs his hands over the curved lid, the particular shape of it fitting his hands like no other object he knows. He flips it in half, revealing the tips of the off-white keys, and then flips it again, and somehow the whole lid miraculously slides its way into the body of the instrument. He loves the weight, the balance of the keys, how when you push a white one it bounces again in readiness for reuse, whereas the black ones are plodding and awkward, objecting to being disturbed from their slumber, hammering out strange sharp and flat tones, grumpy and hulking.

There are piles of sheet music on the top and in the secret section under his seat and spilling along the floor and in front of the fireplace and beside the sofa and on the windowsill and radiators. Mr Leibniz reads music like others read books. Often when Yevgeni comes for his lesson the old man will be stretched out on the couch, his wife in bed, a sheaf of Shostakovich on his chest, and he will hold his finger up in the air to prevent Yevgeni from speaking; *Let me get through this one last section*, the finger is saying, as if he can't wait to find out how it will end.

Yevgeni doesn't have to search for the particular sheet. He locates it instantly. A lime-green cover with a photo of a man who could only be a composer, who looks as if he were born a composer, a great white walrus moustache and a womanly shock of white hair brushed back from his forehead, a bow tie taming his thick neck. He places the sheet on the stand, adjusts his seat and places his right foot on the pedal below and his fingers in the starting position, and brings his ear to the level of his fingers and pushes downwards, letting the vibrations rise from the wooden box and stream through his ear and soak into his body, and he knows he is ready for this, finally, he is equal to the music now, he will no longer buckle to its weight.

He lets the previous night run free through the notes on the page, Grieg's 'Nocturne in C Major', the keys containing any hue he wishes to paint, all the richness of the city: the window frames, the darkened signs, the fake leather on the seats of cars that sit abandoned, stunned, on the pavements.

He plays the drips that splatter down from cracked drain-pipes. He plays the contents of washing-powder packets streaming through the air in white and blue granules. He plays the cards of the poker game, the intensity of the eyes of the looters. He plays Iakov's kindness and menace. Yevgeni looks beyond the notes and time signatures and tonal suggestions and he realizes that the notation is merely a framework upon which to place all this understanding. All things coming together, his knowledge of music and his knowledge of sound, his experience of life, brief as it is but full, bursting from him, searing out in the energy under his fingernails. He plays his Grieg as the room grows lighter, sunlight drawing itself across the pages, until he hears his name being spoken and turns around and sees Mr Leibniz, his eyes soft and watery, leaning in the doorway.

'Have you been out all night?'

'Yes.'

'Your mother is looking for you.'

'I know.'

'You should go.'

'I know. I'm sorry I let myself in. I just, I don't know, missed it. I'm sorry, I shouldn't have woken you.'

Yevgeni stands up to leave. Mr Leibniz's wife comes into the room now, gliding past him, floating in her white night-dress, the ends of her hair catching the faint gusts of her movement, her face gleaming, alert. She sits on a chair and leans towards the piano, drawn to it, pointing at Yevgeni to return to his playing.

Mr Leibniz sits too, takes her hand. 'Perhaps once more,' he says.

And Yevgeni plays it again, differently than before, and then again, each time differently, so much to find within the patterns, his hands working separately and together, like the two figures seated near him, in their nightclothes, left and right, their easy compatibility, the freedom that it carries, the stretches of notes that weave themselves into an intricately complicated formation, fusing and separating, together and apart, timeless and in the moment. He could play this for ever. He will play this for ever. He knows it now. This is what he is meant to do.

April 2011

Silence.

His fingers float upwards, vibrations still running through them, molecules quivering against each other, the sound dissolving somewhere over the orchestra, funnelling into the microphones that dangle above them.

A thousand people exhale.

Yevgeni opens his eyes.

The keys settle in their binary opposition, black and white, returning to stillness, released from his energy. He turns left, to the first and second violins, the violas, the woodwinds in the background, forward to the cellos and basses, black jackets, white shirts, black dresses, white skin, and nods to all in gratitude, and they raise their instruments in appreciation and then he turns right to the audience, the glaring lights, the gale of applause, ranks of them holding up their phones to capture this moment.

It's been several years since he's played in his native city, but still he is not here with them, at least not immediately. He is on the other side of the Tverskaya, back in his old mentor's apartment; Mr Leibniz and his wife listening still.

Some minutes of bowing, alone, then with the conductor, twenty years older than he; a look in the man's eye: pride, gratitude – a look Yevgeni is familiar with. The conductor's grey hair is pasted on to the side of his head with sweat, a night of true exhilaration for him; Yevgeni has demanded that the man climbs to the upper levels of his talent. He has had some minutes backstage to gather himself as Yevgeni played solo, but still he is gliding upon the sensation of his accomplishment.

Yevgeni walks from the stage and through a warren of magnolia corridors. Someone hands him a white hand towel and he wipes the sweat from his fingers, dabs his face, his neck. Technicians and stage managers take his hand as he walks, pat his elbow, his shoulder, as he moves away, until at last he opens the door of his dressing room, and closes it.

Alone. Leaning on the dressing table. Looking in the mirror. The fluorescent light above it buzzing as it gains full strength.

This evening was a lap of honour of sorts, a victory concert. He spent the afternoon in the Kremlin receiving the State Prize for his 'services to the Russian state as a virtuoso of the highest order'. Such idiocy. So many layers to his craft that he hasn't yet discovered. Already, some of the strands of this evening are reaching for his attention, filaments that he needs to fuse together. He knows that later, at dinner, he'll pick apart the technicalities, the unintentional modulations of tone, replicate finger positions on a table or an armrest. Tomorrow, he'll need a rehearsal room before his flight back to Paris, enough time to right his wrongs. Otherwise, he'll be sullen for the following couple of days, he'll allow the lapses of concentration to colour his whole memory of the performance.

Right now, though, he just wants to savour the feeling. The residue of his childhood lapping along the tips of his fingers, the faint surge of an outbound tide.

The Grieg nocturne is only a recent addition to his repertoire. Until a few months ago, he had rarely played it since his earliest days in the Conservatory. He dropped it not long after his audition because of his hunger to learn newer pieces, to stretch his capabilities. Later, as a young man, he was wary of the piece becoming routine. He wanted to retain the frisson that charged him when, doing exercises, he happened to stray upon some of its chord sequences and would then play a couple of bars – like a fleeting glance of a former lover as she stepped on to a bus, or handed her cinema tickets to an usher.

After Mr Leibniz died the piece became too painful to play; it sounded leaden, morose, under his touch. It remained that way until his doctorate students in Paris cajoled him into coming to their Christmas party and he heard it in close proximity, in a small book-lined apartment in the 6th arrondissement, tucked away behind the Saint Sulpice church. Not unlike the old man's place: three floors up, a rickety staircase, the same warm wood-panelling inside. He sat in an armchair with a broken armrest, a ridiculous paper crown perched on his head, a mug of mulled wine warming his palm, and listened to a young Spaniard make it come alive for him again, drawing out its smoky hues. Its patterns seemed more peaceful than he remembered, the two-beat rhythm of the right hand creating a steady, determined tempo, the three of the left wrapping itself around the melody rather than driving through underneath. He cast his eyes around the apartment, with everyone else focused on the keyboard, and what came back to him were not the specifics of that night, but, instead, the atmosphere of the old man's home, the tenderness with which he led his wife between their three rooms, always presenting his forearm for her to lean on, the gentle warmth of his voice when he reassured her in her confusion, extinguishing her distress.

He plucks off his bow tie and bundles his jacket on a chair. A case of fine Scotch sits in front of the ranks of bouquets. He unclasps the lid and flips it open; a satisfying weight to it, a beautiful thing, a wooden box, the triangles of dovetail joints hugging each other. He pours the whiskey into a glass, the warm amber sluicing around. He reaches into the breast pocket of his jacket and takes out a golden ring and puts it on the middle finger of his right hand. His father's wedding band. A graduation gift from his mother which he removes only for recitals.

The communal hum of the departing audience comes through from a speaker somewhere in the corner of the room. It's gratifying to hear his own language being spoken by a large group – a few years since he's heard it in this context. The elongated sentences, a certain curvature to the words, the nuances of meaning that crackle in his ear. Fifteen years in France and he still can't connect with his adopted language in this way, never feels truly comfortable with those throwaway expressions that are reserved for those who took to it from birth.

He listens to people greet each other, inquiring about mutual friends, swapping stories about their children. Of course he's attuned to any words of acclaim that filter into his room, so much sweeter to him when the praise is delivered without his presence. His need for approval lessened as he began to fill large auditoria, but he can't yet bring himself to stand and turn down the volume, quench the chatter. Some day he will be oblivious to this too, his petty vanities finally laid to rest.

Maria sidesteps through the crowd, moving against the flow. She left her scarf at her seat and she's glad of the excuse to grab a few minutes to herself, away from Alina and her husband. Already they're positioning themselves to take advantage of the free champagne. She wants to stave off, for as long as possible, the handshakes and small talk, the feigned interest in who she is. She misses Grigory more intently at these kinds of occasions. No one to link arms with, to exchange ironic commentary with. No one to rescue her from a particularly sterile conversation. The preserve, she remarks to herself once again, of the lonely widow.

She finds her scarf tucked under the armrest and pulls it out, and the seat levers down then flips back up and the sound echoes around the auditorium, emphasizing its scale, the place charged with what it contained fifteen minutes before, the beauty of Yevgeni's encore piece still stirring inside her.

She sits and watches the musicians pack up, quietly. Can she detect a certain reserve amongst them also, a reverence for what has just occurred, or is this simply a natural assumption you make when watching a group of people in formal wear go about a mundane task?

Stagehands come and wrap the piano in a fitted blanket, tie it in place, then move off somewhere else, and the chairs and music stands remain pointed towards it, watching over it as it sleeps. She thinks of her nephew tucked into his small bed, hair fanned out against the pillow as she kissed him goodnight.

That child has become the main accompanist to her adult life. He has always been near. Even in her most difficult times, she has been kept afloat by the currents of his talent. His music, even in his absence, flowing through her, lifting her.

She had once believed that words would be her legacy. A book picked up at a second-hand stall, fifty years after her death. An article that a researcher stops upon, skimming through microfilm files. But language has always been her betrayer. She, as much as anyone, knows its limits, its devious ways. The things that are most precious to her now are beyond articulation. Each has adopted the other, aunt and nephew – Alina is too far away from both of them now ever to bridge the divide – and if, at fifty-seven, she has nothing else to show for her life, then there is always this: Yevgeni sitting on that stage, holding a note in suspension, taking her breath with it, his fluid hands dancing, as they once did, on her typewriter keys, at nine years of age.

How close it all came to never happening.

He clinks the ring repeatedly against his glass, a metronome to pace his thoughts.

Yevgeni has never asked his mother why she kept it for him, why she didn't let his father take it to his grave. Such a question would be too revealing for both of them, would open up too much. Old habits still lingering.

Perhaps she felt guilt at not providing a male presence for him. Perhaps, at his graduation, she wanted to remind her son where he came from, that though he was about to flourish in a new, sophisticated world, he would always be a kid from the outskirts. His wearing of it surely indicates he does feel an obligation, a debt, to his father, but Yevgeni remembers the man so vaguely that he's merely a shadowy presence, a ghost who climbs his walls on long winter evenings.

It's the only possession he has that's older than himself, and he wears it, in truth, out of fidelity to the past. To remind himself that one generation before an artist with his talent, with his profile, should expect to spend half a lifetime freezing in a gulag: chopping wood, laying roads. That the prospect of a life such as his has driven many better musicians, better men, to madness.

The heat of the Scotch licks over him. He takes pleasure in the charred aftertaste, a reward for his work; he can allow himself this. These minutes after a recital are the only time he truly feels at peace, feels equal to his ambition.

The chatter from the auditorium has quietened, the audience continuing their conversations in the lobby, only an occasional stray note from loosened strings as the orchestra pack up their instruments.

The ring has since proven a constant source of speculation for women over a certain age. Almost every day he gets questions about it, little jokes about him transferring it on to the other hand, making it a wedding band once again. Such comments never used to bother him, but now, in his mid-thirties, they carry a sting. He simply doesn't have an answer when they ask if there's a woman in his life. There have been missed opportunities he has seen only in retrospect, too unwilling to compromise his focus, the last of which was a historian who lived in a former hotel that had been through the most superficial of reconversions. The lift had a sliding iron gate, the brass plate outside still announced he was entering the 'Hôtel Jean Jaurès'. He presumed it was no accident that a historian would choose to live in a building named after one of the founding pillars of French socialism. He presumed this but never thought to confirm it with her.

He would call on her late at night, and she would open her door naked, cradling a cat that covered her breasts, a habit she'd developed after searching the building for it one too many times. After their lovemaking Yevgeni would lie awake and watch the ceiling fan, listen to the endless repetition of it cutting the air. He felt at ease with her, felt a possibility stir within him, but they didn't spend enough daytime hours together for either of them to confirm their instincts. At moments like this, she still makes him wonder.

'Find another musician,' Maria tells him. 'A cellist maybe, even a dancer, someone who understands.' But he never has.

Such risks she took. Maria can barely grasp the scale of them in retrospect. Gambling with the boy's future, with his safety.

Alina's too. At the very least he would have been prevented from setting foot in the Conservatory. She would have denied him doing the very thing that defines him. And for what? The Wall came down less than three years later, the Union was officially dissolved two years after that. Everyone got their freedoms and used them to elbow each other out of the way for whatever slice of the country they could get. Screwing each other as much as possible as quickly as possible.

Even her colleagues in the factory had no interest in communal action, in collective autonomy – all those phrases that had seemed so potent to her then – they just wanted more than they already had.

Despite all her worries, Yevgeni's presence turned out to be irrelevant. When the power went out, they guided Sidorenko and the ministerial consort to a guarded room while Zinaida Volkova stood on the stage, proposed a strike and read out their demands by torchlight to cheers and stamping of feet. The euphoria lasted until word went around that there was a city-wide blackout. By the time the emergency generators kicked in, the stripping of the factory was well underway. They took anything that could be ripped out without mechanical aid. Even the supplies of water Danil had secretly stocked in disappeared. The strike organizers fled, opting to stay anonymous. Who could blame them? Sidorenko, the minister and management went home, and a couple of weeks later many of Maria's colleagues were back in the plant, carrying out essential maintenance work.

Production was back up and running within a couple of months. The only gains the workers had made were the piles of scrap metal sitting in their baths and galvanized sheds.

Gambling her family on people who never believed in anything.

What lingers from that night is shame. It still has such a grip on her that she's never been able to tell either of them what they avoided. Who did she think she was, playing God with their lives?

She never went back to the place. While work was suspended, Pavel managed to make enough space in his department to place her in a full-time tutoring position, and she's stayed there ever since. The Lomonosov became her refuge through the new regimes. After the Union disbanded, it was probably the only institution in the city unaffected by the frantic tussle for wealth. Students still carried books, fell in love, turned in late papers, clustered together in the library. Her role, since then, has been in service to them, provoking them, encouraging them. The place has been good to her, perhaps too good. She got comfortable there, while the country needed good journalists – still needs them, now as much as ever.

But something has changed in her in the past few months, a surge of promise. Lately, she finds herself waking in the morning, placing her feet on the bedroom carpet. Curious. Captivated. Ready to soak in the coming hours. All her responsibilities have been played out. She is ready, finally, to live for herself.

The feeling has surprised her, delighted her. The result, she suspects, of something Yevgeni said on his last visit. She was setting a fire in the grate, and he remarked how Moscow didn't seem like home any more. He listed off his grievances: the coarseness of the town, the flaunting of wealth, the teenage girls taking photographs of each other draped over the bonnets of sports cars, the muscle-bloated men wearing T-shirts plastered with cheesy American slogans, the neon-fringed boutiques selling leather dominatrix wear.

'But then again,' he said, 'this has never been our city. It has always belonged to other people.'

She put a match to the firelighter, kneeling close until the kindling began to smoke, then dusted down her jeans, gazed into the hesitant flames.

She paused and looked, taking in the crackle and spit of the young fire.

It was true. She had always been a stranger here. So much energy spent on staying as anonymous as possible.

'You're right, it never has. Half my life I've been talking about leaving it.'

'You don't owe it anything,' he told her. 'Come to Paris. You always talk about how much you love it there.'

'Don't be ridiculous. I'm too old to move.'

'You're too old to stay. Haven't they told you? Anyone under twenty-five isn't welcome. Any time I come back, I feel obliged to get my tongue pierced, just to fit in.'

'Well, maybe I'll do that instead.' She laughed.

What he said has stayed with her, though, awakened her to new possibilities, to change.

Yevgeni showers and takes his suit from the rail, puts on his underwear and trousers and slides the plastic sleeve from the drycleaner's off his shirt, inspecting it for creases, still his mother's child.

He sees her so rarely now. She got married again, ten years ago, to Arkady, an engineer who runs a building-supplies company in Odessa, a cousin of one of the women in the laundry where she used to work. When Yevgeni visits they run out of conversation after the first ten minutes. There are no common aspects to their lives, and they have never been able to speak about the past. So they fill the pauses with trivialities, they argue about politics, pass on any news about old neighbours. Maybe if they were on new ground it would be different, but his mother doesn't like to travel, she's reluctant to shed her old suspicions of the West. She's never visited his adopted home in the fifteen years he's been there.

He was reluctant to accept the State Prize. Standing in the Kremlin, in the seat of power, shaking the president's hand in front of the assembled photographers, was, to Yevgeni, a tacit endorsement of the current regime. But then, he asked himself, what did it matter? No one ever voted according to the preferences of a pianist.

He took the award for his mother's sake. A repayment of sorts, a way to thank her for all she had done for him. When the ceremony was finished, he handed her the medal in its box and insisted she take it, and she did so, her eyes filling with gratitude, and he was glad he had come here, glad he hadn't been too proud to let her have this day.

Maria didn't attend, though, for which, no doubt, his mother would castigate her. But he was more than a little proud of her. Uncompromising to the end.

He'd like to show his mother how he lives now, the things he sees. The beauty, the awe, of his adopted city. He'd like to take her to the Sunday bird market on the Île de la Cité. She would enjoy listening to the red-faced men bellowing out their enticements, cajoling people as if they were trying to offload used cars, instead of budgies and finches. They could wander around the corner to Notre-Dame, she could stand in that building of overwhelming scale, or wander around the museums. Perhaps being exposed to centuries of great art would stir something in her, let her understand him better. She's proud of his success but doesn't have any feel for the music. The music, as she likes to say, is not for her. He's seen her asleep too often at recitals to offer her tickets any more.

He runs a comb through his damp hair and slips on his jacket, adjusting his collar – no tie – puts in his cufflinks. Yevgeni sends his mother clothes, and she sends back little thank-you cards. He knows she still appreciates well-cut cloth, soft fabrics. It's the one small thing that still connects them.

He enters the members' lounge to a rush of applause and upraised glasses, and he nods and places a flat hand on his breast in appreciation and walks to his mother, who makes a great show of her embrace, then shakes Arkady's hand and catches Maria's eye across the room. He approaches her when he has settled his mother and Arkady into conversation with a prominent architect.

'You're not meeting the great and the good?'

'I didn't realize they were here. Alina only introduced me to the mildly compromised and the unashamedly corrupt.'

He laughs, embraces her. 'Usually I'm the only one to notice.'

'That was beautiful tonight, Yevgeni.'

'Thank you.'

'I mean it.'

'I know you do. Thank you. It's so good to have you here.'

A pat on the shoulder from the executive director. Yevgeni nods in response.

'I need to shake hands with some sponsors, do my bit for the scholarship fund. Give me a little while.'

'Of course.'

On their way to the restaurant, the four of them are silent in the taxi. It begins to rain. Umbrellas explode up and down the street, drops on the windowpane descend in streaks.

At their meal, they drink good wine and Alina displays her storytelling skills, recounting tales of her son's childhood to

Arkady, and they laugh and Maria is grateful once more for her sister's abilities. There are some shared experiences that are impervious to time.

After coffee, Alina pulls a package from a shopping bag beside her chair, wrapped in brown paper, rectangular. She hands it to Yevgeni, and he can feel a frame underneath the packaging. A photograph, he thinks, perhaps some certificate he has long forgotten about. But it is neither, so much better than that, surprising him.

An X-ray sheet, enclosed in glass, front and back.

He smiles, remembering.

A fracture on the little finger of the right hand. The hand of his childhood self.

'I still have the bump.'

He displays it, then places his hand over the sheet. All that remain unchanged are the spaces between the fingers.

He holds the X-ray to the light, the inner pattern of the hand so unfamiliar in its negative form. The bones rounded at the knuckles, balanced precariously on top of each other, the fingertips tapering off into triangles.

Maria points to the different parts, naming them.

'Distal phalanx, proximal phalanx, metacarpal, interphalangeal joints.'

'You learned them from Grigory?' Yevgeni asks.

'Yes.'

He lays the gift on the table beside his coffee.

'I remember him that night. His kindness. I was scared, especially after the X-ray – it was a strange experience for a nine-year-old kid. But he talked to me like I was an equal, his voice was so reassuring.'

'Yes, it was.'

They are silent again. Spoons clink against china.

Alina nods to her sister. Maria thinks she won't say it.

Yevgeni won't push her on this subject, he never has – but she can hear her voice uttering the words. 'It's what killed him, you know. Radiation.'

Yevgeni looks at his mother then back to his aunt.

'But that's not possible. It was a heart attack. It happened so suddenly.'

'You know so little.'

When Grigory took his own life, she didn't feel the anger, the confusion, which those close to her predicted would come. She was the one who had forced open the door to their bathroom, found him there, face pressed to the white-tiled floor, the jar of pills standing upright next to the sink. She knew he wasn't doing it to punish either himself or her. He had seen where the illness would lead him. To take his life was a rejection of this end, not of their love. It was calculated, rational, but not cold. Only she could make the distinction. Only she had sat with him in those mornings after his return, when she would make breakfast and watch him eat, as meticulous as ever, and then sit and listen as he spoke of what he had been through, the lives that had passed under his fingers. Talk for an hour and no more, before washing the dishes, passing them to her to dry, releasing the pain in manageable increments.

She knew he was ill from the very beginning, several weeks before he himself did. Something haunted in his look, a shade to his face. She saw it those first few mornings, a physical retreat from the man she knew before.

He came back home determined. He had material: anecdotal, unofficial, but, he thought, valuable nonetheless. Even if he couldn't hold anyone directly accountable, he wanted people to know what had happened.

In his absence, however, he had become invisible.

None of his former colleagues would meet with him. They would barely speak to him beyond the basic courtesies. Grigory sat one morning at Vasily's parking spot at the hospital, waiting until he stepped from his car, and yet, as Grigory approached, Vasily returned to his seat, turned the key in the ignition and reversed. Even as Grigory jogged beside him, red-faced, banging a fist against his window, Vasily concentrated on his driving, refusing to acknowledge him. Even as his old friend was left pleading in the rear-view mirror, arms outstretched, Vasily picked up speed.

Maria tried to give him what help she could. Pavel and Danil and their connections were unwilling to get involved. They couldn't afford to raise their heads again, not so soon after the attempted strike. Eventually she was able to link Grigory up with some journalistic contacts, but of course they wouldn't run with what he was telling them, especially without substantiated evidence.

He talked to prominent artists, writers, asked them to use their position to speak out, but why would they? They all remembered what had happened to Aleksei Filin, in Minsk. Jail was only worth the risk when they couldn't work freely. Now they were able to do so with very little interference, and no one was willing to jeopardize that.

Six weeks after his return there was finally a breakthrough. The European Atomic Institute were organizing a major conference in Austria on nuclear safety. They had invited him to make a presentation. All his frustrations of the previous weeks were cast aside. When the time came, Maria travelled with him. Months had passed by then and, although he refused to go for a check-up, they both knew he was ill: his breathing was laboured, he tired easily. The intervening months had passed so slowly, so painfully, that when they finally boarded the plane and Grigory sat in his seat, she could see the relief wash over him. Finally, she remembers remarking to herself, he could put his responsibilities to rest, he could carry out what he considered his duty and then concentrate on his health. Throughout the flight he held her hand, so animated, and pointed at the rivers and motorways that snaked underneath them.

They took a taxi from the airport, the tall glass buildings of a western city so unfamiliar to them. At the hotel reception there was no record of their names, but it didn't matter, a small complication they explained away, one that would easily be remedied. When, at the conference centre the next day, the same thing happened, then they had no explanations.

There was no listing of Grigory as a delegate. He showed them his letter of invitation and they replied they were sorry for the confusion, but he couldn't be admitted if he wasn't on the list. He showed them his passport, they said they were sorry; even his speech, they said they were sorry. They placed the list of presentation speakers in front of him: his name wasn't on it.

He had ceased to exist, melted into air.

He asked to speak to the conference director by name, but it was a security guard who approached them instead. Again, sorry. Everyone was sorry. When Grigory got angry, started shouting, demanded to speak to someone more senior, they suggested he send a complaint in writing. When Grigory strode past them into the conference room, it was then that they escorted him outside.

On the street, Maria stood beside him holding up his letter of invitation as he approached arriving delegates, told them in his broken English what had happened, took out his box of projector slides, asked people to look at them as evidence.

But no one did. Instead, they held up their briefcases to barricade themselves from him as they passed.

When the last of the delegates had entered, Grigory sat on the concrete steps in his best suit, now two sizes too big for him, looking into the glass lobby from which no one returned his gaze. A beaten man.

Later that day, they spent whatever money they had left on a flight home. Maria found him dead less than two weeks later.

It is just the two of them now, aunt and nephew, sitting in her darkened living room. After the restaurant, Alina and Arkady said their goodbyes and returned to their hotel. Alina held Yevgeni's medal to her chest and promised her sister she'd call, make more of an effort to stay in touch. Perhaps she will.

'And yet you stayed here,' Yevgeni says, 'in this apartment. Surely you think of him every time you walk into that bathroom?'

She takes a moment before replying.

'The past demands fidelity,' she says. 'I often think it's the only thing that truly belongs to us.'

She walks to the window. Tourist boats pass on the river. The dull throb of drum and bass pulses through their silence.

'Is that why you never told me? Out of loyalty to him?'

'Telling you is no disloyalty to Grigory. If it was, I'd have taken his story to the grave. Your generation was gifted with a sense of boundless promise. I suppose I didn't want to burden you with the responsibility. I wanted you to be free to follow your talent.'

She moves to a storage cupboard in the hall and returns carrying two large document boxes. Yevgeni rises to help her, but she gestures for him to sit and places them on the coffee table.

'This is all I have left of him.'

'You don't need to show me,' he says.

She bends and kisses Yevgeni on the forehead. 'I know,' she replies, and then walks to her room.

He turns on her reading lamp and opens the boxes, both of them filled with manila folders, dozens of them.

He reads. He keeps reading, his curiosity gaining momentum. He pulls out the files and piles them in two unsteady stacks. Hours upon hours of ordered black print. Sometimes he pauses to stand and gaze out of the window. Things he half knew, rumours he once heard, are consolidated. A word on the street from his childhood, a muttered side-mouthed comment, becomes here, in their pages, an indelible part of history.

There is no order to Yevgeni's process. He reads something, puts it down, picks up something else. He reads a recounting of dietary routines, cleaning methods, sexual activity. He reads doctors' testimonies, liquidators' activity reports.

It strikes him, amid all of it, that the endless variations of a single life could probably fill an entire library: each action, every statistic, all record of being; birth cert, marriage cert, death cert, the words you had said, the bodies you had loved, all lay somewhere, in boxes or filing cabinets, waiting to be picked upon, collated, notated.

He reads into history, into the conjecture and the lies, into all that spent energy.

He views photographs of firemen and technicians, a plague of black globules spread over their red-raw bodies. He stares at images of infants with mushroom-shaped growths in place of eyes, with heads that have taken on the form of a crescent moon. He reads to gain understanding. He looks and reads and doesn't know how to respond to such things. There is no response. He gazes at the images in awe and curiosity, guilt and ignorance. All of this is his past. All of this is his country.

And when he can look no longer, Yevgeni closes his eyes. And the world comes in.

Acknowledgements

A number of books were important in my research but none more so than *The Russian Century* by Brian Moynahan, *Among the Russians* by Colin Thubron, *Chernobyl Record* by R. F. Mould and *Voices from Chernobyl*, compiled by Svetlana Alexievich and translated by Keith Gessen.

The images contained in *Zones of Exclusion* by Robert Polidori, *The Edge* by Alexander Gronsky, *The Sunken Time* by Mikhail Dashevsky and *Moscow* by Robert Lebeck gave me licence to set my imagination free.

The documentaries *Chernobyl Heart* and *Black Wind, White Land* marked the beginning of my writing. The ongoing and endless work of Adi Roche and Chernobyl Children International continues to astound me.

There are many to whom I am indebted for helping me along the way: Jocelyn Clarke, Orla Flanagan, Brad Smith, Isobel Harbison, Conor Greely, Tanya Ronder, Rufus Norris, Thomas Prattki, Jenny Langley, Diarmuid Smyth, John Browne, Neill Quinton, The Tyrone Guthrie Centre, The Centre Culturel Irlandais, Paris, Anna Webber, Will Hammond, Claire Wachtel, Iris Tupholme, Ignatius McGovern, Natasha Zhuravkina and Emily Irwin.

For their encouragement and support, my thanks to my family, especially my father.

And for Flora, for all of this and so much more.